Singing Innocence

and Experience

Books by Sonya Taaffe

POSTCARDS FROM THE PROVINCE OF HYPHENS

SHADE AND SHADOW

SINGING INNOCENCE AND EXPERIENCE

Singing Innocence and Experience

Sonya Taaffe

PRIME BOOKS

SINGING INNOCENCE AND EXPERIENCE

PUBLICATION HISTORY: "Shade and Shadow" in *Not One of Us 26*, September 2001; "Matlacihuatl's Gift" in *Dreams and Nightmares 63*, October 2002; "A Maid on the Shore" in *Zahir 3*, February 2004; "Clay Lies Still" in *Not One of Us 29*, March 2003; "Storm Gods of the Connecticut River Valley" in *Star*Line 26.1*, April 2003; "Featherweight" in *Say . . . why aren't we crying?* May 2004; "Nights with Belilah" in *Blowing Kisses*, edited by Mary Anne Mohanraj, 2005; "Tarot in the Dungeon" in *Mythic Delirium 12*, Winter/Spring 2005; "Time May Be," first appearance here; "To Everything, A Season" first appeared in *Say . . . what time is it?* May 2003; "Kouros" in *Say . . . aren't you dead?* November 2003; "Retrospective" in *Not One of Us 31*, April 2004; "Harlequin, Lonely" in *Star*Line 26.4*, December 2003; "Constellations, Conjunctions" in *Maelstrom Speculative Fiction 8*, November 2001; "Singing Innocence and Experience" in *Realms of Fantasy*, June 2004; "Gintaras" in *Dreams and Nightmares 70*, March 2005; "Till Human Voices Wake Us" in *Not One of Us 28*, September 2002; "A Ceiling of Amber, A Pavement of Pearl," first appearance here; "Eelgrass and Blue" in *Mythic Delirium 12*, Winter/Spring 2005; "Letters from the Eighth Circle" in *City Slab 1*, October 2002; "Moving Nameless" in *Not One of Us 27*, March 2002; "Courting Hades" first appeared in *Electric Velocipede 8*, March 2005; "Return on the Downward Road" in *Wicked Hollow 7*, December 2003.

PRIME BOOKS

www.prime-books.com

For these stories and poems, my thanks to Mike Allen, John Benson, Alan DeNiro, Scarlett Dvorkin, Dave Felts, Jeannelle Ferreira, Michael Fiveash, Joel Fried, Carina Gonzalez, Peter Gould, Greer Gilman, Jon Hodges, Elliot Kendall, John Klima, David Kopaska-Merkel, Sarah Koplik, Dave Lindschmidt, Shlomo Meislin, Alison McGurrin, Shawna McCarthy, Mary Anne Mohanraj, Lenny Muellner, Tim Pratt and Heather Shaw, Christopher Rowe and Gwenda Bond, Maury Stein, Shoshana Stern, Andrew Swensen, Lawrence Szenes-Strauss, Sheryl Tempchin, Cat Valente, Marc Verzatt, Cheryl Walker, Sean Wallace, Luis Yglesias, and Michael Zoosman. For anyone who ever told me a story: and my family, who read them all.

μέμνημαι τόδε ἔργον ἐγὼ πάλαι οὔ τι νέον γε
ὡς ἦν· ἐν δ' ὑμῖν ἐρέω πάντεσσι φίλοισι.

(*Iliad* Book IX 527—528)

"I remember this deed from long ago, not a new thing,
how it was: and in your company I will tell it, you who are all my near and dear."

Contents

continued

Introduction

The function of an introduction is debatable, but I've always felt it was meant to entice, perhaps to justify, to explain why *this* book, of all possible books, is worth your time. So let's dispense with the preliminaries. Sonya Taaffe is an immensely gifted writer, and may well become a genuinely *great* writer. With this, her first collection, you can begin at the beginning, and have the opportunity to follow along as her career and craft develop.

You could stop reading now, go on to the stories, and you will have the gist of my essential point.

But, to elaborate:

Sonya has the fundamental gift possessed by all the best fantasy writers: to embrace the old stories and turn them to new purposes. She has a gift for showing myths in fresh light, without trivializing them, and of extracting the most resonant parts of a myth and bringing them into the recognizable world, where their continued relevance is made apparent. Even her approach to such mythological figures as unicorns, which might seem wholly sapped of potency through overuse and acquired cutesiness, are fresh, original, insightful, and in service of capital-A Art. She knows that myths have power because they help us to better comprehend our own lives, and her stories are in the service of that same ideal.

I first discovered Sonya through her poetry, when she submitted work to a journal I edited, and she quickly became my favorite new poet—I think I published her work in every issue! (You readers are in luck, as her first poetry book, *Postcards from the Province of Hyphens*, is available from this same publisher.) Soon I discovered that she also wrote fiction, with the same heartbreaking purity of line she brought to her poems. The first stories I read by Sonya seemed almost like extended prose-poems, and while I admired them, I did not feel they did anything her poems did not. Then I read "Singing Innocence and Experience," a unicorn story unlike any other I've encountered (and I've encountered *lots*), and it captivated me. This was the work of an author who understood the full range of love, from infatuation to obsession, and who could be funny and sad and tender and clever all on the same page, and the story *moved* me, it had heart and magic and power. That's the day Sonya became one of my favorite new fiction writers.

She told me once that she'd like to write stories that are both beautifully written and have something to say, rather than being solely exercises in style. She succeeds in that ambition, and the proof is here before you.

Sonya sings—professionally—both classical and folk. I have never heard her sing, but having read her stories, I almost feel as if I have.

Sonya's influences are discernible, but not obvious; though young, she is already very much her own writer. Still, if you're looking for touchstones, her work owes something to Jane Yolen (the simultaneous reverence for and cautious suspicion of recorded history); Theodore Sturgeon (the foremost attention to matters of the human heart); and Angela Carter (the language); and there are hints of Peter S. Beagle, Patricia McKillip, Cordwainer Smith, and Vladimir Nabokov, as well. But she is not derivative. She learned things from those writers, and used those lessons to create work that is entirely her own.

My favorite stories? If I didn't like them all, I wouldn't be writing this introduction. But, if pressed, I might turn your attention toward her wrenching treatment of the story of Orpheus and Eurydice,

"Shade and Shadow;" to her vivid examination of the inner life of a modern golem, "Clay Lies Still;" to the quirky tale of the extraordinary colliding with the ordinary, "Constellations, Conjunctions;" to her recounting of the fate of Adam's second wife—the one between Lillith and Eve—"Moving Nameless;" and, of course, to "Singing Innocence and Experience," deservedly the title story of this fine collection. Sonya takes these familiar stories and figures and makes them new, transmutes them from dusty half-remembered things into bright, wonderful, *important* stories again.

I don't think I've mentioned: she can flat-out write. It seems silly to quote particular passages from her work when you have a whole book of it in front of you, so I'll refrain, but there is music in her lines, and she has that wonderful ability to illuminate her stories with vivid details. It is as if she gets drunk on language, without losing control. She's got style.

Sonya *knows* mythology. Unlike some fantasy writers, who seem to get their entire mythic education from Joseph Campbell-by-way-of-*Star Wars*, Sonya has a profound and complex understanding of her subjects, be they figures from Biblical apocrypha or characters from Classical mythology. There aren't many fantasy writers who study Akkadian so they can read Babylonian and Assyrian epics in their original languages. Sonya does. She started studying folklore and mythology as a child and hasn't stopped since; she's currently earning her PhD in Classics at Yale. This is a woman devoted to *story*. She understands the power of story to shape both cultures and individual lives. She is smart, serious, talented, and knowledgeable, and every bit of that comes through in her fiction. She's not ever going to write third-generation-Tolkien-clones or novels inspired by roleplaying games. She's the real thing, folks. She's got the sacred fire.

Some collections reveal a certain sameness, motifs or themes that an author returns to again and again, and these can come to seem banal by repetition. This is not the case in Sonya's work. Though one can discern her love for the sea (legacy of childhood summers spent on the beaches of Maine), her fascination with sacred stories from various cultures, her understanding of the power of the past, and her interest in the hingepoints and portentous intersections of lives, she approaches each new story with passion and originality. The best of her stories succeed on every level—the language, the plot, the characters. They affect and they entertain. They feel *whole*. Her stories make me feel better for having read them.

I hope I've done my small part to entice you to read them yourself, and see how they make *you* feel.

Tim Pratt

Shade and Shadow

She used to prick her fingertips, but after a few months discovered the pain was much less if she skimmed the soft inner skin of her wrist with a razor. The first time she almost slashed her wrist open, a clumsy horizontal cut that spilled over her fingers and spattered in slow beats on the pavement as she tried to staunch the flow; she was half dazed by the time her companions arrived, and afterward remembered dreamily asking them to call 911, which of course they could not do. For several months she did not touch that wrist at all. A bandage swathed it while she practiced, carefully, on the other arm. Elbow to wrist, light cuts, enough to bleed but not enough to kill. She was not suicidal. After six months, she was expert: she could open the skin with the sharp edge of her nail, if she could not find a knife or a splinter of glass, dainty and precise. The scars built up.

Cairo Pritchard wore long-sleeved shirts even in summer. There was a hollowness beneath her skin, as though the olive tint of her skin and the color in her lips had been applied as carefully as makeup over glass, and her eyes had the bright glaze people call feverish. When she remembered to comb her hair, it crimped like black brambles around the wide bones of her face; there was not enough of her over her bones, she did not look as though she would cast any more shadow than a floating handful of straw. That she cast a solid shadow, and

13

spoke in an audible voice, and was neither drunk nor drugged, came as a surprise to those who discovered it. But she spoke to few enough people to contradict this impression, and drifted sideways through life unless she could not help it. At the library, she curled cross-legged on the floor among the stacks and read until the clock chimed seven and the librarians moved in solemn procession through the darkening rooms, clicking off light switches, replacing books, until one or another discovered Cairo and she rose silently to her feet, vanished out the double doors and down the concrete steps into the evening. The coffee-shop on the corner saw a great deal of her, or would have if she had been a noticeable girl; she could spend hours on a single cup, sugarless, black, drinking slowly as she watched people shift in and out of the doors. Somewhere she had gone to school. She did not live at home. Popular rumor, if any rumor had stuck to her, would have placed her derelict in the wooded park behind the library.

When she was lonely, she took the razor blades out of her wallet.

In winter she walked on the beach, over pebbles crusted with frozen rain and salt, against skies blanched and taut with pale winter light or blocked thick with clouds like crags and combers. The wind gusted from the sea, snarling her hair, peeling it back from her face. Sometimes, when there was no one to see her, she knelt behind a shoulder of earth where the turf softened into the sea and drew red geometries on her wrists. Now she cut a few straight lines, angled her hand and let the blood run down her fingers, trailing into the wind where it blew and scattered on the stones. Skies the color of glacial ice spanned her vision when she tilted her head back and squinted into the thin bright sun. Her hair snagged in her eyes; she pushed it back with the hand that was not bloody, hunched her shoulders inside a corduroy jacket fraying at shoulders and wrists, shivered and flattened her hand against the gritty shingle. "Come," she said, although she needed no invocation, she had never needed the words. "Come now and you will have more later. I need you. Come now."

A seagull spiring high in the empty air cried twice: lost, oracular sounds that the wind caught and threw away. Choppy hedges of waves skinned blue and grey with the sky's reflection smashed to sliding foam on the shore. In the glassy January morning, Cairo watched the dead thicken the air at her side, visible as light falling through smoke or skins of rain down a windowpane: slippery, substantial, intangible. In the beginning she had called only those dead she knew by name—mother, brother, grandfather—then vast drifts of shades, sifting the silent, rustling crowd for the faces she could not name. Those had been the desperate months. Now she summoned only two or three at a time, transparent silhouettes who stooped and sipped from the blood drying on the sand and stones. "Thank you," she said, as always: a custom of the living. "Thanks."

The dead did not reply as they straightened, faint color clouding through their limbs like smoke inside shapes of glass. Cairo was not offended; she said only, shaking away the last drops of blood tightening cold on her skin, "Are you sorry?"

"Sometimes." That was the ghost of Terry, in life Terrence Lansing, voice still returning with his first taste of Cairo's blood. Seen from the wrong angle, like a reflection, he all but vanished; bright against his shade's diluted colors, a ragged smash of pale dusty silver broke among his ribs. He had shot himself twenty years before Cairo was born. "Is, is that all you want to ask?"

She drew up her knees and settled her back against the chill soil. "Do I have to ask you anything?"

"You always do." Cheryl's voice, the memory of Cheryl's voice, was never gentle; perhaps Cairo liked her best for that reason. The ghost licked Cairo's blood from her lips, touched a hand to her temple where the foxfire split of the head wound that had killed her—a break-in discovered, a young man who panicked—divided her smoky hair. Not two years ago she had been Cheryl Cole. "What else do you want us for? What else does anyone want us for?"

"I don't know. I like to talk to you. I always have." The parted skin of her wrist stung in the cold. It would heal soon. She tugged the worn cuff of her jacket over the red lines ebbing closed and asked, "You always know who I want. How?"

"You scatter your wants with your blood. You, you—" Terry's ghost hesitated, snagged on his own words as had always happened when he lived, "you're very clear. Like light. Not like light. I don't, don't have the words. Not for you to hear, alive. Not all the living language c-comes back. Not even now."

"But you like it. The memory you gain when you drink. Your voices back. Don't you?" She heard her voice pitched curious as a child, did not smile—she rarely smiled—but felt the amusement quirk in her throat. "You don't have to come back to the light, do you?"

"It's a hard habit to forget." There was no blood left on the stony shore, but Cheryl's ghost cast a quick glance at Cairo's wrist. New-dead, as reckoned by the millennial count of shades, she needed less blood to revive her voice and memory than did a ghost like Terry's or that of Cairo's great-grandmother; but she liked the taste and the life. With a grin, she added, "Try it someday."

The wind that drove from the sea tasted like old tears. Cairo looked unsmiling from one ghost to the other. "I will," she said.

When her blood began to fade from their faces, she almost took out the razor blade again. Cheryl would have wanted it; Terry would not have minded; and she was lonely, as she had not felt for weeks. There had been times when she had never been without a shade at her side, one of the shiftless dead moving shadowless among the noisy human crowds as Cairo walked her silent paths through the city. Sometimes she had sat for hours in secluded places, bleeding wrists upturned to the ghosts that bent and drank with mouths so light she could not feel them on her skin. Cairo considered it. She was strong enough; she had not let so much blood as to risk an incident like that first, long-ago, clumsy attempt. But the need was not desperate enough, now. She let them fade, vanishing like breath from a cold window, losing color first and then outline: subsiding into empty air. "Goodbye," she called to the last pencil-sketch traces of Terry's lined mouth, Cheryl's fine untidy hair. Another courtesy of the living, meaningless to the dead: "Fare well." They were gone and the waves' surge and slacken, a vast cold heartbeat, crashed where their voices had brushed the air. White against the flat sky, the seagull was crying again; Cairo got to her feet, a little stiff with the cold that had seeped beneath her skin, took a step over the shingle and heard the singing.

First she mistook it for another seagull, then for music wind-snagged from some pedestrian's CD player. When the wind rose and snapped foam from the waves piling toward the shore, she heard another snatch and realized there were no instruments, no percussion, only the voice soon covered by the noises of the beach. A fragment of melody caught her, stuck in her throat, and she picked her way across the grey strew of stone until she stood at the tide-line. With the cold salt swirling around her boots, she looked and saw nothing that could sing; then she looked again, and the breath stopped in her mouth.

In the backwash of the tide where it thinned to foam on the pebbly shore, a man's head was singing. Seaweed tangled in its dark hair, green and brown bladderwrack that might have rooted there tide-tossed years ago; Cairo glimpsed a flash of white under the silted water, thought coral, bent closer and saw bone. There was no blood. The neck had been uprooted from the shoulders, flesh torn, vertebrae snapped, but that was long ago and the sea had washed it clean since then. If the head's eyes were shut against the salt, its mouth opened and closed without rest: singing a language she did not know, words she did not understand, that tightened the skin around her eyes and burned in the back of her throat until she clenched her fingernails into her palms to keep from crying. "Stop," Cairo said to the head rolling in the chill, restless waves. "Stop."

She knelt on the shore, fringes of waves spilling against her knees, and rose with the shins of her jeans soaked through and the severed head in her hands. It was cold as the sea, skin slick beneath her fingertips, dripping salt water and sea-wrack over her wrists. The fresh cuts burned; the old scars, whitened spider-work scratched and cross-hatched from the heels of her hands to her elbows, stung in sympathy. Her eyes blurred with hot tears. Still the head sang. "Please," Cairo whispered, "don't. At least sing in a language I know. Stop singing, you're hurting me, please—" She could not remember the last time she had begged for anything.

Cradling the head in the crook of one arm, she tugged back the cuff of her jacket and the sleeve beneath until she could reach the cuts she had opened to summon Cheryl and Terry's ghosts. She could not get the razor blade out of her pocket, but she pulled at the unhealed skin with her nails until it began to bleed afresh: salt as the sea and warmer. "Drink this," Cairo offered. She almost could not speak around the constriction of sorrow in her throat. "Drink this, and stop your song. I know who you are." She had read much, those long evenings in the library. "Drink—" Blood spiraled over her wrist, chilling fast in the uneven beat of the wind. With luck she would attract no other shades: she did not want their presence now. She whispered, "Please."

The song died as the head fastened its mouth to Cairo's wrist and drank. This was different than spilling blood for the dead: she felt it pull at her, intimate, tugging her strength into the cold flesh that suckled from her skin. She could not imagine how a severed head would swallow, or what would become of the blood. It did not spatter on the stones from the ragged stub of his neck, nor did color flush through his drained skin as his throat worked, but somehow he drank and changed in her arms from a piece of dead flesh, a little battered, song moving in its mouth like a mechanical lament, to the head of a man pillowed in her bent arms as she might have held a lover sleeping on her breast. Beneath the neck he was nothing: how did he sing? His lips left her wrist, no longer cold as the winter sea but never warm as living flesh, and he spoke without life or breath.

"I want to die." An old accent rocked the words, made them music.

Almost it tore at her as his song had; not quite. These words she understood, and so could bear. "If you hear me, kill me."

Open, his eyes were all the same darkness; it seemed to go far back, deep as a shadow or stone, into a place where Cairo's eyes would not see. She spoke to that distance. "I don't know how. If being torn to pieces didn't kill you . . . I can't even kill myself."

"You gave me voice. The speech of this place. You spill blood for the shades."

"They're my companions. My friends."

"The dead are no one's friends." His old, old, young man's voice ebbed and sank. "Friendship is a word for the living. Even love dies in death."

She could not answer that: the hard, sure despair in his voice. Instead she tilted him—lighter in her hands than she would have thought, the weight of bone and flesh and spirit suspended on the threshold—so that she could look full into his face. There was not even blood on his mouth. "About death, I only know what the dead tell me. They come for my blood, for the taste of life they regain, but they also talk to me. Some of them even know your story. How much do you remember?"

"Everything. Everything." The waves ground pebbles into sand, sand into dust, and dragged back into the sea. "If I could forget like the dead, I would not grieve."

"I can't make you forget." The words left her like an apology. "Blood's for remembrance, nothing else. But if I can't kill you"—Cairo's hands were trembling on his skin, her pulse beating in her fingertips—"would you rather come with me, and maybe think of other things, or toss for another thousand years in the sea with your memories?"

"Is that a question for the oracle?"

"No: it's a question for you." She hesitated, solemn-eyed, and added, "Can you still prophesy?"

Perhaps the faintest picked bone of a smile moved the corner of his mouth. "Take me with you; and when you are home, ask me a question and see what comes of it."

Pebbles gritted underfoot as Cairo left the beach, head bent against the cold brightness and the wind. Ice glittered in the crevices between the rocks; when she climbed up onto the narrow stretch of grass that fronted the parking lot, the earth underfoot was hard as stone. To Cairo's eyes, half-closed against the light striking sharp and colorless from passing cars and distant windows, the winter pallor shrank everything: cars, buildings, muffled pedestrians, stripped trees. Only the sea and sky had dimension. Diminished like the rest, Cairo crossed the street when the cars slowed and tightened her arms around the corduroy package she held close to her breast. She was smiling; she flung back her head and stared into the high, winter-scoured sky until her eyes dazzled from the light and she had to look back down at the crusted pavement. Her shadow hurried before her.

A legend bundled in her jacket like groceries, she passed the library and turned left at the coffee-shop. A Japanese fish kite curvetted in the wind outside the store that sold origami paper and local crafts; Cairo lingered at its window for a moment, shivering and careless in her shirtsleeves and the jeans that clung chill and heavy to her skin, before she turned away. Her wrists burned with the salt, she could not feel her hands and her feet felt leaden, her hair was a windy mass of knots. Without regret, she rounded the bookstore on the corner and took the head of Orpheus home.

She did not live in the park behind the library, nor spend her nights on the beach watching the tide fill and drain from the bay. She had a prosaic apartment, not quite hers, on the top floor of a three-story house shared by nine graduate students from the university. Cairo had known a few of them when she was there. Occasionally she saw them going up or down the stairs, or heard their music coming through the floor; she left them entirely alone and most of the time they did the same for her. She kept her wrists well hidden from them.

As her housemates never saw the inside of her apartment—bed, bookshelves, empty walls and windowsills—there were no questions asked regarding her guest. Perhaps one or two of them heard her speaking, late at night, and a man answering in a voice older than the *Odyssey* or Achilles' anger, and smiled to think that the reclusive Cairo Pritchard had finally found an acquaintance, a friend, a lover. She did not care what they thought. She washed the salt from his hair, combed away the sand and the seaweed and the tiny snails that browsed about his temples, and surprised herself with her care for his tide-beaten flesh. There were no bruises on his skin that held no blood. Because it made him uncomfortable to rest on the table or the windowsill, she folded a blanket to cushion his neck, still raw after so many years, and did not leave him where the light would slant into his eyes. She liked the blinds drawn, anyway.

When he ate at all, he sipped her blood. Dismembered, immortal, he did not require the same restoration of voice and memory that she gave the ghosts proper, but it maintained his connection to place and time. Every evening she cut her wrist for him. It gave him strength as well, she thought, and the willingness to interact if not the will to live. He did not sleep. He never asked her questions.

He answered hers. "I was the oracle on the island of Lesbos," he told her, "until the old ways were forgotten and the shrine fell into disrepair. All those years . . . How could I die, when Hades' realm would not accept me? He gave me his trust once. *Take her back into the light,* she said, his sweet wife, Persephone, like a flower. She was weeping. He did not speak, but he nodded. *Take her back.* And I betrayed his trust: what he granted me, I was not strong enough to accept. I failed him. I failed her," his beautiful voice fractured; he was not speaking of Persephone, "I failed her . . ."

That was the closest she ever heard him come to weeping, with his eyes as tearless as all the dead. Against her palm, his skin was cold. She did not mention the subject again.

Without Orpheus, she went walking in the late afternoon dark;

she sat on the beach, read at the library, observed the customers of the coffee-shop. She bought paper and inks under the auspicious eye of the Japanese fish kite and sketched Orpheus when she returned home in the evening. Her drawings were artless; she was never pleased with the results, and persisted anyway. Sometimes she tried to imagine a body for him, musician's fine hands and singer's modeled throat, shoulders braced against the weight of darkness as he descended the paths of the dead after his beloved. She never could. But she drew the lines of his face, young and ancient, pain-polished, until she could have shaped his features with her eyes closed. His voice could make her bones burn with sorrow. She had not summoned the dead in weeks.

In late February, among freezing spatters that never resolved themselves into either rain or snow, he spoke to her like prophetic Apollo's son. "You give too much of yourself."

"What does that mean?" She was sitting cross-legged on the floor, bandaging her left wrist. The new scars were a neat stitchwork over the old: reddened, hair-fine. Every week she switched wrists. "That's cryptic even for you. Do you think I'm going to bleed to death one of these days?"

In the late light, his eyes held no reflection. Quiet, oracular, his voice sounded in the bare room. "More than blood, Cairo Pritchard. You hollow yourself; the dead give nothing back."

"They give me," Cairo replied, not quite defensive, "what I need. More than I get from anyone else."

His breath sighed out like the receding tide. "You speak of love."

She shrugged, and held his gaze. "If you want to call it that."

"You love the dead. You do not know how to love the living."

"I love you."

His eyes were the color of a far darkness beneath the earth but not of it, the rich house, the last door closed. "I am not alive."

"Yes." Cairo did not look away. "Yes. I know. But you love the dead; you still love her. You were singing for her when I found you," not a

22

question, though it hurt her mouth to say it, "you were lamenting her. It was a love song."

He did not answer. His silence was his answer.

"All right," said Cairo. The wind beat on the windows, whining around the edges of the screen. She put up her hands, pushed the black tangle of her hair out of her face, and looked at Orpheus' downcast eyes. "All right. You said to me once, *Even love dies in death.* But you're not living; you're not dead; you hang in the balance and so you can love. You brought your love for her down into Hades, once," and she paused to think of that: the musician in the darkness, carrying his love like a physical thing, like the instrument in his hands or the song in his mouth; the ghosts when her blood brought them up into the light, empty of everything, voice and memory and regret and love; Orpheus always on the wrong side of the threshold, venturing whole into the world of the dead, remaining severed in the world of the living. "Do you"—she swallowed, mouth dry as sand or bone—"do you think, if she could, she would love you still?"

"I do not know." It was like a phrase of his song on the beach, that had hurt her so to hear. He whispered, old-voiced, "I do not know."

"All right," said Cairo for the third time, like a charm or the last word of a spell. Outside the windows, where the snow stung and ran into rain on the pavement, it was almost twilight. She had seen shades the color of that lowering light. On the sill, Orpheus' reflection looked past her shoulder toward some thought of its own. Eyes on the healing fretwork along her arms, Cairo let go the breath she had been holding and said, "Give me a little time."

She put out one hand and combed her fingers through Orpheus' hair. He would not look at her. There was a cold hollow beneath her heart; she felt herself on the beach again, the shades thinned into empty air, solitary, desolate as the stones with the wind beating over them. As she left the room she heard his voice singing quietly, to itself, his heartbreak song for his beloved.

At the end of the week, she was ready.

It was evening again, more the ghost-hour than any midnight, and so cold that the air felt like iron on her skin as she returned home from the library with her hands shoved in her pockets and her shoulders hunched against the frigid wind. Overhead the stars pricked bitter patterns against the sky, dead black as the inside of a shadow with only the city haze to soften it; a piece of moon floated above the skyline, white as pitted coral, and the street was plated with ice. Cairo took the stairs in long strides, stamping her feet to stir the blood in them, careless of the noise. Her heart tapped hard and high in her throat.

She had never been so formal before. Over a bowl enameled on the inner surface with flowers—a little chipped, but still visible as lilies and irises and a butterfly, a gift she had never given away—she opened her left wrist in one long lengthwise stroke, almost to the elbow, and tipped her hand so that the blood when it beat out slid over the flowers and filled them. Almost immediately she was dizzy; the weeks of blood she had given Orpheus, she thought as she steadied herself with one hand on the table's edge, more than she had ever given any shade. How much blood to draw a ghost out of myth? Still she held her arm draining over the flower-chipped bowl and felt something flowing from her with the blood, less a sense of loss than release: the tide that tasted of iron and salt becoming more than a physical liquid, going into the world something like light or love, a beacon, a guide. Only when the world swam white before her eyes did she knot a bandage around her wrist, trusting her quick-healing flesh, and hold up the bowl with hands that left red prints on the glazed ceramic.

"Eurydike," she called, "Eurydike, come up into the light. Don't come for my sake. Don't come for the blood. Come for him." Her throat knotted; old snow from the neighboring roofs slung itself against the windows in the sudden silence, a muffled whisk and rattle on the glass. If Orpheus was listening, he said nothing. Cairo said into the quiet, hearing her voice distant in her ears, "He loves you. You know that. Are you afraid to see him? Are you afraid he'll fail you? He won't, Eurydike, he can't; he's thought of you for three thousand years and nothing else. He couldn't forget you. He tried. All his songs are of you." Her hands trembled and she set down the bowl, careful not to spill any of the blood. "Come now, Eurydike. Come now and I don't know what you'll have later; that's a thing of the dead, and I—I'm still alive. But he needs you," Cairo whispered, "he needs you. If you love him, if you ever loved him, if you remember a fragment of what was between you: come up into the light, Eurydike," and long-dead Eurydike came.

She thickened into shape slowly, plane upon plane drawing itself on the air, the color of glass in water. When she bent to drink from the bowl, she quivered the air like heat-haze: a movement at the corner of the eye never seen straight on. Trying to see her made Cairo's eyes water. Even when the blood was almost gone, she remained ambiguous for a long moment, a watercolor shadow standing upright, before memory solidified and she remembered the form of the woman she had been in a time long since become story. With a young gesture, she ran her finger around the inner rim of the bowl and licked away the last few drops of Cairo's blood. Her face waned and shone in the glancing light. She was not beautiful.

Her throat was not the poet's slender column, white as doves; she was the color of dry earth, bony-wristed, her long hair of an indifferent darkness. No classical statue would ever be shaped to her proportions. No fresco would commemorate her face. Cairo could have seen her on the street and never noticed. A living woman, loved and loving, who could draw her singer down to the underworld for love of her: that was impossible to imagine. She was longer dead than any ghost Cairo had summoned back to the upper air. Her eyes were blank, not quite bewildered; she had not remembered herself in millennia. One bare heel showed a double scar, the cloudy silver of a death-wound, where the snake had coiled among the grasses and struck her down to Hades as she ran. She bent to rub it, childlike, as though it still hurt her; there on one knee, hand touching the punctures that existed only in her memory and Cairo's sight, she looked across the room and saw Orpheus.

Memory shocked into her. Cairo could see it: the spaces opening behind her eyes, recognition sketching her unbeautiful face. If the dead could cry, there would have been tears spilling down her pale cheeks. Her mouth opened on a word, a name, and Cairo could not bear to hear her voice. Its sound would tear her to pieces, as Orpheus' singing had driven tears into her eyes like nails; she had called and Eurydike had come, and the love between them would kill Cairo if she heard it spoken aloud. *Speak of death, Eurydike,* she said without sound. *Tell him what it is like in the house of Hades.* But he had been there, once before; he knew it. Eyes full of white and black static, Cairo sank jerkily to the floor, drew up her knees and locked her arms around them. Neither the shade nor the severed head saw her anymore.

She heard them speak in voices like shadows, ghost voices, the memories of voices—the old language whose words she could not comprehend, the Greek of the mysteries—and she leant her head on her arms and cried. It was ungracious, ugly crying: noisy, inexperienced, hard as rocks in her throat. She might have been weeping for all the dry-eyed dead. Blood clotted her skin to her jeans, she thought something was breaking apart behind her eyes, and when she lifted her head she could not take her eyes away from the bizarre Tarot figure, the Lovers, snared out of time and death into a February night three thousand years too late for their meeting. Cairo swallowed around the ache lodged in her breath and whispered to the woman's ghost, "Take him."

She was very nearly a living woman, Eurydike who turned to look at her with eyes made of the same darkness as Orpheus' gaze, a color-washed pen-and-ink drawing sketched onto the background of Cairo's apartment. Still the edge of her hand slid through the table; no shadow stretched from her feet, and the garment she wore was a colorless memory of cloth; even Orpheus' love, Cairo's blood, could not bring her back to life. Cairo knew this. Even so, she said again, "Take him back, take him down with you. Maybe the dead don't love; but there's enough blood in you now for love, Eurydike," as though the name were a charm, "and little enough in him and he loves you still." She could not say the word *trust*, but she managed without it. Eurydike watched her steadily; Orpheus' eyes were closed, in pain or in hope. "Go now," Cairo told them, "Hades will have to accept you. Go with her; take him. Now. And don't . . . Don't look back."

She said the last words dry-mouthed, light-headed, and loss was a physical pain beneath her breastbone: cold and aching as the iron air of the night outside. There was no breath in a shade to hold or release, no catch or sigh, but the quality of the silence between them was the same. Then Eurydike reached out—a shade whom the wind did not stir, whom heat did not touch, nor cold, nor anything physical of the upper world—lifted the head of Orpheus in her watercolor hands, and smiled. It did not transform her face, it did not make her body graceful or her hair shining, but Cairo saw the smile fill Eurydike's eyes and she saw what had made Orpheus love her: what had made him so mad with love that he would descend into Hades for her; why he had ignored the women of Dionysos, who tore him asunder in their frenzy and threw the pieces into the river; why he had sung her name through the ages until he washed ashore on Cairo's January beach. Eurydike's smile broke in her bones like the sun.

Then she was gone, and the air fractured like glass behind her. On the floor rolled something that might have been a gravel of bone dust, three thousand years crumbled, worried by wind and weather, spiritless and dry. The wind whined in the dark beyond the cold panes.

Somehow Cairo got herself upright, arms and hands streaked with drying blood, and swayed on her feet as vacant as any bloodless shade. Her footsteps scraped loud in the empty rooms. Lamplight scratched at the edges of her vision; a whiteness bloomed behind her sight, dizzied her, and she made a sound in her throat like a seagull high in the wind. She hurt. When her head cleared, she seated herself on the table beside the bowl enameled with flowers, and lifted the razor blade again.

In silence, she cut up and down the inner surfaces of both arms until the blood ran along every finger and dripped onto the floor. Perhaps there was pain. She ignored it. Time had run like rain; she did not know the hour of the night that weighed against her windows, her hand was shaking and the blade slipped from her slicked fingers. She got down off the table to try to find it, kneeling where Orpheus and Eurydike had vanished; and out of their wake, the splintered place in the air, came the dead. Clouds of them sifted toward her, bat-voiced, restless, flickering like an old film: Cheryl with her death-wound shining from temple to crown, Philip shy and distracted, Terry with his heron's stoop, Hannah silted with faint color as she straightened from the rivulets of Cairo's blood, Yanni, Sebastian, Margrete, Jane; she lost count of the familiar faces as the darkness moved at the corners of her sight. Cairo's brother, forever eight years old and smashed silver in a thousand places from the hit-and-run, knelt at his sister's side to drink her blood. Cairo's mother, mouth reddened, nothing of her face in Cairo's memory but photographs and her shade, had one hand that felt like a windowpane in winter on her daughter's forehead.

"Don't leave me," Cairo said, or thought, or tried to say. The ghosts clustered close to her. Her hands went through them, vaguely, and she lost track of their number. "Don't leave," she repeated, as they sipped her seeping blood and remembered, "don't leave," while she slid into the darkness that was the same color as Orpheus' eyes, "don't leave ..." When she could no longer tell shade from shadow, light from dark, she whispered, "Take me with you—" But the darkness had ebbed into her throat, her mouth, and she did not think the shades heard her as she fell.

The shades had not heard her. She opened her eyes to sunlight slotted pale through the drawn blinds; it hurt her eyes and she curled away from it; the arm she rolled onto ran with pain, a dull ache that bruised the bone, and she knew she was not dead after all. Piece by piece she picked herself up and rolled down her sleeves without looking at her arms. The razor blade was under the table. There was no blood on the floor.

It was very quiet in the winter morning. When Cairo pried two slats of the blind apart to squint at the world outside, the sky was brilliant between ribs of white cloud; ice glazed the eaves and flashed reflections from every surface; a sharp chill in the bright empty air. Carefully, she combed her hair and hitched her jacket over her shoulders. Only imagination gave her the smell of old sea-salt lingering in the fabric. At the coffee-shop she paid without speaking, fishing for bills and coins with fingers that ached, and held the cup between both hands to warm them as she walked; steam furled upward, trembling the air like a ghost's presence, warm against her face and gone.

The wind raked her hair as she settled herself on a dry spar of rock, sipping her cooling coffee and staring at the sea. Sunlight glass-shattered from the water. No seagulls circled against the clouds. The beach was silent. Far down the pale curve of shore, Cairo's eyes picked out two figures sitting side-by-side on the cold sand, hand clasped tight in living hand. She tightened her grip on the coffee cup and felt a brief, acid twist of thanks for the wind tossing their words out of her hearing, out to sea. "Come now," she whispered, "and you'll have more later . . ." She had never needed the words.

Between breath and breath it hit her, a feeling too close to crying for comfort building hot behind her eyes, and she had no tears left. Ground glass in her joints, a sunken place in her thoughts, she swallowed the last of her cold coffee. Then she fished her wallet out of her hip pocket, the razor blade out of the wallet, and set its edge against the rent skin of her wrist. Her fingers tightened and paused. For the first time she wondered: what if they would not come? Her breathing hurt and she turned her head away, looking out over the sea where the horizon faded to the color of the mirrored sky: fever-eyed, briar-haired, unused to the company of the living. At her feet, the sun spilled her shadow over sand and stones.

Cairo released the breath she did not realize she had been holding, unbent cold fingers, replaced the razor blade in her pocket. Perhaps she would visit the library. Certainly she would buy colored inks at the arts-and-crafts store, and draw the last night: the tracery of Eurydike's face against her apartment wall, the cloud of shades, Orpheus' eyes poised between life and death for longer than Cairo's language had existed. She did not know what she would do after that. But she rose, wary of the pain that splinted her movements, and left the beach to the lovers and the ceaseless lift and fall of the waves. She was humming before she realized it, pieces of melody rough in her mouth: a scrap of the song she had heard windblown in January. Her throat closed on the recognition.

The cry of a seagull startled her, wheeling toward the sea, and she could move again, think and breathe, and choose.

She was still holding the cheap cardboard coffee cup; she stared at it for a moment, and pitched it into the parking lot trashcan as she passed. Hands deep in her pockets, Cairo blinked sun-dazzle from her eyes and began to hum again as she walked, slowly accustoming herself to the sunlight at her side, the silence of the singing in the wind.

Matlacihuatl's Gift

Be wary when you kiss her: which mouth
you choose to press your lips against
when you meet her in the highlands
where she walks alone. By roadsides,
by moonlight, sway of hair falling dark
down her sinuous back, her steps hold
the grace of shadows, panthers,
and under your touch her skin breathes
like a flower. Be careful when you approach her
as she awaits you in the dark,
when you slide one hand beneath
her riverbed hair, whispering the words
that lovers and liars always use:
por favor, querida, nunca más and siempre,
calling on time and all eternity
to hold fast your love as you lay her down
silent where her arms wind around
your back, where her mouth fits to yours,
where you cannot resist her and she never
says *no.* Her beauty burns the mind.
Printed with your kisses—lip and cheekbone,

throat and palm, vulnerable nape of the neck
when you push her hair aside to taste
the second mouth she hides there,
flowerlike, no more a mouth than what
she keeps between her earth-warm thighs—
moving on you like the tide, she holds you
tight so that you cannot see, as you cry out
into the hollow of her tawny throat,
what smile her face wears in the aftershock.
No time for wariness or regret
when you have left her, under trees' shadows
at the roadside, when you have kissed
both her mouths and burst stars within her
and lied your love to her in the dark:
down in the cities again, you wonder
what made her laugh as you walked away,
why she folded your hand over the coins
you tried to press into her palm, freeing
your fingers with a gesture that almost
pulled you back. Did she foresee
this nausea in the morning, these twinges
in your belly as though a salt sea
shifted within you, while you check
your weight and frown, resolve to drink
less beer and work out more—and you want
to eat the oddest things—does she know how
you never dream her face except smiling,
close-mouthed and confident, sideways
step over what you thought you knew?
Her coin is reversal; she inverts
the mirror, pays you out
in the shadow side of common knowledge
until you no longer recognize where she began,

where you end, until you understand
what she gave you when you took from her,
in nine months' time, to overturn your world.

A Maid on the Shore

Forlorn echoes at the water's edge: he lowered his hands and hunched his shoulders beneath the heavy cloth of his jacket, a little embarrassed that someone might have heard him, that no one had heard him. Out on the water, overcast rain-light turned the waves grey as rough glass, cloudy, wind-scuffed, like something that he might stoop to lift from the tide-line in one curious hand. He bent and gathered pebbles, rattled the wet sliding weights between his fingers like a gambler nerving for the throw; instead he tossed each into an oncoming wave, dull curl and tumble of silt, foam, sand dragged into a still sculpture-curve for no more than a second before it broke and flooded against his feet, covered the sound of the pebbles' striking with its liquid breath and crash. When the pebbles were gone, he stood there with his hands empty at his sides. Wind furled spray off the water, stung his face. He did not move. He did not know where to go.

Already rain was dropping out of the low clouds colored like the sea. The waves hedged him, pinned him to the broken line of stones and sea-strewn weed; rain nailed his shoulders, his hands, his upturned face when he raised his head and squinted into the iron sky, looking for someone, something, anything. He did not have the courage for another call across the water. One shout, no more, as though she would have heard him and shouldered the water aside at his cry: salt streams sleeking her hair that looked pelt-brown in shadow and russet black in the light, crimped leaves of kelp draped slick about her broad shoulders, striding out of the sea with her awkward land gait; feet stamped on the shingle as though she were never sure that the earth would not move under her feet, rock out from underneath her with the flirting sidestep of a wave, chancing element that she loved. He had never been able to love it for more than her sake. Rope and sailcloth and the hauling of nets had scarred his hands, sun and salt winds tracked history around his eyes and mouth, and he could not remember a time when he had not opened his mouth and tasted the shattered-glass scent of fish salting the air; still he did not trust the water that his eyes searched.

Shivering, he pulled his jacket around his shoulders and kicked at the rain-glossed stones, raised his voice once more into the wind and heard the words fall away unspoken behind his teeth. *Come back. I love you. Are you there? Please.* Pleading words, a suppliant's words, defenseless, naked, and the men would rag him without mercy as he tried to drain his pint and pretend that he had not spent that afternoon raining into evening trudging the shore, crying for a woman whose name he had never known, who had given him no more than a dream-handful of her time, not worth his while, never within his reach. He was shaking, bent against rain and memory, remembering: when he first saw her surface from the water that ran from her skin like glass, round-shouldered, bulky, deceptive in her size and her deliberate movement, skin pale against the fall of hair dense and dark and wet as the pelt gathered around her shoulders; she had hold of his trouser cuff for a moment before she turned back into the next wave and he gripped the rail of the boat in both hands, open-mouthed, paint flaking under the pressure of his nails, and he would have thought her a flick of sun-dazed fancy but for the salt stiffness drying in the cloth; he closed his mouth and pulled his cap down against the sun and did not say anything to the men who pressed him for stories,

Tadhg and Micheal and Peadar, drinking men, fishing men, salt-weathered and storytelling, who knew the secret that he did not, how to ride on the sea's back and joke about it afterward, how to wink at the girls behind the bar, how to catch one by the hand and let her go in the same dancing movement, though when he tried the same he nursed a five-fingered burn of shame on his face and walked the shore alone after that.

There he found her, sunning herself on a spar of rock where barnacles and limpets clustered and tough slippery weed sprang in clumps underfoot. Her hair slid unbound over her naked back, hot to his hand when he knelt and touched it, trembling—it felt like silk, though he had never touched silk, only heard the word and seen the weaving; like the fine shawls of his mother and sisters, that could pass through a wedding ring—until the last strands trailed through his fingers and he touched her skin, fever-hot, sweatless, and the sweat started on his brow. Only a little salt had dried along her spine, brushing away beneath his fingers. When she turned onto her back with a lazy, massive assurance that made the breath snap in his throat, his hands brushed across her breasts: the blood jumped in him and he could not speak. Under the hot summer sky, she pressed him down to the shingle and there were stones like fists jutting into the spaces between his ribs, shells crunching under their weight, sand in his hair and all the folds of his clothing; he blinked tears against the sun, blinded, dazzled, his hands full of the pelted richness of her hair, his head full of the sight and smell and feel of her, though she never bent her head for his kiss, he never tasted the salt currents of her mouth, and she seemed to run through his fingers like seawater or rain as light burst in the marrow of his bones. He came to himself because a seabird was crying in his ear, tugging at his hair with a curved and curious beak; he flailed it away with one hand and started awake, sandy-mouthed, sun-struck, sprawled on his back among the rocks with his jersey stuck with dried seaweed and his trousers in a state and a head on him like a week's revelry spent in a night. Shamed, exhilarated and bewildered, he gathered himself together and hurried back to the boats. Behind their hands, he knew, grins and jokes were flashing at his expense; and the girls who looked at him out of the corners of their eyes were measuring him against some standard he did not understand, finding him wanting, and moving on. He did not care about them, now. If he lingered on the shore, she would come: like a delirium dream, as though the furnace heat of her body kindled a fever under his skin, like something out the stories that went around the table when the glasses were emptied, shedding her sea-sleek fur to take him in her arms, strong and broad and depthless as the sea; no matter how many times he reached for the core of her, eluding him every time. He told no one, and haunted the skerries in hungry secrecy.

If he was crying, he could not tell among the curtains of rain; he did not know what tears felt like, though he knew that something clawed in his throat, his breath scraped thin over loss; he did not know how to cry. Still he stood where the backwash of the tide flurried foam and broken bits of weed, staring out over the heaving skin of the sea. Waves dinted under the rain's rough hand; darkness coming fast out of the west where the sun had gone cloud-hidden under the sea's brim. Rain hissed and rattled on the water, drummed on the stones. He had nothing to say and knew it; the storm outspoke him. He clenched his shining-wet hands and felt the nails dig into the calluses on his palms. The only calluses on her hands had spanned the linkage of her fingers, a roughened web at the top of the palm; he had loved to trace the strange skin with his fingers. The color of her eyes defied his gaze, drawing him into darkness, until he looked nowhere except where she was—

Hunched between rain-grey clouds and cloud-grey waves, he crammed both hands against his face and breathed out harsh, angry words into his palms until he could straighten again, could breathe the damp air coming off the sea, could move without feeling his bones splinter against her absence. Let them laugh at him, Micheal and Tadhg and Peadar coiling rope in the sunshine and winking at the girls who walked the shore with their shawls crossed over their breasts and their bright hair like flags in the wind, storytelling men drinking and saluting their clumsy dreamer as he stumbled out of the salt wind and the rain like a half-drowned man: he had touched their secret in the hot sunshine and the salt burn of sweat, and now he could turn his back on the trustless sea and walk against the wind, not pleading for her, not begging her back into his life, masterful. *So she waited for me, boys, and for all I know she's waiting there now: seal-brown, seal-round, out on the shore where the gulls sweep and cry on the wind: and damned if I'm back there again. I've no wish to find myself a drowned decoration at the bottom of the sea. I've no wife to swim down and bargain for my bones. But stand me another round and I'll tell you again how I found her sunning herself on her skin . . .* Long faded from his cheek, the slap still smarted under the skin. But if he caught her hand tonight, when he had drunk his pint and told his story, if he touched her hair threaded ember-red in the flaring light, would she slap him again? He thought of her and walked faster, thought of black russet hair and felt his heart clench, tightened his teeth against memory and hurried over the rocks with long, sharp-moving strides.

Out of the rain-blown evening, crags and slabs of rock jutted black and darkened grey; he almost barked his shin against a fallen stretch of stone overhung with frilled weed, splashed one foot down in a tidepool risen with rain, laughed and came to a halt against a split back of stone where he leaned with his arms crossed, head tipped back to the pouring sky, and grinned until his face began to hurt. Then he saw that one of the stones was not a stone, was pale beneath its shag of seaweed, moving in response to his nearness and his hard panted breath of laughter, turning toward him a face full and broad-boned as the moon that tugged the tides: rain dripped into his open mouth and he could not tell if the sound in his throat was moving toward delight, anger, sorrow as he caught at the rock to steady himself, grit and seaweed slide beneath his palm and a barnacle biting into the heel of his hand; he was kneeling to reach out to her, thoughtless, wondering as the first time he saw the sun falling deep into her five-fathom eyes, his hand almost on the smooth round of her shoulder before he saw who was in her arms, whose face her dense hair curtained, whose mouths had met in a kiss as deep and potent as the turning tide.

Pale eclipse of a face among hair spray-darkened to the color of wet embers, slender hands holding fast to the heavy sea-graceful body that had held him between earth and sea on a hot summer's afternoon: he cried out and felt slick pebbles sliding out from underneath his foot, collapsing like a heartstricken man when it was only the sea tugging his certainties out from under again, all story gone out of his head, all language lost. Blood shocked through him as he fell, rain-pounded, abandoned, remembering when it had been his hands on her secret skin, his fancies of what that long red hair would feel like tangled between his fingers, and it was no kindness that neither face laughed as he clambered to his feet and ran away through the rain, as the men would laugh as he drank bitter pint after pint until he could no longer taste the salt burning in the back of his throat like tears or the sea that had branded him when she reached out of the water to touch him once and make him hers forever, though she was not his, she had never been his, and neither had the girl whose hands Peadar caught and loosed like a game, whose eyes Micheal snagged with a wink, who listened on the breath of Tadhg's spun stories; they would never hear this story from him. Toward the lantern light he ran, choking on his breath, slipping on the wet stone and turf while the rain beat on his back, knowing that everyone knew the secret and he did not: though he did not know anymore what the secret was.

Their eyes stayed with him, though he ran like a madman all the way to the light.

Clay Lies Still

for Lawrence Szenes-Strauss

In the beginning was the word, the word
That from the solid bases of the light
Abstracted all the letters of the void;
And from the cloudy bases of the breath
The word flowed up, translating to the heart
First characters of birth and death.
          —Dylan Thomas, "In the Beginning"

Afternoon on the cusp of September, August's last dog days piling
the sky with haze and heat: dull light from nowhere in the hot
overcast sky, leaves still late green on the drought-crisp trees, and
the boy sitting on the curb took his face out of his hands and shivered. Earlier he had walked until he no longer recognized the
streets without sidewalks, houses set back on their brick-rimmed
stretches of lawn, locust and maple trees shadowing side yards and
driveways; he had closed his eyes at crossroads, turned corners on
coin tosses with a penny he had picked out of a crack in the asphalt,
no good luck at all, all for nothing. Thoughtless, instinctive, he
could still find his way home. Back to Lance shelving books

anywhere he could find space on the walls or floor for just a few more volumes, another bookcase, even a couple of planks on bolted brackets; back to Lance driving to Cartomancy or Stop & Shop or the nearest non-chain bookstore, behind the rattling wheel of his decade-old tan Camry slowly losing the good fight for manual transmissions everywhere; wherever Lance was, like true north tugging at a splinter of iron, a tightening spiral of water down a drain, the center and the core of his prescribed world.

In the street, a plastic trashcan clattered, knocked over; he did not bother looking up. Sweat tagged his shirt to his shoulders, his hair to the back of his neck, the sticky afternoon pressing perspiration from his flesh until he felt his skin sliding loose under the sun's hidden, insistent hand: salt melt down his spine and fingers, viscous slurry warm as blood or riverbank mud. If he raised one hand, he would see his own transient tissue slipping from the fretwork bones, dripping free . . . High on his forehead, close to the hairline, his skin itched; he rubbed the back of his wrist over the minute scars, thumbnail irritation invisible beneath the dense, lank drop of his hair—copper without highlights, cheap baked-flowerpot red—to keep from touching them with his fingertips. His hair was always getting into his eyes. He never brushed it back.

Some blocks down, where the curving residential streets thickened back into main roads and avenues, trucks rumbled construction noises and backup alarms faintly behind the hedges of roofs and apartments; broken piping or gas-line maintenance, jackhammering early in the morning and tamping asphalt at night, that had kept Lance awake or shallowly dozing, fitful, a light sleeper who never went to bed before two in the morning no matter how early he had to get up and get down to Cartomancy, twenty minutes' drive and forty minutes of traffic away. He was not there now, under the icon eyes of Mickey Mantle and Captain Picard; the lodestone pulled a different way, and the boy with the scarred forehead rose and followed.

He found the house within fifteen minutes, though he had been wandering for almost three times that. An overgrown tangle of forsythia backed the front steps, and an abandoned sneaker still dangled by its laces from the telephone wires that strung through the edges of the yard's two beech trees. No one had yet retrieved the day's mail from the box at the edge of the driveway—one black-metal side marked with the street address and *Lancaster Carsey* printed in permanent-marker block letters, index card taped over with transparent packing tape until it almost looked laminated; a very cheap business card—and he stuffed the spilling sheaf of bills and magazines into the crook of one elbow as he opened the door, edged around a stack of records and dumped the mail onto the nearest table, followed the splash and clink of running water and glasses into the kitchen. Against the clinging afternoon outside, the air conditioning felt like the Arctic closing on his skin. He walked through counterfeit winter toward the north in his bones.

Lance was washing dishes and listening to Robert Johnson, the latter with much more interest than the former. In between plates and glasses, he sang occasional lines and lapsed back into easy silence; he would have been talking rapidly or stone-mute if he had known there was someone else in the kitchen. "I went to the crossroad, baby, I looked east and west . . ." He had a slight, true voice and eyes that shaded between brown and hazel, crisp rye-colored hair too short to curl and an incongruous brush of freckles over the sloping bridge of his nose. When he smiled, he always looked surprised and a little rueful, as though laughter granted some concession he had not expected. He startled only a little when he looked up; a mug clattered against the tap.

"Aaron." The name had been a compromise, a default, the right first letter and number of syllables and nothing more, because Lance thought *Joseph* too obvious and the boy with terra-cotta hair would not accept *Adam*: bad in-jokes, both of them. Lance still said it like a question, testing his guest's identity half in expectation of a denial, a correction; waiting to be wrong, and maybe hoping. Hesitantly, the statement as much of an exploration as the name, "I thought you'd gone out."

"I did." His voice echoed Lance's, a little deeper and rougher; broken over adolescence. "I came back. Want a hand with the dishes?"

"What? No, I'm all right . . ." Collapsing bubbles slicked the linoleum as Lance dipped briefly out of the kitchen to switch off the CD—new speakers for the computer since last week, Vero's gift that Lance had been exploiting to the fullest extent of his eardrums; when he put on African fusion drumming, Aaron kept his distance at the other end of the house—wrists and fingers still slippery with hot water and lemon-pungent dish soap. He returned scrubbing his palms along the seams of his trousers, a little embarrassed. "The keyboard needed cleaning anyway," he said, as though Aaron had asked some question: offering his smile like an excuse. "Where'd you go?"

"Around. Just walking." His forehead stung like sunburn or poison ivy, brand-hot chafe digging beneath the flawed skin; this time he ground the heel of his hand over the scars and saw how Lance's gaze flickered. Carefully he lowered his hand and added, "I should have told you before I went out. But you were shelving mysteries over the couch, and you had Dead Can Dance on really loud—Catalan at a hundred and ten decibels. I didn't think."

"Really, it's okay. I should have noticed." Lance ran a hand over his hair, less a gesture of vanity than a movement of nerves and habit, and said abruptly, "Vero gets back tonight. I think we're going out for Japanese food; I couldn't really swear to it. She has some idea that if she offers me a wide enough selection of raw fish, I'll find one that I like. I have some idea that if I so much as look at another serving of wasabi, my head will blow off. Call the paramedics if you hear an explosion from the direction of Cambridge. Will you be okay?" But he was not listening for Aaron's answer, his offhand yes; all his intensity was in his shoulders and his hands that lifted a half-dried plate for a moment before setting it down, his eyes that were watching Aaron.

He had a look of Lance more than a resemblance, like distant cousins or long-standing friends: some likeness in the long nose and blocky shoulders, like a cross between a crane and a stonemason, the deep-set eyes beneath thin, querying brows and a mid-stride stance always tilting toward the nearest bookshelf. In conversation, unexpected flashes of one's face would appear in the features of the other; something Vero had remarked on. But Lance could never keep still, always shifting foot to foot during a conversation, no idea what to do with his hands or his smile, and Aaron could stand motionless until a spoken word stirred him, no more awkward in his stillness than a piece of granite, or asphalt underfoot. Sometimes Aaron thought that Lance was more fidgety since his arrival, that the conjunction of breath and blood spilled had sapped some calmer, cooler place in the man and left him jangling on his bones. No surprise, if that were true. But other than memory, piecework in dreams and useless random eye-blinks of time when he did not know, breath to breath, whether he was seeing through eyes like hazel shells or wet cinnamon, whether three letters etched his hairline or only the old dents of childhood chicken pox, he had no way to know or even conjecture; he leafed through books on the shelves crowded behind the computer, folklore and children's stories filed meticulously alongside Milman Parry and Joseph Campbell, turning pages of David Wisniewski and Avram Davidson, Trina Schart Hyman and Michael Chabon, and wondered what Rabbi Loew had dreamed among his studies, on the Vltava's sixteenth-century banks. Maybe nothing: what dreams did clay have, to spill into mortal thoughts and pull back memories in the ebb and tidal swirl? But Aaron was flesh and blood, sweating in late summer's swelter and cold now underneath the air conditioner's open vent; he had taken more from Lance than life and a family likeness, and like Aaron's need, Lance's guilt, the exchange went unspoken.

Lance said, quietly, "You didn't get lost."

He tried to give Lance the word as an opening, not a stone. "No."

"I didn't think so." Lance pushed both hands against his eyes, leaned back against the half-tiled wall and muttered, "Who thought there could be this many dishes in a house ..." Stopgap for the silence he could not bear to break with truth: in a minute, still echoing, Aaron might have done the same. Water dripped among the abandoned dishes. Behind his caging fingers, Lance's eyes did not close; when Aaron left the kitchen, he neither stirred nor spoke, stopped in some restless, worried thought of his own.

Outside, the overcast was clearing in patches at the horizon; sun smeared through the living room windows, a glare and smudge on the sight, and leaves baked on the lawn. When Lance did not emerge from the kitchen, Aaron put on a Ravi Shankar CD and fingered through the books left open beside the couch, whose bed had been folded out since mid-July; the room no longer looked like much of anything except a bedroom with bay windows, or maybe a sleepaway library. Two of the hardcovers were in Hebrew, as well as one in Spanish and another in what might have been Czech, and a mess of photocopies and printouts annotated in Lance's looping script and Vero's sharply vertical print. *It's actually an interesting paradigm to think through,* the top sheet read: one of Vero's e-mails, three months old and more than somewhat crumpled; water-wrinkled, speckled leaf-brown at the corners. *God takes mud and instills it with His spirit, making man. Man takes mud and, just maybe, instills it with his own spirit instead of with God's. So humans are a mixture of the base and the divine and spend a lot of our time trying to figure out how to lean toward the latter without denying the former. The Golem, on the other hand, is a mixture of mud and man, who is already half-mud. The balance is off, which might explain some of the behavioral problems of Mahara"l's golem.* Aaron's breath tightened between his teeth. With great care, he stacked books and papers neatly, transferred the whole pile to the foot of the unused fireplace, and fell flat on his back with a thump and creak of springs. Vero had hung a suncatcher from the curtain rod; under the air conditioning's current, it turned slowly back and forth, sea-blue glass stamped with a dove and a raven. Aaron could never tell whether it was hers or her gift to Lance; it was the kind of thing she would own, dark-haired Veroniche Feyneman who wore three rings of silver in her left ear and one malachite stud in the right, and had almost literally fallen over Lance in the library of the University of Pennsylvania. An NELC graduate student at Harvard now, she catalogued cuneiform tablets for the Semitic Museum and had never once believed that Aaron was a second cousin or an undergrad with a housing problem. He wished he could blame her.

The sitar planed into silence; Lance was washing dishes again and Aaron heard water lapping somewhere else, much more distant than the inside of a spaghetti pot. *Don't, Vero*— Half-dozing in between glimpses of the rain stains on the ceiling and Vero's suncatcher, he was dreaming argument: Lance's voice in Aaron's memory, earliest blur of Charles River mud drying in spackles on his calves and palms, a seam-frayed quilt wrapped around his shoulders that shivered like a newborn child's, a feverish boy's; sodium light still swam on the water and he breathed in jolting gasps, tasting exhaust at the back of his mouth, city-summer humidity and traffic fumes; he closed his eyes, pressed his head into someone's collarbones and did not remember who carried him unsteadily to the car. *Please, don't. I can't do this right now. My head*— Vero's voice snapped in his ears for the first time then, much lower and rougher-grained than her singing voice that he would hear in a few days, theatrical with disbelief and amazement and fury, *A hangover? You're lucky you still have your head! Half a bottle of cheap vodka and you think you're Rabbi Loew or something. Don't, he's shaking . . . Throwing the name of God,* ha-Shem, *around like confetti and you're worried about a hangover in the morning. This was not,* and she splintered half into laughter at the futility of words, the absolute understatement as a nameless adolescent shuddered between them in the blanched early-morning light, *oh, God—Lance, I'm sorry.* She had a half-nephew Aaron, a thin sandy-haired twelve-year-old with a cracking voice and a struggling, insistent talent for improvisation; for both their sakes, she was wary with the name in Lance's house. But she had told him stories to help him sleep, that first and strangest week when he kept asking where he was and Lance woke sweating from nightmares of incantations he could no longer pronounce; she had seen what he carried on his forehead, three wired fragments of lightning earthed under the shallow flesh and heavy dull hair, and she had never called him Adam.

Rising out of a last haze of dream, an old walled gate hedged within letters of fire, nowhere he had ever been or seen, maybe nowhere real, he rolled half upright on one elbow and found Vero perched on the farther arm of the couch, some book propped open and forgotten on her knee as she gazed at him. "You have the same little skiff of freckles over your nose, you know that?" she remarked, before he could speak or slide back down to ignore her, let the hour and the quiet spin him into Lance's light doze again. Her eyes were as dark as her hair, her eyebrows charcoal-heavy and the angles of her jaw and temple as precise as folded paper. "It's funny. When I don't look closely, you don't look anything alike. But then I'm curious, and I check to make sure I'm not seeing things, and your gestures are all the same . . . I wonder which one of you changes."

He pulled himself more or less upright, tipped his head to meet her gaze. "Are you going out tonight?"

"I thought so. Now I'm thinking maybe we'll stay in and cook, if you're okay with that. I was in New Haven this weekend and I need to decompress."

"I figured. We eat a lot of takeout when you're not around." Vero inclined her head, smiling agreement: points scored. On safer ground, Aaron ventured, "Everything going all right?"

She rumpled her hair with one hand, closed the book and slid one shoulder upward in a shrug. "The same. My mother wants to know when we're getting married, my aunt wants to know when he's going to convert, and my father says, *Lance Carsey? The shy one?* as though he can't quite believe it. After three years, it's still *The library guy?* whenever I mention his name. Some kind of mantra. Someday he'll stop asking—and on that day, I'm telling you, the world ends."

"You could make him a nametag." He could not remember ever being alone with her before, without Lance so much as hesitating in the doorway, locked out and inextricable; neither could he imagine Lance at the house of his prospective parents-in-law, retiring rather than guilt-ridden, an unambitious brilliant student taking the year off from graduate school to follow his girlfriend, though the memories still clung to Aaron's own. Awkward with the humor, and only a little easier for Vero's steady eyes, he offered, "You know, *Hello, My Name Is Lance: I'm The Shy One.*"

"Hey. That's not a bad idea." But she did not continue the thought, and presently Aaron stopped waiting. When she bent her head to study her hands clasped around the book, a jacketless hardcover of *Snow Crash*, her hair tangled forward and hid her face completely; Lance would have pushed it aside, coarse and shining over his knuckles, and touched the edge of her cheek where sweat still tacked from the day's heat. Aaron swallowed the memory and heard her whisper, sharp with frustration and almost silent, "Nobody talks about anything in this house . . ."

The blood shocked, snapped in Aaron's ears. He said, evenly and loudly, "What is there to talk about? There's no such thing as the Golem of Cambridge."

Vero's hands froze; Aaron closed his mouth. The words had startled out of him: he was not used to yelling, to language that did not skirt the cat-ice edges of conversation. What he had heard Lance and Vero discussing in furious whispers, those first few weeks as he wandered through the house, learning equilibrium, time and place, and what he was not, he would never repeat. But she had left a place open for him, as Lance did not; his cheekbones burnt and the letters on his forehead clawed at his skin, and he dared not to look away.

Vero let out her breath in a long sigh, set down *Snow Crash* and drove both hands through her hair in a raking, decisive motion. "No.

There's not. There's you and Lance, and me, and no answers. And the *Zohar*'s a thirteenth-century forgery anyway. What do you want?"

"The impossible." He was shivering, too hot or too cold, and heard his own words angle like broken bones into laughter. "You study this, you don't need— Look. Rabbi Judah Loew creates the Golem, because Prague is such a dangerous city for the Jews in 1580 or when-ever. He has a dream; he takes his students and they chant the words that work miracles, the most powerful names; they write *truth* on the figure's forehead, *emet*, and the Golem came to life. River mud and desperate need and the name of God, and it's ordained. And when the Golem's no longer needed, he's returned to clay again. Take off the first letter, the aleph, and truth becomes death: *met*. Maybe it's still somewhere in Prague, the lifeless heap of clay that was the Golem once. After World War II and now the floods, I don't know. It's what they say."

Vero said, very softly, "How do you know this?"

"I read it." He reached out and caught at the first book under his hand, shoved it toward Vero's half of the couch: a children's retelling in cut paper. She took it from him, gently, and turned the pages as he spoke. A hand of light descended, writing; steam flashed and branched upward; the Golem's shadow towered over the ghetto gates. A month and a half of silence spilling over, Aaron stared past her shoulder at the overcast yard and felt, faint in the compass of his blood, Lance at the supermarket: safely distant. "What did you think? I don't know the things he knew, Joseph, the Golem of Prague; it's not like that. I know what Lance knows. Because he's not the Mahara"l, because he's a UPenn graduate who gets drunk the night you get back from London and thinks it's a neat idea to put your theories into practice, all the ideas you've been throwing back and forth ever since you met, something to surprise you—I don't know, I don't know what he was thinking. And because he's smashed and clumsy, he tears his fingernail getting the car door open and gets blood all over his chosen patch of earth when he kneels, and nobody factored that into the equation. But it doesn't matter. He got it right. What does that make him—a tzaddik, a miracle worker? What am I supposed to do?" He was shouting, up on his knees and his hands clenched on the couch's arm, close enough to Vero to remember how much Lance loved the smell of her hair, like herself and the shampoo she used, some all-natural invention of mountain flowers into soap. Finding his way out of Lance's memories, he got hold of his voice and calmed it; it was beginning to crack, as though he really were some distant teenage cousin, or Lance's impossible son. "Rabbi Loew made his golem for a reason: to keep the Jews of Prague safe. Lance made—me—because he was drunk. What kind of reason is that?"

"I don't know." This voice he remembered, patient, without judgment, listening. She told stories in this voice, and calmed Lance on the stunned, shell-shocked morning after. "*Seemed like a good idea at the time* explains a lot of what goes on in this world."

"Does that make it right?"

"Depends on what goes on."

Aaron sat back on his heels, studied her face until it frayed into separate features: unrecognized, neither beloved nor comfortable, a stranger's mask. Like staring at a printed word until the letters became nothing more than stamped figures, exact and abstract, signifying nothing; until litany and ritual dissolved into shapes of black flame licked onto parchment, unscrolled out of meaning, an alphabet for the impossible, illegible linkage of clay and light. A word that had been Vero looked back at him, mildly. He burnt with the word that he was, that had written him and still remained in pale scars for the reading: aleph, daled, mem; three letters for the oldest shape of earth, the first name of humanity. Low-voiced, shamefaced, he said, "And it's weird … I thought you'd at least have to be Jewish to create a golem."

If she had laughed, or touched his tensed hands in sympathy, or said any of the things she had told Lance as he drank cup after cup of black coffee and fretted over the boy sleeping on their folded-out couch, he might have left: gotten to his feet and gone, past this afternoon's explorations, walked until the sun went down on unfamiliar streets and the moon teased his shadow out behind him, still traveling. Never mind the lodestone blood that snagged like a fish hook in his bones, the memories that would always catch him off guard, the fragility of a miracle made flesh. He would find his way to Prague, demand answers from the Vltava silt that had formed the first golem and the Josefov cemetery where its creator lay, if he had to ... But she did not speak, and Aaron did not move, and the front door opened before either of them could remember what the Camry's engine grinding out of first gear sounded like.

Right on cue and completely off guard, arms full of Bread & Circus groceries and sweat in his rye-crisp hair, Lance stopped on the threshold and said in some surprise, "I didn't think you were back yet." He set the groceries on the table where Aaron had left the mail, passed one hand over his hair, and turned to close the door on the haze of late afternoon, sultry evening coming on. "Are we still going out for Japanese?" His voice was almost steady.

Vero answered slowly, abstracted, emerging from one element into another. "I don't think so. I need to eat something that I've cooked myself, even if we're sick afterward. How do you feel about impro-vised stir-fry?"

"Hey, that's great. I just got some fresh ginger. And I think there's chicken in the freezer—you okay with stir-fry, Aaron?"

He was not looking at Aaron, unpacking the groceries among unpaid bills and the latest issue of *The New Yorker*; watching him, Aaron felt Vero stiffen at his shoulder. He said, as deliberately as Lance bewildered by dirty dishes, "There's no such thing as the Golem of Cambridge."

From the kitchen, Aaron heard the slam of the refrigerator door and Lance said, "Not unless Rabbi Loew changed addresses and nobody told me. Who drank the last of the skim milk?"

"No." For all the vehemence in her voice, she was almost whis-pering. "No. Lance, I'm not going to listen to this. It's almost

September. You can't keep this up. When your parents come out to visit, what are you going to tell them—he's one of my students?"

"He's certainly not one of mine—"

"God!" Her shout slapped the air. Aaron rocked forward and wished desperately that he were somewhere else, never to hear all the secret bindings between them stripped for a stranger's ears; he heard Lance's footsteps from linoleum to carpet, and stared at the suncatcher dangling like a reminder of rain. "You're not a stupid man. I wouldn't love you if you were. You're reckless, you scare me sometimes, but you're not stupid. And you're not Rabbi Loew, and you're not Victor Frankenstein, you are the man my family is giving me hell for and that's not supposed to sound like a guilt trip, and you don't talk anymore. Not to me, anyway. Not to Aaron. If I'd gotten pregnant, you'd be less scared than you are!"

"Do you think I don't know that?" Aaron had heard Lance hungover, evasive, nonchalant, professorial; dissembling, he touched truth from glancing angles, and sidestepped the rest. Now he spoke quietly, and Aaron thought that his words would have been easier on the ear if he had shouted. "If you were pregnant, I'd know what happened! It's a child, and we decide whether we're going to marry or we're going to become some kind of interesting Boston statistic, and we pick out a name, and nobody gets any sleep, and we take care of it. It's not simple, it's not easy, it happens all the time and people deal with it. This—" He shivered, arms tight across his chest and his back to the wall as though Vero's words, Aaron's mere presence, had forced him there; he hurt to look at. "I don't know what to do," he said: the words were for Aaron.

"I haven't known what to do for a month and a half. You get a major in Judaic Studies, nobody says *hey, it's an occupational hazard, you might wind up with a golem, you still want the degree?* Sometimes I think that's why Rabbi Loew destroyed the Golem in the end. Not because it was becoming dangerous, or because the Jews were safe now, the time was past and the world could return to normal—just because how do you deal with something like that? The impossible made concrete. It shakes you up. I feel like a murderer, but I kept thinking maybe, maybe I could, it's not like there's something he's here to do. But how do I know that? There are words I spoke that night"—for a moment, the memory transfigured him: blood and breath and clay cold beneath his hands, and the name of creation that he had known for one lightning-stricken moment and never again; theorizing his way through folklore into the territory of the inexplicable, he had touched the universe entire—"that I can't remember, that I'll never remember, that aren't meant to be kept in the mind; they'd burn you right out, you can't keep a name like that in your head and still stay human. God's name? We call it that; maybe it's just a word for what drives the world, creation and destruction. I'm talking without a safety net here. There's my whole religious life, right in the sink . . . But recreational Kabbalah, that can't work. It shouldn't happen just because you get lucky. I don't know, Aaron: I keep saying that, and it's true. I wrote my thesis on this stuff and who expects to see their bachelor's degree come to life?"

Aaron's voice had shrunk in his throat, a child's high wandering question. "But you didn't kill me. You could have?"

Lance rubbed one hand over his face, hazel-shell eyes hidden again. "Brush away the aleph from *adam*, you get *dam*—yes, I could. The Golem returned to clay. You'd return to blood, I guess: it's what the word means. Appropriate. I didn't think about it that way. Truth to death, earth to blood. A good linguistic golem, you called it," and Vero turned one hand upward in the slightest, wariest shrug of acknowledgment. The pulse in Aaron's ears beat to her indrawn breath as Lance added, "Do you want me to?"

He had been waiting for the question. Still it startled him, how the room turned to silence, as to stone: the absolute zero second when what Lance had asked, what Vero had not said, froze and poised before time slowed and ran again. One smudge of Lance's thumb, to erase the constant compass draw in his bones and the absence of reasons like sandpaper under his skin, calm Lance's mystified guilt and Vero's frustration, return the world to its original, uneasy, ordinary state: Aaron's red-clay hair and folkloric scars lost in a spill of blood like the salt tides of the third day's seas, the iron-marrowed earth. Then Lance could sleep at night without recursive dreams tangling behind his eyes, interleaved memories of his memories confusing him awake; and what remained of his mystery, how half a bottle of vodka and earnest, careless curiosity could turn *yod hay vav hay* into breathing flesh and blood, would not dream at all. The Feynemans would still puzzle over shy Lance who clerked at Cartomancy. The Carseys would never wonder about Vero's live-in student. So much easier to smooth over the strangeness, and move on.

Aaron lowered the hand he did not remember raising, three letters' imprint brushed onto his fingertips. Still sitting on the couch's coffee-stained arm, Vero turned her head for his answer; Lance tightened his shoulders against unspoken words, the syllabic balances of birth and death that charted the world, that changed it. Beyond the windows, a slow smoke-blue dusk was clouding the yard and the empty street; even the air conditioning had gone off momentarily, and he heard sea-tides in his ears as he spoke. "I don't think so. Not yet, at least. I want to see what happens."

There was air in the room again, not glass, not stone; Lance and Vero did not exchange looks, and did not question. Somewhere in Aaron's bones, beneath his breath, a knotted coldness began to ease.

Lance was laughing, softly; a little jittery still, anything would have been funny and nobody cared. "I've got a friend at JTS should hear about this one." His braced stance was already loosening, relaxing into a tentative lean against the wall rather than the target of a firing squad: taken aback by his own laughter as always, unexpected and unfamiliar ground. "I want to see his face when he hears about a golem that eats chicken parmesan."

"Don't start. We are not talking halachah right now. We are

cooking stir-fry." Vero slid off the couch, retrieved *Snow Crash* from the nearest shelf; as she passed Lance, he almost flinched when she took his hand, and followed her without complaint. "Kitchen's this way. Come on," picking a path back into everyday conversation, wary and aware, slowly figuring out where to place their feet, to keep the balance. "Even the Mahara"l ate dinner," she added, dramatic in her annoyance, and Aaron grinned.

Alone in the living room, probably his room now, Aaron tilted his head back and let the light bloom red and candle-yellow inside his closed eyes. Someone would call him when the stir-fry was done, if the smoke alarm or Vero's cursing did not alert him first; he had time and no choice more complicated than whether he really felt like moving or not. Something close to a theory, not quite a reason and still little more than a stray thought, had worked its way into his head: maybe he would tell Lance and Vero over dinner, what he was wondering. *What am I supposed to do?* He was not Joseph Golem, terrible strength to counter violent hate; he did not carry knowledge beyond Lance's memories, his own learning. Another purpose, then: not to protect the Jews of Cambridge, or the eastern seaboard, or America, in any way that traditional story told; but to safeguard remembrance of the unbelievable, the miraculous that earthed itself in the unlikely. *The impossible made concrete. It shakes you up.* No golem ever appeared in a comfortable time. The world needed, or it did not. Perhaps it needed Aaron, odd creation of blood and river mud and alcohol and speculation, to keep possibilities alive: so much more improbable than history, or survival, or peace.

He liked the thought; he put no definite faith in it; his forehead was itching again, and he rubbed at the scars with his knuckles. Skin against skin, nothing happened and he did not expect it. Not even Vero's touch would convert him back to blood and memory: only Lance, reluctant wonder-worker. Someday Aaron would ask him. He wondered how long it would take. In the kitchen, someone was dicing vegetables; oil hissed in the wok that Lance almost never used.

On the edge of September, Aaron dozed on the couch and listened to Lance and Vero improvising around "Walking Blues," background words and wryness that caught a faint smile from his mouth even as he knew just how Lance stood beside the sink, reaching for the spice rack with Vero's hand on his shoulder.

Light blurred in his dreams, as he lapsed and woke; he wondered what Prague looked like, this time of year.

Storm Gods of the Connecticut River Valley

for Michael Zoosman

Around Talcott Mountain and southerly, where
two rivers braid in tandem toward the Atlantic's
cold salt, it's raining hard: air water-shattered,
spattering in shrouds that the wind catches
sideways and buffets at the lightning's branching
snap, harder dint and drive coming over the roofs
like a tide of nails. Cloud to cloud, dense
as earth upheaved into sky flash-frozen, whited
out, thunder rends. Run down by the reservoirs,
the water's wind-scuffed grey as rough glass.
Three hundred years back, elm trees told
war stories—saplings planted to bud memories
green—and names still scatter, literary,
much-handled, like leaves or struck shingles
on the raining wind; broken branches, loose
pages blown free. History unsheaves. Rainstick
music on a grand scale. Storm walks stately,

tumultuous, electric: lay an older name
to its jagged bolts before it clears. No faces
building billowed in the clouds; no thundercrack
of revelation; but sometimes in clearing moments,
when the rain rattles a little less harsh
on slates and asphalt, batters glass a little
more softly, you can see a shape standing
where the flash and clamor quiet, still
and poised as the breath before the first
pitched prayer. Rain washes his spectacles,
patiently, in streams; his hair never
blows askew. Come closer, and carefully,
to hear what keeps wind and tempest tuned
and true: the low notes are thunder, and
all the thousand voices of falling rain.
Stand and wait, though you never see
quite clearly enough, and maybe he'll turn
through shifting sails of rain, gaze caught
on the high note that splits sky like cloth—
but step too near and the storm's hand
will furl him round, leave you rain-blown
trees and the sound of renewed drops dinting
Trout Brook; no answers. Find somewhere
dry to wait out what's left. The oracle
is over; the performance done, exit
made; the curtains of the rain drawn closed.

Featherweight

"It's not the same," Ligeia said. She still pressed one hand beneath her jacket, fingers stiff along the curvature of her ribs that showed stark under grey cotton, denim worn white in patches; her breath came as sharply as her words were dispassionate, quick metallic flashes that made Dominick's throat tighten to hear. Cross-legged on the concrete floor, so oil-soaked that it slicked dully even years after the hydraulic posts had been uprooted and the garage converted to warehouse space, ghosts of rust and speed and travel clinging in the place's heavy, slippery smell, she had not moved since he left and returned again, settling down with a roll of silver-backed duct tape and a wadded handful of brown paper towels. In the sallow light, her skin looked taut as plaster or papier-mache; fragile enough to split if Dominick touched her hard, set his hand against the hollowed plane of her cheek and pushed inward. Her hair had slipped forward in fine handfuls, the color of woodsmoke. Gently he reached inside her jacket, palm against one shallow breast for a moment as he prised her fingers free and curled them inside his own; Ligeia's skin shocked against his and he saw her face close in a tart, momentary smile. "I know," he whispered, and pulled himself closer over the darkened concrete, slow deep cold already fading through the bones in his hand, "I'm sorry," and he did not know what he was apologizing for, which way he had disappointed them, as he took the heart carefully from her other hand.

Handmade glass, lumpen and half-translucent: he turned the thing a moment in the light before shoving it back into his hip pocket; it just fit in his palm, an artsy love token streaked through with blues and aquamarines like a piece of romanticized winter. A few days ago, he had picked it up from a crafts store down the street, one out of maybe a dozen cookie-cuttered hearts tumbled together in a wicker basket on the counter. It had not reminded him of Ligeia; she had accepted it anyway, and now he watched her divesting herself of the gift.

She had already shrugged out of her jacket and slipped her arm free of one T-shirt sleeve, untacking tape from the roll with small noises like static. Fine steel wire glinted the length of her breastbone, curved about her left breast: a neat toothwork of stitches, tiny and precise as embroidery; undone. No blood clotted the pale, hemmed edges of her skin. The first time Dominick had touched her, the metal had made a faint zipper burr beneath his tracing finger, a sound of opening, as he turned one nail inward and wondered whether her skin would part: unpeel like parchment leaves folded back to reveal the armature of bone and sinew beneath, blood-oiled; as though his touch were a moving key, her body a puzzle-box. Ligeia had showed him how to unpick the seams herself, open to the cold place where emptiness nested. Now she closed over the hollow again, smoothing the tape down with the fingertips of one hand, absently; like pushing hair out of her eyes or knotting up a loose sneaker lace, a thoughtless and habitual gesture. A smudge of grime, maybe old motor oil, lay over her ash-fair skin like dust floating on water. Crouched warily at her side, Dominick proffered a paper towel; but she ducked back into her T-shirt, had done up the jacket's flat brassy buttons before her eyes found him again. "No depth," she said. Her breath was easing; the words had the flavor of an apology. "There was nothing to it. Just what you saw, all the way through: transparent."

Dominick shivered a little, put one hand on the floor to steady himself; his palm stuck to the gritty cement and he lifted it with a grimace, gave up and folded into a sitting position against the stained wall. He had a thin, curious face, fair rusty hair and eyes less green than variable grey. Against Ligeia's jeans and leather, he wore corduroy trousers and collarless shirts, sleeves rolled up in the summers and his hair awry; in winter, he donned knit vests like a man more than twice his age and twenty-five years ago, overcoat buttoned to match. A faint pepper stubble made his jaw look like something left out to speckle in the wind and rain. Light beaded on the silver helix spiraling through the upper rim of one ear: pure anachronism, illusion deliberately broken. When he unfolded his hand, palm upturned and no demands made, Ligeia slotted her fingers through his own; from the fourth finger up along his arm, a chill began to seep again. Gelid trace in the veins and capillaries, bleeding his blood's path to the source. He tightened his clasp and asked, "Can you still feel them?"

"Last night. I dreamed—" A shudder hit her, sideways buffet like bitter wind; outside the garage, late afternoon would be melting into evening, shadows sinking in the westering light and everything turning the color of oranges and new bronze where the skyline fractured to black. Dominick shifted nearer to Ligeia, breathed the first crisp edges of ice. "The scales tipped. With nothing there, they tipped," she whispered, "and I was falling—" With her eyes closed, she looked small and very young, all thin bones and downed defenses, holding tight to Dominick as though his warmth could keep back nightmares. Then she looked at him, and the grey of her eyes caught some fluorescent angle of light; a pewter gloss spilled over their granite, duller than silver and more dangerous, and the underside of Dominick's skin turned to fractal crystals.

"I won't let you fall," he promised. The color of her eyes was coursing mercurial in his bones, her hunger inside him; he had never gotten the hang of undoing buttons one-handed. "I said I wouldn't. I keep my word."

Her hair smelled a little like weathered stone in shadow, like old gasoline fumes, brand-name shampoo. The slope and curve of her collarbone exactly fitted where he leaned his mouth, and her hand closed softly on the nape of his neck. "I know," she murmured, "I know," and he did not care whether she believed him anymore.

He kissed her first where she was coldest, before she pulled him close. Beneath his mouth, even through the layers of T-shirt and duct tape that held all the universe together, her skin burnt like winter metal: icewater paralytic, flinching in the roots of his teeth. Her fingers froze in his hair. Warmer, the base of her throat tautened as shallowly with her pulse as a dreamer's flickering eyes; with his thawing tongue, he nudged aside green enamel and silver, a pendant eye and triangle that clicked against his teeth as he mouthed it, Ligeia's only and inseparable jewelry. Occasionally he wondered what eyes she could find more frightening than her own. *Justice is not,* she had answered when he mentioned the necklace, an offhand reference to dollar bills and hamsa hands while her eyes glittered and waned stone-grey again, *always blind.*

Beyond the metal-slatted door that Ligeia had rattled down and locked when they entered, a police siren streamed past in a Doppler wave and Dominick heard his own breath following. Salt burned down his spine; Ligeia's touch laid ice and electricity over his hips; they traded warmth. Stripes of fired light slanted high on the wall, where dust-webbed windows filtered the sunset. The blue glass heart was jamming into his hipbone; Dominick thought of shards, cracked and razor edges, and pressed his mouth blindly to the duct tape over Ligeia's breast, shield for her secret: the hollow where her heart had been, where he had lost his heart.

When he dreamed of Ligeia, her eyes were always grey: in memory, always metallic and mirror-inverse, drawing at his bones. Sometimes he remembered her hair darker, settling around her shoulders like smoke, or her skin less parchment-pale. Once she walked through his thoughts when he had nodded off in an armchair, afternoon sun spilling over his lap and a forgotten book splayed on the hardwood floor, blind as though silver coins already lay over her eyes; daydreaming, he rested his hand inside her hollow places and woke half a heartbeat from orgasm. Some dreams he never told her. She had changed them.

The first night after they touched, after she showed him the cold that rooted in her veins and fragments of story that explained nothing, Dominick thought that he closed his eyes and woke. On a plain of sand and fallen pylons, he walked until all the stars drained out of the sky and the night revolved over him, a woman chained and jeweled in lights, the earth fast in her embrace. A dry, low wind pushed through his hair, hunted for his bones beneath cloth and flesh; he paused once to fit his fingers into the grooves and worn arches of half-weathered writing, hieroglyphs on fallen red granite, meaning-less, and walked on. Then he stopped, saw the figures blurred some-where between smoke and roughed stone and human silhouettes fraying into long, tilting shadows, and heard the voices hissing on the wind. Dreaming, conscious and chilled, Dominick put up his hands against the glow that tricked the eye—ember haze from the first few minutes after sunset when the sun had gone down below the horizon and fiery swathes of light still flushed the sky; western light, dying—and marked a lean cat's profile, a hawk's eye of flaring gold, the gleam of inlaid lapis and the burnish of alabaster, and heard a harsh laughter that no human throat ever formed, that sang and snapped out of the desert, and he wanted desperately to wake.

Hands dark as wet earth rose and fell in the afterglow, lifted clinking ornaments of gold, ties of linen that unspooled to the insis-tent wind. A voice was murmuring, tuneless, tenacious; the jackal cried out again, and the sun's fires were fading out of the sky. On his

63

knees though he had not knelt down, Dominick held onto sand with both hands, clutched at slipping time and place. A ellipse of light flashed hot in his eyes, and another: the pans of a balanced set of scales, holding only the last sideways flare of the sunken day. The jackal's eye, liquid jet, opening inward like a ring or an event horizon, transfixed him. A woman was walking toward him, shivering with heat-haze, in her hands something white and fern-curled that she laid on one side of the scales. For a moment he saw her face, while the others eddied like spindrift in dead currents and the feather sank slowly on the scales: incised and expressionless as a statue, black hair folded back on her shoulders and eyes less legible than the jackal's. At her heel, shadow bulked. Dominick saw the gleam of teeth, muscles that bunched heavily and a hungrier darkness gaping; then the woman had reached him, and laid her hands on his chest, and something broke open beneath his ribs.

The dream was dissolving like sand, crumbling down in cold shadow over wind-haunted stone and faces that were neither animal nor human but immortal. Sculpture and bright paints on tomb-wall plaster were only the barest sketches of ambiguity, of certainty and terror; but he saw the scales swinging, the feather rising and the other pan dipping with the weight taken from the deepest places in him, the record of his heart. *In the Hall of Two Truths,* Ligeia confirmed when he described the scene as something he had seen in a museum—tentatively, jumpy even in full noon sunshine bright off cement and storefront glass. February light split shadows from the chairs and white sidewalk tables outside Where The Flowers Went; her voice ebbed, childlike. *You know them, then.* He tried to protest; she covered his mouth with one wind-cold hand. *They'll always know you now.* The pewter spilled over her eyes then, ghostly overcast to make hummus wraps and tomato-basil quiche unreal; and he did not tell her, though sometimes the image flashed up again in other dreams and he startled sweat-drenched into wakefulness, how he had woken before he saw which way the scales balanced.

He believed, or he did not; he knew how her skin felt against his, what stories she had reeled into his dreams. He brought her the first heart two days later.

Sarah Vaughan was singing "My Funny Valentine" when Dominick snapped the radio on, throatful of smoke and deep, wry longing; the air had cooled abruptly with evening and prickled slightly in the fine hairs on his arms as he closed the windows, little aftershocks of Ligeia still tripping his nerves. Beyond the panes that overlooked a slant of shingles before dropping down into the sodium-lit street, night spread like soot: stars sketching low constellations at the corners of vision, gone when Dominick looked for them; oversize moon in a hazy cove of clouds, one day past full and sinking tawny between the stepped crags of buildings. When he washed his hands at the kitchen sink, lukewarm water scalded over his chafing palms. He could still smell the garage's memories of changed oil and tune-ups, and Ligeia.

Don't change a hair for me, Sarah Vaughan coaxed, *Not if you care for me,* and Dominick put a mug of cold coffee in the microwave to nuke. Employee perk or some kind of barter payment from Where the Flowers Went, cheerful cellar holdout from the 1960's where Dominick served chai and played chess, sometimes both for money; he still avoided open-mike nights. *Each day is Valentine's Day . . .* No one's funny Valentine: Ligeia had never visited him at work. He doubted there was space in the same world for her and vegetarian coffeehouses.

Elaine Stritch on the radio, "You Took Advantage of Me," by the time he coughed a little on the coffee that steamed its way down his throat, fished the glass heart free of his pocket; cool against his palm and mouth, and it had left him a shallow bruise. On the shelf over his computer, he put it down beside a card of Christ's sacred heart, twined around with thorns and erupting in holy fire like the petals of a rose, relic of the Catholic upbringing he had never had. A suite of playing cards had unsheaved almost the length of the shelf, magician's trick frozen in the hinge of pick-a-card-any-card: jack, queen, king half fallen behind one bracket and the ace leaning up against a miniature anatomical model, dyed plastic and little pins holding ventricles to vena cava, truncated aorta and hollow-molded atria. The same tactile symbol repeated in fragrant, unstained cedarwood, in openwork silver wire and polished aventurine, fat stuffed plush and glazed earthenware from a gardening store. Suncatcher glass; painted pressboard. Porcelain chambers marked out like a dissection. Rough pink quartz. An old one slipped to the floor where Dominick stooped to retrieve it, flat red construction paper, lopsided and softly ragged at the edges where it had frayed in his hands and Ligeia's breast; something Charlie Brown might have cut out for his little red-haired girl, painstakingly, and never let her see. A few months ago, he had even spilled tiny, tangy candies into Ligeia's palms: drowning in sugar, breath stopped with hearts. None had fit. *It's not the same,* she had whispered, again and always, words that hooked into Dominick's own heart and set fast; she asked no apologies, and he gave them.

Once, he had wanted to dream of her, before: wherever and whenever that had been. Centuries and wandering centuries back, before time pressed the tint from her skin and tattered her hair to the color of ghosts, when her eyes had no lead in them and blood pulsed hot at the delicate turns of her wrists. If he ever found the right heart, her own or something close enough to fool pursuing dreams and the metal edges of emptiness, would she revert? Slowly warm beneath his hands, shake back her hair and show him a handful of metal threads come free from her flesh as painlessly as old, dissolving stitches? Crumble to onionskin husks and flakes of bone? Another strew of rust where the heavy cast-iron pipes had leaked, the ex-garage's own cardiovascular system breaking down like anything organic and dead: *consign to thee, and come to dust.* Or another girl in the crowd, biker jeans washing out hazily at the knees, God's eye sliding around her neck because she liked the look. Someone to pass by, and remember that you had once known. He had never asked who had closed her breast with dainty steel; what had taken up the time between loss that fractured his sense of possible and a man in an overcoat looking up from slush-clotted streets to a necklace of milky green and silver, a jacket too thin for the gnawing season, and her eyes like the clouds shoaled overhead. *You're a Poe fan?* he asked, hearing her name, some remnants of high-school English or library afternoons still ricocheting where he never gave them much thought. *I read some drafts,* she answered; and though he considered that she might be joking, he never made sure.

"Ligeia," he said aloud, and stepped back from the shelf of failed hearts, makeshift cardiac museum; knowing better than to promise *next time* to empty air, to say the words at all, and still wanting some consolation stronger than the chill of her hidden places soaking up his warmth like stone in the sun, frost invading winter earth, temporary. Down in the street a dog barked, high and baying: sharp moon-cry that turned like a knife on the ear, and Dominick gulped coffee so quickly his throat hurt from swallowing. *And I was falling*— The dream flickered through him, sand and sunset and insatiable judgment, and he felt the realization open in his mind like an eye, a circle of sun lifting from the horizon, so very simple and natural that he wondered why it hurt.

"I love you," Dominick said. Summer rolled down his back in sweating drops, cooler inside the warehouse's memories of old gasoline and stacked tires, industrial paints slapped down the walls and shelves bracketed high toward dull fluorescence, and the words as he pronounced them still made each atom of his skin flush. Did everybody feel like this, speaking cliché or charm? The look in Ligeia's eyes was as blank as new cement.

He wanted a photograph of her, suddenly, one still moment under this insect light as she looked back at him: naked to the waist, the pendant staring from just below her collarbones and the intricate, opened seam of steel beneath the only ornaments on her frail skin. An inside-out T-shirt, dark enough green to look black, lay jumbled up with her constant denim jacket over her lap. "I love you," he repeated; his hands were empty as he kneeled, all the weight of what he had brought her in his mouth instead. Her hair clouded over her shoulders. "You're never going to fall; they're never going to find you. You don't even have to wear that"—wanting to touch the silver triangle, cover the eye that held him no less impersonally than Ligeia—"anymore, not unless you want to. You don't need anything to look out for you."

Her face was like something made from frozen rice paper, but her voice sounded only curious when she asked, finally, "What did you bring?"

"My heart." He felt the shock in his chest, flash of adrenaline in the vulnerable fist of muscle. Setting the offer in her hands as carefully as a thing of living flesh, "I'm giving it to you."

"Why?"

"Because you've had it since the moment I saw you. You get near me, and I can feel . . ." Even a card would have been better than nothing; a ring, a flower, some more tangible symbol than the puzzled patience in her gaze and the static in his blood, the ungainly protestations and promises that someone else had already said several thousand times before. "I had a girlfriend when I was still in college, did I ever tell you this? We only went out a couple of times. Mostly to chess tournaments. I don't know why, but she really liked me—she's probably one of the few people on the planet who ever saw me wearing a sweatshirt. She loved to talk on the phone; she would call me up all the time and tell me all of these random, day-to-day things. She had a whole catalogue of them, stuff I don't even remember anymore, every evening, every time we caught dinner together. And I'd listen. Because I did like her: she was a good person, interesting to talk to, really not a bad chessplayer, and I still hope she's happy. But we went to chess tourna-ments and talked about openings and defenses, and she called me all the time after class, and after a while she stopped calling and I stopped looking for her at the National Open, because it simply wasn't that important. You, if you had a phone," and he heard the absolute banality of the statement, swallowed a tic of laughter like a hiccup, "I would call you every hour until you got sick of me. So my heart is yours, Ligeia, the last heart. Because I want to give it. Not paper or choco- late—something of myself," sure she would hear in the echo, *because nothing else has worked*. Love, that wanted and sacrificed and conquered all. "Because I think it will work," he finished. "If you want it to."

Ligeia's eyes moved over him, harshly grey, and he realized she was looking for knives, scalpels, chisels—something to lay him out flat and dissect past freckles and tendons and ribs cracked open, hinged back to the beating, blood-webbed organ that looked very little like all its popular representations. An infusion to push out the chill in her shallow, irregular heartbeat, the ghost in her veins; to circulate Dominick's love through every cell and capillary until she moved like a native in this world and no longer needed to look behind her for the old pursuit, the hunters of nightmare chasing down those who escaped the scales' final sway and balance. Blood changed for blood, and at last he would see how his own heart weighed. "Not that way," he said, and the backs of her eyes glittered; a misstep?

But Ligeia was smiling like someone he had never seen, sweet and avid, and he did not know if hope always looked that much like terror: the same emotion that spangled bright and dark inside him, that something might finally change. "Blood doesn't stop them, anyway . . ." The smile closed; she was very still. "It won't be the same," she said, the same sentence crowded twice into the thin space of air between their faces, and Dominick watched the smile reappear. "I know," he said, and she echoed, "I know." Not shivering in her own halo of cold, "What now?"

A pulse beat everywhere, throat and wrist, brow and groin. In dream, the woman walked toward him, holding truth fragile as a feather in her hands, before she touched his chest and took everything. Dominick's voice shook only slightly as he said, "Just this," and he bent forward, suppliant at Ligeia's shrine, and kissed each pewter-eddied eye and her mouth that breathed out frost in early May, the unclosing eye of silver and the palm of each hand that he raised to his mouth, and at last, for the first time, the sharp, strict edges of her parted skin.

For a moment, he imagined his tongue freezing to the filigree of flesh and steel—stuck like any idiot who licked a lamp-post in winter—before the mist of his breath filled the dry, vacant space and he breathed back the mixed flavors of time, and Ligeia, and his vow. Bitter pricks of wire caught on his tongue as he described the emptiness, brushed like sparks over his lips. "I love you," he whispered into her. Each word smokily visible and gone, "I give you my heart." Her fingers slid through his sweat-stuck hair and down to the highest bone of his spine, drawing warmth, ley-lines of another season; opened, intent, he waited to realize that he could distinguish her moving fingertips through simple contact and pressure, no colder or hotter than his own ready skin. The granite color of her eyes when he lifted his head, unchanged. All the hearts he had brought her, found or made: his heart settling on her scales.

Above him, as he lay in her arms, small noises that were neither questions nor names moved in Ligeia's throat and she tensed against him. He was murmuring less sense than sound, breathless incantation, "Ligeia, I love you," while he knew exactly the hallmarks of Ligeia that he loved: the pewter, the cold, the alien, dispassionate need. *If it works,* she had not asked, was not asking now, *will you still love me?* If she had a job, a phone, if she could love him back . . . On the edge, shuddering, Dominick kissed his heart into Ligeia and whispered, "As long as you'll let me, I'll love you." Her voice broke, rending as a cry of birth; he listened for a pulse, and hoped he would.

> Set me as a seal upon your heart.
> —*Song of Songs*

Nights with Belilah

Midnight had turned over long hours ago, in the green numerals of the clock on the dresser and the chimes floating downwind of some distant cathedral, far out over the darkened skyline and the clouds smudged with skyscraper light, and Theo was still awake, thinking of Clarity. Before the party broke up, before Theo started counting who had left and making sure nobody had passed out in the bathroom, she had moved between two pieces of perfunctory conversation and he could not understand how he had missed her before: the rich drape of her hair, overcast crimson as the petals of a dying rose, that slid over her shoulders as she turned; the breadth of bone from chin to brow, the rise and curve of her cheekbones; mosaic eyes, inset beneath fluent brows, some dark color that her lashes hid; across his field of vision and gone. He was just drinking, tequila and Triple Sec, nothing that would start up static behind his eyes or steal freeze-frames out of the night, one ear always listening for the words that said *I need*, but looking at her made him forget what they meant: language crowded out by the thing itself, the blind press of desire. He wanted to speak, to draw her gaze, to hear her voice. He wanted to meet her eyes, to learn their color; to look away, before she saw into him, into every bone and flushed breath and rise of sweat from her passing presence, half a room away, probably heading for the kitchen to mix herself a drink and not even noticing the pale man who supplied, who traded, who gave people what they wanted; who was not used to wanting. Old story, and getting older as the night thinned toward morning; Theo's breath hissed out between his teeth, a hard and rueful sound, and he did not dare close his eyes. He wanted to dream of Clarity.

He lay on his back among sheets half drawn up, a bone ghost of himself in the darkness: skin just darker than his milk-white hair that rucked up into afternoon spikes no matter how carefully slicked back in the morning; his eyes closed like a cat's when he smiled, opened into a wash of watercolor blue that eluded direct gaze, no sounded depth and nothing to get hold of, to pin down or pin anything onto. Somewhere his age had slipped a gear, a handful of years misplaced among the deft, whittled angles of his face; twenty or thirty, not twenty-four in August on the date he never told anyone. He wore gestures instead, expressions for every missing month. How old was she—Clarity, whose name he had had to ask from ginger-dark Devi who grew windowbox marijuana in a small act of social defiance, a Canadian flag draped over the sill. "Sounds like a drug," Devi had added, laughing in afterthought; she leaned back on the fire escape, hands braced on the black iron and streetlight glittering on the silver rings braided into her hair. Air blew in a warm draft beneath them; exhaust and sun-tacked asphalt, three kinds of smoke and Vietnamese cooking. "You should like that . . ."

Clarity: under his skin, running livewire in his veins. Bright as cracked glass, his day scored across; on his breath, from tasting even a thread of her hair; full-body flashback. Arms folded behind his head, Theo reeled time back and poised her in the living room again between bassline beats and windows full of backlit skyline, the ghost of some architect's dreaming. Close enough to feel the wake of her long hair as she moved past him, he tensed against the limits now; his hand had touched her shoulder and she stopped between steps, a smile sketched over her icon's face, and leaned into the touch. Too far, too fast; he was trying to picture how Clarity really would smile and she is there, the tensile membrane between his dreams and her torn through without warning, her hand reaching into his fantasies to pull her into the bed alongside him, on one elbow among the rumpled sheets as though she has been there all night. Her hair settles like dusk around her shoulders, black as tar without the oily sheen, as coal without the anthracite glitter, and he cannot tell where it trails off into the dark; she might be all the stranded hours wrapping around him, all the night that lies over the earth. When he raises one hand to find her face in the drifting darkness, her lush mouth that tastes of spices and her eyes whose color spilled out of an immensity of skies without electricity, without light pollution, only the sickling moon and stars thick as milk or scattered seed, she laughs and air moves over his skin as she evades him, no more than the wry corner of her mouth brushed past his fingertips, her hipbone against his for one scalding second. Then her fingers close in his hair, nothing like an owl's claws: dry and drifting as sand against his scalp, a few degrees of fever in her touch; and an answering heat flashes under his skin, expected and unpredictable, as his nerves kindle and his bones bank fires. When her tongue dips to the faint crease between his colorless brows, he jolts; her lightning earthed in his fragile flesh, her hands that make the marionette dream. "Belilah," he whispers, the word she gave him mouth to mouth when she came to him for the first time, and the last syllable of her name is a groan.

Somewhere in fragments, Theo is still trying to remember how Clarity's easy stride lifted her small breasts beneath the sleeveless T-shirt she wore, no bra under the navy cloth, unselfconscious as a comet. Belilah has pomegranate breasts, and the hard nipple he nurses at is the seed that will hold him fast to this otherworld, this fine edge between curse and blessing. Whenever he dreams like this, he dreams of her: there has never been anything else. The night world ends beyond the shared slide of their skins.

Even his words are gone, now; she has drawn them all out of him with her tongue, her teeth, each kiss like something one of them has been starving for. There are soft noises she makes in her throat, little sounds that slip out of him as they move upon each other, nothing more and nothing more eloquent in the world. Briefly, he glimpses Belilah's eyes—the underside of the heavens, the inside of a shadow—before her hair blackens his vision again, pooling against his shoulder as she lowers her mouth to his chest, draws the intersecting lines of collarbone and breastbone, pinpoints the shallow, shivering hollow of his throat: triangulations of desire. Clarity's eyes are some color he never saw, and even that memory splinters when Belilah's lips brush the inner crease of his thigh, when her breath grazes and her tongue tastes his softest skin. Theo gasps; her mouth closing on him feels like being swallowed by the sea, the distant desert shores where her kindred walk, and he gives her salt for salt, blinded and exploded, holding her fast, as the world fades to black.

He woke with the last beat of orgasm, seed spilt into sweat-tacky cloth, not the deep silk of her mouth; cooling fast in the air-conditioned chill and tightening on his skin as his breathing settled, slowly, as he waited for the room to realign around him. Even after years, he was still searching for some waking trace of her, the myrrh and cinnamon flavor of her sweat pressed into his pillow, a strand of sky-black hair in his hand. There was nothing but the clock that showed him two more hours bitten out of his life, oyster-pale light draining around the edges of the windowshade as the city clarified into day. For a reckless moment, he wondered how Devi would describe Belilah; and he knew he would never tell her.

He met Darwin and Devi at the Laundromat, watching boyshorts and bleached linen tumble behind soap-splashed glass. "You shouldn't wear sunglasses," Devi said after the door had swung shut behind him, the thirtysomething woman behind the counter looked up from her paperback romance and looked back down, reassured that the new arrival was not going to steal detergent or overturn the bleach. "Makes you look like the Wachowski Brothers should hold the copyrights on you," and Theo tipped one side of his mouth in a smile, folded the wraparound black plastic into his jacket pocket and did not blink in the late-afternoon flood of light.

Something Darwin might have said then hesitated, settled into as much silence as the chug and drone of washing machines and towels racketing dry allowed. The air smelled of heated cloth and fabric softener, a clean scent hung too long in the same space; a little too warm on Theo's skin. But there was nothing needling in Darwin's look, nothing that touched too deeply; he asked finally, "You all right?"

"A king of infinite space," said Theo, "were it not that I have bad dreams." He picked up a box of some gritty-blue detergent, dusted off his palms in the moment when Devi might have commented, but she was simply watching him, sitting on an empty dryer with one arm around Darwin's waist. Theo had long ago given up trying to figure out which week they were together, which week at each other's throats, which week reconciled and pushing the upper limits of new-couple cute; he said only, to Darwin, "You still doing something this weekend?"

Darwin was combing his fingers through Devi's hair: one long ponytail coiling onto the dryer's white-finished lid, black as ink and still lighter than Belilah's. Theo pushed the comparison back, studied Darwin's round face instead, the oddly delicate bones and eyes like a photograph in sepia, dark-wheat hair growing out from an experimental buzz cut in April. "Unless Mark can't come. He's bringing a couple of new songs. And they've got a real offer now, not just fans. So if he's in town, definitely."

"Christ, I don't know why you're still in school." Theo glanced over at the Laundromat clerk, blind to the world beyond her torrid pages. "You go to more parties than I do."

"You're invited to this one."

"I'll let you know." He might have handed Darwin anything, the gesture not even delineated clearly enough for casual, half a handful of someone's chemical dreams in transparent bubble wrap pocketed before Devi's wash could spin over again; and if he could package even the afterimage of Clarity on the sight, he would be a rich man long before he died. "I'm still recovering from your last one." He lifted wry brows to ease the courtesy, added, "Thanks."

"She really got to you," Devi said, remark snared between surprise and satisfaction, "Clarity."

Theo rubbed the bridge of his nose, thought about putting his sunglasses back on. "I didn't talk to her."

"She'll probably be there on Saturday. I think Mark knows her." The lines of her face were clean as statuary, a different shade of dark from Belilah; he felt trapped between images, folded into too many times and hungering suddenly for even the barest bones of her words. There was still a faint, pinched crease between her eyebrows, even after Darwin had stowed the packet safely away. Maybe she never smoked her protest marijuana after all, just mixed drinks and argued with Darwin; contact high. "I don't know why she shows up. She doesn't even talk to people much."

Darwin murmured, "Shy's not a crime," words nuzzled into the slope of Devi's neck, and whatever fragments of Clarity she might have given him dissolved into her laughter, husky as blown leaves. One hand came up against Darwin's shoulder, to push him off; remained to slide around the back of his neck, fingers up into his fur-short hair, and Theo knew he should have left: no clearer cue than kissing hard and deep in the middle of the Laundromat. Down the row of washing machines, a bulky, grey-haired man was piling a finished load of checkered shirts into a plastic hamper, one after another like magician's scarves. Devi had slipped off the dryer, Darwin turned to meet her; Theo might have become another piece of scenery, irrelevant as the sun moving leisurely across the scratched linoleum floor. He had never touched Clarity like that, never watched a slant of five o'clock brightness search for highlights in her hair like Blake's desire-darkened rose, never fingered her fluid spine through sweat-stroked cloth; or sat somewhere crowded and ordinary, so close and so impossible to reach over and touch the way he wanted that the air between them felt tactile, live as a quickened pulse or heat jangling over summer blacktop. Something that was neither lust nor longing hit the breath out of him abruptly: come up hard against tight black denim, startled by the intensity of his need to know how Clarity would feel in his arms, leaning her weight full against him some afternoon in a coin-op laundry; how Belilah's eyes would look when the light fell into them.

"Jesus!" The word snapped out of him. If Darwin and Devi did not spring apart, they were suddenly separate; their eyes flashed up to him, tracking his shock, and the man with the hamper full of checkered shirts had stopped with a sheet of softener in one hand. Sweat burned down the nape of Theo's neck. "Go . . . you're adorable, get a fucking room somewhere," he muttered, crooked smile for the woman with the romance novel, and watched Darwin try to apologize convincingly while Devi smiled and slid her fingers under his palm again. Maybe they would think that was everything, would not think to look for anything else; not Theo Volpe, cool and remote as the cat-ice color of his hair, his indefinite eyes. His groin felt like a neon sign; he had one hand on the door already, "See you on Saturday, okay?" thrown over his shoulder as he pushed it open, and he did not realize what he had promised until the Laundromat was half a block behind him.

Up and down the street, shadows were melting over cement and asphalt to meet the opposite banks of sidewalks; dazzle of windows and windshields, sun coasting toward slow twilight. Heat clouded the air. Clarity had snapshot herself onto his brain. Under the roaring shadow of an overpass, Theo closed his eyes; maybe thirty seconds she had spent in his sight, forty-five. One hit, and she was plugged straight into his heart. A pigeon went overhead in a clapping whir of wings and he laughed, thinking of the noiseless flight of owls; of the hours until sunset, and Saturday.

Sixteen years old, seventeen in the house where people still called him Theodolus, nailed by his name to a martyrdom two thousand years gone, he had asked her once where she came from. The most naive question, like trying to map an obsession or a wayward thought, cartography of unreal countries; and in the loft where he slept alone among a pantheon of unframed prints and concert posters, white-haired boy lengthening out of childhood fast, she surprised him, and answered.

"I was born on the other side of the mirror, where echoes are louder than the sounds that make them, and shadows fall with no one to cast them, and the dead are more real than the living." Her voice curled around the words, languid and inescapable as her tongue on him, her fingers. She might have been reciting a part or telling a familiar story to a child, words worn almost out of meaning by rote; he wondered suddenly who had heard this story before him, who else she had touched like this as she spoke, casually, caressingly, blank canvas faces and the same need straining between their thighs, and desire tightened so sharply in him that his breath broke. "My father was a pious student, up late and studying. My mother came to him in a dream, as we do; he woke, said his prayers, and never gave it another thought. But nine months later, I was born, in that silvered world, and there I grew. And when I was twelve, my mother instructed me after the fashion of our kind, that I should go out into the human world, the world of the living—where people leave footsteps as they walk and cast shadows behind them, where the sky is not silver and the earth is not glass—and find myself a student of my own. And I wandered the world . . ." She turned over onto him then, all her warm weight across his chest and arms, his ready hips, and her hair drowned him in darkness before he woke.

On the other side of the ocean and her scholar-father a hundred years gone, Theo dreams how it did not happen: in a classroom where he remembers taking a history of the Crusades, winter twilight water-blue and early beyond the windows; but he stares down at paper like old ivory close-set with letters that he cannot read, and candlelight makes them flicker against the sight, blackly shimmering, charged; touch one and feel the static crackle, the spark of elsewhere. "Belilah?" he asks into the silence, the faint radiator murmur; the candlelight stitches a headache into his vision. In another moment, she will rise up from the spaces between the letters—slotted sideways into text and tradition, gathering like smoke where words do not touch—and he will stammer out supplication to the king of the universe, prayers and protection that will reach her mouth long before God's ears, and breathlessly chant the Song of Songs before she has done with him. If he waits those few seconds, this blurred November evening that was never real, every night and all, her hair will furl feather-soft around them and his hands find her secret skin in its dense, blinding depths. But he has no sacred studies, no litany to trail mid-word into silence and no vows to break in her embrace, and Theo pushes his chair skidding backwards against the wall; all the candles gutter and sway, and he wants so badly that he cannot tell what.

"I'm not a student." He casts the words into the room's shadow-clung corners, as loud and passionate as Darwin and Devi's circle have never heard him, as pelting and effective as confetti; if he breaks the windows, shards and shattered panes that do not hold this dream together, will the winter darkness drop down in pieces as well? "Not a scholar, not all that shit, you know that. I dropped out three years ago. I couldn't care less about God. I wash dishes at Siam Twins, all right? . . . And you're still here!" It makes no difference what he is arguing for or against, if he is, or if he even knows; something as small as an echo whose sound has not been shouted closes his throat and he whispers, "I don't know why I'm anything you want."

He wonders if Clarity ever sat in this classroom, rose-black head bent beneath pale winter light or spring sunshine; how far he can follow that thought before it unrolls into Belilah's arms, and how much it would matter, in the end. Somehow he cannot imagine that Belilah's mortal father, the dream-dazed student tumbled among his books and commentary, simply shook off the scent and taste and honey-taut feel of his lover without even the briefest backward look, the smallest knife of regret. Or maybe just guilt; and this time the sound he makes, thinking, does not come close to laughter. Through the glass, Theo sees shapes slipping upward in the swimming indigo shade, maybe crows rising from the snow-stuck skeletons of trees, night birds, and moves before he realizes his hand has become a fist. "Fuck it—" Plate glass splintering makes a louder sound than he ever imagined, each crack like a blaring sinewave note, and the phone slammed him shaking back into his own skin.

His hand flung out into the darkness knocked the phone spinning over the hardwood floor, leather-cased thunk and clatter while the insistent midi turned up "Nervous In The Alley" another notch louder; Theo half fell after it, still looking vaguely for blood streaked between his outspread fingers, lacerations from glass that his physical flesh had never punched through. Cheated; no fix, and everything breaking at once. At least the phone still worked when he flipped it open and snarled, "What? What the fuck do you want? Hello?"

"Theo?" Tinny with distance and thin with surprise, Mark faltered, "Shit, Theo, did I wake you? I didn't think—"

"I sleep occasionally." The clock was still a green smear in the dimness, Theo's sight wheeling with darkness. He breathed carefully; leveled out his voice. "What is it?"

"I just wanted to know if you're coming tomorrow. Because if you are, if it's not a problem . . ." Words for wanting, ceremonial and circumspect, that Theo translated as absently as breathing; phone calls to make, questions to skirt, things to bring up and things to keep carefully out of the conversation, and all the different species of habit. "I can get that for you," he interrupted Mark finally, "it's not a problem, okay? I've got enough time. Just check your goddammned watch before you call next time, that's all."

Cellphone susurrus on the other end of the line and Mark said, less cautious than Darwin and less concerned, "You don't sound so good, man."

On one knee in the pallid strips of light from the window, sweat raked through his hair and the broken-off dream already dissolving, assimilating back into his thoughts, Theo said precisely, "I've been worse." He held the phone like something indecipherable long after Mark had hung up.

Night pressed up against the windows, viscous residue of a sun-drenched day, and Darwin's air conditioner was broken. Theo slouched back in an overstuffed armchair salvaged from Darwin's aunt in Atlanta, thumbed sweat from the hollows of his eyes and shifted slightly, unsticking shirt from shoulders; black cotton doing its best to become a second skin. Darwin's apartment was smaller than Devi's, half the size of Theo's skylit studio, and so cluttered with people that one more guest might sprain the entire building: sheetrock and concrete would spring leaks, panes of glass pop loose and crash out into the humid night air, the whole party spilled like a rain of dropout puppets down into the street for the police to puzzle over.

More likely Darwin's upstairs neighbor, insomniac old man with the voice of a hacksaw, would start pounding on his floor again; interactive percussion, steady as clockwork. Mark would hardly notice, cross-legged on the floor in front of the stereo and the TV, speakers higher than his head slamming out Synthetic Parameter's latest experiment; if there were words somewhere in that mesh of backbeat and layered dissonance, Theo knew only because he had heard Thanh practicing, unlikely fragments of Auden and Eliot and H.D. entangled at ska velocity. Symbolist punk, maybe. "It's going on the album as 'This Wasted Land,'" Mark had announced, "unless somebody can come up with a better title." He had bleached his hair in rusty streaks and smiled tentatively, proud and sheepish, that nobody had yet reached over and punched the music off. Out of sight in the kitchen,

Thanh was echoing his own recorded vocals half a beat behind; at least two girls were laughing. *If equal affection cannot be, Let the more loving one be me* . . . Theo tilted his glass back and drank, throat sore around a screwdriver swallow, and turned a page of the book in his lap.

All that night, Belilah had blown through his dreams like sand folding on the wind; he woke just after noon, aching on the edge of orgasm, the last traces of her presence evaporating too fast from his thoughts, his flesh, for even the pressure of his own weight against the sheets to call back. Sun gouged his eyes as he snapped the windowshade upward, white-hot off the bathroom mirror when he washed his face. The streets filled with heat like deep water. Around three o'clock in Siam Twins' small, steam-crowded kitchen, he tucked the ends of spring rolls neatly over and checked his wristwatch, checked it again five minutes later, glanced through swinging doors when the next waiter passed to see how the shadows fell over windowfront glass. Like waiting for a birthday, precious time pulling like taffy; or the night before an exam, lost in a gush of seconds toward panic as pure as anything Theo might have hoped to score. But he had seen Clarity once since the evening began, no more than the easy lift of her mouth at something Mark said about the upcoming concert, the slight change of expression disarranging all the remembered symmetry of her face into something that made Theo's fingers almost forget how to hold a glass; the response she called up in him so direct and obstinate that he sat down promptly with the nearest book in hand, some coffee-table collection of Klimt paintings, preliminary sketches and photographs, Judith twice with Holofernes' head and Truth lushly red-haired and nude. Mark had not yet put on Synthetic Parameter's demo, and Theo heard his name flashing in and out of the background tides of conversation, a little hook to his attention every time he looked back down at spectral lovers or the dark-haired musician with her gold-leaf lyre. He had always worked well with an audience, but not Devi's smile multiplied across a dozen faces; the certainty in her voice when she spoke Clarity's name. A whole apartment watching the woman with inlaid eyes, placing personal bets on who would approach her, waiting to see the untouchable Theo lose his cool. He propped his feet on the glass-topped table, turned another page, and did not look up.

Out of the stereo, Thanh sang like torn smoke, *And when I promised I'd be yours forever, I didn't know who I'd be,* and Clarity's unseen nearness tweaked underneath Theo's skin: around this corner or through that doorway, out of sight and wholly in mind, as vivid and intangible as something dreamed. Theo's smile bent tartly. Nothing from the drink that he set carefully down, glass clicking on glass; his dreams were closer. What did he have of her—less than the pages underneath his hand, creamy watersnakes and Danaë opening in dreams to a god's glittering passion—that would bind him as tightly as ten years? On the strength of two glimpses, he wanted their names spoken low as an exchange of promises, a kiss so awkward that their noses bumped, the brushfire contact of breath. Sundown to sunup in her arms, her hair strewn over his sweat-tensed skin and her mouth molded around him; the risk of tasting her, all her places and all her flavors, until he forgot that there was anything in the world but where his mouth touched her and whether she felt good. To ask her what she wanted, and mean only what he could give with his touch and his words . . . Probably she was in the hallway, a dozen steps through the inquiring cram of people who had almost all, at one time or another, told him their needs. He did not know hers.

Belilah had always come to him, as inexplicably, as constantly. The color of her eyes was embedded in his bones. But she had stayed, for something she saw in a skinny, vehement adolescent, dazzled in the aftermath of the first dream that told him what *I need* meant: against all odds and reason, someone that she wanted.

Day from dark, the first division. He was not her mother's scholar.

In the darkened screen of Darwin's TV, another urban windfall, Theo's reflection looked back hieratic, a ritual king, keeper of light and dark places. Then a shadow moved over the glass, and Theo's hand stopped halfway above his drink; but Mark finished climbing unsteadily to his feet, bright-eyed, to take Synthetic Parameter out of the stereo and sort through CDs and empty cases for something loud and innocuous, and Theo changed the gesture into a small, dry wave. "Mark, that's really fucking scary," he called, and Mark grinned.

"That's the idea, man. Hey, we're at Morrison's week after next, you want to come and hear? You get a free ticket, because I woke you up."

"Yeah, sure." Theo leaned forward to pick up his glass, Klimt book in hand as he straightened; and felt something in his stomach rise, or give way, or stop, because she had drawn her hair back in a braid the color of roses at evening, because she braided badly, and she had altered his state of consciousness from the first moment he saw her. Another otherworld entirely: she was turning far away from him, toward Devi leaning back into the curve of Darwin's arm, and he did not recognize his voice at this volume.

"Hey, Devi! Want to hear Synthetic Parameter at Morrison's in a couple of weeks?"

What Devi answered, he never heard and did not miss; his veins were channeling lightning, and he knew what he would dream. Still it was nighttime, and he was trembling, and she had looked across the room, finally, to meet his gaze.

> He is in a space somewhere between
> The human and the inhuman. That's a terrible
> Neighbourhood.
> —Christopher Fry, *The Firstborn*

Tarot in the Dungeon

The card turns up, the dice click: in latex and leather
driving gloves, she pushes back night like an armful
of velvet and taciturn brick, graffiti scratches
above the door; and her heels spike the pavement,
stiletto accompaniment to your heightening pulse,
the tattoo of descent on catwalk stairs as she ushers
you inside.

       Perhaps the magician greets you first,
all tailored shoulders and pressed creases, the shine
on his shoes pristine enough to lure in light
and never let it go, but what he flashes and conceals
among his slender fingers—immaculately scarred,
nails polished like midnight plums—clink and throw
back teases of candleshine, each key to a lock
you never suspected you had. Perhaps you spied,
over his shoulder, empress and emperor enthroned
in adoration, posing disdain and no humble display
extravagant enough for their lion's eyes; identical,
faultless predators, whose regard makes you hungry
to offer yourself up, though you cannot tell: what
sex, what gender, on which throne? Flurry of faces,

recognition strobing like an icon slideshow, quick
shuffle of possibilities: the hierophant kneeling
in prayer, profane as a name of gods, to take
in his mouth this ready sacrament; fortune's wheel
where a girl like belladonna and bone china hangs,
a compass to the quarter points of desire; justice
punishes. In a smoke of burning hearts, the lovers
entwine, hand into hand into mouth into groin
like a puzzle, abstracts of wine-soft velour
and a satin choker, and delicate silver chains.
Overhead, the hanged man in full suspension,
trussed and gagged in silk and spinner's fatal
yarn, distaff between his teeth, spider threads
about his thighs, twists slowly in the tides
of deals and scenes and brokered needs; and where
tiles chill your bare feet, temperance pours out
a libation to every exposure you never dreamed
you could admit.

    The dizzying spread, configuration
of contrarieties, paired hands of roles, blurs you
to your knees: there, searching for death or the devil
who perhaps have taken a private room, for the tower
tumbling in ruin from within, lightning-shattered,
she finds you: the high priestess. Only the guarded
brush of her eyes flares desire like a whipcrack
deep into your heart, a ritual of skins that graze
but never touch, closeness never consummated
and all the air between you turns to fire. Sun
outshines moon eclipses sun, time stolen forever
into a painted picture on a card that your anxiety
has fingered, like a talisman, almost to bright smears
and little more, but you have passed the hermit's
hermetic solitude and this knowledge shivers

in your breast like a distant, warming, elusive
star: foolish and innocent, stepping out
on a journey whose end you cannot imagine, you
will never be anything but hers. She has called,
she initiates, she claims: this is the world.

Time May Be

On the other side of the river, the bells were ringing for morning. Already a thin light was seeping between the buildings, eastward where the Aden slid out toward the harbor, the distant spill of waves and the sea broadening toward the sun; low on the horizon, pale as milled bone, the moon dipped onto the points and domes of Aruis' skyline. The sky was turning the color of washed slate. Josza shivered in the early chill, autumn's taste on her tongue like regret or the faint flavor of a memory; she propped her chin on one hand, cross-legged atop a scarp of old brick where small boats sometimes moored, and watched a pair of cormorants slide beneath the river's skin, dark birds in darkened water. She liked to come here, to the open river. Early morning gave her a space for thought, before the sun rose and stirred the city to life—and now, more than anything, she needed the time to think. Between her fingers, she turned a single card of stiff pasteboard. Patterned back and painted face, it caught none of the faint glow from the setting moon or the gas-flare at Josza's back that cast her shadow onto the water a good three feet below; ate light and gave nothing back. Her mouth crooked and she said softly, "Gauven Dystre."

With the name came an image of his face as she had last seen it, wan with exhaustion and whatever secrets he had taken into sleep with him as he curled like a child on her cleared bed: young, slight, rounded cheekbones and tapering mouth; he did not look old enough for his breaking voice, but she had thought him an old man when he tumbled against her doorstep at midnight. First she had knelt and put a hand to his forehead to check him for fever, for plague-ghosts were not uncommon even after summer had passed, after Shadefast when the year died and the Thorns stripped of their greenery transfixed the weakening Sun; she brushed back his hair, discovered his unlined face and frowned in perplexity. His hair fanned over his forehead, fine and loose as flax. His face held close to its bones. Beneath lashes as fair as his hair, his eyes were some soft dark color; grey as soot, brown as earth, sliding open to stare at her only a moment before closing again. "You're safe," Josza murmured, though she doubted he heard her. "Lie still. You're safe." But he moved his face against her thigh, made a small aching noise that might have had words in it somewhere. Against his temples, her fingers prickled as though she were the one burning with fever; something strange in him, something askew from the streets and canals of Aruis as she knew it. But she could not place this young man's strangeness, save that first inexplicable flash of his face; because there was nothing else to do, she stooped and gathered him into her arms, and brought him inside.

Up two flights of creaking stairs, he made no sound or movement, a lax weight in her arms—he did not weigh as much as he should have, even for a boy just getting his adolescent growth—but when she laid him on the bed, he opened his eyes again. "Please," he said. The word was little more than a breath of air and Josza did not hear him at first; she was clearing scrolls and oddments onto any handy horizontal surface, used herself to sleeping among the clutter of her studies and sure that this stranger, sick or not, would not be. As she lifted a double handful of small mechanisms, pins and screws and rings of different metals, he spoke again. "Please. Tell me."

"Tell you what?" She softened her voice, careful not to frighten him. He was staring at her as she had seen condemned men watch the blade, the rope, the fire. "What can I do?"

"Who I am."

Josza said gently, "Who are you?"

For a moment he looked like any young man of the city, his head pillowed on one bent arm as he gazed at her; she had a hemisphere of dusty agate in one hand, a box of frosted glass and silver in the other and a string-tied packet of political tracts tucked into the crook of her elbow; light from the hanging lamp drew shadows sideways over her face. "Gauven Dystre," he said easily, and the disjoint ran pins and needles over her skin again. "Who are you?"

"Josza." He must not have heard of her, for he showed no surprise. Strangers who followed the stories to her door always expected beauty: the porcelain cast of her skin, the polished sheen of her hair, the enameled delicacy of her lips and the lobes of her ears. Surely her eyes would be as violet or blue as stained glass. She must have perfect fingernails. Instead she possessed a face as dark as a crow's and as angled, private, obscure. The scars of some old pox dented her cheek-bones; lines ridged about the corners of her mouth, smiles or frowns grained deep into the skin; her brows were quick, crooked, flyaway ink-slashes that lifted easily in humor or surprise. Her hair was strong and coarse, black overcast bronze. Sometimes she knotted ribbons into its darkness, red and black; small plaits gathered into one long, chunky braid that still reached to the small of her back. The color of her eyes perplexed. Nothing like the stories, everything like herself. She was never sorry.

When he did not reply, she tried his name: "Gauven?" But he had fallen asleep again, or unconscious; he had burrowed deeper into the patched sheets, turning away from her, one hand clenching on the quilt to spill a sheaf of familiar pasteboard rectangles to the floor. Josza sighed, bent to retrieve them. But he stirred again, put out his hand in a dreamer's movement for the last card still lying beside his face; and Josza felt the breath stick in her throat as it fluttered face-up to the floor. Taking the card with fingers that flinched from it, she had locked her door and gone out into Aruis' night.

Now she laid it down on the brickwork beside her, studying its image in the smoky light. A slow chill weighted her stomach and her hairline stung with sweat. Not for its significance: she had never been afraid when the twenty-first fate set its hands over her cards and cast *Death* into the configuration. She had known the cards since her infancy, their habits, their caprices, every faint change of fates reflected in major and minor arcana alike. So her father had taught her. But this was not *Death* as she knew it, the animate skeleton holding the reaper's scythe in one hand and the hourglass in the other, verdant ivy twining its bones in remembrance that every ending birthed a beginning; this was nothing but blackness, unalloyed, opaque, the denial of any image at all. Her father had never taught her anything like this.

Out on the water, a cormorant was laughing. Josza picked up the card, still gingerly, shoved it deep into one pocket. Practical as the stories did not say she was, she wore boots, trousers, a blouse that might have begun life as the upper half of a dancing-gown: rich velvet, gold and russet and green all beaten together like leaves, frayed now across the shoulders and the full sleeves ripped. In one ear dangled a crescent of translucent stone, uncut selene, that skinned milk-blue when the light touched it. She had left Gauven sleeping among her books and orreries, had locked the door with a word; he would be safe still. But if he woke, and found she was not there, what then? She got to her feet in three quick movements, stretched the stiffness out of her bones, chafed her gloved hands together for warmth. Pasteboard *Death* transformed weighed her pocket like a stone.

Though she had been born far from Aruis, she had come to know its streets as well as the slipping stars or her own upturned palm. For a while she followed the Aden where it turned and flexed between the cliffs of factories and warehouses, its stink of mud and filthy water muted now by autumn. Crossing Leukas' Bridge as the bells rang for true dawn, she looked upriver and considered continuing into the upper part of Aruis, broad avenues and houses that terraced down to the water's edge: the dry districts, richer than her means. Certain clients of hers lived there, those whom she could name aloud and those whom she could not. Sometimes she visited the basilica where the city's tyche presided over travelers, councilors, young couples, entrepreneurs: a kneeling woman in painted marble three times life size. In her left hand she held the Moon rayed with rose petals, in her right the Sun hanging on the Thorns. The signs of the zodiac carved a necklace about her throat. Her hair rained over her shoulders. At this hour of the morning, Josza might walk almost alone over the white flagstones, even settle down on the tyche's knees and converse with the statue. On occasion, legend said, the tyche answered back. But the thought of her sleeping guest pricked under her thoughts and she turned downriver again, back toward the sinking streets and the far harbor: Aruis' river-quarters, her home.

Gauven Dystre. Dystre. The echo of her footsteps came back off the cobbles with his name, resonant, incomprehensible.

Within five minutes the river had forked into a maze of canals and the little building-islands that comprised most of the city. Now Josza relaxed into her usual swinging stride, hard-heeled, almost a lope along the dimming streets. Her braid thumped at her back. Here the houses tilted toward one another so far, so steeply, that they shut out the sunlight; morning or evening, noon or midnight, no light changed in the river-quarters. Only socketed torches and hanging lanterns, sometimes open fires built on stone piers at the crossroads of certain canals, illuminated grimy brickwork, flaking stone, tar-black water slipping and lapping at ledges of pavement a scant handspan higher than the Aden's tide-changing level. Hands in her pockets, Josza crossed cobbled causeways or low bridges of wood and stone, once or twice even leapt short distances over the light-rimed water when the roads and alleys ran out. Fitful currents sucked at the piers. Josza did not inspect what floated by.

Fog lifted off the water and made her cough despite herself. The damp clung to her skin, the close leaning atmosphere of the houses around her; the Aden swallowed everything. Especially here, where the older city still showed itself in the upper sills of windows emerging from the water, faces of stonework going down into the cold, silted depths, sunken gargoyles that spat rippling weed instead of rainwater. Josza herself had dived into drowned houses, some that belonged to families she had known, retrieved the fragments of lives long lost to disintegration and the river's slow rise. There were many kinds of fishing in Aruis. She turned the corner of a street where lanterns of stained glass marked every canal-cut block: vermilion, azure, tangerine, emerald, colors too rich for the air that smelled of tide-flats and drainage, houses that had crumbled against one another until sometimes the sky showed through projecting rafters and shingles shed like scales into the canal below, sunlight shafted onto the water in a glitter of broken glass . . . Not at this hour of the morning; not today. Her house craned over the canal like any other, its third story canted against the roof of the opposite building. On its front door hung the image of a man's face, bronze or brass, kept carefully polished of frost and condensation in every season of Aruis' cold year. Josza pulled off one glove, laid her hand flat against the image's forehead. Briefly it warmed to her skin, or her skin warmed its metal, she was never sure which. Under her breath, she whispered a word.

The latch clicked. The door had no handle, only the brazen face, its eyes open and its lips parted on a word unspoken and unheard; perhaps the word that Josza had spoken a moment ago. Now she said, "Thank you," and pushed open the door, spilling faint light inward over grimed flagstones and a whorled honey-colored shell. Beyond, odd shapes bulked: racks of shelves, gleams that might be glass or metal, some of them in motion, terraced stacks that could only have been books. Her house smelled of damp, and library-dust, and fish cooking in a stew. Like her arresting, unbeautiful face, the sense of her house always surprised those travelers who came seeking the stories. Smiling, Josza bent her head to the sculpted doorkeeper and went inside to Gauven Dystre and his mysteries.

She slept until the bells rang for noon. If Gauven had woken during her midnight walk, he had not moved much; she climbed the stairs by candlelight, shadows splayed over the lath-and-plaster walls, and checked on him where he still slept beneath her faded quilt. His breath was faint and even, his skin cool. Until he woke, she could do nothing: Josza dragged her heaviest winter coat out of its closet, rolled it around herself, and spent the morning on the sloping floor at the foot of her bed.

Through the window, dyed lamplight flickered on a view of brick and water. Someday one of the beams would give, a wall would split, and the entire top story of her house would collapse into the canal. Josza had seen this happen before; the survivors built atop the wreckage and in time the tumbled heap became another island. In her dreams, she was walking through Aruis as it slid down all around her, river-quarters tipping and pitching into the water that brightened as one building after another fell and exposed the sky, dry districts shaken stone from stone as though by an earthquake, domes caving, spires plunging, and the Aden washed over it all. Aruis' tyche, painted stone flexing like living bone and muscle, wept until the waters closed over her head. Her marble hair streamed on the surface of the river like weed. Josza's open hands spilled cards whose faces she could not see into the moving water, fluttering from her fingers like an entertainer's trick, bright rectangles melting in the murky swirl. Sorrow ripped at her heart. With desperate, futile movements she grasped after them; her fingers stubbed themselves on wool and well-worn planks, and she rolled over onto her back to find Gauven awake and staring at her.

He crouched at the end of the bed, quilt and sheets bundled about his drawn-up knees, almost intent on her: a sleepwalker's wide, fixed gaze. Josza's braids had loosened during the night; she pulled hair from her mouth and said warily, "Good morning." He did not blink. "Gauven Dystre, good morning!"

He came back to himself then, visibly, awareness tensing his face and deepening the soft dull color of his eyes. The quiet grey of stone in shadow, Josza thought; new-spaded earth. His mouth opened, faltered on a forgotten sound before he said, "Good morning." It was the voice she remembered from last night, older than his face, ordinary enough. "Where did you come from?"

"I live here. You fell across my doorstep last night; I put you to bed and went out for a walk. I don't need much sleep. You, on the other hand, have been in the kingdoms of horn and ivory since midnight. How are you feeling?"

She could not place his age: smooth-faced, rough-voiced, all his movements as steady as those of a grown man. He watched her rise and shake out the coat, fold it and drape it over the bedpost, with almost no expression at all. "My neck hurts."

"Oh, Sophia." Josza bent over the bed, fished briefly underneath the pillow. Straw crunched under the cloth beneath the pressure of her fingers; she flourished a slim, tattered volume before tossing it onto a heap of star and sea charts piled underneath the window. "I'm sorry. You've been sleeping with Lysehadt's *On Politics* under your pillow. You could hurt yourself that way." He did not smile; he had never read the dialogues, the joke meant nothing to him. The silence thickened between them.

Gauven moved before she did, stirred, slid out of bed and shivered as his bare feet touched the floor. The air came through the windows cold and heavy: autumn's wiry winds rarely made it through the maze of canals. Standing there among boxes of books and scholarly debris, he looked too young, his hair ruffled backward by sleep, cropped short as a sailor's or a woman's; he had slept in his clothes. Very pale, his skin in this light, hard and fragile as stone. No light reflected in his eyes; she had a sudden thought of *Death* swallowing moonlight and gas-glow, taking light and giving nothing in return.

He locked his arms around himself, childlike, and said in that first inaudible voice, "I'm missing something."

Josza's hand had gone to her pocket. She pulled her fingers away from the bent pasteboard, steadied her voice before she spoke. "Do you know what?"

"No." His voice shifted again, remote to adolescent in the space of a heartbeat. "I don't know what it is. You spoke to me. In the night. I heard you. Here—in here," and he flattened one hand over his chest, the cage of heart and breath, the seat of reason, "there's something not there. I know my name. I can say it. Gauven Dystre. But it doesn't mean anything!" The last word broke into a cry. He curled his hand against his mouth. "Why," he whispered, "doesn't it mean anything?"

"I don't know." Below her window a boat was passing; she felt more than she heard its wake against the paving, the tap of its pole, strange and silent as the ancient ferryman of the myths who bore heroes over the waters of death to the country of the gods. A hero had stolen a dipper of the waters of death once, bottled it and brought it back to the mortal world, a trickster who carried the boundary between life and death in his pocket and could not die until the bottle was broken and the water ran away into the street, down the grating into the sewers, and what became of it after that the stories never said. Josza had always felt sorry for the ferryman: forever on the boundary himself and no one to break the bottle. Gauven's indistinct eyes pleaded. "Come on," she said at last, "come downstairs. I'll see what I can do."

She cast the cards in her kitchen, though it still smelled of smoke and cooked fish, on the scarred table that held Josza's peculiar finds more often than it held cups and plates. If she had been surer of a clear sky, she would have climbed up onto the roof, into the open air, and measured the angles of sun-shadows against the night of Gauven's arrival. But his nearness disturbed her; whenever he drew close, even when she was handing him water in a cup of knotwork glass and offering him cold chicken and cut bread, she felt him on her skin like the pressure of rough water, tangible static that made her think of the first time she had seen an eclipse, the song of the sea-going mariana of the northern islands, the green guising at Thorntide: the touch of the unknown. *We feel the world with strangers' skins,* her father had said once. On the other side of the table, sipping water with the solemnity of a child or a madman, both hands clasped around the cup, another stranger looked back at her; a different order of stranger from herself. Words dried in her throat. She uncorked a bottle of thin wine, spilled some into the fire for luck: a libation to the fates that would gather over the cards as she cast them. Gauven set his elbows on the tabletop and his chin on his fists, watched as her fingers slotted cards together and apart faster than the eye could follow.

"What will you ask them?"

"Who you are."

"What if they cannot tell you?" He spoke in a stranger's voice again. The smooth planes of his face were solid as marble. "The stars do not oblige every mortal who crooks a finger to make them come."

Almost she let the comment pass; habit stoppered her mouth. But something reprimanding in his tone, in the distance of his eyes, made her reckless. "Then," she said deliberately, "we've nothing to worry about."

For the first time, she saw surprise surface in his face. The texture of his eyes changed; he caught his breath, opened his mouth, did not speak. Josza could not bear to hear what he would say, this pale young man, boy, old man, whose face changed as often as the light fluttered over it: what curiosity or compassion or pity would sound like in that unstable voice. Her voice broke over his as he began to speak. "So. Hold out your hands for the cards, Gauven Dystre—like that, don't touch them." She had put *Death* back into the pack. Something stung her fingers as she lifted the first card; it might only have been his closeness. "On the hearth-side, in the first quarter of the sky—"

She laid the card down with a slight snap of pasteboard against wood, between herself and Gauven and the bottle of wine, and Gauven cried out.

Where the blasted blocks of *The Tower* usually tumbled, lightning-stricken, fire and water consuming stone where the sea frothed at the building's foot, another picture had appeared. This tower sagged under a yellowing sky, grey stone sweating and seeping; white fungus clotted its windows, stranded the stones, a rotten shell that would collapse onto itself if anything so potent as lightning touched it. Josza whispered, "Hiera Sophia . . ." and did not know how to complete the prayer. A thin, sour taste began to rise at the back of her throat. "On the stranger-side," she managed, and touched the second card, "in the first quarter of the sky—"

One after another, the cards showed her a sheaf of fortunes: all changed, all terrible. On *The Star,* a falling fire-drake plunged, trailing sulfurous light and smoke, onto the sketched suggestion of a crowd beneath. For *Temperance,* dull, lumpen fluid sludged from the veiled figure's pitcher. *The Hanged Man* creaked in the wind, flies swarming his gibbet, gore-crows at his eyes. *The Sun* in eclipse, stained and smudged, bruised the sky like a sore. *Justice's* scales tilted, the feather broken in half, the heart cracked black as coal or clinker. *The Lovers* no longer held hands face-to-face but grew into one another, lip and foot and finger, like something softening into mold. Josza's hands were beginning to shake. She swallowed down bile and finished the casting, watching the nightmare take shape under her hands: cankered *Moon* and swollen *Emperor,* *The Magician* hunched over his bloody scrolls and the blasted churchyard of *Strength,* *The Wheel of Fortune* that ground beneath its spiked curve a myriad of tiny, agonized figures. Stone-stiff, silent, Gauven clenched his hands on the table's edge and never looked away.

She had no prayer left in her, no one to pray to. In her hand, the twelfth card that finished the wheel of the sky and the seasons: she laid it down. Beneath his painted mask of red and black, *The Fool's* enigmatic smile had clenched into a skew grin; he stood not at the crossroads but in empty space, the void, a malevolent motley figure turning alone in the dark. At that, Josza swept the cards together and shuffled them until she could not guess at their faces, scrubbed her hands along the sides of her trousers until her skin stung only from the friction. He had never deserted her before, her first, soundest, most mercurial guide—whose colors she wore in her hair, whose path she had walked since she was a child—and now he too had changed. What had she opened her door to?

"I've never seen that before." She was amazed at how even her voice sounded; it might have come from another's mouth. Perhaps the fates that closed their hands about her card-caster's own were speaking through her—she did not believe that. "Not like that. Never. Even casting death, casting destruction, damnation, the cards themselves don't change . . . You can't do that. It's not possible."

His face had fallen into childhood. His eyes were ancient. "Why?"

"What the cards mean—their influence, their symbolism, their nature—it's bound into them at their making. You don't destroy a deck easily. Sometimes you hear stories about people who've tried; it's never pleasant. The image doesn't just represent the fate, it is the fate in miniature. The part that contains the whole entire; the symbol that is the substance. Like working through a shadow, or a reflection, or a name."

"But my name means nothing," Gauven whispered, "and I cast no shadow."

She glanced down, saw without surprise that it was true. The sight of the changed cards had shocked her, slowed her; she did not feel much of anything else. But she was still thinking, speaking her thoughts aloud, trailing a thought that would not disappear. "I know. But the cards respond to something in you. What you are. The way"—her brows drew together in thought, she was not seeing Gauven's strained face—"the way all the casters in a city come to its tyche at Shadefast, and ask her to keep her hands over their work, guiding the fates in the coming year . . ." Her voice ran down.

Distantly, through the impossibility rising like a breath or a tear in her mind, she heard herself asking, "Have you ever been out into the city? Do you remember?"

"The sunsets are beautiful from Leukas' Bridge," Gauven answered. "At midday on Meridian, the Protectors of Aruis process across the basilica under the eye of the Sun in all his strength; they wear gold and green and gold again, for the Sun and the Tree and the season, and it never rains on that day. Slaves may not be sold on Aruisine ground. Go upriver on Solmas, into the hills, and blood smokes in the bonfires to call back the Sun as he dies on the winter Thorns. Sometimes rooks flew overhead and their wings formed fringed patterns against the light."

Once, when she was little more than a child, Josza had heard her father summoned to prophesy. He was old then, slow and dull-eyed, his steps creaked and his voice had almost rusted in his throat; but when he opened his mouth, and the voice came through him that was neither his voice nor the voice of anything human but the language of stars and lives fixed into mortal words, all of Josza's skin tightened with cold and her mouth went dry, her feet stuck to the floor and she shivered where she stood. Gauven's words had the same hieratic, riddling quality: not the pure power, but much of the flavor. She did not know how to read it. Still she could guess.

He added, after a space, "I don't remember any of it."

"No." Josza's blood jolted in her veins. "No, you wouldn't. But you don't need to remember. You don't need to know. That's why your name has no meaning—it doesn't need one, it's a sound, nothing more. Your face, your eyes, all the same. It doesn't matter how you look, how you sound, whether it all changes. And what you—what you think, that's not important either. Only that you are. That you do what you do. But that you don't know—" She bit down on her anger, the sudden sharp leap of it into her chest. "Even the ferryman knew what he was doing."

For a moment there was nothing but mortal bewilderment in

Gauven's face as he stared at her: a sharp dark woman kneeling on the kitchen floor to lace her boots one-handed, the other hand full of slipping cards whose faces showed only the ill side of the fates, her hair fraying out of its foreigner's braids, eyes the color of some indeterminate darkness. He stammered, "Where are you going?"

She had dreamed of a city in ruin. Aruis' tyche wept like a live woman; cards melted in the Aden's rising tide. Josza almost laughed. "Where I should have gone at the beginning. If my father had a grave, he'd be spinning in it. Wait here for me. But even if you leave, I'll find you. You can find a man through his shadow, if you know how to look: and if you cast no shadow, you're still the one who changed my cards."

Sometime during the afternoon it had begun to rain; between the timbers and tiles and bricks that jammed together into constant arches overhead, water dripped and scattered into the canals, sculling the water in joined rings of light. As the Aden rose and fell with the tide, so it lifted and ebbed with rain or snow. But it was not rising unduly, now, the pavements were not flooded. *Thank the Sun and Sophia*— Josza vaulted a narrow canal where a cobalt lantern shed ghost-gleams on the bobbing water, skidded on filthy stone and grabbed at the lantern-hook for support, rounded the corner and ran on. The rain tasted of tar and tin nails, stained her shoulders with soot. Out onto Leukas' Bridge, where it no longer drained through roof-slats and birds' nests, the rain fell fresher in the cold air; but Josza did not notice, did not care, she pushed aside two stately matrons crossing the Bridge with colorful umbrellas in hand and pelted toward the basilica.

The rain had driven away most of the usual trade and passersby from the long court of white marble: the tyche at one end, a memorial arch at the other. Cold gusts furled against Josza as she walked, steady under the statue's broad remote gaze. Aruis' horizon pressed into a sky the color of scuffed steel. Shivering a little, hard-eyed, Josza tilted her head back until she could look full into the beautiful, ponderous face. The Thorn-spiked Sun hung on her left; Sophia's petaled Moon weighted the air to her right. All the fates gathered here into Aruis' tyche: the city's fortune, as favorable and as cruel as every turning wheel. Deliberately, Josza raised her voice and spoke three words she had learned from her father. They sounded like the cracking cleavage of stone from stone, the split of secure rock underfoot: broken certainties. The tyche shone in the rain.

"I don't expect you to answer," Josza said after a moment. "I expect you to listen. People talk to you all the time; you can listen to me for a minute. I've spoken to you before. You know me." Rain dragged her hair into her eyes. She did not bother to push it away. "You know him, too. Gauven Dystre. Though he might as well be nameless for all that it means, all that he is . . . I should have guessed when he changed *Death*. Cards don't change. Only fates do; and the cards reflect it. But you don't expect to meet a fate walking the streets. Or sleeping on your doorstep. You don't expect to find a fate who doesn't know what he is."

She lifted one hand, tugged at the earring that swung beside the hinge of her jaw: selene, Sophia's stone, mined in the Aruisine hills and nowhere else; her father's gift to her when they came to Aruis. *Child of wisdom, child of reason,* she remembered him saying, and his crooked smile at the words. But he had been telling the truth, slantwise as any who cast fates or prophesied; she was a creature of the objective world, much more so than Gauven, than the motionless stone she addressed. "The world breeds your kind—out of dreams, out of visions, out of fears and daylight fantasies, I don't know where you come from and I know you'll never answer. Mortals and immortals, you make one another. No human life without a fate to chart its course. No fate without a mortal to work through. While I"—her face ridged in its wry smile—"I'm within and without. I cast fates and read them; I live, and someday I will die; and no one who knows me would call me human. I live in the spaces between." The smile dropped. "And so does he."

She did not hear the tyche answering, not in words that touched either her ears or her thoughts: rather a sense of reply in her bones, in her marrow, even in the breath that filled and flowed from her lungs. It did not deafen her. She did not fall down onto the rain-slick stones. But there was no room for anything else in her while the tyche was speaking, the fortune of the city and all that lived in it, the summation of the individual fates of every Aruisine citizen, past and present, future and potential, the closest thing to a god Josza knew. It spoke in her and she listened: nothing else was possible.

A great magician, once upon a time, made himself a brazen head to answer all his questions. But he left its keeping to an apprentice, and the apprentice was not as mindful as the master. After a time, the head spoke. It said, Time is. *But the apprentice did not think to call the magician. After a little more time, the head spoke again. It said,* Time was. *Still the apprentice did not call the magician. For the third time, the head spoke. It said,* Time is past. *And then it blew apart into shards and fragments of brass, and the magician rushed in: too late, too late. Time was past. He never built another creation so great in his life.*

The voice lifted from her, freeing her bones and her blood. She blinked cold rain from her lashes, shuddered in her sodden clothes; the wind over the river had an iron edge as the day waned. An unexpected image struck her: herself, ragged, rain-sodden, shouting at a statue. She would be lucky if she did not end the day arrested for disturbing the peace. Then she remembered Gauven, no doubt still sitting at her kitchen table watching the fire go out on the hearth, a wild swing of fate for whoever came near him, unknowing, blessing or destruction without will, and she did not smile at all. Her mouth would not shape the words well, but she raised her eyes to the painted ones and said, "That's a common story. I can name three or four great scholars who've had the brazen head attached to their names."

About this one, said the tyche, and Josza's blood thundered with it, *there is another story as well. Some say that the magician did not built a brazen head, but a man of brass, and endowed him with all the faculties of a*

103

man as well as a magician's knowledge. When he left this man in his apprentice's keeping, again the apprentice ignored the brazen figure's speech and never called the magician, and so the magician's questions were never answered. But the man of brass did not destroy himself when time was past. Instead, he spoke a fourth time. He said, Time will be. *And then he vanished. He left the house of the magician and no one knows where he went. But some stories say that he settled in a city by the sea, a city on the river, built out of the river; and there he built himself a daughter, like himself, and endowed her with all the arts that were in his power. So they lived together for years, the brazen man and his sorcerous daughter, until he ran down at last and only the daughter remained: neither mortal nor metal.*

She could not speak.

You wear the colors of change and crossroads. You live where the river devours and your power is small. You hide, magician's daughter. Your fate must work to find you. Do you reprimand me—and she felt, like the memory of someone else's laughter, the tyche's amusement—*that another fate wanders this city's streets?*

"If he were my fate," she worked her mouth without sound before the words came, "if he were my fate, I wouldn't be here. I would take him into my home. I've heard of it being done. Theriou, at the Shadow's Back, tells stories . . . But not with Gauven. He's no one's fate. Nor one of the twenty-one fates of a card-casting. Nor one of the twelve fates of the sky and the seasons. I don't know where he came from. Do you? The stars crossed at an odd angle of the seasons, a birth or death at an unexpected time, a hiccup in the universe: it doesn't matter. Perhaps he took human shape himself; he had no place among stars or birdflight. He came to me only because we're both creatures of both places and nowhere. Hiding." Even at that, she could not gather the courage for a smile. "But I know what I am; I've always known. Gauven only knows that something's wrong. Fate enough to color my dreams, to touch a deck of cards and change them to catastrophe—and if I let him handle the deck tomorrow, perhaps they will all turn to blessing—mortal enough for a name and a shape, or the credible illusion of both. And Aruisine. All his memories are of the city. Your city. He's part of you, Tyche Aruisi." The old title almost tangled her tongue. "You."

If the tyche had moved, laid down her Sun and Moon and spoken to Josza like a living woman, it would have been easier than feeling this voice possess her, blood and bone. The bells had rung already for afternoon, she knew by the color of the low sky that still poured with rain; she had not heard them. *I cannot unmake him. I do not change fate: I am.*

"You are change."

You are stubborn, automaton's daughter, magician's granddaughter. The statement, the sense of it, was not unkind. *Neither mortal nor metal: you are as hard as either. What would you do? Rip down the stars and disorder the universe to please yourself? The houses of the sky and the seasons feel what happens in Aruis. Change one fate and change all. The path opens both ways.* The tyche's voice swelled and sank like a tide. *Your father was wise. Time is and time was, time is past and time will be. The same for fates and fortunes. You tell me that you know the stories. Then you know: to evade a fate brings it closer. To change it makes it certain. How do you change the fortune of a fate?*

Rain clattered on the flagstones, on the tyche's painted shoulders, on the roofs and windows of Aruis: rainy city, river city, Josza's home almost as far back as her memory reached. In past years she had gone northward, following the spiraling archipelagoes toward the equator, to hear the city's language spoken on far sun-soaked shores and see signs in neat Aruisine script swinging under brazen blue skies. Even in the south, across the Iron Sea, Aruisine whalers hunted among great crags of ice. How far did a fate follow? Her mind felt numb, lost in the feel of the tyche speaking; she swayed where she stood, face and hands burning with the cold; she wanted to speak and could not make her mouth move again. Gauven was waiting for her. She should go back to him . . . What then? Keep him in her house like a familiar, trapped forever half-incarnate, changing all around him and never changing himself? Josza opened her mouth, lost words, tasted rain a few degrees from ice. No less bitter, the thought of him as she had seen him this morning, scant bell-hours and an age ago, sleeping among a tangle of much-mended sheets like anything exhausted and young. She wanted suddenly to touch him, brush back the dull fine hair from his forehead as she had done at midnight, lay her palm along the side of his face: no desire, only simple human contact between two people who were not. Rain runneled her face like tears.

She bowed her head against the sky. Then she lifted one hand, turned her fingers in a weary conjurer's gesture. Between her thumb and forefinger appeared a slice of pasteboard, its back patterned, its face hidden. Rain was already blotting its printed colors. The tyche of Aruis, the memory of the tyche's voice, repeated, *How do you change the fortune of a fate?*

"But he's not," Josza whispered, wry, hopeless, "only a fate."

She snapped cold fingers; the card flicked into the air and floated, turning, drops pelting the absolute black-painted negation *Death* had become at Gauven's touch. Hand still upraised, watching the flimsy rectangle fall, she neither breathed nor moved. She did not look at the weight of stone and destiny before her.

The tyche said, in her blood and bones and breath, *Magician's granddaughter—*

"Yes," Josza said.

Now her hands moved, fast as when she had shuffled the cards for Gauven, catching *Death* before it touched the ground: and she tore it in half, clear across, the inconsequential sound of ripping pasteboard almost inaudible in the rain. For a breath she stood there with half a card in either hand, faintly smiling with her mouth, faintly frowning with her brows.

Sky and earth shattered around her.

Most of the river-quarters' fires had gone out in the rain, torches soaked and smoking, bonfires reduced to half-burnt charcoal shiny with damp; only the lanterns still shone in the perpetual twilight, garish spreads of light marking pavement and tide-choppy water alike. Where the leaning roofs had fallen in and the sky become visible through the patter of rainwater, lightning snapped and branched across the blackened sky. It would storm all night.

On the street of colored lanterns, Josza crouched beside a pier to observe a family of rats swimming industriously down the canal. Her braids had come undone and her hair matted across her back and shoulders, hanging sodden to her thighs; red and black ribbons, some of the color wept out of them by the rain, still tangled the strands. All her bones ached. For the space of less than a second, she had felt the lightning scorch the air before her face: the hand of the sky clasping the hand of the earth. Its aftershock still whitened her vision, blurred her hearing. But she had lived. It was not her fate to die by lightning. At that thought, her face eased slowly into a smile, and then into a laugh. Above her head, a voice began to curse down at her: *for sweet Sophia's sake, will you shut up, holy Sun on the Thorns, shove off!* Josza had no energy left for annoyance. She leaned against the pier and laughed.

Some time later, perhaps five minutes, perhaps half an hour, she set her hand against her father's brazen forehead. Sore-throated, she whispered, "Thank you, father." The metal face said nothing; he had died long years ago, sorcery or electricity ebbing out of him with the years, and Josza had mourned him alone. Still she imagined, sometimes, that she could see him looking out of the soldered eyes that had once been his. Created to answer questions and nothing more, he had changed his fate: the time that might have been, he had made. "What I inherited from you," Josza murmured with a tired grin. At the click of the door unlocking, she knocked aside the shell that served as a doorstop and stepped inside. There were no lights anywhere in the house, save a dim eddy from the kitchen: the fire burning out. Josza peeled off her boots, wrung out her hair between both hands, made her way into the kitchen where embers still flared and dimmed beneath a kettle of prosaic fish stew.

He had fallen asleep waiting for her: put his head down on his folded arms and drowsed off. The lapsing firelight made his hair richer than its true color, soft gold, fair copper. Daylight would show it some light, nondescript shade, fine as a baby's hair. How his eyes would look, she could not guess. Gently, so as not to wake him, Josza reached down and laid her open hand on the upturned side of his face, her palm at his temple, her fingers in his hair. No static, no fever smarted between his skin and her own. Under the angle of his jaw, a pulse beat steadily.

Something opened and broke in Josza's heart. Even if Gauven had been awake, she could not have spoken. She did not have the words for this. It was enough to sit there at her battered table, in her house that smelled of books and fish, and watch him breathing quietly as he slept. When he woke, she would see what he was. They would say what needed to be said, or not, and after that she would have to see. But he would be one thing or another, fate or fated, she knew that as surely as she knew her own name or his; as she would remain the automaton's daughter, neither mortal nor metal, with no regrets.

From her trouser pocket, she withdrew a stack of limp, sodden pasteboard; each card stuck to the next, almost melted; she would have to find another deck. The top card all but tattered in half as she pulled it loose. "On the hearth-side," she murmured, "in the first quarter of the sky—"

Hung in the heavens among stars and watching tychai, the twelve-spoked wheel turned. At each quarter, some conjunction of the Sun and the Tree: Shadefast, Solmas, Thorntide, Meridian, the Sun that sank to its death and rose again, the Tree that turned thorny with winter and gentle as the year waxed anew; Sophia's infinite eyes formed the hub. Living and dead alike moved to its measured revolution. All the world's fates kept it turning.

Josza laid *The Wheel of Fortune* back atop the ruined deck, settled into the chair across from Gauven to wait for his waking. On the other side of the river, the bells were ringing for night.

To Everything a Season

Anachronism, and you know it: the way
you wear your hat, cab-driver's
snap-brim tweed, a cap for hawking
newspapers on New York's teeming corners
more than eighty years ago; button up
your overcoat, cold wind and angled shadow
down your film noir collar, heavy
scarf tucked in neat and shake hands
with the press, off the lot and candid
in the camera's pop and static
flash; but make him a scholar,
rocking forward to a spindling tune
that shapes letters like black flame
licked onto the first day's light,
the wrong side of the sea, in a tongue
too new for translation; cast a few
and catch them back, a thousand
faces and none of this time. Thirty
years past, you might have worn
those damnable lapels with equal
sincerity, might have grown old enough

to don sweaters, convincing cardigans,
for this winter's chill; your skin slips
against older bones. Time folds forward
in wire-rimmed glasses, backward
like a steamer's wake when you hold
the door, politic in photographs
too young for color. But you know this
already: always: how stars turn
and do not turn back, how to stitch
story into self and pull past close
like a double-breasted coat, driving
gloves, against the chill. This snow,
this season, now. This moment, breath
and beating blood. Just think; how
memory makes the man: and without
these pasts to clothe you, today,
what time's face would you ever wear?

Kouros

Wild geese were flying as he came to the reservoir; their calls chased back and forth beneath the low clouds, nasal, breathless, other-worldly, their wings hammering a wild hunt in the cattails. Slate grey where the sky reflected, pale as cloud on the ice, water ruffled beneath a fitful wind; seen piecework through the trees, the shored banks and dikes, it gave him the feeling of something always just out of reach, floating at the corner of vision, near enough for his finger-tips to brush and never solid enough to grasp. He shivered, turned up his coat's collar when the wind ranged over the water toward him: a hazel man, fallow hair and eyes like the dead grasses underfoot, more bones in his face and ungloved hands than should have shown beneath the winter-paled skin. "No," he said aloud, deliberate sound that made no dent in the overcast, the quiet where only geese folded their wings and water pushed against old ice and thawing earth, and walked on.

Winter was sliding off the world, damp earth and rain-darkened granite surfacing through sunken, tracked snow; between the trees, stark and wet-branched, half scaled over with lichen and some still ragged with last year's leaves, meltwater streams idled. He picked his way carefully through an ankle-deep slurry of loosening ice, twigs and dead needles, autumn residue layered and compressed like bog coal.

The air still clung coldly to his skin. Once a fallen branch snapped when he set his foot on its raised twist of wood, brittle, riddled with the chill months, down across his path at shin height like a low gate or an old-fashioned turnpike, and the noise of breaking might have been a shout: his presence, her name. Crows mocked in the leaning branches, raucous, restless, quick-winged flicks of shadow. Another trick of sight; as though he knew what to look for.

He found her between two birches and a broad-forked ash, where a waist-high shoulder of sooty rock humped up out of the soil and glittered with minerals and peeling ice, hair loose to the wind and feet tucked underneath her as neatly as a cat. She had shifted position recently; the shins and knees of her jeans were dark with old rain, leaves tacked to their cuffs. Her feet were bare. A black, hooded sweatshirt wrapped her shoulders. Her head lifted as his footsteps stopped, hesitating where the ground dipped and rose again toward her rock; behind the heavy drape of her hair, lighter than the crows' wings and darker than the reservoir's mirror water, her eyes were a frail, momentary color poised between antique gold and green. He could not remember which way they had tilted, the last time he saw her.

"Cole." She pronounced his name curiously, shifting again on her rock to draw up her knees and link her arms around them, half gamine and half numen, not even shivering as any remaining warmth faded out of the day. Out on the horizon, late afternoon was breaking through the clouds: flushed blue and bronze gilt as an oil painting, layered and lambent, detailing cloud strata; the unknown countries of the air. Their glow burned over her skin. Caught by the burnish on her hair, the fine molding of her throat and her hands clasped one over the other like a stranger's handshake, he breathed, "I'm here," before he meant to speak. Crows' voices worried at the air, riotous as claws and scraping feathers; when she spoke, they ceased.

"You came."

"I came."

At his tone, she pulled back her hair with one hand to see him better. Westering light barred her eyes, gilded over their fragile green. "It still matters?"

The question hit him at the base of the throat; he swallowed something jagged, unwieldy, and only realized afterward that it was anger. "Yes," he said. His voice shook. "It still matters. It—matters very much. I want this. But it's not wanting or not wanting anymore. It's like air, or light. What would you do if you suddenly stopped breathing? If the sun went out?"

Barefoot, blue-jeaned, golden-eyed, she whispered, "Never to see the light of the sun . . ."

Anger still jolted in his veins, headier than fear, and he said, "Yes. What else did you do, when it was you?"

Her face froze, paler than birch or ice. Her lips parted as he braced himself, waiting for the dark to come crushing down or the earth to open and devour him; but the wild geese set up such a clamor that he never heard her answer, or if she answered at all.

For weeks afterward, he had dreamed of Jasper. If he had gone from the world, maybe some nonexistent landscape had taken him in; so his dreams theorized, Cole thought when he was awake. Once he floundered where surf ripped white tumbled endlessly down the slant of an impossible beach, raked so steeply that the sun glared and dazzled only at its peak, and the waves thundered down among slabs and spars of rock dark and tilted as headstones; sand poured away under his feet as he struggled upward in the troughs between waves, searching for Jasper's name in the scrawls of bladderwrack and scaling barnacles, snail tracks and the blown-blue fragments of mussel shells, and each wave smashed down like salt apocalypse, a wreckage of bottle-green concrete. Hollow streets gave up Cole's steps, footfalls echoing on rain-slippery concrete and bricks worn one into another over long, swarming years, sidelong alleys where catwalks crossed out the moon; he followed nothing more than the obstinate, clawing desire to see a familiar smile turning out of crooked shadow, eyes like flaked shale and the long-healed cant of a broken nose, dark hair always rumpled, spiky, rowdy as Jasper's gaze was steady. Waking, he could not remember the names of midnight cities, knew that he had never walked in a desert, never followed a lake-wide river through the crowding overhang of trees, never sat in limestone caverns until the dark hardened against his skin, until even blind fish, pallid and fragile as frosted glass, listened for Jasper's name. Halfway to the corner store to get milk—the last carton gone grainy at the back of the refrigerator, forgotten and sour—he almost lost track of the sidewalk, had to stop and think carefully that he was awake. He picked up a poster, torn across a concert date three months gone. A bottle rolling into the storm drain sounded like the tinniest steel drum in the world: Jasper's hands rapping out rhythm on the nearest sounding surface, the banister, the steering wheel, the bedroom door and the handspan of streaked plaster wall between pillow and windowsill. Never on ice, though they had both stood on the dike and pried rocks from the snow-locked earth, thrown them far out to hear the resonance bouncing through the cold, cloudy panes, the reservoir water running dark underneath. Ice broke; the water seized like iron, gripping, summer-starved and greedy, in winter.

He saw Jasper in his dreams only the one time: deep beneath his skylight of ice and snow grit, bedded open-eyed in silt and slow, settled mud. A cloud of finger-long fish, silver and blue as a January morning, hung suspended above his mouth like a final, frozen exhalation; a frog in hibernation hunched stony beneath his shoulder. No weeds stirred in the motionless cold, and his hair drifted only slightly in the backwash of curving, fleeing fish. Not five full fathoms down in the marble water; far enough to fill veins and chill hearts, to preserve until the transmutation of spring when all kinds of things surfaced. Cole sat cross-legged on the reservoir bottom and felt tears slipping from his eyes like freshwater pearls, moon-silken and misshapen. He touched a fold of Jasper's jacket, dark-green windbreaker new that fall, zipped up over the heavy knit sweater that the hand-me-down years had turned some color between antiquarian ivory and old socks; gloves still stuffed in one pocket, ice trapped around the zipper's metal teeth. Jasper's skin looked paler in the drowning light, blood gone to reservoir water that tasted of decay, the ebb of seasons, fish shit and the choking roots of water chestnuts, willow branches trailing and trapped in ice.

Cole cried out, a word that was a chunk of ice in his chest, and sank both hands into the soft mud that oozed up around his fingers, glutinous, frigid; and the reservoir bottom peeled back. There in the dark, in the inner curve of the earth, she was sitting: back on her heels like someone tired of kneeling, head bent aside and her hair like a curtain he would have to part, to find her. Behind its darkness, her face looked very young, vulnerable, a child abandoned in a dead place. Then she looked up, and for a levinbolt moment Cole forgot that he was dreaming, forgot the dogtag chain still glinting around Jasper's neck and the way silt had dusted the dark, worn grey of his eyes, forgot everything but the years sunken in her eyes like amber, the centuries and the millennia falling endlessly away into past: fossilized time. Dryness caught at the back of his throat, soil parched to powder in the drought of a season like the houses of the dead, bird-faced, bound to earth. The cold rains covered him over, buried deep until the lengthening days. Her eyes were harvest, were first fruits; the tentative fractal of a fern dripping with spring rain, the long, fiery twilights of the burnt-out year. She said, "It's not impossible."

"You did it." He hardly believed that he could speak in her presence, that all his words were not mute as Jasper's mud-stopped mouth. *Shells for teeth and weeds for tongue* . . . CDs stacked beside the stereo, that Cole could not play. "For somebody you loved. You must have."

Their shadows moved with the flurry of crows' wings, feathers ruffled in alarm and smoothed down again under a fussy, preening beak; a dry, dark, autumn sound. "For somebody I loved . . ." She spoke with a lingering precision that might have been wistful or bitter, or both; Cole could not tell, did not dare try to decide. Something in her eyes had scarred over his question long ago, moved now and closed her face against him like a language he could not read: not a barrier to keep out his clumsy, wanting guesses; a place of nothing where no words reached. Her hands plaited her hair, unplaited, an absent, human movement that terrified him. "It's the wrong time. Do you understand?"

"Yes." For a moment she was almost mortal, seconds enough for him to take in breath and get out speech. "Spring."

"It's not a bargain," she warned. "There are no terms. No compromises. Just—" She did not have to raise a hand to show him, this place he had been looking for as he wandered in dreams—not Jasper's chill bed, after all, among the husk-sheltered larvae of caddis flies and wintering bull tadpoles—where shadows rustled, peered with black splinter eyes among the dust and sheaved grain, the fallen leaves, the bones; and nothing, when he opened his eyes again, but darkness and the deep turning of the earth.

"I love him," he said. He chafed his hands, thought of Jasper's warmth beside him in the stranded hours between three and four in the morning, the startling boom of his laughter like the lowest string of a bass, plucked; not the dark star of broken ice, already healing over in December's deep-freeze, the searches that dredged up nothing but mud and clotted weeds, some unexpected current tugging in the water, deeper than they had thought; not green algae furring a sweater's frayed sleeve. "Even half the year . . . Even all the year, all my life. All the lifetimes there ever are." His thoughts bled forward and he tried, "Then you . . ." A chain of wheat stalks, snapped in half; crows moved in her hair, disappeared as she leaned forward, shook her head.

"No. For him, or for no one. Not for you, not for me. There are no terms."

"For Jasper," Cole whispered. "Bring him back into the light."

He woke to the color of her eyes, faded to the thin wash of winter morning over his ceiling, sky and snow the same palest blue: the world between two mirrors. No smell of rot-rich mud in the sheets and pillows, no black feathers broken in his hair, no proof more tangible than the way his blood moved and still he knew what he had done. His bones felt unfamiliar, too sharp beneath his skin; Jasper's father had left a message on his answering machine, baritone rough with fifty years of cigarettes and three weeks of grief. When he walked down to the reservoir, boots crunching an alien script in the drifts behind him, a few crows followed. He had no bread for them. They did not go away.

The cattails swayed at Cole's shoulders, nodding rust-dark and heavy on their bending stalks. Water welled around his boots, pressed upward from the thin margin of mud and gravelly snow underfoot, marshy excuse for a beach where the bank tipped down to the restless water; mud streaked past her ankles, hemmed her jeans and one knee where she had bent to sink her palm into the softening earth, narrow fingers spread among the caltrop seeds of water chestnuts, the roots and stringy leaves of some pale olive plant flotsam-tumbled ashore among kernels of ice and bare, broken twigs. "Not long, Cole," she said, and he heard his name strange in her mouth, a little disbelief still edging her voice: what he wanted, maybe, or the name itself. When he had first told her, she had slanted her gaze—more green than gold, that afternoon, as they watched mallards huddle for warmth among the willow roots—at him, as though he had become suddenly what the sound hinted: something small, burning, intense, for her to warm her hands at and keep her distance. Or to pick up and douse in a bucket of cold water; she had eyed him as warily as though her fingertips already smarted from the attempt, while she planned another try. When she said, "Jasper," he heard blood-grained and clear yellow stone, the smooth curve and cut of sculpture, a piece of rough brightness picked from a hill's rocky flank. He wondered what her own name became, when she spoke it; he did not ask.

He asked instead, "How long?" The need pushed through his voice anyway. Wind washed across his face for answer, little warmer than the water it played over; he heard the small sounds of weak ice breaking up, easing, and a wild goose went overhead like a lost soul out of season.

"Not long . . ." Her hair snapped in the wind, quieted along her spine as she knelt again, eyes open and blind: looking for something beyond sight. A little wryly, something he had not expected from her, maybe something she had caught from him—viral, remembered humanity—over these few hours, she murmured, "It still matters." The crows were screaming in the trees. She tilted her face back to the grey sky, the faint clearing of light at the western horizon; there was a long-dead maple leaf, rain-slick, the color of molasses, tangled just before one ear. "Jasper," she said, clearly and conversationally, "Jasper Bratt," and Cole's blood reeled. When she pulled the leaf from her hair, a faint glaze of slaty mud followed over her cheekbone. She had brushed against a cattail in rising, scattered rust-crumble over one arm and the sweatshirt's laces; in the overcast, Cole could not discern the color of her eyes. Quietly, she said, "It's still your choice," and stepped away.

Jasper stood at the water's edge, clouds and cattails behind him. Whatever Cole had expected, watery ghost or warming flesh hauled untimely up from the depths, he looked most like himself soaking wet and a little staggered, as though Cole had dunked him and then pulled him back into his proper element: almost comical, water-slicked hair in his eyes and his windbreaker dripping from his shoulders, algal strands straggling down his pants legs and wound through his shoelaces in a slippery double knot. Remembrance twisted between Cole's ribs; he heard the name slip out of him, "Jasper—" as their bodies jarred together, and he dug his fingers through sodden, muddy cloth to hold him fast, to keep him in the light.

He rocked in Jasper's warmth, the solid weight of him, his embrace as crushing and tender as though he had been the one waiting three months above ground to see the miracle play of seasons translated into truth. They were almost exactly of a height; they fitted together. Even the crows were quiet, and he did not care whether she watched. He tried to think of the dry, dark place where she had gone down and remained, where he was going; not while holding Jasper, being held by him. Against his neck, Jasper's breath checked; his hands did not loose their furious grip on Cole, but Cole felt the question rising into his voice, had no idea what he would answer. The idiot words fell through his mind: *You've been dead; don't worry about it,* and he half-laughed into the damp spikes of Jasper's hair, pulled back just enough to find his lover's face, find something to say when a resurrected man finally spoke.

Beneath tilted brows, Jasper's eyes were green as the moss that padded the rocks farther out from the dike, green as a chlorophyll skin of pond scum: pupil and iris the same wet, blooming color, and the whites gelid as frogspawn.

Cole had forgotten how to breathe, how to speak; his fingers searched blindly over Jasper's face, the faded scars bridging his nose and the pulse accelerating beneath his jaw, the broad, pliant mouth that had opened on a name Cole no longer knew how to hear. His hair had the texture of matted leaves, the underfoot rags of another year. A faint verdant rust speckled his brows that were drawing together at the look on Cole's face, frozen as midwinter. He said, gently, "Cole...?" and his voice whispered like the feathers of uneasy crows.

Cole never heard that he screamed. The green of Jasper's eyes ripped into his throat and he only felt the sound leave him like metal shearing, torn wide open and rending. Cattails broke under his hands as he stumbled backward, tripped and almost fell to one knee in the snowmelt and shadows of starkened trees; a taste of old pennies was burning up into his mouth, sickening, nauseous as failure. "You promised," he shouted, or thought he shouted, slinging the words at her slight figure standing where the reservoir path ran off into woods again. "You told me—like you did, when it was your brother, when he went down for her and couldn't come back—half the year or always, I don't care, as long as he—" He was strangling on his words, staring at her to keep from looking at Jasper, at whatever waterlogged remnants of Jasper she had dragged up and given him from a cold winter's grave: and that he still wanted to hold until the dark earth turned over them both. Shaking, he said, "You cheated me," and waited to hear the crows laugh.

Sunset had fallen out of the sky, afterglow caught like a thin wash of gold in the clouds and nothing more; from the east, evening moved through the trees' jagged darkness like ice, thickening and chilling the air. Bent over his sorrow, Cole shivered and almost missed when she spoke, as though she could ever have gone unnoticed. "This is not a bargain. You can still choose. But you knew that."

"No." Stubbornly, "No. You just wanted—to come back to this life again, to the sun," while he swallowed tears like bitter almonds, like pearls cramming and choking his throat, "and I'd make any stupid promise, I'd take anything you gave me, I missed him so ... How could you ever have loved anything?"

"I don't know." Now her voice tasted of snow falling on snow, arid grasses and rivers withering in their beds; waiting for six months' respite that dwindled into the long, lifeless dark while somewhere above the stories moved on, a promise broken, a cycle subtly out of joint. One hand lifted, spread muddy fingers toward a point behind him, Jasper green-gazed and silent. There was a crow on her shoulder, its eyes glittering blackly where her hair kept hers in shadow; he could not tell her expression, compassionate or merciless, envious or triumphant, or none of these things at all. "How could you?"

Every morning he had woken, uncreased sheets cold and hollow beside him. He had walked the vertigo shore of dreams, called Jasper's father in Tampa for interminable, undeniable hours that spilled away like tears, eaten his bones hollow thinking of Jasper and the things he should have said, the stupid ways that people died. Any answer sank in Cole's mouth; drowned. Between water and darkness, he swayed, too tired to look at her, too afraid to look behind him. To the ice and mud at his feet, he said, "It doesn't matter. I promised. Changing places: you to this life and me to—whatever; and her to wherever she wants, I don't care. There shouldn't be a world without you in it. Whatever—however you are. I made a promise. I try," and there were thorns in the phrase that had made them laugh together, once, "to keep my word." He raised his head, drew one hand over his face to slide the tears off onto the hard ground. After thousands of years where nothing lived, where nothing grew, would he still remember what it had been like to love Jasper, or only what he had given up for him? "I consent."

There was a wet scent in his nostrils, a flavor of water: not a tidal stink of weeds and fish humus, more like the way Jasper smelled when he stepped out of the shower, or when he had been swimming in the lake up in New Hampshire where they went one summer and shivered in the lazy sunlight and transparent, icy water. Papery husks of grain rustled, dried ears of wheat or barley, half-shucked corn and winter rye, and Jasper said, "I don't."

The crow cawed, raw scrape of claws and beak over quiet air, and she flung it from her shoulder with a quick, angry shrug.

Cole said blankly, "But it's done."

"It is not." If he turned, he would see Jasper's face remote, passionate, only his voice fluent with conviction and something close to anger. "You shouldn't do this."

"Then what?" Cole held himself still, the inches of air between his skin and Jasper's each calibrated, tallied, vivid as a wound; tuned to the drowned man's nearness. "What do you want? The reservoir bottom? This half-life? It shouldn't have been you who died so stupidly, so young—" His voice hurt and he had to stop, finish almost breathlessly, "Christ, Jasper. I would do this for you."

"I know." A crow sidling on a branch; a wry and remembered brush of feathers. "I know you."

Cole felt like his name, burning in the dusk. "I'm not doing this for the drama."

"Neither am I."

"No."

Down in the cold depths, Jasper's watch had still been running, digital face palely printing the seconds for the fish to read, time forever running away; Cole closed his eyes, saw a sleeping face, a dead face, a face he had never predicted. He almost laughed, abruptly and sore-throated. He was not cruel; he only shook his head, and swallowed the last and bitterest pearl, and listened to Jasper speaking past him.

"We'll keep the balance. There are no broken promises here."

He did not look back, into green eyes and the reservoir's indelible mark, the brand of returning; she was there before him, her face like a birch ghost within the black sweatshirt's hood, who had walked down that broad road long ago. "One for day and one for dark. One from the living and one from the dead. You can't go back." The same precision that Cole had heard, dreaming, ached in her voice; watching her made his sight darken and he wanted suddenly to touch her, to know if she would learn again how to move among the living, how to joke and argue and lose track of time, how to hurt people, how to make excuses, how to laugh. If she would remember him and Jasper; if she would speak of them, and what stories she would tell. Still she said simply, "Be very careful," and he thought that perhaps, to her, it also mattered.

Wild geese glided on the dimming water, far out from shore: returned from winter pilgrimage, come back with the sun. Cole whispered, "It's still my choice." Jasper's autumn voice grazed his ear, shaped his name. He was not speaking to her anymore. "I choose this."

He did not look to see her face change, if her face changed; he did not listen for crows or wild geese, for the sounds of thaw or twilight. It was easier, so much easier than he expected, just to turn into the circle of Jasper's arms, and put his mouth to Jasper's mouth, and taste the currents of transformation: water running in dry places; the deep streams of the earth that welcomed them in. In a thousand years, he wondered what color his eyes would be.

> Light breaks where no sun shines;
> Where no sea runs, the waters of the heart
> Push in their tides . . .
> —Dylan Thomas, "Light Breaks Where No Sun Shines"

Retrospective

The phone rang five times that night. Around four in the morning, he rolled over and groped in the dark until he found its corkscrew cord, jerked it out of the wall in a clatter of cheap plastic and a single aborted ring. Far downstairs, sometime before seven o'clock when a colorless dawn pressed around the edges of the window and smeared over the opposite wall, he heard the kitchen phone again. "Go away," he whispered into the pillow, cold hands clenched tight, "shut up and go away." Snow had crusted the windows overnight, melted and frozen again in spidering, brittle veins. When he tugged at the creaking blind, bleached, overcast light spilled over the small room: a Macintosh monitor, a bar stool piled with winter shirts, cardboard boxes of records and coathangers, and the phone cord strung out over scarred floorboards and a raveling triangle of fir-colored carpet. The air closed sharply on his skin as he sat up, half-snarled in sheets and blankets; Eitan Koster shivered in the sunken chill and wrapped his arms around himself, a slight man, shadows bruised beneath his eyes, hair sleep-spiky and fraying grey over dense black. He had not been crying. He remembered no dreams.

Last night's clothes were cold and crumpled on his flinching skin, as oddly-fitting as though some other person had left them on the floor for Eitan to find; somebody else's cigarette smoke stale in the cloth, the rum-and-coke some stranger had mixed and drunk and spilled, salt tackiness of sweat that did not smell like his own. Black jeans washing out cement-colored at the knees and back pockets, grey shirt and an ink-smudge sweater: he should have at least rinsed them out, hung them to dry in the shower overnight, dripping down the transparent plastic fish; should have borrowed a shirt, found his socks, or gone back to bed until he no longer remembered why the phone was ringing. Instead he scrubbed hands through his rumpled hair, washed his face in the bathroom down the hall—cold water from both taps, rust cracks in the porcelain basin—until his cheeks burned and he could not feel his fingertips or knuckles, and went downstairs slowly in the bleak morning light. Step after step, the stairs sighed. His coat hung over the banister, elbow-patched, heavy denim turned icy to the touch; in its pockets, he found one glove and a wadded mess of Kleenex, a paperclip chain, the cap off a bottle of hard cranberry lemonade, clinking aimlessly in his palm like motley dice. December moved in the house like another guest.

Hallie was drinking coffee at the kitchen table, in an oversized men's shirt and out-of-season sandals; he watched the long fall of her hair, almost maple-red, early-morning uncombed and still shining past her waist, shift with the rise and pause of her breath until she turned her face just enough to show the angles of chin and cheek-bone, pale skin flung with freckles, and said, "Matt called for you."

"Just now?" His voice snagged in his throat, slow with cold. Coffee from the pot on the counter burnt his mouth, tasted of nothing except heat and caffeine; he chafed his palms against the mug, head bent over the dark-brown fume, and did not come closer.

"Last night. Several times." She looked at him briefly, over her shoulder; she had put her contacts in, and her eyes were brilliant green, exotic as absinthe or a cat's night vision. "I said you were sleeping."

Eitan swallowed more coffee, almost too quickly; tripped over his own shaming question. "Did you say I'd call back?"

She snapped, bitterly enough to surprise him, "I should have." Outside the kitchen windows, the air flattened with cloud, blank face that the skyline printed but did not touch; old snow matched its dull pallor. Hallie sighed, as careful a punctuation as her final sip of coffee and the mug set back on the table before she turned around, winter sky for a face and meltwater for words. "Give them a call. You can't stay here another night."

"I know." He rubbed one hand over his mouth, his bruised chin, a grit of dark and silvering shadow beneath his palm; small bones in his spine, his shoulders and the nape of his neck, ached at unexpected moments. "But I can't . . ." He did not repeat last night's arguments, half slapdash confession and half rawboned need, that hurt to recall almost as much as the day they had followed. He whispered, "Thanks," and Hallie turned up one hand in the slightest, wryest of shrugs. Her mouth tightened, wordless. She had also known Chris Kimmel. Last night, Eitan had not even spoken the name.

She did not rise from her chair; he did not move toward her. He laced his boots in the front hall, in silence, and let the door lock behind him as he left.

Wind slapped his face, gusted between brownstone cliffs: hard as metal with the deep cold, shattered glass honing itself on this flat stretch of ice and asphalt; the ploughed drifts of sidewalk snow were stone underfoot. Someone had smashed a bottle on the front steps, beer-brown mosaic chips and splinters ground into the sand and salty slush. Eitan's work, maybe; he could not remember. Scarf lost somewhere between Chris' party and Hallie's spare room, one hand gloved and the other shoved beneath his arm for warmth, he bowed his head beneath the wind and headed for the bus stop. His breath smoked and faded on the air, more lively than anything else under the grey, hanging sky.

Few cars passed in the Thursday morning streets, windshields and windows blind in the overcast, but the bus had just pulled away as Eitan rounded the corner. No strength left in him for a curse, he

leaned against graffiti-streaked plexiglass and stirred bus-fare coins
against the litter in his pocket; enough for a phone call, and he tightened his shoulders against the air's dry freeze and waited. He wanted a
shower, badly. Something to eat, something to drink that was neither
coffee nor alcohol; somewhere warm that had no phone lines and no
faces he recognized; a place before memory, or buried deep enough
that memory no longer mattered. Another bus heaved up to the curb
in a creak of brakes and exhaust, the wrong route, and Eitan hung
back apologetically until it had gone. Shoes scraped the pavement
behind him, crunched on snow piled in the gutter. He thought,
briefly and crazily hopeful, that maybe Hallie had come out after
him, tracked him down the cold blocks to say that he could stay, no
questions, no answers; though she had said Chris' name when they
argued. But Hallie was nowhere in sight when he looked up, and the
woman on the sidewalk was no hope at all.

Everywhere he glanced, he had prayed not to see her; as the phone
had still rung in the night, she stood stiff and grittily pale as the frozen
scarp of snow between them, unremarkable in a dull overcoat and
work boots, and he could not miss her. A heavy scarf covered her hair,
hooded her face in rough, almost-white cloth. Beyond its folds, he
glimpsed her eyes held closed for a moment, a slow blink, as though
pressing back tears or a thought; she lifted her head, and said nothing.

The cold was biting at Eitan, pushing through wool and denim to
find his skin and prickling flesh. The woman did not shiver; no breath
plumed white before her. Her eyes were no color at all, leached, stark
as the air. "Go away," Eitan whispered: words said once to turn away
Matt's calls, exactly as effective now. "You're not here. I'm not seeing
you. I'm not crazy, and you're not talking to me. So don't bother;
don't even try; go away."

She had her hands in her coat pockets, as ordinary as any pedestrian waiting for a bus late on a winter morning, not a young woman,
nor old; fine lines marked her eyes and mouth, and the flesh still held
firm to the generous bones of her face. If he could see her hair

beneath the scarf, he knew it would be dark still, harshly wavy. She opened her mouth. One note sounded, struck from the brittle air or the snow: cloudy, crystalline, reverberant. In its overtones, or its aftershock, she said, *Eitan*.

"No." Eitan's breath rasped in his throat, chafing as the jeans cold against his shins, the wind getting under his collar and whining there. Quarters and dimes were stamping hard circles into his palm where his fist clenched in his pocket. "Don't. Get away from me."

You looked back. She might have been puzzled or condemning, resigned or curious. Stone molded her words, the blurring pitches of a bell. *Look back.*

"Get the fuck away!"

Fire flashed up in her nothing-colored eyes, like flame kindling behind a lens, sudden and gone. Sweating now, shaking, Eitan wished for the bar whose name he could not remember, Hallie's hands pulling him out of the dark and the concrete burning his palms with frost and blackened slush, last night all over again if time would fold back upon itself and dissolve this woman: ice in a wash of hot water, dwindling to chill slivers and brief coolness, nothing to grasp and nothing to remind when it had gone . . . She remained. Her eyes were cloud-clotted air again. On the same note, pure and stony clarity of desert or midwinter, she said again, *I saw.*

When the bus came, he was still shuddering, though no longer from the cold. Hands and face, he felt each last touch of the wind or the smack of warm air from inside the bus—too close, oil and plastic and the smells of too many people that the windows had locked in, stuffy in his opened mouth as he folded into the nearest seat and tried to remember how to breathe—like a thrown handful of sand, like sunburn. Carefully, he leaned his head against the speckled glass of the window; ice webbed at its black-rubber corners, a faint seepage of cold air that tasted like metal on the tongue. Hallie's coffee pooled sullenly in his stomach. The bus coughed deep in its gears as the street slid away on either side, and

Eitan slouched down in his seat and thought of places he could go, places he could not: nowhere next. He did not crane backward to see if she still stood there, pale and waiting for no bus. He had seen; he knew.

When he closed his eyes to the bus' stop-and-go rattle, Tuesday night was waiting: Chris' party in a brilliant, inescapable flare. The second-floor apartment crowded close and reveling, a chaos of conversation and books stacked two deep on every wall, David Krakauer on the living room stereo and Celtic revival in the kitchen, a smoke of incense and takeout pizza. Snow shivered against the darkened window, wind's fingernails tracing a sharp tattoo; testing how to get in. Candlelight, softened lamplight, traced shadow-puppet portraits on the glass. Orange juice and coconut rum smelled vaguely like sunblock, tasted nothing like: Eitan's third drink of the evening, hardly his last. Christophine Kimmel had finished her dissertation, a three-hundred-page printout propped ceremoniously among the various kinds of alcohol on the living room table—twin to the bound copy handed in to her advisor earlier that day—and they were celebrating as riotously as though it had been her wake.

"Absolutely," Matt said, when Eitan mentioned the paradox, and tilted his glass until the lime fell off its rim and into his open palm. He had a blunt, dark face, a linebacker's shoulders and stood like a classical pillar: no one had ever seen him lose his temper. "Commemorate an intellectual achievement by reducing said intellect to alcoholic sludge. Now pass me the fuck that tequila." Less than forty-five seconds later, he and a thin, beaky woman, whom Eitan vaguely remembered from some Friday night dinner at Chris and Josine's, were arguing over the use of *fuck* as an intensifier, a particle, and the value of tmesis in contemporary profanity. Eitan laughed so hard he spilled half of his own drink down one thigh of his jeans and swore, knew it would only add fuel to their ludicrous, lovely academic fire. *So why doesn't "unbelievfuckingable" work?* Some minutes afterward, he located a carton of orange juice and drank several swallows before remembering that he had meant to put it in his drink; carton still in hand, he went to look for Chris instead.

To Eitan, Chris Kimmel had always looked like an Earth Mother gone slumming in a Dickens novel: heavy, tumbled hazelnut hair dangling with pins and horn barrettes, never braided except when she slept; a broad face, cat-eyed, skin rich as dark honey; not a tall woman, stocky and rounded, and she smiled like a sunburst to the solar plexus. Against winter's bite, she wore a rusty black greatcoat and gloves wearing through at the fingertips, a flat-brimmed tweed cap and muffler to match. Celebrating and warm, she wore a flower child's shapeless mossy dress, sashed at the waist with another autumn scarf, and went barefoot on the layered rugs. When Eitan last checked, she was hiding out with Josine, hands full of each other's hair, whispering between kisses and hiccuped laughter, so dizzy and earnest—some Tarot deck's Lovers crossbred with their beloved Fool—that no one had the heart to tell them *get a room!* Yellow-haired and angular, tall enough that Chris' chin rested on her collarbones when they embraced, Josine was calling out something about Chris' dissertation, the cities on the plain and rains of sulfur and fire. Chris laughed, rumpled one hand through her hair and caught hold of Josine's sleeve to pull her out of her orator's solemnity. Their mouths brushed before Chris shouted, "Jacques Brel, eat your heart out. Sodom and Gomorrah are alive and well and providing dissertation material on the East Coast!"

Candles on every windowsill, every table where the books had been cleared; origami fretworks dangled from the ceiling on colorless thread, Josine's work. No cranes, precise struts and planed shapes instead, mathematical formulae translated into bright folds of paper. Momentarily stranded, Eitan watched them spin in the candles' draft and tide of conversation, until his eyes watered and he closed them hard, light-headed, light-blurred. Phosphene static swam behind his lids; his balance tilted out from under him and he rocked one step backward, felt for the overstuffed arm of the couch behind him and found instead something broad and stone-smooth, cool when he flattened his hand against its curve, solid among a strew of journals. "A gift from my advisor," Chris explained as he stared, tranced; abruptly at his shoulder, she grinned and disappeared between two biochemists, refilled margarita in one hand and Josine's fingers fast in the other. "He figured it was appropriate—" a salt crystal the size of a loaf of bread, smooth and cloudily transparent, that rang like a bell when slapped with the flat of a hand. Origami forgotten, Eitan stood by the couch and smacked his palm against its smoky-white curve again and again, just to hear that single note: an alien word, a geologic echo, the translated language of frozen time. The sound Lot's wife had made, perhaps, as she turned back for one fatal, inevitable look, as holocaust flashed down from heaven and the earth's molten burn swallowed everything she had known—

He did not turn, back or otherwise: from the distracted corner of one eye, he watched as Chris, jostled sideways, laughed breathlessly and reached over to set down her drink among the bottles and plastic cups, framed photographs of family and friends spliced into the glitters of glass and liquid. "Damn," she said, clumsy, smiling, and the salt note sounded under Eitan's stinging palm. Then the heel of Chris' hand knocked against a fat melon-green candle slumping into its own wax, scent of honeydew and burning wick, and she snatched her fingers back, swearing in earnest. The halo of another candle divided around them, grazed her wrist, the battered watch and hemp bracelet braided just where the bones met; and clung. Matt cried out before she did.

Halfway across the room, Eitan started from his contemplation of the salt crystal bell; the breath dropped out of him, all blood and all thought, and he knew in a single stopped moment that he would remember this. How the flame rolled along her sleeve, licking into the green fabric in dainty sunset tongues; how Chris shouted, pushing at hands and confused chests in a fury not quite panic, trying to find floorspace enough to stop and drop and roll while her hair lit into an autumn heyday; how Eitan dropped his drink and marveled, drunk and heartstricken, at how quickly skin spun into smoke. How someone shouted to call 911, and Lisa Gerrard sang of the wind that shook the barley, while Josine jerked the curtains down to muffle the crawling, hungry flames and books flew broken-winged; and how someone else in the tangling press around the table, faster than Josine and closer, Eitan never saw who, never wanted to, instead grabbed a bottle off the table and upended it over Chris' arm and shoulder and kindling hair, to douse the fire in a rush of Bacardi 151.

He never quite figured out where Wednesday had gone. Twenty-four heedless, aching hours congealed sometime after midnight, almost one in the morning as he vomited into Hallie's claw-footed tub, painted iron anachronism closer than the toilet when he stumbled to his knees and heaved up sour alcohol and bile: the liquid aftermath of one whole day run away into a slur of bruising disbelief. Every bar and every block from the gutted apartment like a safeguard between Eitan and the woman who spoke like salt, shored against memories huddled on a frozen sidewalk while bloody wheeling lights splashed over trash cans and smoke drifted like breath down the biting air, what Matt might say when he finally answered the phone and the comfort that Josine would never demand of him; what he did not know how to bear, what he feared he could not give, what he had seen.

Nausea had outweighed his arguments with Hallie: he was not going anywhere tonight. Still he felt wary ice glazing over the space between them, easily fractured. Over Chris' name and Eitan's refusals, they had torn at each other until he did not know what they would say to each other in the morning, if there was anything left to say that would not wound. But her voice was almost gentle as she said,

"There's a waste. You haven't kept anything down long enough to really get drunk," and she did not leave him even when he choked up a last acid spatter onto the cool pink-sand tiles of the floor.

Then he raised his head, nose and mouth reeking and burnt, and saw her just inside the door, pale and angular among worn maroon towels and the curling Rackham print Hallie had tacked to the bathroom door years ago, and began to shudder again. "Christ. Christ, she's here," never mind that Hallie would not see her, "Hallie, she's here." Words ground his throat like glass, salt in wounded flesh; he almost laughed, coughed painfully instead.

Beside him, hands still lightly on his shoulders, Hallie said, "Who's here?" Her voice skimmed, snapped the ice: "Chris?"

"No!" He jerked away from her, banged his chin against the tub's cast-iron rim; the jolt of pain almost cleared his head. "No. I don't know," choked into a half-gulp of laughter that tasted like pennies at the back of his throat, too many forgotten drinks burning their way back up. Cold, falling, everything felt like old tears. "Can I keep her? She followed me home—" He lost the end of the sentence as his guts spasmed again, nothing left to come up but hurt, and dragged in a breath like rusty wire. In the sickly pause, he heard Hallie's breath check, felt her hands tighten involuntarily on his wincing shoulders.

"Eitan . . . ?" Her voice edged higher, mistrustfully. Between the towel rack and faery revels, the woman fell into sifting white, like snow blown down from a roof, and was gone. "Never mind," Hallie whispered; but she rose, closed and locked the bathroom door, and sat silently beside Eitan until he had finished dry-heaving, until she could make him mild and milky coffee in the kitchen, everything else shelved for the night.

She never said what she had seen. He did not need to ask.

The park lay in a frame of black iron and snowed-over brick, landscaped hills and avenues, bonework trees and trim lake, compressed pale between snow and sky. No toy boats sailed here, relics of older summers.

Just the restive wind, miniature whitecaps kicked into the lead-colored water where ice had not scabbed it over already: thin panes at the pond's margins, clotting inward. Huddled close beneath the willow's stripped overhang, a few disconsolate ducks fluffed their feathers; no bread in Eitan's pockets. He had been thinking of ways the world might end, ice and fire, Robert Frost: *From what I've tasted of desire / I hold with those who favour fire . . .* Josine's voice, Midwestern cadences for a New England poet, and he wondered why he had not simply changed buses, metropolitan transit for Greyhound interstate, and kept on going. In this city, the world would keep clawing at him to answer, phone calls or e-mails, messages through friends or whatever he called the people he had not yet closed out: to look back. The farther, the better. He chafed his hands and watched the pond freeze over.

The wind wrapped ice around his shoulders, drove nails through his hair. No shadows crossed the pocked and crusted snow at his side, though the horizon smudged pallid as a fading bruise; the willow's trailing branches clacked together, deadwood chimes, and he said wearily, "Just leave me alone."

She had sat down on the far end of the bench, as though come to feed the ducks in this bitter season of charity: nothing out of the ordinary, and Eitan did not dare look closer. The air shivered beneath her voice, jarred harmonies out of the wind. *Eitan.*

He could not tell if his teeth were chattering from the cold or from her nearness that scraped against his skin; he almost bit his tongue as he whispered, "Go away. You're not even a hallucination—"

You looked back. Look back.

"God!" Fire choked Eitan's throat, ate his words; he struggled to speak past the fury, the incomprehension and her changeless, insistent voice of salt and desert distance, and flung himself upright from the bench so sharply that he almost touched her before he recovered himself. As raw-throated as the wind, as desperately, he shouted, "What do you want from me?"

Her eyes had no color except when ancient fire moved through them, washed pain to life. But the wind had tugged dark strands of hair from beneath her scarf, and the clouded light showed all the faint lines in her face, sorrow and endurance tracked hard around her mouth and between her dark brows. Softly, she said, *You saw me.*

"No." Eitan shook his head until he forgot what the movement meant. Standing on the other side of the bench—as though snow-barked metal were any defense at all—he slung the words at her furiously, last night's memories piecemeal and vivid. "That doesn't work. Hallie saw you. Why the fuck aren't you haunting her?"

I saw. Before he could protest, drowned in the overtones of her voice, she finished, *You knew me.*

The fire fell out of him, left him shivering on his feet, scoured by the forgotten, gnawing edges of hunger and cold. A man in a bright ski jacket passed them, leash in hand and a slight crease of puzzlement on his face as he stared at Eitan staring at apparent nothing; a golden retriever trotted merrily through the crunching snow before him. Eitan's hands were numb, cold-pinched. He exhaled into cupped palms, watched his breath fall in clouds; covered his face briefly and knew she would be there when he took his hands down.

"I don't know you," he whispered, more than half an easy lie. "I didn't . . . I just saw you," because to speak even her story meant to acknowledge what he had seen, while fire enfolded shelf after shelf and alarms shrieked in the corridors, and Josine plunged through thickening smoke for the woman no longer screaming at its core. Too fast, this transformation: soon the double-paned windows would snap, caught between winter and inferno, and shower glass like hail into the street. Eitan should have run from the building already, out into the night that was deathly cold and safer; deafened, stunned, sirens slicing the air and smoke filing at his lungs, he clung to the doorframe and shouted for Chris and Josine, somewhere back in the apartment, in the burning city.

Through pleated leaves of fire, its devouring roar, he saw her. Like a sandspit where tides washed an island into being, salt gathered upright, glittering white and rough: moon sandstone, mannequin crystal. The fire did not touch her. Within the pale, broken planes, her face shifted like an optical illusion, gone when he searched for it, there when the fire and anguish took his attention again. Then she moved, and he knew her: two thousand years of rocky grief, tears desert-dried into this woman's form. Called up, impossible, the hallucination of a city whose sins had survived its history, and Chris would have wept to see her. Her voice parted the air, one note drummed from pure lamenting crystal, from cataclysm—

Hands were pulling at him, sleeve and shoulder. Coughing, he never saw who hurried him down the smoky hall, the stairwell where red alarms bolted to the wall flashed like hell's own strobe lights, out into the night that shocked over him like icewater until he thought that his face would crack like glass or misfired clay. Slowly his vision returned in blotches and streaks, as he sat on the curb across the street, careless of the ice under him and the wind flaying beneath his sweater, his unbuttoned coat. The figure on the stretcher was Josine, hands and arms cracked charcoal past the elbows, as though she had tried to gather all the fire into her grasp. Matt was shouting at a policeman, blue-white glare spinning over his face, the tears freezing fast on his skin. Eitan swallowed, throat scoured from smoke and salt. He felt the wind cutting inside him; his heart hung in rags from his ribs. Clumsily, cold-fingered, he buttoned his coat and got to his feet. Each step was no easier than the last, but he kept walking, until the sirens and the light receded behind him. Her face, Chris' face, took longer to fade into the dark. Somewhere, he drank.

"What do you want?" Eitan whispered, bitterly. Now she looked nothing like Chris, who was beyond all words; this woman might never have been human, anything more than a conjuration of loss and salt and fire. Her eyes were as blank as December air. Not alcohol, panic, tear-tricked vision, and Eitan wanted suddenly to touch her. Beneath his fingers, would he feel grains of slipping salt or breathing human skin? Maybe nothing: air, cloud, distance. "Chris. Chris knew you. Six years . . . So what should I look back for? Her, burning? Josine in the hospital?" He shuddered: something Chris might have seen before the smoke or the flames took her sight. What had Josine seen, as someone else dragged her away? Matt's voice wearing itself raw over the phone, calling friend after acquaintance after somebody someone knew, trying to find Eitan and what had happened to him. Chris laughing, books and candles and the immense mineral bell. No punishment. "What good does it do, looking back?"

Sweat stiffened his hair, slid beneath his shirt as he trembled. The man with the golden retriever had gone, carefully not glancing Eitan's way after that first startled stare. What did he look like—another crazy man in the park, dirty hair and two days' stubble, a drunk or a junkie railing furiously at his own private demons? Somebody would find him tomorrow, frozen solid as rock salt beneath his grimy clothes, and marvel over the driver's license of an assistant professor in the pocket of a homeless man . . . Hallie had seen her. But she had followed him.

You looked back. I saw you. There was nothing human in her voice but the words, patterned phrases; they hurt. The shoulder of her overcoat was cold cloth, her dark hair chilled where it brushed against Eitan's hand. No lightning, no torrent of fuming sulfur engulfed him; the ground did not open beneath their feet. The woman on the bench, her face a barren plain where cities had burnt and her loved ones had walked on, said, *Nobody looked back for me.*

Her face was paler than snow and sharper. Eitan's fingertips touched her chin, the curve of her cheek: like touching sand just before it ran into glass that would cling and scald him, or frostbite that felt like flames stiffening on his skin. He did not take his hand away. He was crying. "I didn't mean to. God . . . You. I don't even know your name. I don't know if anybody knows. Just that you looked back, that you turned back and turned into salt, God's punishment for not leaving everything behind—"

Wind split and sang around them, drove white tracks over the water and loose, gritty snow against Eitan's jeans. Beneath his hand like a grounding wire, a woman's face regarded him, encrystalled in cloudy bright angles and beginning to fold apart into fine, shaken grains. Time ran through her, salt for hourglass sand, desert seconds. Eitan's ears rang like struck crystal. She said, *Look back.* A benediction or a curse, or neither, *You saw me.*

"Chris," he said, "would have loved to see you."

His tears were freezing, falling on empty hands. They melted, left palms and fingers streaked and glittering in the hungry cold; he was on his knees, shaking, could barely catch his breath as he clambered to his feet. Salt ran in his eyes, in his veins. The sky was bearing down on him, dirty yellow where late afternoon light filtered underneath the clouds, weighing down glass-eyed buildings and crusted streets. At the nearest gate, where he halted to lean against the rimed brickwork and flex his fingers until the blood ached in them, a pair of passing students asked him for the time; he had no idea. He wondered absurdly if he had lost another day.

When he fumbled change out of his pocket, scattering paperclips, pain bit through his fingers: cracked, blistered, fire-seared. "Shit," Eitan breathed, and almost called a local clinic instead. Past the phone booth's scanty windbreak, he saw the shade of her eyes settling over the roofs: Josine's hands had looked much, much worse. But he had not looked at her long, had not dared. Had Lot ever been sorry? Wondered what he had lost, what he had not seen, obediently blind? Turning, looking, the act of vision making what he feared into what was real . . . The phone number he punched in felt almost as alien to the touch as Chris' name in his mouth. The receiver leaked ice against his ear and denim-guarded shoulder. One ring, two rings, tinnily electronic and the salt note sounded on the darkening winter air; Eitan tucked his hands beneath his arms, the hale one and the hurt, and waited to hear Matt's voice, to see the city burnt.

Harlequin, Lonely

for Marc Verzatt

Harlequin, lonely, thinks it's a good idea
to try another mask for a change: been long
enough as checkered Arlecchino, servant
on the sly, duping Il Dottore out of his letters,
Pantalone out of his bride, courting the girl
who's later Columbine (pale Pierrot moons
over her) though she's tricky enough herself
to see through him like paper, like glass,
like the eyes of the mask he's been wearing
since he first drew breath onstage or off.
Years since he's seen her, since he's walked
upside-down or tumbled handsprings
for his own delight, traded wit and insult
with the braggart Captain (sword in his hand,
limp where it counts) or pulled Pulchinella's
sausages from his hands; he's seen his cousin
dwindled red and ranting on the English
stage, Punch pitching the baby window-wards,
knocking Judy down and the doctor too,

constable, undertaker, hanging the Devil
till there's no one else left; that's not the route
he wants to take. He's flash words and dazzle
but he's not without a heart, Harlequin
who feels his skin like a stranger's,
touches chin and cheekbones to measure
the face he forgot he owned (remembering
Colombina's kisses, stolen between scoldings
like Les Amoreux silly with young love
and the trust that the world will never end)
peering at himself in water, in cracked
mirrors, to see slantwise what disguise
he's grown into; a hollow in his heart
like the space that should be hand in hand
clasping a bargain, even if it's sleight-of-hand
next minute, hey presto and too late now,
there's Harlequin gone and snacking on stolen
goods, seeing self-congratulatory what's
next on the horizon: he can't see now.
Take off the mask; it crumples like ashes
in the hand, left with a mothwing palmful
no better than some of what he's paid
captain or doctor or rich old fool: stir it
with a curious finger and watch his past
flake into moonlight. Like wind smoothing
water, hands on clay: no grin or solemnity
on his facile face, no words ready on his tongue
that told so many lies he might have circled
round to truth eventually; he waits to see
what happens now. No script for this:
he's always been good (he'll tell you
whether you want to listen or not)
at improvising when there's someone else

to play off; sharp enough to cut himself
when he's not looking. Red diamonds
gone with the mask, old pattern slid
with the shadow into nothing, and he
who was Harlequin stretches into himself,
yawning, it's getting late and he has someplace
to go before he sleeps, who knows where?
He doesn't plan that far ahead. Brushes
his hands together, scattering mask-dust
like the grit in your eyes from dreaming,
picks a road that turns a corner he's never
been: long and long since he didn't know
who he was when he stepped out into sight
and laughter and heckling approval, long
since he had to put up his hands, pat
angles of brow and nose, discerning
shape beneath second skin, inventing
(he's never at a loss for invention, though
it's killed him nearly as much as it's saved
his skin) self at a breath or a word: this time
he doesn't know. Harlequin, no longer,
walks his road as the sun goes down. Time
enough to find Colombina, and who
she's turned into; find a mirror, and find
what mask he put on when he took off
himself— By morning, he'll figure it out.

Constellations, Conjunctions

He woke beside her in the night to discover that she had reversed.

Pelle Fisher was thirty-four years old. He had long ago decided that there are varying levels of happiness, proportionate to the life and needs of every person, and his life was not one which required great bounding joys and exaltations: a fortunate thing, since he received none; thus, if not exactly happy, he was certainly content. By day he worked as a teller in the small bank two blocks from his home, a modest if perfunctory occupation. By night he wrestled a complicated and beloved telescope out onto the black iron bones of his apartment's fire escape, where he watched the stars, recorded various celestial phenomena, and read the poetry of T.S. Eliot and the short stories of Shirley Jackson.

His voice over the telephone, his words in neat script or e-mail, confirmed him as small and slight, punctual, with glasses: a mild, absent, archaic personage. In reality he did wear glasses; he was also six foot four, slender as a dancer, and his eyes were the precise shade of the sky between showers of rain, a soft wandering watercolor grey. His hair was a simmering blond; he had a shy smile and clever hands of which he was very proud. Those who met him often found him both more and less worldly than they would have expected: more, because he could, with reasonable equanimity and great affability, balance a checkbook, manipulate a computer, find his way in and out of a supermarket, and carry on a conversation; less, because the conversation would invariably circle back to astronomy. He was also inclined, in the course of a discussion, to lose track of his current context. That was how he had lost his prior job, that of bookseller in the stores of a nationwide chain, because he would converse extensively with a prospective customer, hold in his hands a volume he liked and read a few paragraphs to the customer, and then never sell the book at all. His present job, at least, offered no such opportunities. The only stellar thing about the bank was its clock, which had old sun and moon faces that passed beneath the hands as the hours turned: the one yellow, rayed, and smiling, the other blank and white, eyes closed in sleep.

At the bank, his clever hands—with ragged nails awkwardly disguised by some filing, since Pelle in a meditative mood also bit his nails—were transforming a check into a neat sheaf of bills when he chanced to look at the hand into which he placed the envelope. It was not a very large hand, narrow and finely tapered. The nails were like moon shells, unbitten; the quick was the palest-pink color of the smooth inside lip of a conch shell. On its back, set among the filament tendons that ridged and sank as the fingers closed around the envelope, were seven dark freckles that formed an exact replica of the configuration of stars known as Lyra.

Pelle's gaze snapped upward. The star-printed hand, now securing the envelope in the inner pocket of a gray winter coat, belonged to an equally narrow wrist; he skipped the intervening spaces of sleeve and lapel and hunter-green scarf, marshaled as bland an appearance as possible, and located the owner's face. She was smiling at him, a nod and thank-you as mechanical as his usual own, and even that was a white moon-slice of beauty. Her hair was dark and curling, nebulous, spilling in a loose billow from the thrown-back hood of her coat. Along each of her cheekbones ran a high flush from the slushy streets and the bank's warmth, though elsewhere her face was as pale as her hands: a classical oval with a cat's slanting bones and short nose. Her eyes followed the line of her cheekbones; her eyebrows reminded Pelle of the careless pen-slashes used in childish drawings to denote distant flying birds. Then he thought they were nothing like that, it was a stupid comparison; but the pen-image persisted, for the beautiful calligraphy curves, and her eyes too looked as though they had been carefully inked in. The flush was dying from her face, and he thought that among the fine bones he could now glimpse freckles spicing her pallor, perhaps another group at the outer corner of her eye, along the delicate round of bone, or at the base of her throat where the scarf wrapped, or there, beneath the tilted edge of one cheekbone—

"Excuse me," said the freckle-starred face in a voice that was not music but certainly some haunting or haunted instrument, "is something wrong?"

Caught off balance, becoming for a moment the shy social inept indicated by his voice and his written conversation, Pelle blurted the first fact that came to mind: "You have the constellation Lyra on the back of your left hand."

He could feel his world contract to the tide of embarrassment washing across his face. The teller to his left, a decorous middle-aged woman, turned on him a look of shock equal to that of a prim Victorian matron suddenly transplanted to a Las Vegas strip joint. Behind the woman with the constellation on her hand, a harassed young father, whose heavily-bundled child was already tugging at his parent's jacket and making urgent incomprehensible noises, rolled his eyes and exhaled in audible exasperation. Pelle wilted. But before he could speak, attempt an apology or pretend that he had said nothing out of the ordinary, the woman smiled. The simple beauty of the expression, not gorgeous, very distinct from prettiness, shocked him back into silence.

She asked, in that same tuned voice, "Are you an astronomer?"

144

"Yes. When I'm not being a bank teller. It's what I love."

The woman nodded. "When do you get off work?"

"Half an hour." He glanced past her shoulder to the clock, then to the windy blue darkness settling over the frozen sidewalks and crusted roads. "Why?"

"Do you want a cup of coffee?"

Caffeine gave Pelle headaches; he nonetheless nodded. She turned and was gone before he could ask for a name or a place, pulling the hood over her cloudy hair and throwing the scarf about her neck, and the harried young father said swiftly, "Have you got a bathroom in here?"

By the time he had finished the last transaction of the day, it was fifteen minutes past the time he had given the woman and Pelle despaired of ever seeing her again. He was buttoning his coat on the front steps of the bank, shivering in the indigo wind that skidded along the narrow street in flurries of kicked-up snow, when a gloved hand put itself on his sleeve and a voice said, with a faint edge of wariness, "Sir?"

"Yes?" He turned with some comment about closing hours ready in his mouth and swallowed it with a start as soon as he saw the inky eyes under graceful calligraphy brows, long blue-jeaned legs and hands stuffed into the pockets of a quilted gray coat. Despite the long trailing scarf and the hood, a few streamers of dark hair coiled in the wind. She was shorter than he, which he had expected, but not by more than six inches, which surprised him. "Pelle," he said then. "Pelle Fisher. I dispense with the honorific during off-hours."

"Good. Coffee with Mr. Fisher, Sir, feels too much like an interview. Where do you want to go?"

They settled for a small place on the nearest corner, crowded with college students in various stages of freezing or thawing; Pelle retrieved some esoteric brand of coffee and a hot cocoa and feared that the star-handed woman had disappeared until he saw her waving from a table in the corner. He did not remember what he said to her.

The usual affable exchanges, thoughtless and almost unnoticed, until she mentioned having seen in some magazine a recent image of the sky: a field of stars, she supposed, and then she looked closer and saw that every star was a galaxy, unimaginable distances compressed into a single page by the sheer volume of stars, comets and nebulae and the glowing shells of exploded supernovae, each no more than a single shining point in the eye of the telescope lens, lost among thousands of matching, minute, immeasurable points. Less than a speck of dust, the human eye in the universe. The spaces between the stars dazzled.

"Yes," said Pelle, his cocoa cooling in its cardboard cup. "Numbers mean nothing. That the eye looks through space, not at it—equally as meaningless. One looks up into the night sky and still sees only the concave of a great dark bowl tilting with the seasons, figured all over with fiery designs drawn by some god's hand." He added, "I saw the same picture. It jolted me: there was no place to stand anymore. Nowhere solid, nowhere fixed, only adrift within the expanding boundaries of what we call real ... Wheels within wheels." The cocoa was now entirely cold and the woman was watching Pelle with more than polite interest.

She asked abruptly, "Do you have a telescope?"

Pelle, swallowing his cold cocoa, nodded. "Yes. In my apartment. Do you want to see it?" There had to be better lines, he thought: less blunt, inviting without leering. But he could not think of anything else; a spatter of freckles at the corner of her right eye resolved into a delicate miniature of Cassiopeia and he blinked, still hesitating to believe his eyes; hesitating to believe his ears, because she had said yes.

The clouds had cleared by the time Pelle and his guest returned to his building, leaving only the everpresent film of smog between them and the stars. Snow crusts snapped under their feet as they crossed the parking lot under the white eye of the moon, the yellower eye of the streetlight; he gave her the annotated tour of his apartment and worried he was babbling, but steadied as he removed the telescope from its corner and gave it into her hands like a treasure. Now the cold did not bite, it pressed like a weight against every inch of his skin as he climbed carefully through the living room window and out onto the fire escape—its metal ribs lightly fleshed with ice, slippery underfoot—and took the telescope from her, tightened various pieces and adjusted lenses as she ducked through the window and joined him.

"There." Without looking, he felt her presence at his shoulder. "Mare Imbrium, Mare Frigorum, Copernicus—go ahead, look. The Moon looks as perfect as a model."

With an appreciative laugh, she bent and set her eye to the first lens. "Ah—that's beautiful. White as a bone and as dry, and you can't stop looking at it . . ."

His breath was a nebula, blooming between them as he leaned back against the frozen railing. In the cold lights she was a sketch of shadows, like the moon still caught in the telescope's glass eye; its shadow slanted across her face, dipped over the bridge of her nose and one eye. Just by her mouth, dark and clear against skin that seemed pale as the moon's sun-struck highlands, three melanin stars belted Orion's waist. Betelgeuse at his shoulder pinpointed the high angle of her cheekbone, the stars of his right wrist printed her temple, his archer's left hand was lost in the shadow that touched the inner corner of her eye. No cloud marred the air between their faces as she rose; Pelle released his breath, spoke in a whisper. "You wear Orion on your face. Lyra on your hand. What other constellations? Where else?"

He was prepared for denial, flight, laughter: not for her mouth brushed across his, lightly, like the touch of their gazes as she moved back a pace. Her voice was quiet in the still air. "Do you want to see?"

Common sense should have had him thank her for her company and guide her politely back through the window and out his door. She was a stranger, accidental, beautiful; he did not even know her name. The constellations on her skin intrigued him. He spoke to her aware of every word; her beauty lured him into anecdotes, confidences beyond the usual reach of his incongruous pleasantry. But that meant nothing . . . Pelle thought of levels of proportionate happiness. Where did she fall? Did he need her? His life contented him.

A car turned into the street beneath them, skidding a little on the rimed asphalt, scratching its headlights along brick walls and grime-pocked banks of snow. Set among the strange stars that patterned her face, her eyes watched him in steady silence.

Into the winter air, his words spoken in spreading drifts like the tides of stars, he said, "Yes. But it's cold. Come inside."

His bedroom was papered with photographs of the solar system, maps of constellations and deep-sky objects, like a shrine to the world beyond the blue or black skies. The pieces of clothing scattered across its carpet and chair were intrusions from some more mundane world; there was nothing of vast silent spaces or the matchless forge of a star's heart in a sock draped over a bookshelf. But the woman at Pelle's side, her nakedness pinned with figures of the night sky, might have stepped from the far reaches of the long-observed cosmos: fallen in fire like a shooting star, earthed in the body that held him and roused him, impossible, indisputable.

There was much here for Pelle's clever hands to do. Her hair fanned between his fingers; her eyes closed briefly and he saw, on the soft skin between eyelid and eyebrow, tiny Canis Minor like an afterthought. He touched the pattern gently with his thumb. The miracle of her starred skin made him laugh, amazed. "They can't be real. Paint, or ink."

"Try and remove them."

So he tasted Lyra on the back of her hand, Leo at the inner joint of her elbow, the Coma Berenices in the hollow of her right collarbone. Orion remained fixed beneath his moving mouth. At the hinge of her jaw he discovered the Pleiades; pushing back her hair to kiss the single mole, like Polaris, on the side of her neck, he found Ursa Minor nestled at her hairline. "They seem stuck fast," he said, half in humor, half in wonder. "Every detail, perfect—" His thoughts flashed to the star charts pinned to the walls, the reference books stacked and spilling along his shelves. But he was not, despite any appearances to the contrary, a man to abandon his lover for a *Field Guide to the Night Sky*: he trusted his memory, and continued to explore.

At the ridge of her hipbone, just beneath the taut span of her belly, he marveled at his birth-sign, Libra. "This is unreal. You're unreal," he murmured. "Unreal and beautiful. Why can't I wake up?"

"Into what?" she laughed. "A dream?" Hydra he discovered in the palm of the hand that caressed the ridges of his ribs and scattered fire across his tensed flesh. Draco glided along the inner curve of one thigh. Even the sole of her left foot—ticklish, as he quickly learned—harbored Auriga stamped into the callused skin. "You're awake," she assured him, even as he shivered with an excitement too material for any dream, "you're not dreaming me. I don't think you're dreaming me. Maybe"—her breath hissed between her teeth when he found and traced subtle Virgo—"maybe I'm dreaming you."

Pelle had never been called anyone's dream before. He had never hoped, in the most far-flung of his own dreams, to find his beloved constellations drawn from the shifting skies and minted in perfect human flesh. He felt himself a comet swinging close to the sun, swallowed by the heat and flaming corona: pulled toward the inferno, flashing to steam in the curve of solar wind, plunging inward, exploding—

Later, when they lay intertwined with the streetlight sodium glow striping their bodies and the tangle of blankets, he turned the thought into a poem for her. It was a terrible poem; he knew it. The imagery was outlandish, the language worse. He was a better astronomer than writer. But it made her laugh, fondly and without malice, and a small warming fire-seed like the vestige of an exploded comet burned steadily beneath his breastbone as he sank against her shoulder, turning his face to the drifts of her dark hair, and fell asleep.

He did not expect her to stay past that first night. He had barely expected even the first night at all. But stay she did; she was making hot cereal in the kitchenette when he rose the next morning shivering and muttering at the thermostat, and he discovered with pleasure that he was not the only person in the world to eat honey instead of brown sugar on his oatmeal.

"Do you have a name?" he asked as he watched the honey slide off the spoon in impossible elongated teardrops. "Or am I to shout 'Hey, you with the constellations!' every time I want to speak to you?"

"Not so far off," she replied. "My friends call me Stella." Her hair was loose and she wore last night's shirt only half buttoned, showing where diamond Aquila stretched beside her breastbone. She was smiling at him, drizzling honey into her oatmeal. He smiled back and asked her whether she had read "Ash-Wednesday."

He dressed and left for the bank with a kind of formless trepidation which finally resolved itself as the worry that she would somehow disappear while he was out. But she did not. She was there when he came home, working at a table strewn with books and scribbled notes; she was there for dinner, stirring the tortellini as she told him about the local university where she had been teaching, while Pelle cooked down the tomatoes and searched the spice rack for bay leaves, said a bad word—which did not surprise Stella, as it usually surprised most people of his acquaintance—and added another item to the grocery list. Even after dinner, perusing Pelle's small collection of fiction and impressive conglomeration of all things celestial, arguing ice-cream flavors with him while she turned the browning pages of an old copy of *The Lottery and Other Stories*, she remained.

It was beginning to snow when he kissed each of her fingers and discovered a miniature miracle on the knuckle of her right ring finger, Cepheus sketched in the tiniest and faintest of freckles. "Are you sorry?" he asked. The living room lights were out and through the window spilled the filmy city light reflected from slopes and brittle edges of snow, across Stella's lap, across their hands clasped together.

"About what?"

"About me. I am hardly—I'm really not much of a boyfriend." He stumbled over the high-school terminology, the precision of his language faltering; he was unused to fitting words to emotions, and it showed. "That is . . . I can cook, I can converse, but you know me—I'd rather read 'The Waste Land' or a Carl Sagan article than see a movie. Not, I think, what most people look for in a relationship."

Snow freckled the window; the ghost-colored light illuminated a quarter of her face, the valleys and rises of an alien landscape. "You're fishing for compliments," she said, kissing the corner of his mouth. "I refuse to bite."

"But if you don't want to move in—"

"When I leave," she said with an ominous edge, smiling in the speckled light, "you'll know it." That night he found Canis Major, Bootes, and Gemini. He thought he glimpsed Taurus as she moved above him, her face an eclipsed moon among the heavy clouds of her hair, but it could have been the snow-shaded light. The foot which held Auriga was still ticklish.

He loved all of her: the dark roils of her hair, her musician's hands, her lunar-crescent smile that was all the sweeter for its rarity, the sound of her voice like some undiscovered instrument. Her conversation, her insight, the things she said that surprised him, the way she would come out onto the fire escape to watch the stars with him even when their breath crackled in the bitter air and the constant city haze seemed to have frozen and dropped in pieces out of the hard black sky—all of these caused a feeling that was very much like tears to well into his heart and throat. He was forever picking up the socks she left on the floor by the laundry basket. She made him see *Casablanca* at a small local theater that ran classics every Friday evening, with popcorn. Simple actions like that made him smile for no reason. Her knowledge of astronomy startled him at first, then pleased him; it seemed there was no fact he could mention that she had not already, at the very least, brushed in passing. One evening they strung extension cords out onto the fire escape and there, beneath a futile electric blanket, spent the night naming stars. "Like two love-struck adolescents," said Pelle, with a laugh for himself. At nine o'clock his breath froze on his glasses and they went indoors.

Most of all, he loved the universe scattered across her body like rare, strange jewels, celestial love-tokens. She was his beloved sky incarnate; each lovemaking discovered a new pattern hidden somewhere in her pale flawless skin. Sometimes he swore they moved when he was not looking. Aries beneath the point of her shoulderblade, Cygnus to the side of her knee: it would not have surprised him. At night, he joked, they multiplied.

He did not mention the word love. He understood the superstition that prevented him—fear of tempting the Fates, that only those things that can be lost are loved—and kept it to himself. Instead, when he felt the feeling-that-was-not-tears push itself into his throat, he pointed out some conjunction of planets or showed her the latest of the photographs he had taken, ardently and inexpertly, through his telescope. For without a doubt, Stella came under the heading of "great bounding joys and exaltations," none of which the life of Pelle Fisher had heretofore required, nor which, he feared, were intended for him. He imagined some cosmic register buried behind the stars, ticking off names and destinies and all the little random occurrences of peoples' lives. A glitch in the program—and there was Pelle, Stella at his side, sure it was all a mistake, a temporary aberration, loving every minute of it. He was no longer content. He was happy.

As he avoided the mention of love, he did not count the days. They might vanish all the faster for his counting.

Now he lay beside her in the winter night, his back to her side so that their bodies touched at shoulder and hip beneath the loosened blankets. Thin slices of light pierced the blinds and broke across the far corner of the room, darkened but for the red numerals of the clock on his dresser, and beneath the slow measures of Stella's breathing he heard only the distant rush and ebb of city traffic and his own slight movements as he shifted away from the chilled air and toward the warm skin pressed against his own. Something had woken him: not a sound, nor any stir from his sleeping lover, more like the change of light that often nudged him awake in the mornings before his alarm sounded. In the soft darkness he shifted, reached for his glasses and felt his fingers brush their cold rims. The vague changed state of things pushed at him, and he turned and raised himself on one elbow, curious in an unruffled drowsy fashion, and looked at her.

She had reversed. On her skin that had been pale as the white chipped coin of the moon, the constellations of her body burned colorless and bluish and faintest dimming gold; only those sudden stars made her visible, delineating the absolute jet blackness of her sleeping body. Her hair had become a froth of stars and glowing tides, luminous as something of the deep sea and sky, that spun in drifts across the pillows and sheets. Even her lashes shone, and the fine pen-lines of her eyebrows, while waking suns seemed to smolder beneath her nails. A galaxy lay like a goddess at his side.

Pelle could not breathe. He had dropped his glasses; he heard them clatter on the floor. When he bent over her, his hands denting the mattress, he thought the sounds would wake her. In his own ears, every movement was loud, even his own renewed breathing that began in a gasp. One hand sifted through star-surf that felt like her hair, the fine cloudy silk it had always been, but its light turned his skin the color of pearl. He touched the line of her cheek; Orion rode across the familiar planes of the face he could not see for its color like the absence of all light. The distant coal of Betelgeuse glowed beneath his fingertip, without heat, inset into her skin like a jewel.

"Stella," he whispered, almost afraid to speak the name, to see her wake, rise, turn away from him with all the stars of the night sky scattered brilliant across her body . . . She rolled over slightly, exposing a new glitter of patterns along her face and throat, and her eyes slid open between the milky fringe of her lashes.

"Pelle?" Her eyes were the color that people call moonlight, as if the moon provided its own effulgence and not the sun's borrowed glow: luminous liquid silver, eddying as her eyes lifted to find him in the darkened room. "You're trembling. Whose ghost did you see?" Only her voice was her own, her voice and her shape and everything but the changed colors of her.

"No ghost. You." His words had gone again; he stammered and his hands shook as he put on his glasses. He felt cold and bewildered. "You were written with stars. Now you *are* stars, that's all you are. Look at yourself."

She lifted her hands to study them and made a small sound in her throat. When she slid upright, an overlarge T-shirt tumbled around her shoulders, he thought for a moment that the clothing was moving by itself, the night itself had thickened and taken form and pushed the covers aside as she left the bed to pace back and forth in the sparse filtered light in the corner of the room. It did nothing to lessen the gemmed brightness of the birthmark constellations he loved, nor the sheer black of her skin. One hand combed through her hair in distraction, a gesture that annoyed him as much as he was fond of it. Stars could form in that hair, tidal forces drawing gas into fire, dust into light.

A single fact crystallized in his thoughts. Even superstition had not prevented it. He said, his voice very steady, "You are going to leave me."

"I thought I had more time." Wan light ran across her radiance as she returned to the bed, sat beside him with her long legs drawn up and her arms locked about her knees. Stars winked out and reappeared as she shifted slightly. "I would have warned you."

"Demon lover." He was relieved to see her smile draw the constellations of her face slightly awry, the moon smile he so loved. "Will I find you tomorrow with some other man, closeted behind a door that never opens?"

"No. Oh, no. You underestimate yourself, Pelle Fisher." Her voice was an alien instrument playing in the darkness. He wanted to touch her; he did not know what she would do under his hands, whether she would keep this changed shape or fly apart like a star gone nova. She added, like a confession, "I didn't mean to meet you. I didn't think I would; you can never choose who draws you." She shivered. He thought it was the air and had already opened his mouth on an invitation back to bed, his hand on the blanket edge, when she turned and kissed him. "Now, Pelle," she said, against his mouth. He heard the ache in her voice, or wanted to hear it and imagined it: believed and did not question. Perhaps tears ran from her eyes down his cheeks. The moon-quicksilver of her eyes looked liquid anyway. "I'm leaving you now."

"I love you," he said. He had said it all wrong, as he knew he would: like an accusation or the opening line of an argument. Like the terrible sun-and-comet poem of their lovemaking, it did not seem to bother her. He tried, his hands tangled in her star-froth of hair, "I want to ask, will you remember me? But everybody asks that, in movies or romance novels of the trashiest sort. 'I'll never forget you' is just as bad . . . I will be forever looking at the hands of women who come into the bank, looking for Lyra everywhere I go. That's your fault," smiling shyly as he said it, so that their parting should not be the spiteful affair he had feared. Her hands felt as they always had, fine and thin and a little nervous, intertwined with his hands. The ghost-light shed from her skin turned his own unruly hair the color of sand under moonlight. "I will always be looking for stars."

"You were always," Stella said, both of them conscious of the line like something from a movie or a poem, "looking for stars."

Musician's hands and slender wrists, spangled with Lyra and Hydra and Cepheus, he held them for a heartbeat, a breath of time frozen and fixed as the winter stars. Then he remembered about the distance of stars and the speed of light, how every star that shines in the night sky might have died long ago: and she slid through his fingers in streaks and jewels of light, and even Pelle's hands, clever as a conjurer's with their bitten nails and their need, could not hold her.

Heartbroken, he did not retreat from the world. As he surprised others with his competence, he surprised himself with his resilience: the next morning found him dressed and walking through the crusted slush to the bank, where he cashed checks and discussed accounts and handed money to strangers, always keeping his eyes resolutely fixed on those strangers' faces lest he begin to dart glances at their hands, looking for constellations, looking for miracles. He did not take up drinking, he did not walk in front of passing buses, and while he sat one evening for forty-five minutes on the edge of the vacant bed, weeping into his hands, he also tossed her discarded socks into the laundry basket and treated himself to a double literary feature: "One Ordinary Day, With Peanuts" and, Stella's recommendation, "The Man Who Rowed Christopher Columbus Ashore."

Memory hurt. He had expected it would: a knowledge which did nothing to diminish the pain. When he climbed out onto the fire escape a few nights later, panting frozen clouds as he maneuvered the telescope through the window without the familiar help of her hands, he could not watch the stars at all. The glittering traceries in the sky were remote and impersonal; he could not touch them. Viewing the moon with his eye pressed against the chilled metal, he imagined her face among the shadowed hollows and rises. He turned over half-asleep, expecting to find her warmth at his side, and almost fell out of bed. A few days gave him back his joy in the night skies, but each constellation reminded him of some point of her body, some line of her flesh. It disconcerted him.

He continued his job at the bank; there was no reason to quit. After a few weeks he gathered his courage and began, on his off days, to frequent the university: specifically the Department of Comparative Literature where Stella had taught classes. He asked after her, painfully conscious of knowing only her first name, and was surprised by an answer. The secretary remembered her well: "She was really popular with the students, did you know? There was practically a movement to keep her here, but it wasn't like she was being fired—she left herself. I don't know where she is now. Teaching somewhere, writing a book, researching ... She loved what she did. It was her life."

"Yes," said Pelle, "I'd believe that." He went out into the bright blue-shadowed day and came back four days later when the bank's hours permitted.

After a while he became a fixture, without realizing it, and laughed with surprise when he noticed one student pointing him out to another as he leaned against the wall, reading an astrophysics text and making pencil notes in the margins. By then the professors were used to him; he no longer disrupted classes by opening the wrong door, and it had been several months since anyone called the police. A few of the students even spoke to him regularly: about star mythology, close enough to astronomy for Pelle to keep on topic. It was spring now and he sat on a drying stone wall outside the science complex, listening, amazed. One student told him about the goddess Nut of Egypt, whose starry body arched over the earth, swallowing the sun every evening to give him birth at dawn. Another mentioned Ourania, Mnemosyne's ninth daughter, Muse of astronomers. He dreamed that night of Stella in his arms, her reversed self, aflame with stars and her hair wrapping him like a comet's tail. *I didn't mean to meet you*, the echo of her voice said as he rocked between waking and sleeping in the grey dawn. *I didn't think I would; you can never choose who draws you*. He woke and wondered.

Memory still hurt, but now it hurt a little less; and not because he was forgetting her, either.

Pelle Fisher was thirty-six years old. He had celebrated his birthday two weeks ago Saturday, quietly, by himself, then come into class on Monday only to discover an impromptu chorus of students who presented him with "Happy Birthday" in a variety of keys. The gesture touched him; he had been at the university for a little over a year, tentatively undertaken to teach a semester of undergraduate astronomy under the auspices of his professors, and had not expected any such fondness on the part of his students. He flushed with delight, took his glasses off and polished them on his handkerchief, and that gesture reminded him briefly and unexpectedly of Stella, who had teased him about the care he took with his glasses. He smiled then, and wondered if his students would think he was smiling at their display.

Stella had not returned to the college. Somewhere in his bones, Pelle thought when he considered the matter, he had known she would not. Wherever she had gone, it was not back to teaching. He did wonder whether she had been to the one to teach the myth of Nut to the young CompLit major, the story of Ourania to the student who spoke two kinds of Greek; how much of his new job had been his easygoing interview with the head of the Physics Department and how much had been something—he was not sure what to call it—else.

Perhaps goddesses rewarded their devotees. Muses looked after their own. But the universe was composed of chance as well as design. A planet swung in its prescribed orbit until a wandering star came near, pulling gravities awry and resettling the order of the spheres, and all an observer would see were two lights in the sky, close for a moment, immeasurably distant for all the years to come until the sun burned cold and died in shrouds of light ... Pelle believed in the inexplicable. He believed that Stella had loved him; that was, perhaps, all he needed to believe. Her nature did not change his emotion: she had been joy beyond his expectations and now she was gone. He dreamed of her less often now. Once he startled at a student who handed him a midterm exam: freckles spattered across her knuckles like the arm of a tiny galaxy. But they formed no patterns; there were no constellations on her sunburnt skin. As he had promised Stella in thoughtless prophecy, he was always looking for stars. The edge of the heavens had brushed him in passing and, whether or not he noticed, he was no longer the same.

He liked what he did; he was liked for it. Sometimes he sat at night on the fire escape, watching the stars through the smoke-screen city sky, and wondered whether this too would vanish in a night like Stella from his arms. He was afraid, as he had feared her leaving, that some day his class would be interrupted by a summons from some administrator that would end his professorial career with a faint expiring whimper. The banality of budget cuts might ruin him, or some failed student might complain, or a better contender for the post might appear— But his fears had not kept Stella; why should they keep his job? He bit the ragged edge of one thumbnail and watched autumn leaves scrape through the streets. Nor had she vanished in any of the expected ways. He liked to think that made him less afraid.

He never told his students of Stella, and they, with no grounds for curiosity, never asked. Sometimes he thought of the story she would have made, and wished for someone to tell it to: how Pelle Fisher had loved a woman made of stars, chance-met at the teller's window in an undistinguished bank. But he did not speak of her to anyone, though he remembered very well and with great love the precise slant of her cheekbones and her voice tuned to some haunting scale, and his students were forever bewildered by the way he paused with a faint distance in his eyes at the mention of Lyra, or smiled with reminiscence at the constellation Virgo.

Singing Innocence
and Experience

The unicorn said again, "You know you want it."

He was reading on the bed, naked, chin propped on one fist while he turned the pages with quick, incurious flicks of his fingers. Morning light rinsed his skin the color of ivory, pale slate where shadows touched him and the same smooth pallor everywhere; even in summer, he never tanned. A faint silvery down, like the silk on a nut, traced the length of his spine. He had the look of a dancer or an acrobat; his face held unexpected hollows and angles, the spacing of his eyes, the tilt of his cheekbones, moved almost past exotic into alien. His hair where it spilled over the pillow was whiter than his skin. For some time he had kept it short; now it was growing out and fell constantly into his eyes, silk shag always cool to the touch; he smelled a little like sunlight, and a little like snow, and his hair had the taste of dry violets. Without looking up, he closed his book and laid it on the bedside table, rolled over onto his back and folded his arms behind his head. "You're a virgin, after all," he added, and blinked eyes like evening air, "not a nun."

Isabeau Reisse, called Beau and inclined to damage anyone who tried any other abbreviation, leaned back on her hands and laughed. It still hurt. She had corn-colored hair to her chin, one eye more blue than green and the other more brown than hazel, high rough bones in her face and a trefoil tattoo on the inner turn of her left wrist; she was sitting on the end of her own bed, watching a unicorn try to seduce her for the third time in a week. "I read once that the unicorn used to represent Christ. Like in the Unicorn Tapestries, at the Cloisters, he's purifying the waters with his horn after the snake poisoned them. Also the association with virginity: as Mary was a virgin to whom the Holy Spirit came, so the unicorn comes only to a virgin. The purest and noblest of living beasts. Butt-naked on my bed," Beau added, "and you don't get any more explicit than that. So much for purity."

The unicorn's smile, like everything else about him, was both beautiful and unsettling. Even his mouth had little color; his teeth were very white. "And when the unicorn laid his head in the virgin's lap, what did you think was happening there? Freud would have had a field day with the symbolism of the horn and the maiden. You should program less; read more. As Daniel keeps telling you, there's more to life than coding."

Her shoulders had flinched taut at his mention of Daniel, who had never said any such thing to her; now she snapped back, "Like getting into that bed with you?"

The unicorn said practically, "You'll have to sleep somewhere." When he brushed the hair out of his eyes, Beau glimpsed again the stain on his forehead: shapeless, smoky as a fading bruise, the only flaw anywhere on his impossible skin. "You'll be safe enough. The unicorn is also a peaceable beast, as you've no doubt read. Have I hurt you in any way, these past months? I will do nothing that you do not want. More accurately, I can do nothing that you do not want. You touched me; you're virgin; you've read enough for that. When she brings in the hunters, he never runs."

For a moment the color shifted in his eyes, darkening to an indigo even the sunlight could not clear. His beauty had gotten into Beau's throat; it closed her breath, fractured all the bones around her heart. She swallowed an emotion she would not name and said, unevenly, "There are no hunters here. No nets. No spears."

"A walled garden and a pomegranate tree and chains of gold."

Beau did not dare touch him, fresh as sprinkled salt or snow. Beyond the broad window over the bed, crows were fighting in the ash trees. Her backyard opened onto a scanty wood, thin stand of trees and scrub that spread between her block of houses and the town reservoir; the unicorn liked to walk down there, around the perimeter of the water where ducks nested among the cattails and the occasional pair of swans made their home. Birds crowded out of the trees and beat the air about his head. Dogs whined like puppies and yearned after his footsteps, or crouched to the ground until he had gone. In the tapestries, Beau remembered, the unicorn's spiraling horn laid open the stomach of one hound until more fastened on its white, speared shoulders, and brought it down in its own pomegranate-red blood. Even the squirrels quieted momentarily as they passed, the mortal girl and the immortal man. "I'm sorry," Beau murmured. "You're not laying your head in my lap."

"No," said the unicorn, "not yet." He turned over onto his side, unselfconscious, easy in his skin, and began to read again. Beau unknotted her hands, breathed out, and watched the unicorn take no notice as she slid off the bed and went downstairs to make lunch. He had been with her almost half a year now; she did not know how to release him. Rather, she knew how to do it: she did not know how she ever could.

She had found him sleeping on a park bench, among the plane trees where she liked to walk in the evening on her way home from work. Even in April, the streetlights came on early among the trees, and she walked through cross-hatched shadows still dripping rain from that afternoon's showers; she had not thought to find anyone else in the damp, lowering evening. At first glance, she did not even see him. But she smelled, out of nowhere, sunlight, snow, violets, and stopped where she stood, among the rainy grass and branches beaded with electric light, and stared. Perhaps the shape on the bench was human, hunched on its side in sleep. It stirred, raised its head and Beau's breath snagged on sudden panic: the odd scent caught her, calmed her, and she did not run. Old violets, she thought, pressed dry for the keeping in a diary of loves fifty years past. Summer sunlight, rich as sap or honey, that soaked into the bones and eased the muscles; first bitten-metal taste of snow on the wind, stirring the bones of brown leaves, wakening winter; violets again, preserved, brittle, like a memory treasured so long its origin had become unimportant. Curious now, unable not to look, Beau opened her eyes and discovered—unreal, unmistakable—the unicorn.

She did not see the lion's tail, the cloven hooves, the beard and mane, the seashell helix of the horn. She saw a slight hard man, not much above her own height, kneeling on an ancient bench with one hand still along its back to steady himself as he came upright: startled, composed, resigned. In the streetlight's sodium flare, his hair reflected bruised orange, burnt neon; his brows were as pale as his hair, his lashes, or perhaps a faint shade of silver darker than both. His eyes were the color of the air between dusk and winter twilight.

"Oh," Beau said. The sound slipped from her and she did not call it back. "Oh, you're beautiful."

The unicorn lifted his head: it was not a human movement, and it did not look wrong on him. "You," he whispered, "I felt you. The hunt's close, isn't it? You never come alone."

She lost language in the color of his eyes, shook her head dumbly before she remembered how to say, "No. Just me."

"Then," said the unicorn, "you are the hunt."

A wind came out of the western half of the sky and shivered rain down from the young leaves, the branches blackened with damp, onto Beau's shoulders and the unicorn's light-dyed hair. Neither noticed.

She said then, "Let me touch you." Afterward she squirmed at the memory of that breathy, breathless plea: high-school wallflower begging for a dance, a date, for the bare brief regard that passed over her and passed on. Beau had never been shy, or overlooked, or needed from anyone what she could not get herself. Twenty-six years old, she heard herself pleading and despised it; but the color of the unicorn's eyes, his skin, his ragged shadow that might be changing shape at the farthest corner of her vision, when she was not looking, loosened her throat and she spoke without thinking. "Just once."

"Never once."

"I won't hurt you."

"You don't know how," said the unicorn. A slight smile changed all the lines of his face, so that Beau caught her breath and almost laughed for delight. The smile left him and he bent his head, dipping his horn into the poisoned stream; his movements had nothing to do with her. "You can't know."

"I know," Beau said, and did not know whether she was agreeing or arguing, "I know." Gently, she reached out to him through the damp April evening and laid her hand on his forehead.

Beneath her palm, a faint pulse ticked between their skins; it might only have been the blood beating in her hand that slipped a little against his brow, but warmth came and went with the rhythm, steady as sunlight, as though she held the afternoon like amber under her hand. It neither sped nor slowed as he breathed. He did not move at her touch. But he allowed it; he did not pull away, he could not, her touch fixed him fast to the park bench beneath the buzzing street-light, to her. She had no need for a golden bridle, a chain of gems around his throat: nothing but her hand and her desire and the sorcery of inexperience. She knew what she did without knowing how. It was not quite innocence; it was close enough.

Her fingers were beginning to prickle, pins-and-needles waking, as though the sun-glow out of his forehead had gotten into her bones and her blood was bristling with light. Beneath her spread hand, his twilight eyes watched her without blinking, without judgment, without yielding. "You're very beautiful," Beau whispered, helplessly.

The unicorn rose, and followed her home.

He never changed shape. Perhaps Beau's first blurred impression had caught him into this form, or some truth in a spiral of story made him as real a beautiful man as a mythical beast, and he never answered questions she left unasked. While she typed, he read; sometimes he cooked dinner, a better cook than Beau and gracious enough that she rarely felt insulted when he leaned over her shoulder and commented on her choices, and often went walking with her on weekends or odd free afternoons. He discussed poetry. He told stories. He tossed around odd bits of philosophy, never unkindly, and monopolized the remote control when they watched television. At night he slept on the futon in her living room, and she often woke with her alarm to find him already awake and reading by the thin light before dawn.

That no one else on her block noticed he was a unicorn—though she could not imagine what they would have said, had it happened—gradually drew further from her thoughts, as nobody seemed to notice the white-haired man who was living with Beau Reisse anyway. Other pedestrians greeted them, when they wandered together beneath the plane trees; at the supermarket, the check-out clerk nodded to the unicorn and handed him a paper bag full of French bread, tuna fish, carrots, and organic fruit juices; none of Beau's neighbors asked her about the beautiful stranger, or cared to consider him when he was not there before their eyes. Perhaps, she thought, they did not see him. Or perhaps they saw him as something other than he was, less evocative, more explicable. Why she had seen him, then, she did not know. She did not think about it much; she did not really want an answer. "Innocence," the unicorn said once, a *non sequitur* to something she had asked him, idly, about his life before he came to the park and the plane trees. "We're drawn to it. Youths and maidens, the unknowing, the untouched, who are beautiful because they do not know they are beautiful . . . Here and there, Beau. Around and about. We never go twice where we've been once. Does that answer your question?" It did not, quite; and at the same time answered the ones she did not touch. Now she stood beside the sink that dripped only at night, hands flat on the linoleum of the counter, feeling her blood rise at the thought of touching his forehead as she had only that once beneath the plane trees. *You know you want it . . .* She turned angrily and jerked open the refrigerator door, listening to the sound of pages turning in the bedroom, refusing to hear him.

She put together sandwiches, vegetarian for the unicorn and turkey for herself, hands moving without thinking about it. When she glanced into the bedroom, he had not moved from his statue's effortless pose. To Beau's eye, something between smugness and a dare polished his immobility. Let him come for his own lunch, then: she left the plate on the kitchen table and wandered into the living room, sandwich in hand, to settle cross-legged on the abandoned futon and wish there were somewhere else she could go. A hotel was ridiculous. If she spent more than one night at the office, people would begin to ask questions. As for Daniel— She entertained two and a half seconds' thought of calling him before she remembered that he would probably spend half of their stopgap, stunted conversation dropping the receiver or losing track of whatever he had been working on when she called. Besides, she did not even know he was home. He kept even odder hours than she did. He would have reverted, gone tongue-tied again or fallen back on trivia; and more than that, Beau had no idea what she would say to him.

Daniel Carter had come into her life perhaps a month after the unicorn and much less spectacularly, a graceless, shock-headed young man with the most beautiful eyes Beau had ever seen. Maybe they balanced everything else about him. He dropped coffee mugs. He tripped over sidewalk curbs. He spoke as though he feared his words might be taken away from him at any second. But his eyes were the color of burnt gold, champagne-translucent in direct light, and he could not keep them off her; she wanted to tell him to get a haircut, and then she wanted to talk to him, for no discernible reason except that her face slid into a smile when he called her name in the hallway, and he had once handed her a paper cup of water after a four-hour coding stint, before she even remembered how to open her mouth. For reasons that she did not name to herself, she did not speak of him to the unicorn until almost three months had passed.

One afternoon, he put out his hand and did not knock Beau's elbow into the keyboard or spill a stack of papers to the floor; he was holding a book, a paperback volume of Rainer Maria Rilke's poetry, and asking her whether she had ever read the *Duino Elegies.* Beau had not; she borrowed the book and surprised herself three days later by asking about Rilke's other works, as much for the language as for Daniel's delighted golden eyes. He gave her the *Book of Hours* and two hours of his own at a local Indian restaurant. Afterward, he walked her to the bus stop: he was not her first kiss, but she thought him her best, and told him so. They had Japanese food the next week, and the week after that Beau confessed that she had run out of restaurants to recommend and they ate competent stir-fry in Daniel's disastrous clutter of an apartment. The week after that, Daniel stumbled on the stairs and all but flung an assortment of flowers into her arms, and though she did not know how she would explain the unicorn—*We're just friends, really . . . ?*—Beau invited him home for the evening.

In the end, she did not explain the unicorn at all. He greeted them at the door, Yeats in hand, did not embarrass Daniel by extolling Beau's virtues as a housemate, as she had feared, and then retired to the porch. Whatever he was doing—waving away moths in the lingering summer air, Beau suspected, and reading—it was out of sight. She had apologized to him more than once, about inviting Daniel over without warning him. He had grinned at her outright, looking up from a translation of Rumi, and told her not to worry. "Do I look offended? You're the maiden; you can bring home whatever knight you like. Besides, he has good taste in poetry. Just tell me whether you're going out for dinner or eating in: if you go out, I'm eating the Chinese leftovers." Presumably he did as he had said; when they returned from a Sicilian restaurant Daniel had hunted down in the phonebook, Beau did not bother to look in the refrigerator and Daniel did not care to remind her. Beneath her palm, his hair felt exactly as wildly springing as it looked; when she reached for his hands, she was surprised at how strongly he gripped her fingers, almost enough to hurt, more than enough to make her smile for nonsensical reasons more beautiful even than Daniel's eyes. He was watching her as though he had a question stuck between his teeth; his eyes were buttered amber in the lamplight. She was trying to think of how she might suggest Daniel's own apartment to him without making either of them blush or crack up laughing, because she could not imagine inviting him upstairs while the unicorn placidly read through that week's library haul on the porch, when she looked past Daniel's shoulder and through the sliding glass door to see the unicorn moonlit and smirking over the pages of Rilke's *Sonnets to Orpheus*. She whispered, "Daniel?" Kindly and carefully, with much more regret than she let him see, she pointed him to the door with her phone number scrawled on a half a notecard and an open offer for lunch. She closed the door behind him before starting to swear.

"How could you?" she demanded, when she had run out of immediate expletives. "As soon as I fuck him, you're free, is that it? For God's sake, you're not even subtle! Just push us into bed, why don't you? Here, you can stand outside the doorway and make sure we do the job right. Want to listen? Just don't come in—we're busy. Jesus! What kind of unicorn are you?"

She had flung the door open, so violently it rattled in its frame and she spared a brief moment from her fury to wonder whether she would finish her evening picking splinters bloody-fingered out of the carpet, it might have been fitting; the unicorn had never moved. Now he finished the fifteenth sonnet, closed the book with one

168

finger between the pages to mark the place, and asked, "Do you know what happened to the maiden who snared the unicorn?"

"I don't know," Beau said sourly, "you tried to get her into bed?"

"She was wed, yes. Usually to one of the huntsmen, if she was not the lord's daughter, or the daughter of a king: thus breaking her binding over the unicorn. Do you think I'm joking? Innocence is powerful stuff. Even physical innocence. A little learning may be a dangerous thing, but not knowing can be far more dangerous. You can hurt me far worse than any hunter with a lance or a gun. You know that, and you don't." The unicorn rubbed at his eyes, a startlingly human gesture. "I'm tired, Isabeau. Go see Daniel tomorrow. Apologize to him. He didn't deserve to be thrown out after such a nice evening; he didn't even spill coffee down your shoes, and that's a great credit to his love." When she came out of the shower, he was finishing the *Sonnets* on the futon.

They did not speak for almost two days. Daniel mumbled an almost inaudible good-morning and all but shied from her as she passed him in the corridor, on her way to make herself some chai; staring after him, Beau drank three swallows before she realized it was only hot water. He was typing when she returned, easy-fingered for once; she reached forward to touch his shoulder and curled her fingers back in memory of the unicorn's beauty, Daniel's courtesy, a night spent wakeful and furious and alone while the unicorn read Rilke downstairs. Instead she finished her work in silence, and returned home to find that the unicorn was more inventive than she had thought.

The first time she saw him naked, her blood almost stopped. He lay on his side, weight on one folded arm; it was afternoon and the light gilded his skin that she had never seen beyond his hands and his face, sleek as marble to the eye, vulnerable, luring. Just the way his hair parted over his eyes, a careless snowfall with twilight looking through it, made her want to touch him. She would have knelt beside him, crushed pomegranates against his pale mouth and eaten the seeds from his lips, combed his hair with his fingers and laid her hand against his throat, like a maiden picked out of fifteenth-century threads; there were no hunters; he was not the prey. Beau blinked and felt herself smiling in surprise, shifting her weight to step toward him.

She closed her hands tight against her sides, and made herself see the scene as it was: the beautiful white-haired man lounging on her bed, expecting her to melt into his arms, never in love with her and most likely scornful of any clumsy attempt she might make in his direction: a recourse, an artifice, a last resort. She tried to imagine Daniel doing the same thing. The antidote worked; she began to snicker, and lost the laughter with a sinking sickness when she remembered that Daniel might never enter her house again. The unicorn lifted both silver brows and asked, "Is something wrong?"

"What you're not wearing." Her voice swayed only a little. "You're a unicorn."

"Which means, I suppose, that I should not look as I do. Unicorns possess the cloven feet of goats, the tails of lions, and the horns of narwhals, which few people had seen at the time of this description's invention. Everyone knows that."

"Get off my bed!" Beau shouted. Her voice split, out of anger or hilarity, she was still not sure which. "I'm not losing my virginity to a mythical creature. God, this is starting to get on my nerves."

"Imagine," said the unicorn, "how I feel." He left the room on noiseless feet; she found him half an hour later, still stark naked, peeling an orange on the back steps. Beau cursed him and burst out laughing. The unicorn grinned at her, offered her a piece of orange, and came inside. At dinner, she could not have told from his manner that anything had happened; he was clothed, friendly, reserved, unreachable as ever. The smell of lost summers' violets drifted on her pillow as she fell asleep.

Three times he had tried to seduce her now, if this blatant, ridiculous dare could be called seduction, and three times Beau had ignored him.

In a folktale, she thought, that might have freed her. Instead the unicorn remained in her house, chained by a breathed word and his forehead burning against her palm; she had not spoken to Daniel in more than a week, except when one bumped past the other in a hallway or close corner and muttered *excuse me*; Beau crumbled the crust of a turkey sandwich between her fingers and thumped one fist into the futon. Faint from a flight of stairs away, the sound of turning pages scratched the air. When she called Daniel, at last and awkwardly, she clenched her teeth hard on the sound of his voice, fumbling over the worst voicemail message in the world: "Hi. It's me . . ." and after almost fifteen seconds of painful silence, "leave a message?" Beau's words lay in her mouth like stone that her teeth bit into; she could not say any of them. She hung up, and went upstairs to find the unicorn.

He must have come downstairs for his sandwich while she was clinging speechless to the phone, because he was picking beansprouts off the plate when she opened the door. He had put on a bath-robe—hers, faded blue terrycloth out at the elbows—and settled back against the bed's headboard, legs curled beneath him, looking like a sculpture any way he moved. "Hey," Beau said, and could not go any further. "Hey." Her voice stuck, like Daniel on his answering machine, and she leaned against the doorframe, arms crossed tight over her chest as though she might slip away.

The unicorn put down the plate, raised his head in the gesture she had seen first by smoky sodium light. His face was turned away. His untrimmed hair fanned forward and screened his profile from her; he spoke without expression. "Once, in the thirteenth century, I spent a winter in the company of a monk. He was a good man, I think; he was kind to me, even at the beginning when he thought I was only one of God's fools, a white-haired lunatic wandering barefoot in the snow; and when he learned what I was, he neither revered nor feared me. He passed me some honey to put on the bread we had been eating, saved from the summer's store, before thinking to ask what unicorns eat. He wanted to know if I had a soul. I could not answer him. But I stayed in his hermit's cell all that winter—and it was a bitter year, people dying of plague and cold, and though I healed whom I could, I could never heal enough—and he did not care whether I went on two feet or four, horned or naked, he did not ask whether I was his or the world's. In the spring, I left. Nothing bound me there. Even the monk's celibacy was not a chain on me; he had not touched me as you had, to possess, as innocence reaches out without knowing what it is taking and holds without knowing what it has. He knew. For all his religion, he knew. And he did not touch me as though I had been born only for his hand, his eyes, his wonder. Do you think I am beautiful, Isabeau Reisse?" His voice broke over the name. "Then take what you desire, though you'll tell me you don't, and set me free. Never mind the last tapestry. I am not made to be kept."

Beau's blood pounded out all thought. "I don't believe this. You. I do not believe this. Are you listening to yourself?" She had never been angry with the unicorn before. Exasperated, irritated, bewildered, yes: never this slow weight of rage moving in her bones, jolting her blood until she opened her mouth and she did not recognize the words she was saying. Even over Daniel, she had never been so furious. "Is that all you think innocence is? Wanting without understanding, blind self-assurance, the confidence of the foolhardy—you think the innocent are stupid, is that it?"

"What you do not understand," the unicorn whispered, face turned from her like a door slammed into stone, "makes you dangerous."

"Then explain it to me! You, who don't even know what you're talking about—Because I don't know what something is like, that means I don't understand it's different, right? Because I haven't been you, inside your skin every moment of your life, I can't reach out my hand and hope you'll take it? Fine, I'm a virgin, I've never fucked anyone—that's all the innocence there is, sure, that's all that matters. I'm not worldly. But there's a world out there. You think I don't know?"

The unicorn shouted, bugle of trumpets and the horn swinging up white as lightning, "You *don't* know!"

The air burned. Into its concussion, the blasted silence where a pale man sat stiff as iron in a worn-out bathrobe and a virgin's touch blazed on his forehead like a scar, Beau began to laugh.

"Oh, Mother of God on a motorcycle." She shook, tearless, hands to her eyes, bent double with the impossibility of it. "I've met a cynical unicorn."

The unicorn shuddered. His eyes had closed like bruises in his salt-white face; he reached forward and picked a piece of shattered plate off the quilt, turned it between his fingers blankly, as though he could not quite recall what it was or how he had come to hold it in his hand. He whispered, "Half a year, Beau. Autumn's rising, and still you hold on to me. I waited for the hunters. Only you. You, and that boy who brings you poetry—what do you want the both of us for? Me at your beck and call, and him to prove that you're worth having: he has to come of his own accord. The lady and her knight go walking in the garden, and the pomegranate seeds fall down like tears. Break one and bite one, Isabeau. Let me go."

Beau had stopped laughing. "I've eaten pomegranates before. They're a symbol. Virginity's a symbol. I don't hold you here."

"Then who does?" He turned his face to her, bitterly. His eyes were the color of ice after the sun has set; his hair stung white as a plague winter. "Virgin. Innocent. Who else chained me that night?"

Beau said, so quietly it hurt her, "Six months." She shivered in the warm fall of late morning sunlight, early September: feeling her way through memory toward the unicorn's rigid, wintry figure. "Did you hate me then, too?"

"I don't hate you. Unicorns come in adoration, to lay their horns in their ladies' laps—"

"Stop that!" He blinked, more than slightly jolted: a crack in winter's face. "The only thing worse than a cynical unicorn is a passive-aggressive one. If I were a mythologist, I could make my reputation with this . . . When I touched you, in the park. You didn't flinch from me. You didn't run."

"The hunt had run me down."

"No hunt." If he had a name, she could have touched him with it; he did not, or she did not know it, and it might have come too close to whatever trembled beneath the boundaries of his skin. When she rested her weight on the edge of the bed, he did not move away. She did not know if that was a good sign. "Just me, like you said."

"The virgin."

"Another virgin. I want to think they didn't all hurt you. Maybe the rest had hunters following them to round the story out, I don't know; you could tell me. But I remember you said this, *we never go twice where we've been once*, so once you go, you stay gone, a memory, a myth, something to turn over in your thoughts at night and tell to your children's children until maybe you doubt that it ever happened to you, a unicorn glimpsed and touched once long ago when the world was young: I believe you. I believe that you stayed all winter with a celibate monk, maybe a virgin if he'd been raised in the order, and I believe that you left him in the spring. I believe that you want to get away from me. I want you to believe that I want to release you." Her breath burned in her throat. "I didn't know. That you were hurting. That I was hurting you. I didn't know that I was keeping you here; I thought you stayed for your own reasons, the way Daniel—the way you talk to someone you like, ordinarily, with no chain or binding, just people. You were kind to me . . . I didn't know. That's ignorance, not innocence. And I am sorry."

She saw the movement of the muscles in his throat as he swallowed hard, terrible in its beauty and how natural it looked on a unicorn, whose movements were not human. The broken bit of pottery dropped from his fingers, clinked against the other fragments. He should have gone from her house long ago. "You can't know what it's like."

"I know," Beau whispered. "I don't. I never can. But you—" She turned up her hands, palms and fingers empty and open. "You can't either. But we hold out our hands anyway."

The unicorn's gaze sank and darkened. He dropped his face, and Beau began to rise, turn away, leave him to his walled garden and the pomegranate trees whose fruit she had picked though he never saw it; his hand on her wrist stopped her. He drew her back down with little more than the warmth of palm and fingers, almost casual, unexpected, opening something inside her bones where his nakedness had fired her; his touch was very light. "I am holding on to you," he said. The words were ritual as the lowering of his head. "Loose me."

In dreams, shameful smudges of imagery and tactile imagination that she woke and tried earnestly to forget, she had felt her mouth pressed against his pale mouth that would taste like snow, and sunlight, and violets; she had slid her hands through his hair, and drawn the snowy strands between her lips, and felt the breath-beat of his lashes against her cheek. Now her hands shook as she set them to either side of his face, cupped over the tilted cheekbones until her fingertips rested at the outer corners of his eyes and his growing hair slipped over her fingers as fine and cool as she had imagined it. His eyes had closed as she bent her face to his; she tasted dry violets as she set her lips to his forehead, where her touch or a horn's conspicuous absence had smudged the skin, where sunlight beat out of him to the rhythm of their moving blood, no more than a brief brush of their skins; it burnt her. The unicorn said, "Isabeau . . ."

She held falling snow, rising light, flowers growing in a garden whose door swung open to the wind. An uncoiled spiral, whorled and shining as the inner curve of a mussel shell, wheeled and glanced over her shoulder; a slight-boned, compact man little taller than corn-haired Isabeau Reisse raised his face to hers, like a child. She held something from a young world, to remember at night and retell. Quietly she straightened the empty quilt, and leaned forward to pick up the pieces of the broken plate.

In the lightening silence, something beeped downstairs, waited forty-five seconds, beeped again. Beau hit the play button with her knuckles as she crossed the kitchen floor in champagne-colored sunlight, hands full of white shards.

On the answering machine, a message from Daniel was waiting.

> Again and again, although we know love's landscape
> and the little churchyard with its mourning names
> and the terrible secretive ravine in which the others
> end: again and again, we two go out
> under the ancient trees, again and again we set ourselves
> among the flowers, opposite the sky.
>
> —Rainer Maria Rilke, "Immer wieder"

Gintaras

Resinous tears, that the split bark
sheds: sorrow's fixative, slow caulking
of time preserved in potential, seconds
between sticky newness and decay. Waves
beat these beads ashore, hardened glosses
of legend over grief; Jurate under Baltic
currents, the fragments of her palace
as splintered on the sea-bed as mortal
bones, drowned and thunder-stricken,
wails like the storm churning her tears
up from the silt: syrupy bits of sun
salt-frozen, flotsam treasures to adorn
the hair of women whose lovers are yet
living. In and out of her drift-net hair,
fish gleam and vanish, memorial, silver
as she does not cry. Tide spumes milky
between stones, amber clicks on the wet
shingle, one sibilant and consonantal
rattle: *Kastytis, Kastytis.* At the mouth
of the Sventoji, fishermen cast nets,
haul in their day's catch, untroubled

by warnings popped to the surface
like bubbles, maidens with skin of nacre
and cold kisses surfacing like dry-land
dreams, by the love of the sea herself
gathered into a knot of sorrow and amber
deep within her kingdom's shattered tides:
stories are for hearts, not for hands
and backs that strain again to this unmythical
work, herring scales and early mornings
and trawlers chugging over the waters
that keep their secrets, as everyday as
the slow track of sap down a fissured face
of bark, the fossilized traces of loss.

Till Human Voices Wake Us

Dylan's sister was swimming with her lover. It had been a full hour since he lost sight of them, two wave-sleeked heads glimpsed occasionally, like seals, among the breakers that constantly crested and constantly sank; her hair the color of old parchment, spindrift pale against the marbled water, his hair wet and black as the jagged rock of the shore where the waves spilled and broke. Far out on the horizon, they had seemed to sink under the curve of the world: out of human sight, out of reach. Dylan had no such mystical recourse. Monday would find him back in school, two states away, far from the bright bitter taste of salt on the wind and the sea's plain glittering where the land dipped toward the rising sun, far from his sister and her house cluttered with a melange of objects, old books and bits of jewelry, sea charts, fishing floats, fans of feathers and flowers dried into papery immortality, clay candle-holders, coffee mugs, the aftermath of a typhoon in a curio shop. If he could have dived out of the world, he would have done so without a backward glance, if only to escape the schoolwork he had been avoiding all week.

The thought made him scowl at the papers he held pinned against his knee, wind-snatched and crackling. He had already finished his math assignment; he was halfway through the week's allotment of *Great Expectations* when boredom abruptly rose and swamped him.

179

He dropped a rock atop his trigonometry book to keep the problem sets from blowing away, checked his watch—an hour and six minutes since he had last seen Mariana—and abandoned all hope of actually doing any of his work. Instead he threw pebbles into the oncoming waves, wrote his name in the thin paring of sand available between the rocks and the sea, sang while the wind peeled his voice thin and out to sea. If he had a girlfriend, he pondered, would he leave his family to go swimming for hours with her? If his girlfriend was anything like his sister's lover. If he had a girlfriend. That was, Dylan conceded, a more immediate question. He picked his way out onto the rocks, slippery and tide-cracked underfoot, and seated himself on a promontory high enough that not even dry barnacles scaled the stone. The sky curved down to the sea, brilliant with heat; there were white cliffs of cloud over the water, piling toward rain, but not tonight. Mariana never went swimming when there was danger of storms. Sun soaked into his shoulders, wind furled spray from the water and scattered it cool across his face; he shivered between the sea and the light, wholly thoughtless, entirely happy.

He was fifteen, shaggy-haired and stocky; he looked older. Often he was mistaken for a college freshman, which delighted him. He needed glasses, slightly, and sat in the first row of every classroom rather than wear them; his voice had broken late; he was not handsome. His own face in photographs always startled him. Twelve years lay between himself and his sister: he was the beloved child of carelessness. When he visited Mariana, people thought they were cousins.

The waves lifted, subsided, and between a steep downpour of salt green and a broken glitter of light he saw his sister. Her hair rose with the swell of the wave; he saw her laughing. Dark as a cormorant, her lover parted the water that slid like glass over his shoulders as he lifted half out of the waves, caught her hands in his own, rolled forward with the drag of the comber and pulled them both into a scatter of foam and water all the patched colors of the sky. Near the rocks he tugged at her hand, and together they drifted to a halt in the still hollow between two long spurs of stone. "Mariana!" Dylan shouted, waving. She pulled her arms from around her lover's neck, wet hair from her eyes and her mouth from her lover's mouth, and he slid away with the backwash of the tide. Dylan had one last sight of the dark-haired man as he curved into an impossible dive, water closing over the planed muscles of his back; perhaps his shadow moved beneath the surface, darting in the eddies, gone before the eye could grasp its direction. Mariana was swimming toward the rocks. Dylan dashed back for the bundle of clothes and towels he had stashed beside his broken-backed Dickens and his sandy sheaf of mathematics, and ran out to meet her at the edge of the sea.

"I thought you were never going to come back," he said when she drew near enough to hear him. It was almost an accusation. "Almost two hours. What happened to you?" Kneeling on the damp rock, looking down into her face, he realized he was shaking. She looked less like his sister than a stranger out of the sea: her hair spread on the surface of the water like foam; her hands gripped the rock heedless of sharp barnacles or thick mats of seaweed that slid between her fingers, tight as limpets; her eyes, not green, not grey, only a shade lighter than Dylan's own, seemed to catch their color from the waves. Salt water streaked her face like tears.

Then she grinned, shook her head, transformed into Mariana Beck again. "Nothing happened to me. Come on, what did you think? I'm not going to swim away and abandon you. Can you hand me a towel?" The wind curled the water about her shoulders and she shivered. Back turned, Dylan proffered the towels and listened to the sounds of his sister emerging from the sea.

She was not Aphrodite, flawless and foam-born, but she might have been mistaken for a nereid. All the family's rather inconsequential height had somehow burst forth in her long bones, so that she overtopped her entire immediate family by at least four inches, and if she was not slender as a poured drink of water she was graceful enough for the illusion. Nor did she look much like her brother. The bones of Dylan's face were stamped prominent beneath the skin, heavy-minted as the profile of an ancient coin, and he often looked sullen when he was merely being quiet; Mariana had inherited the look of something classical without the dense bones, a quick study for a Greek statue, and with water sheening from her skin as she climbed out of the sea she looked smooth as marble. Even water-heavy, matted, knotted with twigs of driftwood and seaweed snarls, her hair hung past her hips. She would be combing it for hours when she got home. For now she wrung it between her hands and tried to pick out the worst of the debris. "You can turn around now," she added.

She had her jeans on now, and made faces as the denim stuck to her wet skin, but Dylan noted the extra, almost wincing care with which she pulled at the cloth. In the early spring, even proud as she was of her birchwood skin that never sunburnt and barely even tanned, she had stopped wearing anything other than jeans or long skirts. When she swam, she was careful to let no one see her as she slipped from the rocks or waded from the water. Dylan, being visiting family and unavoidable, had thought at first that sand from the pounded shore speckled her skin, or there were ribbons of weed tangled about her legs, or perhaps she and her lover had been on the tide flats where the mud was pitch-dark and stank of salt. Then he had understood, and she had confirmed it, and now he tried not to stare as his sister settled onto the rock and toweled her feet dry.

Below the knees her pale skin was invisible: a fine mantling of scales, rusty green, the tough flexible sheen of kelp, lapped her from shin to ankle. They did not seem to impede her movements, though their color grew a little dull and stiff when dry. Translucent fans of skin, the bottle-glass color of a cresting wave, linked her toes. When she fitted socks and sneakers back onto her carefully dried feet, Dylan saw her flinch.

He asked softly, "Does it hurt?"

"No more than usual." She jerked the laces of her sneakers tight, picked with an absent hand at her salt-stuck hair. *I see the lights of Casco Bay,* her T-shirt read, sea-green on grey, *Coming home to Portland Town.* When she worked at the art store on Exchange Street, she always wore scarves around her neck and pieces of antique jewelry; pins and inlaid combs tangled and glinted in her hair. For a moment he imagined her swimming, mermaid-footed, drowned gold at her wrists and throat. He could not hold the image; it frightened him, and he let it go. "Sometimes, in the middle of the night, it itches. I think the skin dries more easily now. I tried hand lotion—you know, like you put on in the winter—but that only made it worse. I've begun taking showers before I go to bed and when I get up."

"That helps?"

"I think so. I'm not sure. Fresh water doesn't work so well ..." Her eyes caught the color of the sea again as her gaze lifted, like a bowl of glass held over the water; she was not seeing him, nor the sky where seagulls swung and circled, but some place beneath the shifting skin of the waves. "Are you afraid?"

The abrupt question startled him more than the words. "Of you?"

Mariana shrugged. With the heavy pale weight of her hair laid over one shoulder, her fingers working fragments of driftwood and weed free of the tangle, her face looked still sea-submerged. "Of me. Of him. Of—this." She lifted one sneakered, indistinguishable foot. "Does it matter to you?"

"I don't know." The question made him uncomfortable; it required articulation. "I guess not." The waves washed against their silence.

"Dylan?"

"Yeah?"

Mariana had risen to her feet, the towels bundled under one arm. He always forgot how much taller she was, and how much younger it made him feel. "Thanks for doing this."

Dylan mumbled, "No problem." Why should she break her

weekly engagement for a younger brother's visit? Every Saturday afternoon, she swam with her lover. When he had come to visit last summer, she had been doing the same thing. He would have visited in February, if he had not come down with the flu, and he suspected that even an ice-rimed sea had not kept her away from the dark-haired man who never said a word, never came closer to shore than the rocks where they stood now, never walked on land. "Did you," he hesitated, "do any of your friends know? What's happening to you, I mean?"

"No," she answered over her shoulder, striding over the rocks toward the thin beach and the parking lot. Sunlight split from the water still clinging in her hair; the air over the asphalt swam with heat. "Only you."

Her trust stoppered his mouth; he said nothing as they drove, damp towels on the back seat, Dylan's summer work piled between them and shedding sand onto the floor. For lunch they stopped at the same clam shack where they ate every summer and had fried clams, oysters, tiny curls of shrimp that Dylan speared four on a plastic fork and ate with tartar sauce. Once he lifted his cup for a swallow of root beer, and over the cardboard rim saw a girl looking at him; she sat with her family at the next table, legs swung over the side of the bench, an open book between her hands. Her smile was a sheepish reflex, quick and shared, but she did not take her eyes away and after a few seconds Dylan ducked his head and broke their gaze. Some sand clung to her skin; she had been on the beach, the bright strap of her bathing suit visible where her T-shirt slid from her shoulder, her cropped hair spiked with salt. Her legs were tanned, paling in a line around the ankles, her feet bracketed by sturdy outdoor sandals. A light downing of hair, water-darkened, traced the contours of her skin.

"You're staring," Mariana murmured, and Dylan felt his face burn. The girl was reading again. But he found himself watching her as he ate, waiting for her to raise her eyes again, touch his sight with the color of sand smoothed dark by a wave. Below the table, Mariana rubbed one foot against the back of her leg; her brows, light as her hair, twitched together in a brief grimace that could have been irritation, or pain, or a sudden perplexing thought.

"What's wrong?" Dylan stabbed at the last oyster; he was looking at Mariana more than at the cardboard container, streaked with crumbs and grease and odd dabs of tartar sauce, and missed it.

"Nothing...I was thinking, I might go swimming again this evening. Do you want to come? We'll go back to Crescent."

Something moved coldly in Dylan's stomach, nothing to do with the fried food. "You don't swim at night. Not with him."
"Since when don't I swim at night? I went swimming before I met him, you know." The name, unspoken and unknown, clung in the air like the sharp flavor of salt. "Besides," Mariana said, delicately dunking the second-to-last shrimp, "I've always come back."

He had no answer for her, not that he could say face-to-face in the hot August afternoon, and so there was nothing more to say. Dylan tossed the last shrimp into his mouth with a theatrical flourish that the girl at the next table, now shoving the book into a backpack as her family prepared to leave, completely missed; Mariana rose and dumped the cups and cheap plates into the trash; two seagulls landed at Dylan's feet and sidled accusing, unsatisfied looks at him. "Not my problem," he told the seagulls. "I ate my shrimp. Go bother someone else." Then Mariana called him, and when he looked back from the car, the girl and her family were walking away. She had taken off her sandals and her feet moved easily over the stony ground.

Mariana glanced in the rear view mirror, at Dylan. "Who's she?"

Dylan made a noncommittal noise, clarified it as, "No idea." Under his sister's scrutiny that might have been amused or might have been serious, he felt the blood rising along his cheekbones and refused to look down. His sister was not unkind; she turned the key then, and said nothing as the barefoot girl and her family diminished behind them.

Dylan rolled down his window, rested one elbow on the frame so that the wind slung his hair into his eyes. Two pages of trigonometry had vanished between the beach and the clam shack, and he did not really care. Summer reading—even summer mathematics endured for the promise of senior year calculus—dwindled in comparison to Mariana and her lover. He opened his mouth, breathed in salt and sunlight, exhaled a question. "You love him?"

"Yes." Mariana angled a brief look at Dylan, drummed her fingers on the wheel, some aimless accompaniment to one of the old tunes that was always going around in her head; she hummed when she thought no one was listening. "I do. More than anything else in the world. You know I love you; I love our parents. But I love him, too, and I don't have the words for that. Did you ever notice that? If you're not the one in love, love poetry, love songs, all sound like saccharine slush. I think the true language of love is unspoken. Unspeakable. Unable to be spoken. That's it." She grinned, hair fluttering in the wind from the open window. "Like that girl at the clam shack."

"I don't even know her!"

"I know, I know; I'm teasing you. Kindly. It's one of the prerogatives of an older sister."

"Yeah," Dylan said sourly, "I feel so much better now." But he thought of her reading on the shore, dipping into the waves that showered foam into her short, sea-smoothed hair, running barefoot on the sand; or maybe she would not run, would only lope long-legged over the pebbles and tide-cast seaweed, gawky and graceful as any adolescent; and he put the wishful twist of thought away before Mariana could divine it from his face.

On the other side of Dylan's sandy homework, Mariana lifted one hand off the wheel and scratched at the side of her neck. A faint, rough pinkness hid beneath the angle of her jaw: "Sunburn, I guess," Mariana offered, when she saw Dylan staring, "or sand fleas. It'll go away. I really need to take a shower; I feel like a tide flat." But Dylan saw how her hand lingered on the abrasion that grilled her skin like old scars, and wondered: how long? The question sank in his mouth and he could not ask it. Mariana pulled the car into the driveway, stopping as always scant inches from the twenty-foot pussywillow tree that Dylan had once recommended to the *Guinness Book of World Records* in seventh grade. When she swung her feet onto the ground, her breath caught briefly between her teeth; she walked faster than Dylan's tentative, reaching hand, and had the front door open before he had gotten all of his papers and books out of the car, her mouth tightened on something that might only have been a stray memory, a forgotten promise, a lamp left on.

All the pipes in Mariana's house made peculiar noises. When younger, Dylan had been convinced that malevolent spirits inhabited the radiators and clattered their way toward his bed at night. The shower running downstairs sounded like iron shuddering in the walls; pile-driving water. In the guest room where he always slept, papered with photographs of family and friends until all four walls and even the closet doors had become a collage of reminders, Dylan tried to ignore the sound of imminent plumbing explosions and read another chapter of *Great Expectations*; it was not working very well. Instead of Dickensian language, he kept seeing Mariana's lover sliding among the waves with no swimming stroke Dylan had ever learned, teaching Mariana to do the same. Cormorant hair, eyes like water where the sun never reached: when he kissed Mariana, it had looked like love. He must know how long she had, how many times the moon must pare itself thin and swell again before she gasped in the air that knifed her lungs like salt, before she could not walk on her double tail that flexed with great strength and fluidity underwater, collapsed and shot with pain on land. Would he love her then, welcome her into the water, or leave her stranded where the waves washed, trapped between the tides? Dylan slammed the book shut on Pip's second meeting with Herbert Pocket, made a sharp sound that did not quite resolve into a swearword, and stared at the wall until all the faces blurred into a mosaic colored like memory, meaningless. There were no photographs of her lover. Never any tangible proof, Dylan thought, but for Mariana's sea-change. Only stories and rumors; never any explanations.

The shower had stopped its tremors downstairs. Soon Mariana would come upstairs and find him, or stand at the foot of the stairs and call his name, her voice clear through the air as a song out of the sea. Maybe he would watch her as she repaired the clock that had sprung a cog, an old necklace whose pinned chain had come undone; she was good with her hands that way. As afternoon waned towards evening, she would begin to look toward the sea again. Probably she would drive out to Crescent's long swell of sand, that sloped into the sea as softly as the sea-ripped rock of Kettle Cove or Two Lights never did, walk into the water until the waves combed her hair and her lover found her there. Dylan lay back on the bed, stared at the swirls of plaster on the ceiling, the rain cracks that mapped out the brown rivers and deltas of some childhood country, and tried not to think of his sister toweling her beautiful scaled legs dry.

She did not call his name; he took his book and wandered downstairs, settled on a bottom step and stared at the cheap paper and print until he found himself looking beyond the letters to a long twilight-colored skirt, loose pleated fabric printed at the hem with dolphins and crescent moons cresting upward, brushing the floor as she stood there; a good camouflage. "I decided," Mariana said when he did not look up, "I'm not going swimming tonight. I thought, if you wanted, we could rent a movie. Wasn't there something you wanted to see?"

"I don't remember." He did not; he could not remember anything, except the fluid slide of Mariana's lover into the deep sea, the girl from the clam shack and her darting smile. "Maybe. I'll think about it. Thanks."

"Dylan—" She knelt in a fall and slip of cloth, finding his gaze as it slid away from hers; her parchment-fair hair was wet again, clean, straight-combed over her back and the towel she wore draped over her T-shirt. "I'm sorry, Dylan. It's not you."

"You didn't tell our parents." His mouth did not fit around the words; he stumbled on the sounds. "I thought you'd told them. While you were showering, I called. I mentioned your boyfriend. Mom said, *You've met him? We were beginning to think he was mythical. Todd Merrow. A fisherman, right? A lobsterman. Like an Andrew Wyeth painting.* That's what she said. A fisherman. What was I supposed to tell her? *No, a fish-man* . . . Merrow. I don't read as fast as you do, Mariana, I know that"—his voice was heating despite himself, slow to gather anger, the building tide underneath his voice—"but I'm not that stupid. You used to tell me stories, when I was younger and I could only come visit you for a couple of days. You gave him that name; you know what he is. And you think they won't find out? When you come home, they won't notice?" Outside, summer rain was beginning to spatter on the pavement; he heard it clattering on the shingles and the driveway, darkening the air; weather changing with the wind from the sea. He did not know what had made him angrier: the lie, the assumption, or the name that was so slyly wrong. "You know what's going to happen."

Blue light cracked the windows: lightning, and the immense rasp of tearing air that followed. Both of them jumped. Mariana smiled first. "I'll tell them, Dylan. Okay? I promise you, on my lover's life," an oath out of a story, like her lover, like her change, no less real for all its ritual, "I will tell them. I haven't drowned yet. I'm not going to drown; I'm not going to leave you. Dylan, come on—Dylan—" He burrowed his face into the angle of her shoulder—her hair that smelled of shampoo and faint salt stuck to his cheekbone, his arms locked around her waist—refusing to cry under the tear-fall noise of the rain, close within the circle of his sister's nereid arms, shivering and resentful and unable to let go of her shoulders as long as she held him. Now she was whispering to him, nonsense sounds soft and sighing as seagulls on the wind, tide on the shore, calming him although he was not weeping, perhaps calming herself; but over his head, he knew, she was looking

189

through the windows where the rain tacked and streaked the old panes, looking east, toward the sea.

If he had the skill, he would go out himself: kneel on the rocks where mussels scarred the soles of his shoes and barnacles printed their toothwork into the palms of his hands as he held tight against the booming tide, wait until the thin beach-curve of the moon lifted out of the blue darkness where the sea lapped against the sky, and shout into the seagulls' wind the incantation that would chant the dark-haired man up out of the water into the moonlight, the song to pull him ashore with the tide, the handful of words to make him come and listen and answer. But Dylan did not know them; he doubted Mariana did. How she had drawn her lover to her, he did not know. Perhaps it was the other way around. He wished he dared to ask her. He could not ask her lover. *Do you love him?* he had asked, never doubting her answer. But he had not been brave enough to go on, *Does he love you?* He had not known how she would answer; and what he would do with his answer, if he had it, he did not know now. He could only wait, as her lover must be waiting: there as long as she needed him, when she pulled herself from the sheeting water and winced a little as her feet found the unfamiliar land, when she climbed on hands and knees from the sea that dragged at her kelp-skinned ankles with threads of running foam, when she could no longer speak his name; perhaps she would sing it.

Todd Merrow. Mariana Beck. He tried to imagine calling the words onto the wind, to catch them both out of the sea: the merman and his lover that had been Dylan's sister. But he could not speak the names, any more than he could speak the unknown name of the barefoot girl with the book. He whispered, into his sister's hair, "Don't go."

Mariana said, "I don't swim when it's raining."

It was not an answer; it was almost a promise. When she let him go, he dragged himself back a step and held onto the banister with both hands. Fifteen years old, often mistaken for a college freshman, he felt his face falling into childhood as he stared at her: a stranger out of the sea. He did not say, *You will.* The words lay between them and did not need saying.

"Come on," Mariana whispered, regaining her voice, "I'll make you some chowder. No movie. We'll sit on the porch and watch the storm. Okay?"

"Yeah." He ground the back of his hand across his eyes. "Okay. Give me a minute—" as he climbed the stairs to throw Dickens' masterwork onto his bed; no more homework for tonight. From the closet door, over the desk, above the head of the bed, his own younger face grinned out at him: shock-haired, bulky, a toddler in the arms of parents and grandparents, sprawled on his grandmother's lawn beside a white-haired girl whose face would grow into the sketch of a classical statue; already she pinned her hair back with a mother-of-pearl barrette. Her feet were bare, pale against the springing grass, striped with a sandal tan. Mariana had not added any new pictures to the bedroom for almost a year.

He did not throw *Great Expectations* after all; he set the book down on the bedside desk, switched out the light and watched lightning split the sky over the houses across the street. Light filtered through the rainy glass: drowned blue, dim, submerged. Raindrop shadows darkened his skin like scales. Somewhere out to sea, beneath the storm-shredded surface of the water, Mariana's lover was waiting. But Mariana was waiting for him downstairs, heating the chowder she had promised him; he had two more days before academia would reclaim him until December. He might see his sister then; he might not. Sometimes she came over for the holidays, sometimes remained with her friends: ever since she graduated, she had always been an intermittent visitor to her parents' house; that had not changed. A sharp smile cracked Dylan's mouth: the only thing that had not changed. *The true language of love is unspoken.* But if he heard her voice singing, over the rim of the ocean where his sun-squinted gaze sank down into the sea, he would know what she was saying. If he heard her. If she sang to him. He wondered how old he would be, and if the girl from the clam shack lived in town, and whether he would still be listening for her voice, after all the changes, after all the years.

Dylan pulled down the shade and made sure he had left none of his trigonometry proofs where the rain would slant through the screen and soak them—though he would grieve for those drowned pages no more than he had for those lost at the beach; this was summer vacation—and went downstairs, to his nereid sister, to watch the storm.

A Ceiling of Amber,
A Pavement of Pearl

Frankie went to see Elias Haden on Friday, after rehearsal ended. She had left the other musicians in Dave Felder's apartment, taken the bus and walked down past art galleries and tourist storefronts out onto the wharves, where the city clasped fingers with the bay and the sea rocked beneath every piling. Like accidental buoys, the places she passed showed her how the land slid away from itself: from steep streets and close-set stores, windows cluttered with junked treasures that might have changed every time Frankie looked back, to the bank where she no longer had an account; past a white-painted flagpole flying semaphores and windsocks that racketed back and forth in the warm, erratic wind, to the fish market where Frankie's grandmother had taken her to buy halibut and salmon on distant summer vacations, where the dried skin of a sturgeon hung leathery on the wall and raw shrimp and scallops rested like jewels on ledges of crushed ice, and crevices in the floor's scuffed planking showed the brindle of light on moving water, five or six feet down. The air smelled so sharply of salt, Frankie thought she could have held out one hand and watched glittering crystals, come abruptly out of solution, scale around her fingers like coral or a crust of ice. Sun soaked everything, cloudless, burnished by heat. High overhead, seagulls traced the currents of the sky.

There was a piece of sailcloth in Elias' window, hung crosswise in a rough curtain; it moved aside slightly as she watched. Behind the sun-struck pane, she glimpsed the darting, circumspect movement of a small startled fish: Elias disappearing briefly to unlock the door, returning to gaze down at Frankie for another moment before the sailcloth dropped back. Plain white blinds hid the lower windows, drawn now after five o'clock; the accounting office of a small fishing company, Elias' landlords. Between the buildings, down the narrow street, sunlight wrinkled like amber off the bay. Sometimes she wondered if he had taken the apartment only for somewhere to sleep, a fragment of land to hold his dreaming moments rather than a rack of weed-softened stone, a rowboat overturned on the sand. Tide and moonlight made a cold bed. He would have slept in the skeined reflections of dawn on the waves if he could, Frankie thought. Shouldering her guitar, she opened the unlatched door, and went up the stairs to Elias' seafloor.

All the lights were out, and most of the windowshades down; Frankie moved through slants of late sunlight and afternoon shadow, picking her path between boxes of clothes and shelves jumbled with sliding books, CDs and records in stacks against the walls, an opened suitcase shoved behind the door. She had been visiting Elias for almost nine months, and the apartment still looked as though he had moved in last week. One of the glass-fronted cabinets against the farther wall had broken a pane in transit and Elias had patched the crack with masking tape; behind the scar, she saw shells and dusty pebbles, a dry spray of blackened seaweed, sand dollars like undersea coin and starfish slowly crumbling to ochre rust; a pink-lipped conch, a brass sextant and the blade of a tarnished knife, the spine and translucently mummified tail of a fish. When she set her guitar down against a seam-sprung armchair, a glass fishing float wrapped in twists of newspaper rolled off the seat; she caught it awkwardly, one-handed. Sand slid back and forth within its salt-green curve, a whisper of desiccated seas. Circling a battered dresser, all nicked varnish and brass handles, she laid the float carefully down in one of the drawers, half pulled out and mostly full of black and white socks, and came up behind Elias.

In worn-white denim and a jacket full of pockets and salt stains, Elias sat at his computer among a flotsam of books and printouts, one hand on the mouse, clicking, the other rumpled through his hair. He looked like something weathered early, spare and silver-grained as driftwood, too thin for his bones and the breadth of his shoulders; but his eyes were rich as blue shale, and Frankie only thought of him as middle-aged when he was not in motion. He had not turned at the sounds of the opening door or Frankie's footsteps on the bare floor-boards, or even the fishing float's near miss that had caught Frankie's breath between her teeth. Only his fingers moved, and his eyes. Sea charts tacked to the wall beside the window sounded depths offshore in hand-lettered fathoms; a wildlife calendar recorded daily high and low tides in Elias' lopsided script, each major phase of the moon circled in green marker. Over his shoulder, Frankie glimpsed a screenful of weather forecasts for the Atlantic northeast. Sunken in his own world; five fathoms inward. His feet were bare. Gently, she said, "Hey, Eli."

His glasses were frosted with salt at the rims; margarita lenses. A smile lengthened one side of his mouth and he pushed them up on his forehead to rub at his eyes and the narrow bridge of his nose, scattering dried brine onto the keyboard. "High tide at 4:39 AM, 5:13 PM," he said when he had resettled his glasses, all the lantern lines of his face expressionless now, "low tide at 10:54 and 11:24." For a second she watched him warily, looking for the giveaway—capable of a perfectly standard greeting, and they both knew it—then grinned as his own mouth slanted up again in his uneven smile, far more jaunty than his eyes or the fractured stories he told. "How was rehearsal?"

"Pretty good. 'Cruel Sisters' lends itself surprisingly well to clarinet improv. And Dave Felder thinks there's some kind of open mic on the beach, just sign up and show up, so we're planning on that, and I'm translating another Golden Peacock ballad." Cliffs notes for the life of A Dybbuk Adrift and its composite members, walking their precarious tightrope between music and scholarship, trying to fuse three kinds of folk tradition into one and not drop out of college in the process; steel strings tuned to "Eyn Mol" and "Anathea," "Di Zun Vet Aruntergeyn" and "The White Seal Maid" like some unholy love child of the Klezmatics and Steeleye Span, balladry from beyond the Pale. "Catholic Dave's still working on it," she added, and watched Elias' gaze resolve again from the screen to her face. She was shorter than Elias, her bones heavier, landbound; she had flighty, clove-colored hair that streaked with unexpected colors—copper, ash, pale bronze at her temples—under a summer's sun, and eyes like one of those highlights as her mood preferred. "He's even dropped his setting of 'Tog Broyklikh,' and that was keeping him up nights. So I wanted to ask: did you want to sit in next week, tell us if you actually like what you're hearing before we go any farther? Seriously."

"I trust you," Elias said, and checked the forecast for Tuesday.

She had found him beachcombing in August, or something like enough to fool her until she came closer: picking up everything to inspect it, broken moon shells, cloudy sea glass, crab claws mottled blue and brown, mother-of-pearl mussels, and then lay it back down in the sand or surf and walk on. His hair was longer then, ruffled back like windblown water, and he wore ancient hightop sneakers that filled with seawater and trailed dark runnels in the sand as he roved up and down between high and low tides. Tucked against a corrugated shelf of rock with a spiral-bound notebook and pencil printed with absent toothmarks, Frankie had watched him occasionally as she worked on "The Ballad of Night's Daughters," half a verse and chorus puzzled out of nightmare and desire and she still heard Dylan rather than the words she wanted. *And it's night's black daughters when the sun's gone walkabout / Studious candles and the screech owl's cry / Demon moon falling like the sea's salt bones / When she's dreamed you hungry, she'll drink you dry* . . . She had not thought he could hear her, until she looked up. *Is that yours?* He had a clear, abrupt voice, deep enough to surprise her; the sun was behind his head, glaring out over the green marble water and the dunes bristling with tough grass and beach roses, and she narrowed her eyes to find him within its dazzle. Cautiously, she answered, *It is, if it's any good,* and his reply came back like the next wave, *I think it's very good.* Wind pulled a skein of hair across her mouth and she caught it loose with the edge of her hand, wondering where the conversation went next, this late morning on a mostly deserted beach, if she should have started worrying when he got close and she never noticed; when she should scream. But he was hesitating, as though the next words mattered more than a random question from a stranger to a stranger, *Do you write a lot of songs?* and Frankie eased; shop talk. *Not that many. At least, not that many I like. I mistrust everything I've ever written until at least a dozen other people have told me they don't hate it, and even then, sometimes we're rehearsing and I wince. But mostly we sing folk stuff, so it's not that relevant. Also,* confessing with a wry raise of her eyebrows, *we've had exactly one gig at this point, and that was at school. So it's not like we're so greatly famous, either.* She folded the notebook over, hiding the half-cursive spikes of her careless handwriting, whole stanzas blackened out rather than erased, the surviving and reconstructed lines down at the bottom of the page in a marginally neater hand. Question for question, *What are you looking for?*

Nothing much, he said, slight and self-deprecating smile; and she knew, although she did not know his name, or his age, or what had drawn him to her, that he was lying. *Shells, driftwood. Flotsam and jetsam. I'm Elias Haden, sorry,* as he held out one calloused, broad-palmed hand, apologetically. *I have no manners.* His grasp was cool, dry as the high sand, shy of her touch. *Frankie Bale. I probably don't either.* They talked for another few minutes, about folk tradition and songs of tall ships, exchanged well-wishes as he returned to his patient, fruitless examination of the shore and Frankie opened her notebook again, crossed out two more words; she did not expect to see him again. Toward the end of the month, skipping stones with Catholic Dave over the early-evening waves, she had spotted Elias standing ankle-deep in the swirling foam, and hailed him. Six months later, A Dybbuk Adrift was working on his song.

Now she said, recklessly, "I wouldn't. Trust me, I mean." Elias, making notes in a journal full of graph paper, precise measurements and cryptic identifications that Frankie had never bothered to riddle out, glanced upward over his glasses; waiting for the explanation. On the facing page, he had drawn, in painstaking inks, the extended wing of a cormorant and the pop-top off a can of soda. "You've never seen what I've written. It could be she-sells-sea-shells limericks for all you know."

"I don't care what it is," Elias said, "as long as it's true." His eyes shifted from her face back to the screen again; he was reading a list of retired hurricane names, *Hugo, Ione, Inez, Janet, Joan, Keith,* lips moving silently to the litany of destruction. "As long as it goes deep enough ..." By the time she had cleared herself a place on the floor, selected a volume of sea lore and ghost stories from the nearest shelf, he had forgotten her presence again. When he needed to speak of his findings, he would remember; she opened to a chapter on mermaid sightings in the seventeenth century, and waited.

Legally, Dave Felder's apartment above the all-night grocery also belonged to Catholic Dave and a pillowy PoliSci student named Asher Graham, whose housemates had knighted him an honorary Dave on one of his rare forays out of his room. But Frankie had met Dave Felder first, spinning the same peacock-blue fountain pen around his fingers in their freshman seminar as in junior literary theory, and visited his parents in Manhattan long before she was aware that Asher even existed; when she took the bus over to rehearsals, no matter who she saw, the apartment always had his name on it. This afternoon, she opened the door onto secondhand furniture and one of Catholic Dave's CDs in the stereo, *There and Now* or *Rehearsals for Retirement*, lyrics like she might have traded her heart to write, if she was sure that would be enough.

Sunlight filtered half-overcast through the broad windows, sky like a pearl-colored backdrop for the other two-thirds of A Dybbuk Adrift scattered across the common room, a pair of reversed coins. Catholic Dave Carroll correcting his own sheet-music scrawl with a ballpoint pen, hair almost the same chipped dark as the street's sun-beaten asphalt and he still limped slightly on the ankle he had broken in high school, trying to climb back into his own bedroom window after a prom; Dave Felder cross-legged on the couch with his violin and rosin, an angular collection of long, spider-dancing fingers, fairish hair that coiled like wire if he did not keep it short, and eyes the startling color of morning glories between lashes too pale to be seen, except up close. Frankie had thought he wore contacts, the first time she met him. But Catholic Dave had the glasses, black-framed shorthand for physics or math, and half a semester left on a degree in composition and theory. He greeted Frankie first, as she locked the door behind her; Dave Felder looked up, and yawned.

Frankie stopped next to the couch, grainy blue cushions and an ancient coffee stain half-hidden under Dave Felder's bare foot, and said acidly, "Thanks."

"I didn't sleep," he protested. The window unit made a wet, gravelly hum under their words and Phil Ochs' tight-strung prophecies and protests. Frankie could smell dust and faded incense, bread ash from the toaster in the kitchenette that had no settings between inferno and off: not the sea. "All night, I kept waking up," and as though in self-defense, he yawned again.

From the chair he had pulled up to the long windowsill, makeshift desk, Catholic Dave said, "The sea getting into your dreams now?"

"Careful, Freud." Dave Felder dropped the rosin back in its container, leveled a wry glance at Frankie. "It's this song. By the time we actually perform it, I am going to be in serious danger of drowning. Possibly while I sleep." He was speaking lightly, but a shiver walked spider-footed down Frankie's spine. Head bent away from Dave Felder's dreams, she knelt and unfastened the catches on her guitar case, dry clicks like the hinges of snapped shells; she ran through half-learned melody lines in her head, song after song, and still heard him saying apologetically, "Just this deserted underwater city, and me walking through it. That was about it. I never said it was an exciting dream."

"No," Catholic Dave agreed, capping his pen and tucking it back into his pocket. Occasionally one leaked; cuffs and pockets, his shirts held geographies of washed-out ink stains, territories of absent-minded inspiration. "Especially for a wet dream."

"Chowderhead."

"Come on, I dream of lines like that."

"I dreamed," said Asher, sharp-voiced reminder from around the doorframe, tortoiseshell hair rumpled from too many nights awake and a scowl that scared nobody, "that I failed the LSATs, and everybody I knew laughed at me. It was traumatic. I think I went on a murderous rampage and killed everyone who had ever kept me from studying. So, please. If you're going to rehearse, rehearse. If you're not, shut up!" His door slammed so conclusively that the windowpanes rattled.

The thousandth iteration of this scene since A Dybbuk Adrift formed, accreting around shared tastes in music and disliked movies and nights spent talking until dawn smudged up out of the sea, so old and well-handled a routine that they could have performed it between sets: the chill that had slid through Frankie at Dave Felder's dream began to drain away, and she did not even bother to complain about the clashing opera that Asher cranked up a few seconds later, sonic wars through the thickness of a locked door. *You loved your love*

200

so much that you'd strangle her madly . . . Verloren! Ach, verloren! Ewig verlornes Heil! Out under the cloudbanks, light broke and ran in lines like rain, and brightened in panes on the old sand-grey carpet. Catholic Dave tilted his chair back far enough to reach the stereo and switch Phil Ochs off, began gathering up pages from their spread across the windowsill; Dave Felder was putting his violin tenderly away, trading instruments. A curiosity winked at Frankie, something that the conversation had glanced off and moved around: a fracture of light across the water's surface or a shadow sliding underneath. She sat back on her heels and said, "Dave. Catholic. What did you dream?"

"First of all, I fell asleep over your song. This would have been a lot easier if you could actually write music . . ." The air conditioner coughed and gurgled to itself in the stillness as his voice fell away. "I dreamed cold, and green light," he said finally, the words pronounced as deliberately as the answer to a dare, "and salt like a fresh wind off the sea. I woke up and for a minute, I swear to you, I couldn't remember how to breathe air. I really didn't want to go back to sleep after that. But around three in the morning, I passed out again and dreamed I was doing counterpoint exercises. Except I was writing them in the sand with a shell. And then I woke up and figured it just wasn't worth sleeping anymore, so I worked on the lead-in to 'Break the Mirror' until Asher got up to make breakfast. Why?" His eyes were oddly lighter than his hair, a clear river-water brown, narrowing in an interest that was not yet suspicion. "What are you dreaming about?"

"Nothing much." She heard in her voice an echo of Elias' dismissal, and wondered if her own lies were as obvious. "The usual nightmares. You know, playing naked and you don't realize it until the second chorus . . . Elias said he's not coming today, by the way," shifting the subject as casually as possible, misdirection that must have fooled neither Dave. One had leaned forward to pick up his clarinet, dark polished wood and nickel-silver keys; the other was halfway across the room, from composer to drummer in less than six seconds; but their eyes were watching her identically, unthreatening and dangerous. She did not know what question they would ask; she did not want to hear it. *What are you really dreaming? Where do you go between rehearsals? Frankie, what's going on?* She wanted suddenly, impossibly, to be rehearsing somewhere else. Not in a practice room, among thumbtacked plasterboard and fluorescent lighting, a cappella covers of bygone pop songs as audible through the walls as Asher's operatic resistance now—instead out on the beach, in the sunlight and the wind and the depthless sweep of sky over sea, braiding their song back into the landscape from which they had woven lyrics and music alike. Fiddler crabs around their feet, the dunes spilling over with their castanet dance; terns and sandpipers like notes on a stave of sand. The ocean itself for an audience, and the waves riding in to shore would sound applause.

"Is he all right?"

Frankie blinked at Dave Felder and his concern, wondered why she felt cheated. "Yeah. He's fine." Pushing down the daydream, momentary flight of fancy, "He just says he'd rather hear the song when it's finished. When we're ready."

"In which case, boy and girl," already moving into performance mode as she watched, letting go whatever question she had feared behind his eyes, "I suggest we start rehearsing. Dream analysis will resume next week, mental stabilities permitting—and sometimes, you know, a drowned city is just a drowned city." Seated now among his drums, Catholic Dave knocked one knuckle against a cymbal in answer, the audible tilt of an eyebrow. "Don't smirk so loudly. I wasn't the one who forgot how to breathe . . ." Frankie smiled, half listening, drawing her focus back from the sea to A Dybbuk Adrift: to first waltzes and prophetic crows that bickered over the dead, the lines she always confused and the sideways fingering that would trip her up if she was not looking out for it, and the song that no one had named yet. The guitar's weight over her shoulder, in her hands, was an anchor.

"Enough with the Valkyries!" Dave Felder rapped on Asher's door with his knuckles, called through the white-painted wood, "We're actually working, all right? We don't have all day. Time and tide, like they say." He glanced back over his shoulder at Frankie, all his face folded into the grin that she never remembered to expect. "Come on, Frankie. Meet us in the morning," as Catholic Dave shivered a noise out of the snare drum like the smack of waves together and Frankie checked the guitar's tuning one last time, a thousand stories within her fingers' span. Her heart lifted in spite of itself, or perhaps as it should. "Take us down."

"I drowned," Elias had told her, that night in bitter January, winter's gales slashing snow across his windowpanes like spindrift in a storm, and the shells and skeletons of sea-things watching them in the yellowed lamplight around his desk, "maybe ten years ago, when I still thought the ocean was only salt water and fish, I drowned." He had been showing her around different maps and charts, pointing out the locations of wrecks, ships gone down in storms or circumstances still unexplained, when he slid into his own story so idly that for a long moment Frankie thought he was simply recounting another strangeness of the vast, studied, unpredictable sea. "I was stupid; I thought I could sail at night, steer by the stars—me, who'd never even learned to swim until I moved out here, can you believe that? But I loved it, cold water and everything, paint on the houses peeling from the salt, hauling up lobster traps and imagining my family had lived like this for a hundred years, I loved the sea. I just wasn't very good with it." His mouth made a faint, rueful shape that Frankie had not seen before; she had known that Elias could dissolve himself in fascination and desire, that he could apologize and pass for untroubled, but not that he could regret. "I didn't understand."

Perhaps because she had never heard him say more than two direct sentences about himself, the first person a rare, alien form of speech that Elias occasionally used when discussing likes, dislikes, and the song he had commissioned from A Dybbuk Adrift, she listened even as her skin chilled and prickled with the impossible, unarguable honesty in his voice; drank honey-soaked tea and felt the winter night close around them, as trackless as the wasteland of water and the mute stars overhead that had trapped Elias Haden between fronts of darkness, heaven and the deep black sea. "I shouldn't have gone out so far, should have stayed where I could see the channel buoys, the lighthouse, anything. Or I should have radioed for help, once I realized I was," half a laugh at the words, something in his face younger than Frankie had seen it; memory surfacing, maybe, "out of my depth. But I thought I could turn around, retrace—what steps? Whatever I was doing, it wasn't walking on water. I wasn't thinking." Then he had let go the sail, rope whistling out of his clumsy hands before he could even realize what he had done, distracted by the lack of shore lights in any direction and the constellations that gave him no more clue than their reflections rising and falling on the waves' surface, and the boat pitched over; he remembered the water breaking around him like cold concrete, the spluttering burn of salt in his throat, coughing up seawater and swallowing it back down in the same frantic gasp, and the waves buffeted his groping hands and the boat apart before he could catch hold of anything that floated. The sea folded itself around him, and the next inexorable wave dragged him down.

"This is the part," Elias said carefully, "that's hard to explain. Because I know what happened, after. A couple of early-morning beachcombers found me tossed up on the sand under the lighthouse, of all places, bruised and bleeding from a head wound—probably the rocks, I think I'd remember if I'd smacked my head into the boat—and looking like a corpse until I rolled over and started groaning. They told me my first words were, *Holy fuck, what the fuck happened to me?* Some mantra for a resurrection," and Frankie, who had never heard him swear, either, swallowed a quick mouthful of tea to stifle her grin. If she laughed, she might lose this tenuous thread of past that he was giving her, clue to the coral labyrinth where he wandered even while awake; she would not mock him. "But I also know what happened when I went under. What I saw; and what I lost. It's not…There are two ways to see everything. And if I tell you that I saw a place under the water, that a light opened up in the blackness and the cold, that my lungs were full of water and I couldn't breathe and I knew I was going to die, but there was this place more frightening and more beautiful than anything I'd ever seen, you'll tell me I was suffering oxygen deprivation and I saw whatever fantasies my brain called up right before I passed out and floated up to the surface and eventually ashore. If I tell you that I felt my last breath arrow out of me, just like a fish, darting home to that place and the—the things that were in it, you'll probably say the same. I've read about near-drowning experiences; I know about rapture of the deep. And I'm here, of course. But I wasn't anywhere near the surface; I couldn't see moonlight, starlight, anything except blackness. Strangling with my lungs full of water and I felt like I was choking on fire, the wrong element. And—"

He opened one hand, fingers loosing belief, trust, a dying breath. In the sideways light, his face looked as harshly weathered as the sea-gnawed rocks where Frankie wrote; less familiar. "I drowned there, down under that water, down in the abyss with whatever I saw. I died and I should have stayed dead. One more skeleton for Davy Jones, one more husband to the sea. They say the ocean will one day give up its dead. It spat me back too soon. And I can feel it, here"—one hand to his forehead, his breast, dismissive flicks of his fingers like a fish turning back into the rippling safety of weeds—"I know where I belong."

The intensity of his gaze weighed on her like miles of water, pressure enough to crumple a sunken submarine's hull like tinfoil, reduce surface-born flesh to a smear of settling blood; when she spoke at last, her mouth opened and closed against the yielding tension of liquid. "That's why you want the song." The words left her like bubbles, strung one at a time from her submerged lips, her drowning lungs.

"Song got Orpheus down to the underworld; why not the bottom of the ocean? *Married to a mermaid at the bottom of the deep blue sea . . .* The sea is woven with songs. There are so many stories." Elias reached for his own tea, gone cold hours ago, dipped in and out of the lamplight and became familiar again, a man maybe forty years old and skinny as a rake, his hair the color of storm-roughened water, his eyes distant behind wire-rimmed lenses that he took off for a rib-cracking stretch and yawn while Frankie watched, cold and tense. This was the danger she had sensed in him, in those first seconds when nothing more than an unfinished song and the sea wind lay between them; the riptide under their conversation that had drawn her down. "You don't have to," he said into her stillness, surprising her. Snow keened at the edges of the windows, pale as blowing foam; Elias' voice had gentled, and she remembered that he was not careless or blind. "I know there are other ways; I just have to find them. People don't look, you see; they stumble into the strange places, they glance off them, they say it was just sunstroke or daydreams or staring at the water too long, it wasn't real. And they go home and they never know for the rest of their lives what they almost found. But if you're looking, if you're looking hard—I'm asking, Frankie, that's all. You don't have to say yes."

"I know." The words were too dry for sound. Her body had tightened, gathered itself for sudden movement: as much on guard as though a wave might sweep out of him abruptly, curl tight around her and draw her down to the lightless, unmapped regions where his dreams had sunken long ago. Like the hungry sea out of one of her own songs, tide creeping higher to reclaim the body of a drowned man, gathering in whatever of the land lay in its way, his need could engulf her as easily, as thoughtlessly, smooth her away as casually as a name written in damp sand. Nothing left but a blank space at rehearsals while the stagnant, salt-rot smell of tide flats soaked out from underneath her door, filled the hallway with memories of pitch-dark mud and fish picked to ivory slivers by raucous gulls, the deep, soft places of the ocean spilt out onto the shore. Tenants would check under their sinks, drop cakes of blue freshener in every maligned toilet bowl, complaints piling up the phone lines until the super came with her clatter of keys and unlocked the apartment where Francine Bale had lived, where nothing remained but salt water sopping in puddles on the linoleum and scuffed, sodden carpet, ropes of kelp tumbled over the bed and fish scales glittering on the water-slicked windows, sequins after the ball was over. Or nothing so visible and unmistakable, only her thoughts turning inward to brine and deep shadows, possession stealing beneath the skin of her land-locked husk, roaring black water behind her eyes and the sound of retreating tides whenever she opened her mouth to speak. Contagion; a fever of the sea. Trying to find in her songs the place he wanted, she might never shake it from her blood.

She pictured Elias as she had gotten to know him, trading sea chanteys and historical accounts, sitting on the roof to scan the moon-washed horizon like a sea captain two hundred years ago, recording the colors of sunset and sunrise over the water, the patterns of seaweed at the low-tide line and the migrations of humpback whales; sifting the known world for splinters of the unknown, charting the fragile geography of winds and currents and seals who slipped their skins to dance as women on mortal shores. Crazy, a lunatic as much under the ocean's sway as the tides bowed to the moon, seawater streaming in his veins and his bones already cleaned and rolling in the deep sea-swell—nothing she had not already known. Only this last knowledge made any difference, the innermost chamber, the secret inside the shell. Her unwritten song dangled in her mind, flashing, too silver-bright to ignore.

"I can't promise anything," Frankie said. "We have a campus coffeehouse show next Tuesday, and Dave Felder might actually have come down with flu. I'll write something when I can. I don't know—I don't know if it will be what you want," exorcism, validation, whatever she thought he was looking for without knowing; skirting the whirlpool's rim. Elias was already gathering up the empty tea mugs and rising to look down at her from just outside the light, a medieval map of spouting whales and Latin names at his back.

"Thank you, Frankie." For the smile on his face, the gravity in his voice, she might have handed him all the sea like a teardrop then and there. "Thank you so very much." He turned and disappeared into the kitchen, walking as loping and light as over the pebbled strand; Frankie listened to the wind crashing against glass and shingles, seawater returning as snow to the harbor and the welcoming sea, and thought that if Elias Haden was not crazy, that was no comfort at all.

Elias came for his song in the first week of June, among thundershowers and broiling days when even the breezes from the olive-green sea were sultry. His apartment, that had no air conditioning, had turned into a two-room box of heat and close shadow; he kept the shades permanently drawn against the light and spent as little time within its walls as possible, came home to doze and drink tea poured through crescents of freezer ice. When Frankie saw him, he looked wilted, brittle at the edges, like thick kelp toppled ashore and left to parch. He was keeping a daily record of temperature and humidity, correlated against a value she could not read when she checked over his shoulder; the height of the tides, she thought, but did not ask. In the relative cool of Dave Felder's apartment, she experimented with "Sheyn Vi Di Levone" as a solo and watched Asher pass back and forth from the kitchen to his room, refilling the same glass of water time after thirsty time, his face shining with sweat and less than two weeks left before he blazed himself a path to law-school glory or exploded; his housemates were not sure which. Frankie twisted her hair into a knot at the nape of her neck, to keep it off her sweating skin, and tried not to sunburn. The sea slid in and out of the bay, possibly the only cold thing in the city.

There had been a storm the day before, a brief squall that did nothing to lighten the sticky, unseasonal highs; the air outside shimmered, so glutinous with heat that Frankie half expected to see the gulls' wheeling paths slice it into falling chunks, blue as glaciers and cohesive as Jell-O, sky minced jigsaw into sea. Even Catholic Dave's hair, like the streets, was looking tacky. With the rest of A Dybbuk Adrift in his room, playing the newest composition off his computer, she was pouring herself a glass of water in the kitchen when Asher came in; he stopped in front of her, took the pitcher from her hand, and studied her for a moment. "You look haunted," he said. His hair was spiky, uncombed, and he had acquired a constant five o'clock shadow in the last few days; she was mildly amazed that he could still register people, rather than simply questions and answers on a page. "You look like you haven't slept in a month," she replied, and Asher glanced down at himself as though it had just struck him that he was standing in front of a friend of a friend in a slept-in undershirt and cutoff sweatpants; for answer, he tilted the pitcher carefully until he had a palmful of refrigerator-cold water, and threw it against his face. He flinched slightly when it landed, blinked water off his lashes, and said reasonably, "Yes, but I can always sleep. What can you do?"

Startled, she forgot her intended comeback about insomnia and said, "I don't know. Finish this song, I think . . ." She watched him fill another glass in endless succession and asked, prodded into the question by the level look he gave her, "Since when are you so lucid?"

"I'm usually lucid. We're not generally in the same room long enough for you to notice. Or," he conceded, "for me to notice that the backs of your eyes look like someone else's living room. You're thinner than I remember, I think. I can't be sure. You used to come around more than once a week." His own eyes were darker than Catholic Dave's, Guinness-colored; the ends of his hair, his chin and nose, were dripping onto the linoleum, and he worried her far more than either of his housemates. "Nevertheless," he added, "you sound very good. All three of you. Even that one you're always working on, *meet me in the morning,* it's grown on me. Not that you need my endorsement, okay? But you should keep doing this."

"You don't know what you're asking," she warned, teasing, truthful.

"No, probably not." Very possibly, she had never seen a full smile out of Asher before; it almost made him look not tense. Then, raising the glass like a salute, "Good luck with the song. Snap an E-string, or whatever you musicians tell each other."

"Thanks. You'll probably hear the performance, unless you've managed to soundproof your room since yesterday." She wanted to ask him, *At night, if you ever sleep, what do you dream?* Asher, who played no instruments, who loved opera and sang like a deaf man, who had only heard the song she had written for Elias through a closed door and plaster walls; who put words to the idea she had lately seen hanging back in Dave Felder's glances, in Catholic Dave's silence. *What have they told you? What do you think I look haunted by?* But she said only, and genuinely, "Good luck with the sleep."

"Plenty of time to sleep," Asher said, "when you're drowned." He put the pitcher back in her hands, a slide of condensation against her fingers and she almost dropped it, and his mouth pulled sideways in something closer to his usual harassed sarcasm; less edge to it, now that she had seen how his smile could look. "I've been wanting to say that for about a month now. Thanks," and Frankie was sure he had never made her laugh like this before: as much from tension as from his slyness; something she had thought he knew, or maybe he did. Then someone was knocking at the door, uncertainly; Frankie set her glass down beside the sink and stepped around the corner to see Catholic Dave sliding the chain off and undoing the lock, a faint squeak of damp-swollen wood when the door popped free of the frame. On the other side, where the hallway still simmered and Catholic Dave hastily waved him in, Elias said, "Hello."

He looked less crinkled and more like a recent cast of the tide, his hair wind-wild and sweat gleaming under his cheekbones and in the furrows of his throat. The cuffs of his jeans were thick with sand the color of sugar, brown and white; Frankie had wondered occasionally if his landlords ever complained about bits of sand and shell trickling down through lath and plaster into their offices, he brought so much of the beach home with him. "It doesn't really have a name," Catholic Dave was explaining as she crossed the room to her guitar, a seasick and ready anticipation beginning to rise through her stomach into her throat, a shot of burning liquor through her veins. "The working title has always been 'that song Frankie's writing for Elias.' Even though Dave calls it—hey, Dave," as he emerged from Catholic Dave's room, clarinet already out of its case and his eyes flicking back and forth between Elias and Frankie, "are you ready?"

"Of course," he said finally. "I have no hesitations whatsoever about premiering a piece we've composed just for someone, especially when we're never done anything on demand before." He did not clarify the name that Catholic Dave had alluded to, quickly glossed over in the small scramble to perform; *that song that gives me nightmares,* he had called it a few days ago, smiling so that no one would take him seriously and Frankie did not believe him. "But I have faith in Frankie." Over his shoulder, theatrically growled, "Don't you dare disappoint us now."

"I'll see what I can do." Catholic Dave had seated Elias on the couch, homegrown audience; and though she had worried, he looked no more than curious, awaiting whatever maelstrom gate to the underworld she had written for him, whatever sun-traced road home. Dave Felder twisted the air conditioner off, shoved up two of the windows with glass-shivering creaks; a gull swung past, dirty-white and the colors of dry slate, balancing its wings taut against the sweltering air. In the heat haze, the roofs and gutters that fell downhill toward the sea were blurred, gravel and shingle miniatures seen through streaky glass. Dry-mouthed, a quick swallow of water before she ducked her head and slung the guitar across her shoulders, Frankie said, "Elias." Words as consequential as sand blowing over a beach; too late now, and she had not thought of anything else that she could say. "This is for you."

Her chest was too tight, nervousness in the way of her breath for no reason that Elias' questioning, shale-colored gaze could explain. Out of the corner of her eye, she saw Dave Felder resettle his fingers, nod slightly; the first notes were as circling and melancholy as the flight of seabirds beneath the sun. Her hands remembered the chords before the words, but she had written these lyrics months ago, in the tangle of wariness and wonder that Elias' confidences called out from her, and they were already in her mouth as Catholic Dave reached for the downbeat.

Meet me in the morning where the tide runs slow
Where the sun spills up from the world below
Where the dragon back of the ocean curves
Out to lands I'll never know

Meet me in the morning, there's a following wind
Where the tracks of terns and gulls begin
To trace the path that veers and swerves
To somewhere I've never been

She did not dare look at Elias, as the clarinet slid a dissonance against the three-cornered, rocking progression of notes under her fingers, the drums slowing, syncopation to tease out the moment when worlds fragmented against one another. If he approved, if he hated, she had no time to stop and check and begin to worry. This was her core, as real and unlikely as Elias' consuming hunger for the sea: this moment of words and breath and melody, even performing for an audience of one, adrenaline as brief and heady a blaze as phosphorescence on midnight water; her nautilus core and her obsession. Through the windows, sun flashed metallic-blue from the distant harbor. The waves were swarming with light.

There's broken gold in your eyes
When you tell me
And there's salt upon your hair
You show me riptide
And crushing black
Five fathoms in a story's snare

Meet me in the morning, as the waves recede
And leave me stranded with the disbelieved
And it's only drowning that at all assures
That there's anything to see

Catholic Dave's sticks spun the cymbal's rim into the rustle of sand, the hissing of a wave rushing in and away, and the last drumbeat was a heart stopped with wonder before the everyday fell back like a cheap curtain: one glimpse and never more. Sweat like a deluge pasted Frankie's shirt to her spine, every strand of hair to her scalp, her temples, the nape of her neck where the pins had come loose between the second verse and the bridge, when Dave Felder twined restless, windborne circles into one downward gyre and plunged. He was grinning, surprised into exhilaration; Catholic Dave's face was temporary stone, performance aftershock, poised to break into any one of a dozen emotions. On the couch, Elias was holding his head in both hands, bent forward under the weight of dreams or memories, so still that a cold panic flashed through Frankie's chest. *I died and I should have stayed dead* . . . Then he lifted his face, and a different panic went through her. His face glittered in lines; tears had run between his fingers and tracked down the outer turns of his wrists, a divergence of salt like currents or veins. He was smiling as she had never

213

seen before, even when she promised him in January, and he was still crying as they stared.

"Oh, shit," Catholic Dave said, and dove for the dented box of Kleenex on the windowsill.

Dave Felder said conversationally to Asher's locked door, to the air that still trembled with music, "We're not that good. There is no way we're that good. You're running out of tissues. There's more in my room—hang on."

Frankie stood with her hands still on the strings, the fingers of her left hand flash-frozen around a minor chord, and felt something snap in her chest. She would not cry, but she did not know what would come out of her mouth if she tried to speak: a child's screwed-tight sound of disappointment, in herself? Or that the sea had not flowed through Dave Felder's windows and taken Elias down to its bottle-glass heart, that he had not dissolved into bones and red seaweed as they watched, a change of elemental states? Perhaps only that she had thought, once and too many times, that their music could move heaven and earth and sea; that the song, her lyrics and Catholic Dave's arrangement and Dave Felder's guidance, was even that good. "I'm sorry," she whispered. "I'm sorry, Elias. I'm so goddamned sorry," but he was crushing a handful of Kleenex against his face, and she did not think he was listening. At either end of the couch, Catholic Dave and Dave Felder were anxiously hovering with their boxes of Kleenex like a pair of mismatched guardian angels; Dave Felder looked up at her long enough for a smile, no obligatory comfort or papier-mâché reassurance, a real and tender expression, and she could not decide how it made her feel. Elias' shoulders jerked with his silent, terrible crying. Helplessly, Frankie repeated, "I'm sorry."

In the time it took her to swallow whatever fierce, edged feeling had clotted her throat, Elias was on his feet, new streaks of salt down his beachcomber's jacket and his face like something the tide had taken out, scoured, thrown back to shore. Head bent as though scrutinizing the carpet underfoot for some trace of shells or fossils or secrets, he crossed the distance to her in a few long strides; laid his hand over hers so quickly, skittish as always of contact with things of the land, that she wondered for a minute if he had even made the gesture at all. There was no expression on his face that she could read. His eyes were millennia in a sea-bed, time embedded in the depth of water; his mouth opened, and she stopped breathing to hear what he would say.

His mouth closed; he looked away, face raised as though into a sudden, stirring wind. Before Frankie could call his name, he turned and pulled the door open, stepped out into the blazing afternoon that poured in from the hallway to fill the space he had left behind, and was gone.

June cooled, burned again into July; the sky clouded over with heat, and sunlight lay on the ocean like gilding. A Dybbuk Adrift was still performing locally, traditional repertoire and lately some of Catholic Dave's instrumental pieces, the odd bulgar or freylekh built around Dave Felder's improvisations, one or two of Frankie's songs that she could be coaxed into writing down. A few notices in the paper, a few people who showed up to more than one show, nothing that would catapult them to fame by September and little that made them unhappy. If Dave Felder still had nightmares, he no longer felt compelled to talk about them; if Catholic Dave ever dreamed again of his cold green place, he never said so; and while no one knew exactly what score Asher had gotten on the LSATs, he smiled and showered much more often, and was heard swearing at applications for Yale, Boston College, and the University of Pennsylvania. Frankie neither dreamed of Elias Haden nor saw him. In late June, she had walked down once through the waterfront maze and seen the hand-lettered "For Rent" sign in his window, stripped of its sailcloth and washed clean of dust and webbed salt for the first time in nearly a year, and never gone back.

She was not reading, writing, or talking about the sea.

"It was crap," she said harshly, the only time either Dave tried to discuss the song for Elias, still formally nameless, that Frankie had obstinately refused to perform at open-mic night on the beach. She had sung "The Maid on the Shore" and an improvised cover of "Fogarty's Cove," but not "Sule Skerry," despite requests. "We were just showing off. *Look, look, I can write you anything you want—just as long as it's really about me, about what I can do for you, what I need.* God damn it! I wanted to make him something real."

Dave Felder removed the violin from underneath his chin, looked at her for a minute instead of tuning. His eyes were a richer color than the sky outside, less easy to glance away from; he reminded her unreasoningly of Asher. "I wasn't showing off. I don't know about our esteemed drummer over there; I don't know about you. But I am fully aware of when I'm showing off and when I'm playing—and when I'm doing both, mind you—and you can sell yourself short all you want, but don't insult me. It was real enough."

"No," Frankie insisted. "We never should have done it." She said nothing else, and no one argued, and that afternoon they went through two sets, from "The Ballad of Night's Daughters" to "Thomas and the Queen," without a halt.

In the third week of July, when Dave Felder had gone home to see his parents and Catholic Dave was in Montreal, she lay awake until nearly five in the morning, staring at her ceiling patterned like a giant waffle iron and listening to the sounds of tires and passing voices on the street that fronted her windows. Earlier she had been playing a tape that Catholic Dave had given her, but it had run down. Sweating in the darkness, she had thrown off the sheets and set the fan right at the head of her bed, but its droning half-circles kept her more awake than sleepy; she dozed, but could not dream. *A white flag in my hand, a white bone on the sand . . .* She rolled over onto her stomach, closed her eyes to trade one form of sleepless dark for another, and opened them to sunken, overcast light and the slow breathing roar of the sea. Wood flaked under her nails when her hands tightened, a weather-eaten smell clinging to her skin when she held them up and stared: warped and salt-bleached logs of driftwood built into a dock, a bridge, this awkward structure spanning a stony beach where the tide spilled and broke. But the water was drawing lichen-green and smoke-blue out from the shore, like a tide perpetually pulling away, only a little ebb and backflow where rocks and grey branches tangled the water's edge. No whitecaps, no breaking tumble of waves; Frankie looked, and saw only a ceaseless, crestless recession toward the horizon like the faint line of a mirror between the overcast sky and the clouded sea, a place of nothings meeting. When she stepped down to the beach from the last step of the pier built up over no water, bits of driftwood and shell and broken fragments of dried-dull stone crunched beneath her bare feet, grinding, and she danced a wincing step aside when something sharp came jagged against her heel.

Something else broke under her weight at the movement, a thin distinct snap, and she bent to retrieve it: a little clipper under full sail no longer than her finger, ship-in-a-bottle released back into the wild and beached on this desolate shore, painted and rigged out in meticulous detail. It weighed very little as Frankie tossed it in her hand, and she almost threw it into the flat, sliding-out tide. Then she looked more closely, and whispered, like Catholic Dave, "Oh, shit ..." With the tiny ship in her fist, she crouched down and began to sift through the litter of the shore. The driftwood was not driftwood, and neither were the stones—toothpick spars, handkerchief sails, mylar twists of propellers and hulls that would dent at the pressure of a fingernail, oars like splinters and anchors she could have worn for earrings. Every ship fitted in her grasp, some cradled in a cupped palm, others balanced on outstretched fingers, none longer than the full length of her hand. She was afraid to look for their names, to read *Marie Celeste* or *Flying Dutchman*, anything she would recognize from stories that Elias had told her; she raised her eyes from the wreckage of ships, all the lost flotsam of the ocean, and listened to the waves lifting and rolling away, draining to the edge of the world and beyond.

"No," she said. She spoke to becalmed air, windless as the doldrums, neither cold nor warm. "No. Not this." Under the grey sky, the sea's surface was opaque, and she saw no reflections. She wanted to hurl one of the ships into the water, to see the liquid shatter and splash, but the thought of touching that slow-curling, foamless tide-line kept her from moving closer; to sort through the vessels, triremes and coracles and junks and liners, but the thought of discovering their crews, their captains and their passengers, was almost worse. The name escaped her like a held mouthful of air, bleeding to the surface, "Elias—" But she was alone on this beach that curved shallowly as far as the eye could follow, ages and legends cast up and drying on its shingle, and she whispered bitterly, "That there's anything to see . . ."

She had no time to breathe, to dodge or even finish the last, hateful word. The sea roared: ravenous, driving in to shore, an explosion of dragonscale crests and troughs that smashed Frankie over into the spiky welter of ships that shattered under her weight, the tiny spines of masts and anchors and prows jabbing into her flesh, and she cried out in the same moment that a wave filled her mouth with ramming salt. The sea pounded her, its fists coral and clamshells and the backs of breaching whales, and she stared through its distorting flanks at the sun like a fire of prisms on the water's other side. Then she understood: she was not looking out into the air, but down through the depths of the ocean, where the abyss should have waited, sperm whales diving for giant squid and their kraken's entangling arms, fish that dangled their own photophore flesh for lures and the encrusted city that Dave Felder had dreamed; the light burned colors that had no names above the water, a beating heart, the last spiral working of a shell, and a lost schooner as long as her ring finger hove tumbling up against her side. Breathless, her blood unfolding like her name in the wild water around her, she reached for the sun beneath the sea until the ocean finally flung her up into darkness, gasping heat, unwounded, and the shore was desolate and barren with the sea's discarded prizes again.

Alone in her efficiency, sluiced with sweat like seawater that cooled slowly as the fan turned back and forth, Frankie lay on top of her blankets and did not think now about Elias, or what she had dreamed those long months while she wrote his song, or where he had gone, if anywhere that she did not know. She was listening intently, for the blood-familiar percussion of her heart in the distant chambers of the sea, as lost and strange as the memory of a life before her pearls were eyes and her coral bones; and for the words that, some day, some shore, might bring her back.

> Out of sleep
> Something of our own comes back to us:
> A drowned man's garment from the sea.
> —Archibald MacLeish, *J.B.*

Eelgrass and Blue

for Jeannelle Ferreira

I. Three of Scallops:
   These skins of silk and ocean, silver
   as coins laid gently on the eyes: all
   new-minted, scalloped bone and spine
   like a chain uncoiled up from the sea's
   oyster heart, sinews cat's-cradled
   to the drive and churn of breasting
   waves, the break of salt upward
   and the deep roll down, blinded green
   over a moonscape of shoulders
   and pelt like the frieze and filigree
   of silver over night tides: these
   skins slip off, slip easier on.

II. Five of Driftwood:
   Salt grass and shallows. Heron, stalking: slate mud, serpent's neck,
signature against the blue. Gulls in the sky like chips of whitecaps;
crabs at the roots, moss-green, kelp-brown, sideways through the ebb
of shadow and sun-strike. Ancient, this smell: tide layered on tide,

shells turned to silt, scale to sludge; germination, rot. Peat ocean.
Brine edge of wind. All the sea is waiting.

III. Eight of Whales:

    The ocean is metamorphosis: rain draws up, occludes,
    falls, a moonful of water to wax and wane its air
    arid or juicy, storm or sun, red skies at night and morning
    and St. Elmo's fire plays in the crosstrees like a beacon
    for ghosts. Sand smooths out under a wave retreating,
    a ripple of grit and pearl: sea spells itself
    over and over across the same shore, never twice
    the same name. Cormorants sew the water, phosphorus
    drifts in skeins, luminous diatom tangle that rising
    mouths sieve, devour, transmute, become; swallowing
    its infinite, mirror-backed tail, the ocean revolves
    upon its core: casts itself up on the broken teeth
    of rocks, slides back into itself, strains itself through
    salt marsh and delta and coral crusted like a fossilized
    dream of sand. Spindrift folds lace into skies' crushed
    and endless reflections, stonewashed waves, cloud
    shadows skimming: there and gone, here and nowhere,
    look and wondering look again; a trick of the light,
    a snare of the sea: the alchemy of stories told.

IV. The Configuration:

    The wind came off the water and snapped your hair like a banner,
and the clouds and the wave-crests were the same color as the salt-worn
rocks underfoot. You said, "Well, if I drown, we'll know it's all just
stories," or something as flippant and shivering, and I studied the scale of
ivory barnacle under my left palm while you put your clothes in a neat
pile on the dried-black seaweed, sand and bits of shell already in the folds
of cloth like something abandoned to the shore. The slap and swirl of the
waves covered any sound, and when I looked out over the water, I saw

only the green-grey ridges of ocean, falling; but presently the seal's head came up, and, eventually, you came back.

V. Queen of Moons:

The last card laid down. The last mesh of sunset drawn up from the water.

The last rock to walk out to, farthest sunken spar: mare's tails of seaweed hang down, rust-colored bundles; iron, copper, slick to the touch. The last glimpse of the land, lighthouse circling its convex blaze around the harbor, past the channel lights, out where the terns fly black against blue-black: mussel sky. The last word, that the wind catches away.

The last step, toward the rising stars.

The first breath. Home.

Letters from the Eighth Circle

Se tu se' or, lettore, a creder lento
ciò ch'io dirò, non sarà maraviglia,
ché io che 'l vidi, a pena il mi consento.
—Dante, *Inferno* (Canto XXV, 46—48)

He woke before the sun rose, startled into his own skin and sleep-forgotten name, the murky dreams still swimming behind his sight no comfort against the dead hours before five o'clock, the wind rasping blind and bone-cold over pitted brick and glass. Half a word, an ache, slid out of him as he rolled over. Faint fever twinges came and went in his bones; his skin tightened on his flesh, drumhead-dry, scratchy as though he had been rolled in sand overnight. But it was almost December, icy grit and dead leaves packed into the crevices of his locked window, and he felt the dull chill of the air weighting his veins as he moved. His bones were slow with it, his fingers as they found the switch and snapped a wash of warm light across pillows and sleep-jumbled sheets; he wanted nothing more than to sink beneath the covers and subside into sleep again, not move until the solstice had passed and the seasons tilted back toward a higher, brighter sun. Wind hit the window with an audible thump, winter's fist slamming him a reminder. Shivering, fear growing stony and constant in him as blood or breath, Gary Bresson crawled out of bed.

In boxer shorts and an ancient bathrobe frayed at every possible seam, he twisted the thermostat as far toward summer as it would go. The radiator clattered at him as he passed, siphoning steam in a rattlesnake burr and hiss that made him start as though his foot had come down on an actual serpent: lunge and recoil, pain flashing in his ankle where the fangs set like fish hooks; nothing that simple. At this hour, there might have been nobody else awake in the entire building. Only the sounds of the wind and winter coming on, seven floors above the sodium static of streetlights, traffic lights, shuttered storefronts and cars pushing past ramps and bridges where the skyline bent toward the river, light-slicked, sliding out to the harbor and the sea—Gary braced both hands against the bathroom sink, suddenly fearful of mirrors and light. He was not a small man, but stocky, and always looked shorter than he was. His hair was fair brown, tending toward sandy in the summers and thinner than he liked, the angles of his face as neat and compact as his shoulders or his hands. His eyes were almost the color of the heavy November sky. Of late he had become obsessive about his reflection, peering at it in every mirror he passed, trying to memorize his own shape. Now he scrubbed handfuls of water across his face, blinking in the sallow fluorescent dazzle, until his reflected eyes cleared: bruised and gritty from too little sleep caught at odd hours; lashless, and his eyebrows were gone.

"God . . ." He put one hand up to the mirror, fingertips digging glass and reflection for the certainties buried under its mercury skin; he could not bear to touch his own face and his likeness yielded nothing. Then his reflection's eye burst inward, coin-size icework fracturing light and blood that beaded from the heel of his hand, and Gary heard the sound he made, small and final as stone cracking. He blinked at his hand, throat caught in a sudden knot of love for his receding, dusty-brown hair.

It took him three tries to dial Rika's number. Even then, he did not cry. His new shape had no recourse to tears.

The scientific reports had christened it Dante's Syndrome or systemic ophiomorphism—as though fixing a name to unreason would make it comprehensible, predictable, safe—but Gary's friends had always called it going naga. Britte's coinage, one of the careless catchy phrases she flung out into a conversation and never remembered afterward, so that somebody always had to write them down for her. Nobody was writing down anything of hers right now.

Gary had gone to see her little more than a week ago, the shameful anxiety crawling in him that someone might catch him tapping furtively at her door and pounce on him with all the vindictive terror of the plague-time healthy, contaminated outside the apartment of a known ophiomorph, a naga. Crossing the park, he had seen few enough figures moving in the cloudy afternoon; snow sifted out of the low sky, melting before it touched ground, and the passing cars troweled sand and salt slurry up onto the sidewalks. Fewer cars than Gary remembered from last year, fewer buses and almost no one on the streets save the shapes that huddled in doorways, the concrete windbreaks of subway mouths, buried from the cold in husks of cloth and newspaper. No one dropped coins at their feet. People skirted one another, clustered in groups; Gary walked alone and began to worry, halfway across the overpass, that maybe he should have cajoled Cas or Rika along with him. *You don't have to outrun the bear,* he was thinking, a terrible joke that more than one acquaintance had dropped into thoughtless conversation, stone to shatter a pool and leave no ripples behind, *you just have to outrun your friend.* On the second-floor landing, a coffee-skinned woman crouched against the metal banister, weeping into her hands. Tears glittered over her fingers; then Gary thought perhaps they were not tears, and he averted his eyes as he took the stairs to the third floor two steps at a time.

Paul opened the door, wary in an old university T-shirt and running shorts where Gary had just taken off his gloves and unzipped his fleece. His dark hair looked as though it had been brushed the wrong way, like a cat's fur; damp salt, sweat or tears, shone over his cheekbones. "She won't recognize you," he said before Gary spoke. There was no anger in his voice, only a slow bone-weariness thickening his words. "Or maybe she will. I can't tell anymore."

"I know." Sweat stung his scalp, the small of his back, as much from tension as from the heat that filled the apartment and pushed out into the white-lit hallway. No wonder Paul was dressed for high summer, sun-glare smashing back off sidewalks too hot to touch and asphalt turning sticky underfoot: the air baked his skin like a furnace. He swallowed dryly. "Paul. Can I come in?" For answer, Paul swung the door back.

Almost, for a few stopped seconds, Gary could imagine that nothing had changed. There were the rows and racks of books, Paul's pottery displayed between volumes or press-ganged into bookends, the two African masks that hung cowrie-eyed over the desk, even Britte's collection of china animals that she had once called her porcelain Penates visible in the glass-fronted cabinet in the dining room. Homemade curtains bursting with tropical leaves and toucans swagged the windows. None of Britte's usual clutter anywhere in sight, half-full glasses propping hardcovers upright and open in place of bookmarks, jackets hung over light fixtures or clean unmatched socks set out on the keyboard—so she would remember to organize them, she had explained once, when she sat down to type; Gary, grocery-store clerk who liked the occasional historical novel, nodded and said nothing—and otherwise it looked much the same as usual.

Then he had seen Britte, piled on the couch in a fetal hunch that was almost a coil, motionless but for the faintest flicker of her tongue when she breathed. Light glossed from her spine the color of ripe chestnuts, like her dense hair that she had kept army-short for as long as Gary had known her, stippled here and there with broken shadow lines; he could no longer trace her features submerged in the stream-lining of bone and beaded scales, and even her eyes had become black and opaque, sealed behind transparent lids. He was no herpetologist, he could not have told her from any large snake seen in a zoo or a film, any brown-black serpent made a little ungainly by the presence of vestigial arms and legs like the bulk of an undigested meal: she was no longer Britte.

Polite conversation felt as unhandy on his tongue as a scientific name. "When did—" He tried again, trembling, words too loud and misplaced in this room, this cataclysm, "How long?"

"She lost language last night." The heat was soaking Gary's shirt to his spine, salt precipitate on his skin like a peel of scales. "It went pretty quickly after that."

"You didn't call anyone?"

"To do what? Stand around and watch?" A faded, furious grief angled through Paul's voice, and he turned his face from Gary to the heavy serpentine form at the other end of the couch. It gave no sign of recognition: its tongue shivered in and out, tasting the changing world, and its eyes were blind and black. "I couldn't do anything, Gary, she wouldn't listen to me or she couldn't hear me, and I kept offering—You know Nathan's going too, Nathan Mays, not Berger, plays the saxophone and thinks he can play the piano? The way every-body worries it'll happen to them and it never does, it happened to him. Some crazy on the street. He thinks it was a girl. Doesn't really know, she was that far gone . . . She bit him. Grabbed his hand, practi-cally took one of his fingers off, she was so scared and desperate. He showed me where: the scales were scabbing over it already. And nobody"—cold tautened the bones in Gary's back at the way Paul's voice went raw on the word, even fatigue stripped back by hurt and rage and no explanations at all—"nobody did anything. People on the street, of course, and all of them too scared that if they didn't let her have Nathan, she'd go after them instead. Scapegoat. She's got her own shape back and I don't think Nathan can even stand upright anymore. Cas and Rika are looking after him, I think. I don't know. I should go see him again . . ."

Gary said, no comfort in the words and no way to remain silent, "Take care of Britte." His voice faltered on the name and he reached out awkwardly, felt Paul's hand seize around his own so tight that all the small bones popped and clicked together.

"I'd give her my blood," Paul whispered, "if she'd take it . . ."

The snake slid its head forward on the couch, a slow incurious movement, and its tongue darted on the air.

He hurried home in the gathering dusk, idiot out late and unprotected, chancing his shape for an old friendship's impulse: gunfire on the other side of the park, or somebody's car backfiring, and the thing he stepped over as he stepped down from sidewalk to street looked far too much like a dead blacksnake, whip-shining skin split and blood-crusted in a molt without renewal. *Dies irae, dies illa* . . . Gary bent his head against the wind coming raw off the river, steel and concrete shouldering out the sky behind him, and almost ran into a tow-headed man in a navy overcoat who shied away from him with a breathless gasp. *It's all right,* Gary wanted to say, almost said as the man slipped out of sight, *I'm safe, it's okay.* Nine days later, his reflection watched him from a splintered, tearless eye as he bandaged his hand and waited for Rika to answer the phone.

Close to five in the morning and he had a sudden terrible presentiment that she was sleeping: he should have known better. Plastic clattered, a hollow rustle and mutter in the background, before Rika said easily, "Hey." She had a high voice, deceptive as the curved bones of her face or the color of her eyes: still shadowed water, transparent brown silted olive green and gold. "Hey, hello? Is there anybody on the other end of this call, or am I talking to dead air? If you're a telemarketer, I am going to find out where you live and break your neck."

He could not make his voice work. Pain ebbed through his hand, fine splinters in his bones and sluggish flesh; he tasted a tinder rasp of loss, held on to the receiver and whispered, finally, "Gary." The name lumped oddly in his mouth, two syllables of identity sliding fast away into flexible scale and an impenetrable stone-glaze stare. Swallowed by myth and old poetry, subsumed into a Dore woodcut. He kept glancing at his unbandaged hand, searching for the diamond indents of scales; it was nothing more than his hand, a little callused, chapped across the knuckles, and he drove his nails into his palm to make himself remember. "I'm . . . Can you come over?"

"Christ. Yes. Twenty minutes." Her voice blurred as she shifted the phone against her shoulder or a thought reached her, and she added, "Stay warm." The word gave him a sudden memory of Paul, sweat-soaked, high desert heat wavering the air and the serpent mounded indifferently where the last traces of his wife had smoothed away, and Gary's laughter broke like glass.

Nineteen minutes later, or twenty-one, Rika was leaning in his doorway: a slender graceless woman with rust-black hair, her skin the shade between steeped tea and teak, the faint twist of a smile grained always around the edges of her mouth. Over one shoulder she carried an olive-green backpack so plated with buttons that it clacked and rattled to itself as Rika unslung it, dumped it at the foot of Gary's secondhand, dirty-white couch, and knelt to retrieve three glass bottles wrapped in a checkered scarf Tom Baker might have envied. "Hard lemonade," she explained, "since I know you won't drink anything that actually tastes like it might get you drunk, and you sounded frankly fucking awful. But who knows how alcohol affects snakes anyway? We can run a couple of experiments. Here." Her deliberate, sardonic distance steadied him where condolences would have scarred; he took the bottle from her hand, condensation sliding against his skin colder than he expected, and something else that she put into his fingers without looking.

229

He turned it over: a religious card, flimsy incongruous paste-board, like something she might have gotten from Ashwini vanished now into a church's vaulted shadow, bulwark against apocalypse and metamorphosis alike, the Punishment of the Serpent, chanting confession and penitence among incense and altar candles to keep the scales from her soul. *There are few more frightening sights in this world,* Rika had said thoughtfully when she told Gary, a bite of broken ice in her voice that the sinking season could not match, *than a born-again heterosexual.* He could not imagine Rika asking anything of her now. Then it struck him, what he was seeing, and his voice tipped upward in amazement.

"Saint Patrick?" At the brink of a rocky coast, a white-bearded man in green bishop's robes, staff in hand and a gilt halo behind his solemn face, pointed toward the sea; serpents twined jade-green, seaweed-green, about his feet. Solemnly, Gary replaced the card in Rika's narrow hand. His skin flinched from the touch of hers; the steadiness of his voice amazed him. Perhaps his emotions were already sealing over, like bead-black eyes under glass lids, shingled beneath scales the color of fine sandy dust and November's guttering skies— "Good luck getting the snakes off this island."

"Idiot. Tell me when I turned Catholic, okay? That's Danbala. From Haiti, a *loa*, ever hear of them? He's the serpent, Saint Patrick's one of his faces and sometimes Moses, and he bridges water and earth; weaves the sky and the mountains together, cradles and crosses the worlds." Slightly shamefaced, she added, "I took a course on this stuff in college. Amazing the random crap you remember. He's—look, he's a theory. That this isn't what we think it is. That we're all fucked up over the wrong thing: it's not loss, it's transforma-tion, transmutation, like alchemy. You go through the impossible and out the other side, and then you know things. Don't look at me like that, it works. Britte talked about this with me, before—" For a moment she faltered, turning Saint Patrick-Danbala between her fingers like a cardplayer, about to lay down her hand on odds and intuition. "Serpents guard secrets, the hidden places of the earth and doorways; they hold knowledge, where did you think the Jesus people got that idea? The Tree of Knowledge, that's just the spine of the world linking above and below—the center pole that Danbala spirals up and down. Cast a skin and find out what it's like to go through death and back. Even if it's a human skin and there's no guarantee you'll ever get it back without trading somebody else for it. Tell them. Pass it on. You never know. And if that doesn't work"—stooping to fish another bottle from her backpack, slight sarcastic flourish that had nothing unkind about it—"this tastes mostly like lemonade."

Words crowded his tongue until he forgot all of them, stared at Rika poised glib and reckless in too-bright electric light, talking to ward off the inconceivable with a saint in one hand and a bottle in the other like her own ironic icon; what she believed, what she told him, meaningless against the single fact that she had come over half a city's blocks and bitter windblown streets, the darkened river oil-smeared with lights, alone, to find him. He tried for her name, "Rika—" and citron spirits splashed and almost spilled on the couch as he reached for her arm, her hands, human in his grasp and holding him as though he were; her fingers hurt his shoulders, gripping fast through cheap terrycloth and fever-crisp skin, and neither one let go until tears smeared both their faces. His eyes burned, dry as sand or scale.

Some blurred time later, still dull as old iron outside, as closed and cold, Gary was beginning to think that Rika's experiment had failed; the hard lemonade tasted like nothing much, a tang at the back of his teeth, and he killed one bottle while Rika leaned her elbows back on the opposite arm of the couch, feet propped over his own, silent audience for the horror stories he told to keep his thoughts from his own. "Two days ago, Christ, I nearly went home. Some guy unloading artichokes almost got his skull beaten in with a tire iron because this passerby he banged into thought he was going naga." He could not bear for the next sentence to be a punch line; he said flatly, "It was acne."

"Shit."

"And the revival tent on the corner, you couldn't walk that way unless you wanted to hear about the Mark of Satan for the next day and a half." A teenager in snakeskin boots, tasteless, hardly demonic, had provoked a screaming onslaught of prayer that had kept Gary from going out to the Laundromat; he washed his socks by hand and hung them out to dry in the shower, stood at the window to watch the figures in black and white exhorting, condemning, Bibles and homemade signs held aloft to the thin bright sun, God's insomniac eye, fiery regard measuring distantly the fall of sparrows and angels and cities. An absurd, spendthrift anger had stirred in him then as he considered slamming up the window in a shower of paint flakes and frost and yelling down into the street, near-deserted except for the righteous and terrified, something, anything, words that Rika might have shouted at crucifix-carrying Ashwini if she were a woman who shouted. "The dragon," he muttered, "that old serpent . . ."

Rika said mildly, "So what's the temptation here?"

"Not turning into a fucking snake." The last word grated sharply and he leaned back, shoving the heels of both hands against his defenseless eyes, his forehead skinned of eyebrows and expression. "Sorry. I'm sorry. I don't mean . . . I'm scared."

"Yeah. So'm I. So's everybody." She pushed one black-socked foot against his ankle, local approximation of a hand on the shoulder, and added, "Plus, you're in shock and you never drink. It's okay."

"No. That's not it. I just . . . I saw Britte last week, I told you, and Paul told me about Nathan, and I don't even want to ask you about Cas or Johanna or, or, that redheaded girl that Kieran was seeing, the one who was scared of photographs, I don't even want to know. I don't even call my parents, my sister; I don't want to find out. They're on the other side of the country, for Christ's sake, and how do I know the same thing's not happening there? Everyone I know, practically, and me." He dragged in a breath, air like gravel, and his voice tore over the sudden sympathy in Rika's gaze, the hopeless futility of this recitation, holding on to camaraderie while moment by moment the strangenesses sharpened between them. "I was careful. I was so careful, my God, so fucking careful—no shadows in the alley, no sharp teeth—careful and it doesn't matter after all, doesn't make a bit of difference, because blood binds. Just think, your hands get chapped, skin cracks because it's cold outside, and maybe they don't even know—I could have handed somebody change for, God, I don't know, avocados, and handed over my—my humanity with it—" He whispered, "Damned if I'll crawl with Ashwini to the altar, but you tell me: the world's not ending? And nothing to do but look in the mirror and wait."

Soft-voiced across the couch, shoulders braced equally against his mention of Ashwini and litany of friends gone naga, gone, Rika said, "I'll be here."

"I know." Heat clanged in the pipes, distant in the concrete guts of the building; he clenched one hand on the other until pain strobed his palm, no snakeskin shield against this, three words shaking such fury through him that he wondered Rika could not feel it in the air, like an earthquake, in the foundations and the street and the marrow of her bones. "You'll be here. Lucky you, with Saint Patrick and Danbala watching out for you. You and your philosophies, you with your shape that you get to keep while all the rest of us go naga," hearing the words spattering from his mouth, vicious as though he had already sloughed Gary Bresson's skin to gain poison and bite and the precision to place both as fatally as possible, "go crazy, and no one to give us our selves back. But you, you'll be fine. I mean, who'd take care of all of us? It's winter; we'll get cold; we'll die. We'll need you. That must feel good. Rika Cherayil's Free Serpent Clinic, you ought to open up a business. Keep yourself busy while we all go to hell."

She said tightly, "That's not what I'm doing here. You called me, remember?"

"Well, it was a stupid thing for me to do, then, wasn't it? I should have just bitten you when you walked through the door." He heard her breath stop in her mouth, drove his spite into that silence. "You said yourself, maybe we're all fucked up over the wrong thing. So prove me wrong. Come on, here's my wrist, you can bite me if you want: better symbolism that way. Take the naga's communion. Don't tell me a little blood turns you off. It's secret knowledge, right, it's alchemy. Just shed your skin; it's good for what ails you. And it'll come around eventually. If not me, it's going to be somebody else, and they probably won't give you the option. We're all in this together."

He was kneeling on the couch's uneven cushions now, worn sleeve pulled back and palm and wrist upturned as deliberately as she had handed him a hard lemonade, a dare and a slap in the face: nothing in her look but blank revulsion, staring at something unrecognizable, sickening, inverted from the familiar until there was no way to find what it had been. Were scales printing his face already? Had his teeth thinned, his eyes glazed black, were his fingers cleaving into braided, beaded flesh so fast? Or maybe she was seeing nothing but Gary, her friend, himself, and that repulsed her most of all. Slowly, she put one hand on the back of the couch and one hand on its thread-snagged arm and levered herself upright, never breaking Gary's gaze from her own that had darkened in the shadow of her hair; momentarily a stranger's face. He swallowed, sore-throated. Silence weighted him like stone.

"All right," she said, without emphasis, and he remembered that she never raised her voice, "so I'm going." She slid one foot off the couch, rising to leave; beyond the latched windows, a vague pallor clung to the edges of the horizon, smearing the dying night. "You cold-blooded bastard."

He caught her as she turned, moving before he knew whether he meant to apologize, to hurt her, to make her listen or simply gain one more moment of time, and then it no longer mattered: his fingers closed hard around her wrist and he felt the fine bones shift under the skin, grating; her breath snapped audibly and his weight pulled her half sprawling across him, wrist skewed at a wrenching angle, sound-less even as he felt her jerk with the pain. Beneath his driving finger-tips, her pulse drummed, strong and frightened, and he knew then what he could do to her.

Her skin burnt his hand, his mouth. Tilted toward the light, Rika's gaze unfolded sudden color, a quiet loop of the river where willows trailed and no currents ran. Her eyes tightened with pain. Very softly, she said, "Go on, if you're going to." Her breath was warm against his palm, an edge of lemons to the flicker of his tongue. "We're all in this together."

Cold day growing outside to sink comfortless back into the dark: the world devouring itself in an ouroboros loop, skin to scale to skin again, circles within circles and no exemption, only the bitten, bitter knowl-edge of endurance. His bones opened and ached under her riverbed regard. Danbala coiled over his thoughts. The first reported case that made the tabloids before the scientific journals, lurid *Shape Rape!* though who knew how many others before that; the day that a riot trashed the reptile house in the zoo, left chameleons burning and so many bullets in the thirty-foot anaconda that there was scarcely enough left to make a wallet; Britte's eyes, evening blue, seed-black. *I'd give her my blood, if she'd take it* . . . Nathan had played excellent saxophone.

Warmth jangled in Rika's veins. Gary lifted his head and whis-pered, "Go."

His voice would not take the word, little more than a rust-ratchet of sound, and he had to repeat it. Ashen light moved over the carpet where lemonade and liquor had spilled into the sandy shag, the threadbare couch at whose foot Rika's backpack leaned, narrowed Gary's eyes against the brightness: no lashes to screen them, and water trailed like tears across his temples as he blinked. He smeared the wetness away with the back of his bandaged hand, thoughtlessly, taped gauze scratching his skin. He was not sweating. Rika had risen from the couch; she did not rub her wrist or speak, neither condemnation nor acceptance, as she knelt to lace scuffed sneakers and collect the empty bottles, one drunk and one spilled. Wind buffeted the windows. Somewhere in the icy street below, seven floors down, a car alarm was keening.

Head bent, Rika studied the floor for a moment before leaning forward to retrieve Saint Patrick tossed like confetti to the floor, face-up and disregarded, trumped. He took the card from her silently: the man between states, land and sea, heaven and earth. Serpents tangled where his staff touched the shore. Gary's voice was a fracture, a husk. "And if it's not true?"

She straightened in a radiator rattle of slogans and smart-aleck statements, shrugging to settle the backpack on her shoulders, no answers in the motion. Rising light scoured the window behind her, grey as the stripped inside of a shell; sweat traced fine ink-lines of her hair against her forehead. Neither of them glanced down at the marks still printed like a shadowy rash around her wrist.

"I don't know. Nothing, maybe. Or maybe we're all fucked up over the right thing." She spoke evenly, her mouth a plane without humor or yielding, without cruelty. "You'll know sooner than me." She stepped across his threshold and was gone, solitary, into the morning.

Cool air slid around him as he closed the door, locked it, an unexpected beat between every movement and the next. Even the pale sunlight felt warmer across his shoulders, his hands, as he settled onto the couch, eased the slight aches still shifting bone and muscle-deep; he scratched at the back of one hand, absently, and did not explore the texture of the skin beneath his nails. *How long? She lost language last night. It went pretty quickly after that.* "Not yet," Gary whispered, "not yet, Patrick," and closed his eyes, drowsing, while the blood sank in his veins and slowly turned cold.

Moving Nameless

"Don't be afraid," Adam whispered. In the sloping afternoon light she could see the sweat shining on his cheekbones, half from summer, half from her nearness; he had shaved that morning and already there was shadow grained beneath his skin. She wanted to touch him, put one hand alongside his jaw until the faint sandpaper sensation rasped against her palm and the tips of her fingers. If she tilted her face, she could make their mouths meet. But sorrow like stone weighted her movements, dragged at her blood, and instead she stood very still as Adam murmured again, "Don't be afraid." His reassurance made her smile. He was the one afraid: shy and fearful of getting it wrong, not pleasing her, scaring her away. What could she fear? He would not hurt her. He could not. But she would hurt him; that was the way of the world, and her bones ached with the knowledge. The old mantelpiece clock, now transferred to a sideboard in the miniature kitchen, ticked out time in the stillness softened by their breathing. She did not know how many seconds she had left. Despairing, desiring, she took Adam's hands in her own.

He had been showing her his apartment—not really his apartment, his grandfather's, but his grandfather was visiting Adam's aunt in Topeka and his parents had allowed him the month's experimental use of the three rooms and storage closet—and now they stood together in the sunlit living room, as careful and awkward with one another as all first-time lovers. Earlier they had eaten Thai food across the street from the bookstore where Adam worked, browsed the used book store where Adam spent all his paychecks, and walked back to his grandfather's apartment with their hands clasped and swinging between them. Nothing had happened; she was still a little surprised. Over their heads the sky had simmered rich with the season, clouds blossoming out of the haze feather-white against heat-soaked blue. Their shadows had paced one another on the sidewalk. Asphalt stuck to their shoes. Fortunately the apartment was in the basement; shadowed, but not subterranean, and light streamed over the floor when Adam flung up the shades. For a while they talked, as Adam showed her pieces of his life and his grandparents' that had settled about the apartment: sculptures his grandfather had done before his eyesight went, old books that slid household to household depending on who wanted to read what, photographs of Adam and his family at varying ages, childish drawings, dried flowers, detritus of memory that she absorbed through his words. "It's amazing that your parents trust you this much," she remarked. "Not to mention your grandfather. Handing over the apartment to an adolescent— You must really get along."

"Yeah." Adam shrugged, unimpressed and a little embarrassed. "They're good people. I like them. How about yours?"

"Oh," she said, quietly, "we don't talk much anymore."

"I'm sorry." They were sitting side-by-side on the couch, beneath a charcoal sketch of Adam's grandmother holding her first child, Adam's father, in her arms. In the blurred lines she could find familiar traces of Adam: broad, raised cheekbones, peaked eyes, mouth that widened easily into a sharing smile; unbeautiful in repose but more than attractive when animated. Roughed in, his grandmother's hair was braided and piled about her head. Adam's hair sprang over his shoulders, dark and unruly. He looked nothing like his maternal great-uncle, for whom he had been named. She could grow to like him very much.

Suddenly it hurt to breathe; it hurt to hear Adam's sympathy. "It's all right," she managed. "I'm doing fine." But she was not, she was lying, and Adam did not know. He did not even know to look for the lies, as when he called "Eva!" because he wanted her to see a book he had found, because that was the name she had not denied when he guessed at it. He liked the cheerful, impossible allusion. She did not have the heart to discourage him; it had been his own name that first caught her attention.

He looked nothing like his oldest namesake, and only like any of the other countless Adams she had met in all the years since as one human man looks like another. Adam Harrow, the great-uncle who had been her friend, had been earnest and red-headed—gone springing white in later photographs, an unblown dandelion with a shy smile—thin and bespectacled, the very archetype of a weedy scholar. In fact he had been a newspaper editor, a well-read one, and had known her name before she told him. But an earnest short-sighted editor had not helped her, nor the banker who had borne his name before him, nor the courtier, the alchemist, the monk, the madman . . . After the first few millennia, she had learned to disregard the years, but she had never learned to disregard the pain.

Whether she thought Adam Loukides could help her, or whether she merely felt the hopeless smile cross her face as soon as he introduced himself and she knew she had made her decision, she did not know. But the irony was wonderful, and he was cheerful and meticulous when she asked after a book that had caught her curiosity. "Robert Graves' *Hebrew Myths?* Out of print," Adam apologized, "but I know this great used book store around the corner, and I can run over and check and see if they have it. Do you like Robert Graves? I've only read his Claudius books. You know, the Roman ones. Only because I'm a Derek Jacobi fan, really, which is kind of sad . . . My mother was a classics major in college." From the moment he spoke, she loved the sound of his voice: informal rambling phrases said with crisp ease, a classically trained actor with a high-school vocabulary. "Look, I'm off work in fifteen minutes. Do you want to run over to the bookstore with me? We can get lunch from the Thai place—they've got amazing coconut soup—or there's this place that does sandwiches, really nice ones, and we can sort of poke around. There's a plethora of restaurants in this area. Not enough bookstores, but a lot of restaurants." Suddenly shy, he flushed beneath his fair olive skin and said almost too loudly and too quickly, "How's that sound?"

Already she liked him; and because she knew it was hopeless, she was safe in her liking. Adam's eyes were the color of ancient amber, dark until the light tipped into them and clarified to a smoky, concentrated almond. His fingers tapped an arrhythmic tattoo on the countertop. Before he could speak again, she nodded. "It sounds wonderful," she said. "I'd love to."

She did not find a copy of her book that day, although she had a very nice sandwich eaten on the green outside the library, but she had found Adam. "Adam Yves Loukides," he said grandly, gesturing with his own half-eaten sandwich, "and if that isn't a name to make you cringe, I don't know what is. My parents were trying to name me for each side of the family. Pity that everyone in my family has names no one's ever heard of."

"I think most people will recognize Adam," she said dryly.

"Fine, but Yves? The last person I saw named Yves was in a medieval mystery."

"Sorry."

"Don't apologize to me," Adam sulked, sprawled full-length in the sunlight with half a tomato sandwich in one hand and the other folded as a pillow behind his head, "complain to my parents!" Then he grinned. When she came back to the bookstore the next day, it might have been for the care he took over her book, his sandwich recommendations and his speeches about names, or even his kind, spontaneous grin that eased a little of the worry collecting cold beneath her heart; but regardless, she came back, and Adam was very pleased to see her.

A week later they finally made it to the Thai restaurant, where she tried the coconut soup and agreed that yes, it was amazing, and almost destroyed her sinuses asking for red curry extra hot. After that, he invited her home. This was an idyll, a dream. She had loved every swift-running second of it. Now she stood beside the glass-topped coffee table where she had risen to escape his kindness—his understanding that could never really understand—holding Adam's hands in fear and tenderness. He had put on one of his grandfather's records for her, Benny Goodman's famous 1938 Carnegie Hall version of "Sing, Sing, Sing," but it had ended almost ten minutes ago. The melody was still going around in her head. She was listening to the clock tick.

Clocks and watches were useless to her, long before their invention; she measured time in the silent geologic roar of cracking continents and rising seas, mountains lathed to desert, stone pried from stone, the winds that swept from every quarter of the globe save that one forgotten place. She had not forgotten it. She never forgot. But mortals forget, men forget, Adam had not been able to find Graves' book and did not know her name. Scant inches from her face, amber eyes fractured with the light filtering through the dust-glazed panes, he was trying to comfort her, trying to kiss her, drawn to her for reasons he would never be able to explain. She knew them, of course. Made for love, to love, she could not help but want to hold him; she could not hate, only sorrow. She was sorrowing now.

Adam drew one hand free of her clasp, combed fingers through her hair; lifted the dense fall from her face and touched the angle of her cheekbone with his lips. He was very gentle. With equal gentleness, she turned her face and closed the distance between them with her mouth.

Adam's body tensed against hers, eager, undemanding, and she felt more than she heard the soft noise he made under his breath as her hands slid to the nape of his neck. Her mouth tasted of nothing at all. Did he find that odd? Lost in the taste and texture of him, she could not tell; his mouth moved on hers, his hands traced her body; blurred with the scant distance between them, she saw the dark fan of his eyelashes closed against his cheekbones. Between her fingers, his hair curled soft and wiry, and his skin heated beneath her fingertips. There were tears packed behind her eyes. With the certainty of millennia, she kissed Adam and waited for it to happen.

It came like a galvanic flash, a lightning stroke driving into him through her body, and it smashed them apart. His head jerked back and she knew he had seen, she saw it in his eyes, not the last sight of a dying man but the last image of dying love. Imagination flayed her, skin peeling from flesh, veins stranding from muscle, disclosing blood that seeped, saliva that spilled, jellied globe of one beautiful disconnected eye; he saw her constructed from marrow to breath, the cartilage fretwork of her throat knotting with ligaments, ribcage filled and pulsing to the spasmodic double beat of heart and lungs, hair sown in her scalp over the thin zigzag bones. Metamorphosis without physical change, realization and recognition: the rooted stubs of bone his tongue explored, the sag of glands his hands cupped, wet meat, slick bone, membrane and gristle waxed with fat and corded with sinews, all the fascinating sickening strata of flesh that slid beneath her faultless skin. Adam made a sound in his throat—not the same noise, so much the same noise that she felt the wrench like bones breaking about her heart—and let her go. One minute their mouths were fastened, the next he stood halfway across the room, disgust smeared and stamped on his features so clearly that even he felt it and tried to smooth it away, wiping both hands over his face, shaking, too shocked even to swear.

"God," he said when he could speak, the words heaving out of him, "oh, God. Eva—"

"Don't call me that." In his moment of understanding she had drawn into herself, receded from beneath the margin of her pristine skin. She felt a physical distance between herself and her bones, her flesh and the air that pressed against it; she moved as jerkily as a marionette as she got herself to the couch and folded onto it. The ancient sorrow ate at her breath and she gasped a little, between words. She whispered, "It's not my name. I don't have a name."

Adam leaned against the wall. The blood had run out of his face, leaving the bones pressed white against the skin: startled out of himself into a stranger's look. He swallowed shock and croaked, "What are you?"

Her face bent in a smile without humor. "That book knows, the one we couldn't find. The nameless virgin. Adam's second wife. After Lilith left, threw him over for Ashmedai on the shores of the Red Sea, God made— You have to call her a woman, she wasn't anything else. But not a woman like Lilith was a woman, like Eve was a woman, made out of earth or flesh. He made her out of nothing, out of his will, before Adam's very eyes: bones, muscles, tendons, flesh. Piece by piece. Layer over layer. You saw. What's inside everyone, that's all, but Adam had never looked into a living body. They didn't have Gray's *Anatomy* then. And he saw her and sickened. He couldn't touch her. So Eve was made while he slept, so that he should not see her creation; and on waking he managed to forget what he had learned from the sight of the second woman, the forgotten one, the surface of Eve's beauty so enthralled him. Maybe God helped him to forget. God was kind to him. The second helpmeet— Some people say God destroyed her. Some people say he only made her leave Eden. Gone out into the world like Lilith; not like Lilith, really. Lilith had her anger and her beauty, her immortality and her power. The nameless woman had beauty and immortality only. No gifts, those. Nor did she fall, like Eve. Adam wouldn't get near her: how could she ever leave her innocence? No one touches her. No one can bear it." Her voice crumbled under the burning tears. "I can't touch anyone. Ever."

"Eva..." Adam swayed; his precise, slangy voice wavered and he sat abruptly on the floor, collapsible as a string-cut puppet himself, to sink his head forward and shudder. "I'm sorry. I'm sorry. I didn't mean that . . . I don't know what to call you now."

"There isn't anything to call me. In any language. I've learned so many," she whispered, "so many." Of all those who had tried to touch her, men and woman both, the kind ones were the worst. She did not care when a groping hand stiffened as though stung, a mouth rummaging over hers yelled in shock, but she flinched from the anguish scoring Adam Loukides' face: that he should see her suffering and could not ease it. He could not even press her shoulder in a friend's caress, could not even hold her hands as she wept. "No name. Nothing. God made me so."

"I don't believe in God." His voice shivered on the edge of crying. "But people breathe, bleed, shit, all of that, I know that; I've got hydrochloric acid rattling around in my stomach, it's no big deal; but I couldn't, I, I saw— I saw you, Eva!" he cried, and she did not stop to correct the name. "I shouldn't feel like this, I shouldn't. It's not reasonable. But I can't— I don't understand it. It's not God. I don't know what it is."

"God or no God," she said, desolate, definite, "what does it matter? My memories are the story. What I remember happened in someone else's words, the words of the storyteller who took the tale of Adam and Eve and filled in the spaces, the words of the man who translated the midrash, the words of the editor who proofed the book for publication, and all the generations in between and after—but still it happened to me. My creation is the story." Sunlight warmed her shoulders; it did nothing for the ache of ice branching in her veins. She closed her eyes. She did not want to see if Adam was looking at her in fascination, away from her in revulsion. In his eyes she would see the knowledge of the first Adam, what he had learned from her and then forgotten: another kind of fall. She murmured to the red-washed darkness behind her eyelids, "God doesn't have to exist. Only the tale. Only me."

"So change the tale. Tell the story differently. Say the nameless woman, Adam's second wife, found a boy she loved who worked at a bookstore and spent the rest of her life with him. Say she kissed him and nothing happened except what's supposed to happen when two people who're attracted to one another kiss." Hope made his voice raw. "Tell the story that way."

She shouted, "Do you think I haven't tried that?" There was no anger in her voice, she could not be angry, only a great and tearing grief. "Your great-uncle tried it. He wrote stories—not very well, but he loved doing it—and he wrote me a story where we stayed together until our deaths, side by side in the same bed, breathing out our last breath on the same sigh. And here ... Here I am, Adam. Adam, if I could touch you—" She bent her head into her hands and tasted the tears that ran between her fingers. "I don't know how not to want to."

She heard the catch of his breath, as it struck him: the ceaseless journey, a different country every time, a different face, a different courtship, but always the endless repetition of the same story over and over past all human limits; but she was not human, not mortal, lost to Eden before its gates closed. Adam's first failure that had stamped her into this changeless mold still held true.

Adam Loukides, her dark-haired garrulous Adam of the bookstore, whispered from across the room, "What now?"

"I don't know." Now she lifted her head, ran a hand over her face and pulled tear-wet strands out of her eyes; he was not watching her with horror, nor with interest, but steadily and with pain. "People love me. And they are always hurt. Everything we've ever tried"—she and all the thousand thousand friends, lovers, companions that might have been—"has never worked. Each one thinks he'll be the one to change things, she'll break the curse, we'll live happily ever after. Nothing changes. Our lives go on. Adam, I have to leave. It will get worse. You can look at me now, but soon you won't be able to do even that. You won't be able to stand being in the same room as me. Soon you won't want to think of me; and then, like the first Adam, you'll wake one morning and forget. You'll never know I was here. Or if you remember, you'll remember only that something terrible happened, that it didn't work out in some awful, sickening way. Like the first Adam. Only I remember."

"I . . . I understand." Adam's mouth worked over a word he did not dare to say. Then he rose, clambering to his feet with one hand against the wall, and crossed the room in hesitant strides. "Come on. I want to look at you. I want to remember."

"You don't."

"No, I do. I mean, it hurts somehow, to see you. But I keep thinking, if I look hard enough, it'll stop hurting. Like eating that red curry you ordered, remember? I thought the inside of my mouth was going to peel off. That's a disgusting image . . . But I kept eating it, because I figured it couldn't get any worse. And shoveling in the rice. And maybe it worked, because I still have my tongue and all my teeth . . ." Rambling as when she first met him, he stooped and held out one hand, and she took it to pull herself to her feet.

He flinched. His hand snapped out of hers, his feet took him two stumbling steps backwards before he realized what he was doing. Immediately a brick-red flush slammed into his face: shame and guilt burning beneath the skin. "I'm sorry," he gasped, "Christ, I'm sorry. I thought— I hoped—"

"It's all right," she answered. Of course it was not. "It's not your fault." He hovered at her elbow as she left the living room, passed the bedroom and the kitchen where the light fell in late dust-grained slants through the high windows; he unlocked the door for her and followed her up the stairs, close enough that she could feel his presence stir the air against her skin; but he did not try to touch her again. Though she heard Adam make soft choked sounds from time to time, she was not crying. Her heart had broken open, and all her tears run out.

On the steps, he paused in the doorway and raised one hand in something between a farewell wave and a summons; the gesture hesitated, and he let his hand fall. She was already walking away when she heard his voice and turned.

"Come back." A sallow ghost of his sympathetic grin twitched at his mouth. "You know where I am. I work all through August, and in the fall I'm back at college. I'm easy to find." Tears glassed his amber eyes, turned illegible black by the fall of shadow from the yew hedge beside the door. "If . . . if I don't remember you, tell me. I'm not your first Adam. I want to see you again."

"You won't. It'll be the same. It's always the same. Don't you understand"—though she knew he did, and would have kissed him for his daring if it were possible—"I can never get close to anyone!"

"Stories are never fixed." A spasm of disgust tightened his face; he had seen her again, fat and muscle cased around bone, beauty stripped to reveal the nonsensical repulsion that seized them all. But he did not look away, though he blanched with the effort, and when it passed he was still watching her. "It's one of their great virtues. They don't tell themselves: they are told, and change in the telling . . . Please, nameless woman, Adam's second helpmeet, I don't know what to call you and I don't know if I ever will, come see me again. When I've forgotten. When you can bear to see me." He added, broken-smiled, "At least we'll get another crack at that curry."

She could give him no promises. She did not know if she could ever learn to see him without the memory destroying her, if she could endure the same loss a second time, if she could bear to do such a thing to him; or whether between this moment and next summer she would meet someone else and be drawn to this new one as surely and fatally as to Adam Loukides, to enact the old pattern once again in pain. Across the road, the sun was settling a film of gold across the late cloud-trailed sky. Four or five children were playing in a yard; she tried not to see how casually, carelessly, they touched. Her mouth still remembered the particular flavor of Adam's kisses, her fingers knew the curl of his hair and the roughness of his jaw. Better to walk away, to keep walking, continuing the endless journey of story sealed onto life. But no one had ever asked her to come back. She had never waited to see if they would.

"All right," she said quietly. "When you've forgotten." What she would do then, she would have to wait and see. But it was enough now for Adam; and, perhaps, for her.

She left him as she had come to him, solitary, carrying nothing but the gathering weight of memory, her beauty and her immortality, and her despair. Walking away from Adam, she walked down the street that led away from his grandfather's apartment, going east. Her shadow splayed before her. She followed it, past the used book store and the Thai restaurant, over the scrubby green and the parking lot outside the library: moving nameless through the streets, lost in the world, and loved.

Courting Hades

No pomegranate, comb of bloodied
jewels and honey-pale pith, passed
hand to hand like an entrusted
heart: not in this underworld.
We choose; earth turns, grasses
underfoot no matter who walks
aboveground, who waits below;
sun poised beside moon, half-light
that reveals everything, halfway
from here to nowhere. Here,
now; no bargains sealed in sheaves
of tears, frost-blackened flowers
left to fall among the burning,
binding seeds. Only our hands
hold this river's shores apart,
together: we walk our own ways.

Return on the Downward Road

> The descent to Avernus is easy:
> black Dis' gates stand open night and day.
> But to recall your steps and escape to the upper air,
> this is the labor, this is the task . . .
> —Vergil, *Aeneid*

There was no point in looking for it; she knew that she would either find it this evening, as the sun burnt the skyline black against the western sky, or she would go home in the streetlit night, empty-handed, and rise the next morning to sunlight and an ordinary world. What choice she had in the matter she had already made. The rest was out of her hands. That did not stop her from pausing every few feet and peering through the glass, into a bookstore, a coffee shop, a law office, ice cream cones, racks of designer clothing, searching for the old signs: the schoolmaster who limped, the books whose letters burned, ten startled scholars and the old cry *Devil take the hindmost!* The idea made her smile, a little shamefaced at her own imagination; the school would not have survived the centuries if it had been so obvious. Might as well look for blood dripping pentacles down a wall or diabolic anagrams scrawled on the sidewalk, the stuff of cheap horror flicks. She did not, in fact, know what she would see

250

when she came to the school at last; but she would recognize it when she saw it, that much she knew, and it would not look like anything she expected.

She rounded the corner of the Indian theater, streetlights coming on overhead like fizzing stars. A newspaper went past her feet in the wind from a passing car, crackling across the asphalt; her eyes followed it until disappeared into the shadow between ice cream and a computer store. In that momentary pause of curiosity, a man's voice said, "Come over here, Jena Reese." The sunset had faded to a faint peach-colored haze lingering at the edge of the sky; the air had the almost tangible translucence of summer twilight, dimming blue as water. Without hesitation Jena Reese crossed the street, and went over there.

Shadowed by the brick flank of Ben and Jerry's, she blinked through drifts and dabs of afterimages. Eventually a face cleared out of the darkness, younger than his voice. Loose brown hair and indeterminate eyes, a bony, changeable face: no one she knew, and smiling as though he expected her to hit him. "Looking for the Scholomance," he said. Jena had enough time to nod and not enough time to answer before he hurried on. "Thought so. You have a look about you—students paying for scholarship with your souls. You've made your choice before you even cross the doorstep. Why else did you step into this alley with me? Tell the truth and shame the Devil. Learn enough and challenge God. Don't tell me it doesn't appeal. Learning's a devilish business." He added, "In all senses of the word."

She waited for his fit of oratory to subside before asking, quietly, "How did you know my name?"

"Saw you in Gratia Artis, across from the realtor's office. You like origami figures." His smile was losing its placatory quality, relaxing into the shape of his face; it made him look older, and more innocent. "You paid with a check and gave your name. That's all. Nothing mystical."

Jena said, with certainty and a little disappointment, "You're not the schoolmaster."

"At the Scholomance? Oh, no." He shifted against the brick, folding his arms against his chest, and shook his head in a gesture only a little more dramatic than necessary. Night was coming up, and the lights of storefronts and passing cars shone hard and edgy against asphalt and concrete. She wished he would step forward a little. He leaned into the darkness casually, but it camouflaged him well; even the color of his eyes, hazel fading to brown, lost itself as an angle of shadow slewed across his face. "Mortal as you. I'm sorry."

"Don't be," Jena said, or started to say: tires gritted on the pavement behind her and she looked over her shoulder into a glare of white light. Within seconds the car had reversed and careened off into traffic again, a wrong turn hastily corrected, leaving Jena to blink tears from her lashes and think over what she had seen when the sudden light stretched her shadow across the feet of the man beside her, printing his face with dismay and the asphalt behind him with nothing but bright, unhindered light. She did not even have to meet his eyes to understand.

"You were at the Scholomance."

"The Black School, the Devil's School, yes, I was." Violet dazzle filled her vision; she could only listen to his voice, soft and hasty just beyond her reach. "It was in Germany then, in Wittenberg. It moved to Romania the year after I—after my class. Amongst the mountains over Lake Hermanstadt," he was quoting something, although she could not tell what, "where the Devil claims the tenth scholar as his due." The lift and linger of the words sounded exactly like a wry twist of a smile.

"It was in Boston when I heard of it," Jena offered. Her first real encounter with the Scholomance, a year ago, had been as matter-of-fact as it was unexpected. Her interview with the alumna from Harvard had been nerve-racking, much less from anything the woman said than from Jena's own expectations; her store of small talk and academic statistics exhausted, she watched her interviewer's eyes grow remote and readied herself for the polite dismissal. But the woman only remarked, "I was intrigued by your description of yourself as a 'storian.' You said you loved 'all the world's legends, the secret knowledge of stories, and their intersections with reality as we know it.' Did you really mean that?" When Jena stammered that she did, the woman wrote two things on a strip of paper and handed it to Jena. "You might be interested in this program. Don't worry about applications: I'll see that you're recommended. If you're still interested—" and Jena had gone home, and checked the term *Scholomance* in various dictionaries of folklore, and waited for Saint John's Eve to circle around again.

"It's been in Boston before. About the only place in the New World it returns to regularly, although as you see—" Her night vision had returned enough to show her a hand moving in a careless, descriptive wave. Overhead the sky had turned the color of crumbled charcoal, filmed with reflected light. "I was in Paris on exchange. A librarian at the Sorbonne told me ... He doesn't have to do anything, you know. We tempt ourselves, with our books and papers and senior theses: you know a little, you have to know more. A little learning is a dangerous thing, a little more learning is a lot more dangerous, but that's half the fun. How could I resist? There are books in that library that don't exist anymore. Maps of places that never did. Accounts of the afterlife, the roads forward and back and how to take them. The real rules for alchemy—I've seen what happens when the Dragon devours his own tail, when Mercury opens the way . . ." He came forward a step—a slighter man than she had thought him in the flash of the headlights, standing now where the alley lightened—and no shadow trailed him. He whispered, "The best teacher in the world."

"That's why I'm here." She kept her eyes on his face, away from the untouched pavement beneath his feet; ignoring the sickness, not mentioning the deformity. "If he'll have me."

The student grinned, unhappily. "Oh, he will."

Hesitation, not silence, fell between them. Across the street, someone seemed to have parked and left the car playing Gregorian chant at a hundred and twenty decibels. Presently Jena said, "The tenth scholar."

"Yes. The seven years come due and the students run—like hell, if you'll pardon the expression—and the last one out the door the Devil catches to claim as his pay. The hindmost. What happens to them afterward, I don't know. No one really does. And, no surprise, nobody wants to stick around to find out. So I ran with the rest." His hair had fallen into his eyes and he brushed it away, absently; the lights from the street fell onto his face as though through his hair, through his hand. Only his fingers obscured his face as he rubbed at his eyes with a weary, theatrical motion. No shadow meant no shadow at all. "Do your clothes cast shadows when you're not wearing them?" Jena asked, but he had not heard her; he was still speaking, unstoppable, telling the story he had exchanged for his shadow.

"Now this, this is diabolic. Seven full years you spend with your schoolmates: you learn with them, you share everything with them, you spend your days and nights breathing the very same air and breaking the very same bread: then the term ends and you'll kill one another to get out that door first. I got Sarai's foot in my kneecap and Jan's elbow in my mouth, we were so crazy to get out. Maybe that's part of the lesson, the disillusion. The last piece of knowledge, one of those cold, hard, real facts that settles like a stone in your stomach. Those other nine are so thankful they're not the one the Devil's got hold of, they'll let him have you—and you're doing the very same thing.

"You know the story. Saemundur did it. So did Michael Scot, some say. Maybe others. It doesn't matter. Whatever you think the Devil's like, Jena, nothing's like feeling his hands on you. And he holds fast. And you scream, like he's got your living heart on the coals, and you'll give anything—your schoolmates vanishing out the door, your grandmother turned eighty-two last Tuesday, your lover, your sex, your sight, your sanity, everything—just to get away from him. So you do. There's your shadow, cast on the wall by the light that you can't reach, and you scream that it's someone else. *I'm not the last! Look, see, there's another behind me—take him, take him, take him!* That's your shadow. Your single inseparable companion. As close to your soul as

254

you're going to see in this life. And you'll give it to him gladly, and everything else you love besides, to get free of his hands. The Devil. The best teacher you'll ever have."

Dry-mouthed, shaken sick, Jena could not speak; she had lost her voice, robbed by the spare rise and fall of the scholar's words. Knowing the story did not make the hearing any easier. Dimly, she heard the owner of the Gregorian-chanting car slam the door and wheel away into the street, blasting *Kyrie eleison!* She thought the *Dies Irae* would have been more appropriate.

When he touched her on the shoulder, gently, she shied from his hand as though he had turned himself into the Satan of his story with her shadow in his fist. "What do you want me to do?" she whispered. "Are you telling me not to go? To go home now? Leave it—leave all the knowledge, the secret arts, the sorceries, the stories—just forget it?" She could not imagine coming so far, the Harvard alumna's scrap of paper long worried to inky shreds, only to turn and flee home. But neither could she bear to imagine standing in the sunlight with the Devil's grip knotted onto her shadow, tearing her between her safety and her soul, the final inexorable price of seven years' study: and if the day dawned cloudy or the old trick failed to fool him, to feel that hold, so desolate it hurt her even diluted through the lens of the scholar's language, tight on her soul until the death and resurrection of the world and maybe beyond. "Is that what you want?"

"No!" The earnest, vehement appeal in his face startled her almost as much as his missing shadow. "No, not that at all. If you go, Jena, if the Scholomance takes you—and it will, I don't know why it wouldn't—tonight, if you see that doorway, you walk through it, do you hear me? What you'll study at the Scholomance, you can't learn anywhere else. You can't miss the chance."

"What do you want, then? There has to be something. Get your shadow back? Trade my soul for yours?" Tipped by confusion into anger, she shouted, "You knew I was looking for the Scholomance. Why are you talking to me?"

"Stop!" He did not thunder the word. Yet her ears rang and her vision blackened—and none of the passing drivers or loitering pedestrians, she knew, would have heard anything more than the usual rutabaga mutter of a conversing crowd. "That," he said with thin humor, "is a Scholomance trick. You'll learn it. But listen to me first. Yes, I knew you were looking for the Scholomance. There's more of us than you think. Nine students every seven years, throw in the odd tenth scholar and remember that we live longer than most: not an insignificant number. After a while you learn to sense who's been and who hasn't, who's going and who's refused, I told you that before. Nothing special about you. I knew the Black School had moved again, I found out where—never mind how, you'll learn that too—and I knew there'd be candidates enough wandering around. As for my shadow, you can't get it back and I'm not asking you. I can live without my shadow. I don't," he hesitated only a moment over the word, "need it so much. This isn't the nineteenth century; I'm not Peter Schlemihl. I don't go back on my bargains."

His voice had a defiant, spine-broken pride. He ruined the effect by combing his hair out of his eyes again with a distracted hand; still her ears hummed with the aftershock of his command. In this half-seen world that shadowed her own, he was not without power. Jena had been thinking that a shadow instead of a soul came too close to a broken bargain for her comfort. But she did not say it, because he had shown her that one glimpse of the perilous arts and because she saw how he trembled now, with fear or expectation or sorrow, or something that had no single name. Much more gently, she repeated, "What do you want?"

Distant over the broken line of the roofs, the midsummer moon was rising: apricot full in the warm air, magnified by the skyline's proximity and observers' credulous eyes. Saint John's Eve, she thought, when the world unhinges and pivots through darkness into summer. All the hidden doors of the world open and the unexpected appears. If the Scholomance did not show itself now, she would never see it. A little anxious now, she walked the length of the alley twice, the shadowless scholar following her always a pace behind, always just to the edges of the lights. "To go back," he said when she halted, answering the question she had asked and forgotten, "I have to go back."

"Why? You barely escaped with your soul the first time."

"I can't— You'll understand when you're there. No, you understand already. There's more at the Black School than a thousand students could learn in ten thousand years. In seven years, I tasted it. I learned more from that cloven-hoofed professor than any student of the arcane, no matter how clever, no matter how patient, could learn in a lifetime. A taste. No more. There's always something more to learn." He spread his hands in an elaborate, helpless shrug. "Seven years. That's all you're allowed. And that roulette risk waiting for you when they're up. But I'd go back in a heartbeat—to feel those books under my hands again, dust undisturbed since Johannes Faustus, since Heinrich Agrippa—to wake in the morning in my room that had no windows, in the place where no sun shone by day and no moon by night, and only the letters of my studies illuminated the darkness—even to hear his voice again—" He gestured in the darkness, hands moving in and out of the slanting light, theatrics pain-stripped to truth. Jena could not take her eyes from him; he had become as compelling as the Devil himself.

Because she was not watching for it, the Scholomance chose that moment to appear.

Between word and word, it was there. She did not see it, as she made another concerned circuit of the alley; and then she stopped at the opposite end, in the overgrown parking lot where the streetlight had died. Beside the dumpster heaped with cardboard boxes, in the brick back of the computer store, stood a door that had not been there when her eyes last passed over it and had clearly weathered there for years. Despite herself, Jena had been anticipating something a little more ornate—carved with the letters of dead languages or a relief of significant symbols at the very least. Instead she saw a door of some old dark wood framing a blank panel of glass, a brass doorknob with no keyhole;

it looked as though it should open onto a front hallway, a scuffed carpet and an umbrella stand, but no light shone from the expected ceiling fixture and the glass lay darkened. There was no mistaking it for anything else. Darkness did not seep over the threshold, gargoyles did not grin from the lintel, but merely looking at the door was very much like standing at the edge of a chasm in the dark: vast space, silence, age, and imminent and impersonal danger. Her breathing told her; the blood jumping in her veins said it; her human skin felt the weight of strangeness pressing against it like the tides of an ancient sea. More than anything, she wanted to set her hand on the cool brass and turn the knob. A different kind of wanting, Jena thought, than the usual scholarly passion. She wanted the knowledge of the Scholomance like she wanted sleep or love; and it scared her fully as much.

Behind her, the scholar without a shadow whispered, "If you asked, I thought he might let me in . . ."

In the wan light of the parking lot, he had the insubstantial appearance of a ghost, a folded paper, something elegant and flimsy; his hair had blown into his eyes again and he smiled in expectation of a blow. Now he was trying to reassure her, saying, "You like stories, you said? You'll love the summoning of the dead. They know stories only the earth remembers . . ." and Jena wanted to take him in her arms and hold him until he had finished weeping for the companionable elbow that drove into his ribs, the friend's foot that trampled his instep, as ten students stampeded toward the light he would ever after shun: so his love of learning had been repaid. She could not, and he would not permit it. But neither did she say that it was hopeless; that he would wander the world hunting knowledge and never finding enough, the unfulfilled taste of the first apple ever in his mouth; that the Devil had taken not only his shadow but his heart: she knew these things and she did not speak them. Instead she reached out her hand and felt his own bony hand close about hers, sliding, slicked with both their sweat, and because she could give him nothing else, she said, "Tell me your name."

He gave it to her with a sad, smiling solemnity, standing among empty parking spaces and the distant neon haze. "Justin Saint-Etain. Graduate of the Scholomance. Luckier than many, more foolish than most," and he bowed, a deliberate anachronism in the brick-and-asphalt lot, "and pleased to have made your acquaintance." It added nothing. She would always think of him as the tenth scholar, the shadowless student, before she remembered his name: stranger than the strangest of schools where he had studied. But she found herself sizing up the doorway as he spoke, considering how many students could fit through its narrow frame at once, whether the door would even retain the same dimensions over seven years ... "It doesn't matter whether you reach the door first or last," said Justin Saint-Etain quietly. Out of the light, his eyes held as much texture and expression as the blind obverse of the moon. "He's got you anyway."

"Yes. I know. I know." She shivered with the Scholomance's nearness, feeling in every bone and muscle the pull of the darkness beyond the doorway, her own hungry, questioning darkness. She could not forget the lesson learned from the dim-lit asphalt under Justin's feet. But she had already chosen; only the act itself, the taking of the single step, remained. In terror and desire, she whispered, "Why, this is Hell ..."

Justin Saint-Etain nodded. A smile dipped across his mercurial face as he finished: "Nor am I out of it," and with a reckless sweep of one hand he showed her the parking lot, the lifting golden moon, the world.

There was nothing more to say. Against her palm, the well-worn doorknob was cool and did not, as she had been half expecting, sear her hand with fire or even prickle with static electricity. Still it drew her like a lodestone. Excitement drummed her blood. Quickly she made her farewell to the moon as it climbed the sky, the moving air of the upper world and the light, even electric, that she would not see for seven years, while Justin Saint-Etain watched. His silence held secrets of its own. When she lowered her eyes to his, she knew she could not apologize or offer sympathy; she said only, "Goodbye."

Justin answered in the oldest form of the phrase, with only a trace of melancholy irony, "God be with you."

The doorknob turned beneath the pressure of her hand; the door swung inward. Beyond the scuffed wooden step, darkness lengthened toward some infinite point, a corridor going back as far as the first question, the first answer, the second curiosity kindled. If the Devil waited to greet her, she could not see him. Perhaps he was out and wandering this Saint John's Eve—dancing on a mountainside, perhaps, to the music of Mussorgsky—but his school had admitted her. Jena Reese entered without reserve. Her shadow moved behind her in the glow of the faraway moon and the clouded city light, and vanished, crossing the threshold, in the dark. She did not look back. Not that she thought Justin Saint-Etain would fade into a flitting ghost if she did, but she could not bear to see the ache in his eyes as he watched her descend, following the light of knowledge into the dark; she did not turn to see him lingering thirty seconds beyond the closing of the Scholomance's door and thirty seconds beyond that; waiting, hopeless and patient, outside the gates of hell.

for Andrew Swensen

Story Notes

Shade and Shadow:

This story began life under the title "Thresholds," which John Benson wisely vetoed when he accepted it for *Not One of Us* in 2001. (I knew not from Caitlín R. Kiernan in those days.) Although I have no regrets about the name change, the original title did point to one of my long-standing obsessions, of which this story contains a number: the sea, the underworld, storytelling and memory, and liminal spaces. ". . . Orpheus always on the wrong side of the threshold, venturing whole into the world of the dead, remaining severed in the world of the living." The people on the wrong side of the threshold attract me, as do the people who stand always in the doorway, at the crossroads, between states. Cairo Pritchard, whose primary relationships are with the dead. Orpheus, whom even the sea throws back. Even Eurydike, always pulled up out of her dark and into the temporary light, and maybe he should have let her go centuries back: but that would have been someone else's story. I always wanted to write more about the ghosts.

Matlacihuatl's Gift:

There are not enough female trickster figures in the world. When I discovered Matlacihuatl in April 2002, in the pages of Lewis Hyde's marvelous *Trickster Makes This World,* how could I not write about her? She is herself a liminal space, where assumptions confound themselves and biology works backward, and the last thing any man would expect should be the first thing to watch out for. She walks in the Chipas Highlands of Mexico, and they call her *Mujer enredadora*—Entangling Woman. Don't say I didn't warn you. Luis, Alison, Peter: this one's for you.

A Maid on the Shore:
Jeannelle Ferreira, whose friendship informs several of these stories, asked me one wintry day in 2002 for a selkie story with a redhead. I was listening to a lot of Stan Rogers that semester, so I took a title and atmosphere from his rendition of "The Maid on the Shore," and things went from there. I still like how it's stories that really screws up the unnamed protagonist—not what has actually happened between him and the russet-black woman, but what he thinks, from all the ballads and folktales he knows, should and thereby must have. He's so busy seeing one myth that he trips over another. I think it's not an uncommon phenomenon.

Clay Lies Still:
"Clay Lies Still" came straight out of a lengthy e-mail exchange with Lawrence Szenes-Strauss, to whom this story is dedicated. An excerpt from his side of the conversation appears in the text as the e-mail attributed to Vero. Not only did he cheerfully and learnedly support my obsessions with Rabbi Loew and kabbalah, gamatriya and variant golem legends, he confirmed my speculations about the *adam / dam* paradigm that became the core of the story and added his own theories. (He is not, however, responsible for the line about chicken parmesan: *mea maxima, maxima culpa.*) Although I lived outside of Boston until the fall of 2003, Lance, Vero, and Aaron are the only characters of mine who I know for certain live there. Their story was written in August and October 2002.

Storm Gods of the Connecticut River Valley:
This poem is an in-joke. It is also the only piece of mine for which I have needed recourse to a map. "Storm Gods of the Connecticut River Valley" was written in August 2002 and Michael Zoosman knows why.

Featherweight:
Despite its epigraphs, the initial impetus for "Featherweight" was neither William Shakespeare nor the *Song of Songs,* but an image from its opening scene: kissing a woman whose metal-sewn skin was colder than her jewelry, so cold it burnt, and no heart in her breast. I didn't intend for the story to end up anywhere near as allegorical as it did, especially since I had no idea what heart Dominick would find for Ligeia, if any, until one cold afternoon in New York when I thought, "Oh: *right.*" And promptly felt stupid. "Featherweight" was written in February 2003 and January 2004, mostly to Bob Dylan's *Blood on the Tracks* and *Blonde on Blonde,* and the Dresden Dolls' self-titled studio album. The blue glass heart that Dominick tries is real, and I know who has it. I still cannot read hieroglyphs. I may be the only person on the planet who thinks that the ending of this story is ambiguous.

Nights with Belilah:
In the summer of 2003, Jeannelle Ferreira and I challenged one another to write stories for Mary Anne Mohanraj's *Blowing Kisses: The Best of Blowfish.* The only restriction, as per the anthology's guidelines: a blow job, of either gender, somewhere in the text. Jeannelle's contribute has since become the first chapter of her extraordinary novel *A Verse from Babylon* (Prime Books, June 2005). "Nights with Belilah" was my answer: Theo, Clarity, Darwin, and Devi had all been drifting around my head for nearly a year, in fits and starts of unsuccessful fiction, but it took the catalyst of Belilah to draw their story into shape. All that month, I had the daughters of Lilith on my brain. Two poems, "Lilim, After Dark" and "Night's Black Daughters"—which worked its way into "A Ceiling of Amber,

A Pavement of Pearl" as a fragmentary song—also date from that July. The story that Belilah tells Theo, about life on the other side of the mirror, was originally a storytelling improvisation of mine drawn from Eastern European folktales and the short stories of Isaac Bashevis Singer. "Nights with Belilah" was written primarily to Less Than Jake's *Borders and Boundaries* and *Hello Rockview,* and Yehudi Wyner's incidental music for *The Mirror.*

Tarot in the Dungeon:
In July 2004, at Union Station in New Haven, I was waiting on the platform for the regional to Washington, DC when the Hanged Man of this poem turned up. (Figuratively, although a literal manifestation might have made the ride much more interesting.) My laptop was safely stowed away in my backpack and the train was due to arrive at any minute, but I had a bank envelope in my jacket pocket and I carry a mechanical pencil everywhere. About a stanza and a half of "Tarot in the Dungeon" were scribbled on that envelope, and the rest written on the train. Thanks to Mike Allen for its appearance in these pages.

Time May Be:
In high school, I wrote endlessly of alternate fantasy worlds, and very little of the mythic in this one. From college onward, I have stayed mostly within the fields we know—denizens from beyond them just occasionally venture over. "Time May Be" is something of an exception, written in October 2001 in part to see whether I could work outside of my usual pattern, partially to give me somewhere to put a particularly grim Tarot that had occurred to me one night while looking over a friend's decks. (As this was the same summer that I discovered Mary Gentle's work, I also suspect that its setting that looks like a collision between the fifth century BCE and the eighteenth CE is something of a hangover from *Rats and Gargoyles.* I can hope only that it is not too obviously derivative.) Admittedly, the plot does concern itself with people who are outside; in between; and

Roger Bacon's brazen head snuck in there somehow. I am still pleased with the mythologies that I invented for Aruis, Sophia whose Moon blooms like a rose, the sacrifice-Sun and the Tree. So far I have had no more stories out of this city, but I keep hoping.

To Everthing, A Season:

There is nothing fantastic about this poem. It mythologizes, but there is no myth here—at least, I don't think so. I could always be wrong. "To Everything, A Season" was written in December 2002, while listening to a lot of Robert Merrill and staying up very late.

Kouros:

"Kouros" is all Yale's fault. On the train down from Boston to interview for graduate school in 2003, I started writing to suit the late-winter landscape I saw outside my window; I did not know what Cole wanted, how Jasper had died, or who the nameless girl with the green-and-gold eyes was. By the time summer had come and my plans for the next five years had been finalized, I had some idea. Stories of katabasis intrigue me almost as much as liminal spaces: descent and return, thresholds crossed. As the title suggests, a number of them went into this story; primarily Persephone and Demeter, Kastor and Polydeukes, and Geshtinanna, the sister of Dumuzi whose lover Inanna handed him over to the under-world in exchange for her own freedom in the world above. Half the year, Geshtinanna substitutes for her brother in the dust-dry countries of the dead. Kastor and Polydeukes share mortality between them, one above, one below. The Canada geese took me by surprise.

Retrospective:

This story was written for John Benson, on the last day of 2003: fire and winter and Robert Frost. No one I know has ever caught on fire. There was no music involved.

Harlequin, Lonely:

Written in May 2002 after an encounter with Midori Snyder's *The Innamorati* provoked several weeks' research into commedia dell' arte, "Harlequin, Lonely" taps into much of what intrigues me most about masks. As a very small child, I was terrified of them: I knew absolutely that if I put on a mask, I would stop being myself. Whatever the mask depicted, that would be me. I couldn't deal with the thought. Imagine my relief when I got a little older and read about Hopi kachina dancers, and realized—*see! Ritually, that's exactly what happens! I had a reason to be afraid of those things after all!* So naturally, all these years later, masks—godhead, deception, self-creation, identity—obsess me almost as much as the sea. "Harlequin, Lonely" is dedicated to Marc Verzatt, whose reprinting of this poem allowed me to become, so far as I know, the only person ever to have a poem printed in the program of a Yale School of Music opera production (Charles Gounod's *Le médecin malgré lui,* April 2004).

Constellations, Conjunctions:

In the side yard of my parents' house in Lexington, there is a homemade radio telescope. My father and I built it, my junior and senior years of high school, out of an eight-foot dish that a hospital up on the North Shore had been using to get educational programs off satellite feeds. The next highest bidder had wanted to turn the dish into a goldfish pond; but we rescued it, tuned it to 1.42 GHz, and from our somewhat inconvenient latitude of 42° North, I happily mapped a small slice of our galaxy through the redshifted patterns of drifting neutral hydrogen. When last I checked, my brother had retuned the telescope to pick up meteors during the Leonid showers. There are some morning glories and red honeysuckle growing up its side.

Of all my stories, I think "Constellations, Conjunctions" is the only one to catch some of the wonder I feel for science as well as myth—that stars and galaxies in their immense, indifferent turning are every bit as miraculous as the gods we invent to hang them in the sky. It is also the oldest piece in this collection, written as it was in July

2000 and then seen through several badly-needed drafts by Dave Felts, who eventually accepted it for *Maelstrom Speculative Fiction* (R.I.P.). The language no longer quite feels like my own, and it probably doesn't help that I wrote the story while reading, simultaneously and for the first time, Peter S. Beagle's *The Rhinoceros Who Quoted Nietzsche and Other Odd Acquaintances* and Harlan Ellison's *Slippage*. Peter Gould, who saw this story in its earliest stages, has also remarked that Pelle Fisher is really easy. But it's close to my firstborn, in terms of viable fiction, and it is still dear to my heart.

Singing Innocence and Experience:

I would like to say that I wrote "Singing Innocence and Experience" just to see if I could get away with the first line, but unfortunately I have no idea where this story came from. Schenectady. I read *The Last Unicorn* while in elementary school, and imprinted immediately on Schmendrick the Magician; my parents took me to the Cloisters to see the Unicorn Tapestries in early high school; *Black Unicorn* was the first Tanith Lee I ever read; beyond that, I never loved unicorns. (Dragons, yes. We will not get into that.) I know the technicalities of the legend attracted me, what innocence means when considered from different angles, whether virginity is at all the same thing, and exactly how someone would go about trying to maintain normal relationships with a vegetarian unicorn starting up a one-man nudist colony in the bedroom. Unusually for me, I knew the ending of the story before I knew how on earth I would get there. "Singing Innocence and Experience" was completed in Rome in June 2002, the first piece that I ever wrote outside this country, and has since generated at least one piece of online fanfiction that I know about. The Rilke epigraph marks my first serious attempt at German translation. All complaints are to be addressed to me.

Gintaras:

Gintaras is the Lithuanian word for amber. Amber are the tears that Jurate, chained (some versions say) to the ruins of her seafloor palace, weeps for the mortal Kastytis: she saw him casting his nets one day where the Sventoji River pours into the Baltic Sea, and took him as her lover down beneath the waves; but oak-and-lightning Perkunas destroyed him with a thunderbolt and splintered her home, and now she mourns her fisherman forever as her tears wash up on the shores where once he drew his catches from the sea. See *Odyssey* 5.116—129, *Gilgamesh* 6.42—79, and the *Homeric Hymn to Aphrodite*. The lovers of goddesses rarely fare well. Ever since I learned that the language has cognates with classical Greek, I have wanted to learn Lithuanian, but so far I have studied only the mythology. "Gintaras" was written in September 2004, after hearing a lecture on Myrrha in Ovid's *Metamorphoses:* an entirely different story of resin and tears.

Till Human Voices Wake Us:
Dreams of mine do not often provoke stories, but every now and then I get lucky. From February 2001:

> *Last night I had three or four dreams, all of which I remembered very well just after I had woken, but they're fading now. The first concerned mermaids. Specifically, a boy's sister had been seduced by a merman and gone out to sea with him, and now the boy was following her, trying to bring him back. In this dream I was more of an observer than anything, though once I dived into the sea along with the boy and tried to catch hold of his sister. She was very beautiful; her hair was golden and longer than mine, down to the backs of her knees when wet, and it swirled in the water like a net or feathers. There was kelp in her hair, green and red streamers of it, and her legs were scaled from the knees down; her toes were finned; the longer she stayed with her merman, whom I don't recall that we ever actually saw, the more she became a creature of the sea. The climate was somewhat nineteenth-century. I do not remember if the water was cold or warm.*

In January 2002, I was asked to write something about the sea: dream-imagery jumpstarted itself in the back of my brain and "Till Human Voices Wake Us," written in the space of an evening, was the result. The setting is Portland, Maine, where my grandparents lived and where I spent most of my summers until I was fifteen. I hope the art store on Exchange Street is still there. The lines on Mariana's T-shirt come from a song that my mother would sometimes sing as we drove into Portland, invariably at night, with the tide in and the city lights shining on the water; as though we were a ship coming in to harbor after a long voyage out, home at last from the sea.

A Ceiling of Amber, A Pavement of Pearl:
The first few pages of "A Ceiling of Amber, A Pavement of Pearl," inspired equally by Matthew Arnold's "The Forsaken Merman," the *J.B.* quotation that later became the story's epigraph, and memories of the same summers in Maine that went into the prior story, were written in July 2003: and then sat there, looking truculent. I didn't know enough about either of the main characters to get past "low tide at 10:54 and 11:24," and neither of them was forthcoming. In the spring of 2004, the story abruptly restarted itself while I was reading Demosthenes, developed a further cast and crucial scenes on a night bus from New Haven to Hartford, and was completed at the Villa Vergiliana in Cuma, Italy. Elias' apartment owes much to the China Sea Marine Trading Company on Fore Street in Portland. Frankie's final dream is another one of my own from 2001. Music that enabled the writing of this story includes the Klezmatics' *Possessed,* Dave Carter and Tracy Grammer's *Drum Hat Buddha,* and most of all the Mountain Goats' "Palmcorder Yajna" (*We Shall All Be Healed).*

Eelgrass and Blue:
In July 2004, I offered to write a piece for Jeannelle Ferreira if she would give me a color to start with: she told me, eelgrass and blue. This short cycle was written on the same Sunday afternoon, and takes some of its

color from an afternoon spent on the sea-wall at Newport with John Benson earlier that month. Part IV, "The Configuration," was written originally for a livejournal meme; all hail the internet. Thanks to Mike Allen for the appearance of "Eelgrass and Blue" in these pages.

Letters from the Eighth Circle:
The concept behind "Letters from the Eighth Circle" goes back as far as 1995, when I still ran cross-country for Lexington High School and came up with too many ideas that I could never hold on to long enough to write down. The idea of stealing skins, shapes, identities, bothered me almost as much as it interested me, but I never wrote anything coherent on the subject until July 2002. I had submitted "When You Came to Troy" to the first issue of *City Slab,* and Dave Lindschmidt wrote back and asked me if I had anything longer and more traditional. By the end of the week, I had written "Letters from the Eighth Circle." (As things turned out, he took both stories: and for the first time in my life, I was paid professional rates for fiction.) Because of the 5000-word deadline, I kept having to excise small side stories about Rika and Ashwini, Nathan Mays, and the girl who was scared of photographs, always on the assumption that I could go back and finish them later. None of them so far have materialized into real stories, and I suspect they never will; still, I think it helped "Letters from the Eighth Circle" that I knew what they all were.

Moving Nameless:
When I borrowed Robert Graves' *Hebrew Myths* from Cheryl Walker, to whom this story is indebted, I was looking for Cain and Abel variants to put into a poem. "Moving Nameless" was what I got instead. The midrash of Adam's three wives snared me; both Lilith and Eve were familiar figures and fairly well-represented in the literary world, but I had never before run across any mention of Adam's second wife. For several months the story hung around as four or five dissociated scenes, going nowhere, mostly because I couldn't tell where the narrative was

supposed to start or even who the viewpoint character was. Not until a family trip to South Carolina in August 2001 did anything like a plot cohere: one afternoon on Isle of Palms, instead of swimming, I wrote. If "Moving Nameless" has a soundtrack, it's Dead Can Dance's *Aion* and Benny Goodman's legendary *Live at Carnegie Hall 1938.*

Courting Hades:

In my sophomore year of college, I realized that Wilson Farms down the road from my parents' house carried pomegranates in season. Every semester after that, I went to winter showings (Brandeis University and Harvard Square) of *The Rocky Horror Picture Show* with sexual-underworld fruit in hand. Shlomo Meislin remains the first person to whom I gave a pomegranate, admittedly with none of the usual implications, and some of "Courting Hades" is his fault. The poem was written in April 2004.

Return on the Downward Road:

In the spring of 2001, I took a class at Brandeis entitled "Night, Death, and the Devil"—an entire semester's worth of literature, art, and music of the fantastic and the grotesque, and there is no way that I would have written "Return on the Downward Road" without it. Most of the artistic influences that went into the story are (I hope) credited in the text: Bram Stoker's *Dracula,* Christopher Marlowe's *Doctor Faustus* and echoes of Goethe, Vergil's *Aeneid,* Dante's *Inferno;* Scottish and Icelandic folktales about the Devil's School and the price exacted for studies there; Mussorgsky's "Night on Bald Mountain" and Enigma's *MCMXC A.D.,* and the medieval *Dies Irae* that resurfaces in Berlioz's *Symphony Fantastique,* Liszt's *Totentanz,* and Saint-Saëns' *Dance Macabre.* E.T.A Hoffmann and Oscar Wilde. Hieronymus Bosch and Gustave Doré. Kevin Spacey. Orson Welles. Like the metamorphic faces of the Devil, Justin Saint-Etain fascinates me precisely because he exists on that unsteady boundary between the tantalizing and the terrifying, what is wicked and what is evil, and what is only and achingly human. I wouldn't trust him with anything, and I would like to write more about him.

"Return on the Downward Road" is dedicated to Andrew Swensen, who taught all of us about knowledge. *You are more our Van Helsing than our Dracula.*

Printed in the United States
40195LVS00013B/26

9 780809 544790